Warrior Avenged

"Alpha heroes, strong heroines, paranormal plots, gods and goddesses, and terrific storytelling await you. Don't delay. Try these books today!"
—The Good, the Bad, and the Unread

"Addison Fox has given her readers one more Warrior to fall in love with . . . a fantastic series."
—*The Romance Dish*

"The latest superb Zodiac Warriors urban romantic fantasy is a terrific tale of love, betrayal, and (readers will hope) redemption."   —Genre Go Round Reviews

"Powerful and sexy . . . with a twist of Greek mythology that is exciting and fun."   —Fresh Fiction

"This is an up-and-coming series with a lot of potential. The story lines are complex and the characters are multifaceted."   —TwoLips Reviews

"Intriguing and promising. These ultimate alpha men are hardheaded and love hard."
—The Romance Readers Connection

continued . . .

THE SONS OF THE ZODIAC SERIES

Warrior Ascended
Warrior Avenged

WARRIOR
BETRAYED

THE SONS OF THE ZODIAC

ADDISON FOX

A SIGNET ECLIPSE BOOK

SIGNET ECLIPSE
Published by New American Library, a division of
Penguin Group (USA) Inc., 375 Hudson Street,
New York, New York 10014, USA
Penguin Group (Canada), 90 Eglinton Avenue East, Suite 700, Toronto,
Ontario M4P 2Y3, Canada (a division of Pearson Penguin Canada Inc.)
Penguin Books Ltd., 80 Strand, London WC2R 0RL, England
Penguin Ireland, 25 St. Stephen's Green, Dublin 2,
Ireland (a division of Penguin Books Ltd.)
Penguin Group (Australia), 250 Camberwell Road, Camberwell, Victoria 3124,
Australia (a division of Pearson Australia Group Pty. Ltd.)
Penguin Books India Pvt. Ltd., 11 Community Centre, Panchsheel Park,
New Delhi - 110 017, India
Penguin Group (NZ), 67 Apollo Drive, Rosedale, Auckland 0632,
New Zealand (a division of Pearson New Zealand Ltd.)
Penguin Books (South Africa) (Pty.) Ltd., 24 Sturdee Avenue,
Rosebank, Johannesburg 2196, South Africa

Penguin Books Ltd., Registered Offices:
80 Strand, London WC2R 0RL, England

First published by Signet Eclipse, an imprint of New American Library,
a division of Penguin Group (USA) Inc.

First Printing, May 2011
10 9 8 7 6 5 4 3 2 1

Copyright © Frances Karkosak, 2011
All rights reserved

SIGNET ECLIPSE and logo are trademarks of Penguin Group (USA) Inc.

Printed in the United States of America

Without limiting the rights under copyright reserved above, no part of this
publication may be reproduced, stored in or introduced into a retrieval system, or transmitted, in any form, or by any means (electronic, mechanical,
photocopying, recording, or otherwise), without the prior written permission
of both the copyright owner and the above publisher of this book.

PUBLISHER'S NOTE
This is a work of fiction. Names, characters, places, and incidents either are
the product of the author's imagination or are used fictitiously, and any resemblance to actual persons, living or dead, business establishments, events, or
locales is entirely coincidental.
   The publisher does not have any control over and does not assume any
responsibility for author or third-party Web sites or their content.

If you purchased this book without a cover you should be aware that this
book is stolen property. It was reported as "unsold and destroyed" to the
publisher and neither the author nor the publisher has received any payment
for this "stripped book."

The scanning, uploading, and distribution of this book via the Internet or via
any other means without the permission of the publisher is illegal and pun-
ishable by law. Please purchase only authorized electronic editions, and do
not participate in or encourage electronic piracy of copyrighted materials.
Your support of the author's rights is appreciated.

For Amelia,
my little Melmo Schmelmo

ACKNOWLEDGMENTS

My deepest thanks to:

Mom, Dad, Beth, Eric and Amelia—for everything.

Kerry Donovan—I absolutely love working with you. You have a wonderful ability to draw out the right nuances of the story and help make it shine and working with you is such a privilege and a joy.

Holly Root—your enthusiasm and all-around loveliness are truly too awesome to adequately express. As always—*thank you*.

The Writer Foxes—Alice Fairbanks-Burton, Lorraine Heath, Jo Davis, Tracy Garrett, Kay Thomas, Suzanne Ferrell, Julie Benson, Sandy Blair and Jane Graves. You guys never fail to make me laugh, and you are the most amazing thing that has come out of my dream to pursue writing. To pursue a dream is a gift—to pursue it with the support of such wonderful friends is a dream come true.

And to Jo Davis—you have championed the warriors from the very first day I told you about the idea. Thank you for your support and for all the "brainstorming" on appropriately delicious adjectives for one's hero.

Roxane, Carley and Christine—my most excellent partners in crime. You keep me sane, you keep me honest and most of all, you keep me in stitches. You're my *Sex and the City* Girls—I'll leave it up to the three of you to figure out who's Samantha, who's Charlotte and who's Miranda. . . .

Taurus Warrior

Determined and forceful, my Taurus Warriors lead by their obstinate, unbending will. Filled with quiet pride, a Taurus Warrior will never back down and never give up.

His enemies will feel the mark of his dogged pursuit, for once in his sights, he will never rest until they are eradicated.

Private and self-contained, my Taurus will not let others in easily; rather, he hides his vulnerabilities and needs under an impenetrable mask of stoic strength.

Sensual and unerringly faithful, my Taurus will cherish the woman who wins his stubborn heart. For the woman who can capture him—with a heart even bigger than his—will know a love for the ages . . .

— The Diaries of Themis, Goddess of Justice

Prologue

"Mother. You're the only one who can help me. Surely you can understand my need to do this?"

Themis watched her daughter Eirene pace around the small residence before stopping in front of the now-dark Mirror of Truth. The very same viewing screen where Themis had watched the young goddess fall in love in crystal-clear detail.

Pushing aside her distaste for the subject of Eirene's affections, Themis pressed the one advantage she had. "You have a role, Eirene. Along with your sisters, you are the Horae—the Hours. Diké and Eunomia depend on you."

"I know very well what I am, Mother," her daughter spat, the words raining down on her like hail.

"The world depends on you to maintain the very fabric of society. Moral justice, governance and law and peace. Surely you don't believe you can simply abandon them and your duties?"

"The world's abandoned us, Mother. Why should I continue day after day in my role as worldly peace-keeper"—Eirene flung a hand outward at the dark screen—"if these miserable humans you've chosen to focus on can't do their part? Besides, Dee and Nomy are okay with it. Happy for me." The last part of that statement—*which is more than I can say for you*—hung between them, unspoken.

Themis brought the mirror to life and a dismal scene of war in a jungle filled the room. "The humans. They live in a time of confusion, Daughter."

"They live in a time of selfishness and greed, liars to themselves and to one another. Truth be told, despite your best efforts, they always have."

Where was this coming from? Such sudden hope-lessness from her daughter who had always lived a life devoted to peace and mutual understanding. "So that makes your act—abandoning them when they truly need your guidance—acceptable?"

A small, harsh laugh bubbled past Eirene's lips as she turned her back on the mirror. "You can do guilt with the best of them, Mother."

"Why now? Why *this* man?"

The slash of Eirene's lips gave way to a small, happy smile. "Jack is everything to me."

Themis chose her words carefully. The battle with her headstrong daughter would be lost if Eirene knew her mother had kept tabs on her mortal love. "He is a power-ful man. A shipping *magnate*, the human's newspapers call him. Surely he's made some choices—some poor choices—on that path to power."

The smile vanished. "Jack runs an honest business. He lives an honest life."

"But how can you be sure? You just said yourself, mortals are helpless."

"Not this one."

Gods save me from young love. Even as the thought crossed her mind, Themis had to admit her daughter was older—millennia older—than any human living today. Yet for all her years, Eirene was unschooled in the ways of human life. While her role as universal peacekeeper ensured her constant interaction among humans, it also meant she viewed their worldly problems from a distance.

Her Eirene. Goddess of peace. Forever absentminded with her dreamy belief in the ability to find a common ground in the face of any conflict.

So where was her little peacekeeper now?

Attempting a different tack, Themis tried for something that would express the grave consequences of her daughter's impending decision. "Diké was born a mortal and tried to live among humans. Your father brought her up to Mount Olympus when it was evident she couldn't execute her duties. Couldn't fulfill the promises of her birth if she didn't have immortality."

Eirene's voice quieted, but her vivid blue gaze remained firm on Themis's. "I accept mortality. And maybe I don't want my duties any longer."

With those words, Themis's focus shifted. As she lost ground to her daughter's stubborn will, concern morphed into a deep-seated anger she was unable to hold back.

"You dare to turn your back on your gifts? To abandon who you are? For a *man*?" Themis's voice rose on the last word. She knew her ire had gotten the better of her, but she was beyond caring.

Had her children learned nothing from her mistakes?

Had they not seen how fruitless love could be? How easily a faithless man would betray his supposed beloved if given the opportunity.

Had Eirene not lived with the consequences of her father's abandonment, too?

"If it's turning my back, it's only to embrace a new gift. A love like nothing I've ever known. I want Jack."

"He is not what you think he is, Eirene."

Even as the words left her lips, Themis knew they would do irreparable damage.

A cold, harsh mask descended over Eirene's porcelain features. "Have you watched us? There?" She stabbed at the mirror. "Spying on us?"

"You are my daughter. It is my right—my *duty*—to protect you. To watch out for you."

"You know nothing of him. Nothing of the life he has or the life I wish to share with him. You just sit here on your throne of justice"—Eirene swept a hand around the room—"like this can protect you from actually living."

The words struck Themis's heart, but she pressed on. "This is not about me, nor is it about my choices. It is about Jack Grant. He is not the man you believe him to be."

"No, Mother." The deep hue of Eirene's eyes blazed like blue fire. "You are not what I thought you to be."

Great, hopeless waves of sorrow swept through her, centered in the roiling pit of nerves in her stomach. Shifting tactics yet again, Themis pressed her daughter. "You will not be moved from this course of action?"

"No. A life with Jack is what I want."

"And what of your duties as peacekeeper?"

Although the flick of her wrist was casual, Themis took some small hope in the quaver that tinged the edges of her daughter's voice. "Find another."

"And where would I do that?"

"You'll think of something. Knowing you, it'll have something to do with balance."

Before Eirene had even finished speaking, Themis knew what must be done. Calm now with the strength—nay, with the balance—of her decision, her voice was steady as she delivered an implacable order. "Your daughter. If you persist in this course of action, I'll have your daughter."

"And what if I have sons? Or no children at all?"

At that, Themis raised her eyebrow as an image of the youthful vigor and determined swagger of her daughter's beloved filled her mind's eye. "Your man will be content to live a childless life with no heir to the fortune he's worked so hard to build?"

"I'll make it so. He loves me. He'll agree. I won't damn another to my lot in life."

A tinge of desperation edged the words, but still, her daughter's gaze held firm.

"You dare more than you should, Eirene. Now you don't simply defy me, but you dare the Fates."

"My Moirae sisters will protect me. They will understand."

"Your sisters do their duties."

"You think they'll behave just as you have? Placing duty above love? Above family?"

"They'll do their duty," Themis insisted.

"Is this it, Mother? All you have to say to me?"

Her chest clenched, the feeling so like the day of

Zeus's abandonment, Themis hardly knew how she'd stand it. Unwilling to show weakness, she pushed through the pain, her shoulders rigid, her voice stiff. "So this is it? Your decision is made?"

"Aye. Forevermore, I shall be a mortal. I shall no longer hold the keys to peace. I shall no longer be a member of the Horae." With that, her daughter turned and walked the few small steps across the width of the cottage. Long, flowing flames of red hair cascaded down her back, so like her mother's. So like her sisters'.

A sense of finality pervaded the room, yet Themis refused to back down. Refused to acquiesce. As her daughter's hand reached for the door, Themis's voice rang out through the still air. "I will have your daughter, Eirene. She will replace what is lost this day."

Her daughter's steps never faltered. Never slowed as she moved through the doorway.

Chapter One

Quinn Tanner reveled in the night air as it whipped around his body, battering him with the force of an oncoming subway train. The late October night was unexpectedly chilly, the blustery air a clear indication winter was on its way.

He wended his way up Fifth Avenue, the heavy foot traffic of Midtown giving way to a tonier look and feel as he crossed into the Upper East Side. Despite the evidence of increased wealth and more sedate foot traffic the farther north he walked, the vibe of the city wasn't completely lost.

Three teenagers in matching plaid school uniforms squealed in a huddled mass over the middle girl's cell phone.

A food deliveryman fought in a mix of English—and was that Italian?—with a doorman as he juggled a cardboard box of food on the handlebars of his bike.

Several taxis let up a cacophony of horns when a

Ford Focus in the lead didn't move the moment the light turned green.

Gods, he loved New York.

He'd lived in nearly every major city in the world at some point in his life in service as a Taurus Warrior to Themis, the great goddess of justice. From ancient Rome to London during the Dark Ages to a brief stint helping to colonize Australia and even more places that had blended into a mental soup of blurred memories. None came even remotely close to New York in the early twenty-first century.

Wild energy, pulsing with life.

As he crossed over the next crosswalk, Quinn's gaze scanned the large apartment building that dominated the entire block. His mental tally accounted for four video cameras and an eagle-eyed doorman whose harsh, craggy face and hulking body screamed "bodyguard" far louder than it did "I accept packages and visitors."

Stepping into the ornate marble-arched doorway, where he noticed his own frame was about two inches larger than the doorman's, Quinn stated his business. "I'd like to see Ms. Montana Grant."

The doorman's face never flinched, but his blue eyes went flinty and cold. "Ms. Grant doesn't accept visitors."

"Not even those with appointments?"

Again, not a flinch, nor did the man even glance at the calendar in front of him at his station. "Ms. Grant doesn't have any appointments today."

Quinn moved a few inches closer, tossing a pointed stare at the date book. "You didn't even check your book."

"I know."

Quinn was impressed with the man's stoicism. He had the exact qualities Quinn looked for in his staff—firm, harsh demeanor and a don't-fuck-with-me attitude that would keep most people from thinking twice about making trouble. Alas, Quinn wasn't on a hiring spree at the moment.

He was on a fact-finding mission.

The elevator doors opened across the lobby as an older couple tottered out, the woman in a large fur that touched the floor and the man in a hat that had gone out of fashion sometime in the fifties. To the untrained eye, it would look as if Quinn were observing the couple, but what he really saw was the open elevator.

And as the lobby doors swished closed, Quinn knew he had what he needed. Now that he had an image of the inside of the elevator, he had the visual he required to port back to the apartment later that evening.

Quinn left the sullen slab of meat at his post in the lobby and whistled a light tune for effect. He had no doubt his image would be reviewed on the apartment cameras later. While he itched to remedy that small fact, Quinn left things alone.

The bodyguard had seen him because Quinn had wanted him to.

Later, he wouldn't.

Moving swiftly for the street corner, Quinn nearly tripped over a bag lady before righting the two of them. The fragile bones of her shoulders felt as if they would snap in two with the barest pressure of his fin-

gers and the frightened look in her eyes had him dropping his hands as soon as he was assured she had her
balance.

As he searched her face to confirm she was okay,
her frightened visage morphed as the light of recognition filled her clear blue gaze.

"You came." The words rushed out in a reverent
whisper.

"Excuse me, ma'am?"

"You came. To help me. Just as I knew you would."

The city's homeless problem was well known, and
Quinn paid little attention to her words, his focus on getting her resettled where she'd been—or, even better—
into a public shelter for the evening.

Which was why her next comment had his breath
freezing in his chest.

"Themis sent you, didn't she? I just knew all wasn't
lost."

Themis?

Quinn stared deeply into that crystal-clear gaze again,
searching for answers that would surely explain how
this feeble homeless woman had any idea who he
worked for.

The woman leaned in to him, relief palpable in her
exhale of breath. "She sent you. She's not fully immune to my pleas."

"What are you talking about?"

"Montana is in danger. You're the only one who
can help her."

Danger?

Several missing pieces fell into place in the mental
puzzle he'd been trying to solve.

Was this woman the reason Montana Grant had made an outreach to him?

And why would one of the world's wealthiest women listen to or confide in an ordinary bag lady?

Quinn had spent the last month dialing up his watch on the heiress. She'd come to his attention a few years back when her firm had tried to hire him and, for reasons he'd never been able to fully understand—and despite turning her business down—he'd kept an eye on her.

What had been, up to now, a bit of keeping tabs had ratcheted up to a full-blown investigation. For no apparent reason, Montana Grant had magically appeared and diplomatically fixed a political problem in Africa, which, on the surface, suggested corporate leadership mixed with a benevolent soul.

That was the suggestion, of course, until Quinn also got wind her company was responsible for a very large shipment of smuggled diamonds that arrived one week later on the black market in New York.

Seeing as how he put absolutely no stock in coincidences of any kind, Ms. Montana Grant had landed smack on top of his watch list. What he still couldn't quite puzzle through was why she'd made a call to him the day before, making a new, personal outreach to hire his services.

Now he had a bag lady standing outside Montana Grant's apartment connecting him with Themis?

Quinn felt her small hand at his forearm and he looked down again into that clear blue gaze. Although he recognized pain in those bright blue irises, he saw no hints of madness.

In fact, the clarity with which she stared up at him sent a jolt of awareness down his spine.

Whatever she may appear to be, this woman wasn't playing around. She *knew* who he was. And she *knew* who he worked for. The only question was, if he spent a bit more time with her, could he erase whatever memories she was so fixated on?

"Come on, ma'am. Let's get you into a shelter for the evening."

Quinn turned and walked about ten feet to retrieve her possessions from where she'd left them against the side of the apartment building.

When he turned back around, she was gone.

With a glance out at the crowded hotel ballroom, Montana Grant took a deep breath and smoothed the waistline of her evening gown, her fingers snagging on the heavy sequins of the bodice.

She hated these things.

Thousand-dollar rubber chicken dinners with a side of lumpy mashed potatoes and a serving of vegetables that presumably grew out of a garden somewhere, yet often looked like they were grown in the marshy grasslands of northern New Jersey.

Of course, the food was hardly the worst part. It was the obsequious fawning from the crowd, desperate to "get on her calendar," or "plan a lunch," or worse—invite her to speak at the next one of these events.

How had her life turned into one gala after another?

A row of flashbulbs went off as she mounted the dais at the front of the room.

As she walked toward the podium, the clear screen

of the teleprompter offered her a small moment of comfort. Although she could probably give the speech in her sleep, Montana believed in always having backup.

At least professionally speaking.

Matthew Stone, the celebrity spokesperson for the environmental organization honoring her, held out his hand with a small, flirty smile. She took it as soon as she was within arm's length of him, then tilted her head up to place a small peck on his cheek. The action ensured the next round of popping flashbulbs would be tied to at least half-a-dozen newspaper stories linking the two of them together in the morning.

The month prior, the borderless, worldwide goodwill organization now honoring her had contacted Grant Shipping. Peace talks had taken a decided turn for the worse between two North African nations after a pirate attack off the southern coast of the smaller nation. The attack was seen as an act of aggression and battle had nearly broken out before Grant Shipping stepped in and helped settle the dispute.

Even now, Montana couldn't understand how it had happened or why anyone thought her interference was worth honoring. While she'd fully believed in offering her help—Grant Shipping's vast, worldwide resources made it easy enough; her belief in being a citizen of the world made it necessary—the fact that she was being credited with avoiding war between two countries was a tough one to swallow.

Matt finished his remarks and stepped away from the podium to allow her access.

Another round of camera flashes, coupled with a standing ovation, greeted her as she said hello to the crowd. Montana held her remarks and fought to keep a serene smile pasted across her face. Despite her discomfort—or maybe because of it—the moment seemed to stretch on interminably. And with it, a small kernel of unease whispered up her exposed backbone.

"Thank you. Please—" She held up her hand when the crowd wouldn't quiet.

Another whisper-light frisson of apprehension followed the last and she focused her gaze, seeking a clearer view of the audience standing before her.

Was someone out there?

Although Montana hated public speaking, it was a part of her job—a part of her life—and she accepted it as such. So why did she feel this weird, almost preternatural sense of discomfort?

The clapping slowed naturally and the crowd began to take their seats. Montana took another deep breath, eyeing the clear teleprompter screens that flanked either side of the podium. As she shifted to focus on the screen to her right, her gaze skated oh so briefly across the far end of the ballroom.

And into the dark, dark eyes of a man who embodied every sinful thought she'd ever had.

His frame was draped in the finest-cut tuxedo, clearly custom-made. The black fabric stretched across his shoulders, making them look enormous where he stood at attention against the ballroom wall. She followed the line of the suit, admiring the muscular look of his body and the long legs encased in black silk.

Wow, was this guy a piece of work.

Was he the reason for her unease?

Even as the thought flittered across her mind, she had to admit he didn't set off any internal warning bells.

Montana did a quick scroll through her mental Rolodex. Who was this guy? And why did she have a vague sense of the familiar, like she *should* know him, even as she knew with certainty they'd never met? And why was he standing up, looking as if he were guarding something?

She knew she'd never seen him before. That wasn't a body a woman forgot easily. Add in the thick, wavy hair that was a luscious sable brown and the impressively corded neck that looked like a very nice place to grab on to and, well . . .

With a startled glance, Montana saw the videographer standing below the dais wave at her to begin.

With another quick thank-you, Montana shifted her focus toward the teleprompter and the opening lines of her speech. The words scrolled as she spoke, the visual a welcome distraction from her thoughts of the large man across the room. Switching to the cadence she reserved for public speaking, she vowed to ignore the mysterious stranger as she extolled the virtues of the organization that had invited her.

"The continued efforts of this organization to bring and keep peace the world over are to be commended."

A small bead of sweat ran the length of her spinal column. The unease that had gripped her upon taking the stage spread through her again, morphing distinctly into fear as it did a merry dance along her stomach lining. What was wrong with her this evening?

"Th-the belief in the equality of all humanity isn't simply a noble cause—it's a necessary one."

Montana made a pretense of pushing a lock of hair behind her ear as a way to wipe at the moisture covering her hairline. The move did little to make her feel better as the moments ticked by along with the words on her teleprompter. The normal rhythm that took over after her nerves calmed simply wouldn't materialize. Instead, the small waves of panic began to grow larger and more pronounced.

Feral.

Shifting her gaze from the teleprompter to scan the rest of the room, Montana fought to keep her voice even and level. The words of her speech were so practiced they were virtually memorized and she used that shift into mental autopilot to her advantage.

Quadrant by quadrant, she scanned the room, searching for something out of the ordinary as she allowed the benign words about corporate responsibility and what it means to be the world's largest shipping company float toward the audience. All that looked back at her was a sea of smiling people dressed to the nines and in various stages of happy, glowing, open-bar inebriation.

Even as she told herself this reaction was silly, Montana's gaze sought the corner where *he* had been. The tuxedoed man no longer stood against the wall and for some reason, that small fact made the fear coursing through her system spike uncontrollably.

Suddenly, unease morphed into a desperate need to get out of there.

The flicker of the teleprompter drew her attention brief moments before two things registered.

A loud scream pierced the air as the room went black and a wave of static electricity washed over her with harsh, piercing needles. Montana reached instinctively to protect herself, wrapping her arms around her midsection and bending at the waist to stop the jagged pain coursing through her.

Before she could even utter a sound, Montana felt large arms wrap around her just as her knees buckled from the pain. The last thing she felt before going utterly numb was the sensation of falling against a very large, broad chest as the man cushioned her suddenly lifeless limbs and dragged her to the ground.

"Shhh. Don't say a word."

Quinn felt the long, supple lines of the woman in his arms and—for the briefest of seconds—forgot the danger that surrounded Montana Grant like a haze of noxious smoke.

Her luscious breasts pressed against his chest and his inner thigh lay against the taut lines of her outer leg where they sprawled as he'd fallen with her in his arms.

What the hell was this woman involved in?

Every instinct he possessed suggested she was anything but the peace-wielding, beloved-by-all heiress of Grant Shipping.

The static that had taken hold of her body when Quinn first touched her was gone. The effect of his body, as well as the room's sudden plunge into darkness, killed the field of view of her attacker. Almost immediately, she began to struggle, pushing at him, hissing in a dark throaty voice still trying to recover from the unexpected electric charge. "Get off me!"

"Shhh, heiress. Not yet."

"Who the fuck are you?" Her words spewed anger, but she could do no more than whisper them.

Quinn tightened his grip on her, well aware the He-man routine wasn't going to win him any points in the "trust me" department. "Your savior, unless you insist on struggling away from me."

"What do you want?"

"A really good corned-beef sandwich. An ice-cold beer. World peace. I'm relatively easy to please."

The hotel's generator kicked in and a dull, grayish wash of light filled the room. Montana's bright blue eyes never left his, her long lashes framing a stubborn gaze. "Who *are* you?"

"Quinn Tanner, Emerald Security. At your service."

He shifted slightly, moving off of her but still keeping her body shielded from the ballroom. He suspected her attacker had moved on, but he wasn't taking any chances until he could check out the room himself.

Extending a hand and helping her into a sitting position, he couldn't resist adding, "I'm your new shadow, sweetheart."

Quinn shook the leaded glass tumbler in his hand, considering the clinking ice at the bottom of his empty club soda. He had to admit surprise—and was that disappointment?—at the lack of fight Montana had put up.

Despite the late hour—the society holding the benefit had oh so thoughtfully refused to shut down early once the lights had come back on—Montana had allowed him to accompany her out of the ballroom and to her limousine, where they now drove in a winding, roundabout path through the city as they headed in the direction of her home.

"Are you going to tell me why you've taken a sudden interest in me, Mr. Tanner? Especially seeing as how I haven't actually retained your incredibly expensive services."

"You know who I am?"

"Why else do you think I let you in the car? I couldn't place you until you said Emerald Security. Then it all came tumbling back."

"It?"

"Grant Shipping tried to hire your firm two summers ago, yet you had no interest in bidding on the business. I remember investigating you at the time." She waited a beat before adding in a prim voice, "I also believe I have an unreturned call awaiting your attention."

Quinn recoiled inside, his gut clenching in a tight fist. While the information age had been very kind to him, both in his business and in the Warriors' ongoing fight with Enyo, goddess of war, he loathed the fact that there was data—both visual and written—on him. Although he sought to minimize it—and erase or tweak said information wherever possible—it simply wasn't a realistic goal to steer completely clear of the grid.

The reprimand on the unreturned phone call didn't sit all that well, either.

When he didn't say anything, she continued. "I do my homework, Mr. Tanner." Montana folded her arms, the action pressing her breasts even higher above the luscious neckline of her dress. He gave in to an appreciative glance, then shifted gears to focus firmly on her face. "Yes, well, I didn't appreciate the scope of work the assignment entailed."

"Didn't appreciate it? That's awfully diplomatic of you."

"Your people had too much power. I don't take

jobs I can't control as I see fit, Ms. Grant. As to the second call. I wanted to do a bit of research before calling you back."

"How kind of you. Based on the line of business you're in, I'd have to imagine you lose a lot of customers that way."

"There aren't many who do what I do."

Her voice held all the smokiness of good, aged whiskey; the notes were threaded with steel. "All the more reason you likely lose customers. Death threats have a way of coming true if there's no one to counteract the threat."

"I was going to talk to you tonight. In person."

The lift of one delicate eyebrow over those bright blue eyes conveyed her skepticism as clearly as a shouted retort.

Quinn couldn't help the slight quiver at the corner of his mouth. Damn, but this woman had some fire. And she proved it with her next words.

"So why are you here? Or, perhaps more accurately, what do you now think you can control?"

Quinn stopped clinking the ice in his glass. How to play this one?

Honesty was out.

No one liked to know they were being followed as a person of suspicion. And based on the attack in the ballroom, he certainly wasn't sharing the small tidbit that he needed to know how she was mixed up with Destroyers. Those supernatural assholes didn't make their own decisions—they simply took direction from others—so clearly she had pissed off someone with very powerful connections. With a Destroyer attack, the likely candidate was Enyo.

Lately, it seemed like it was always Enyo.

"Mr. Talbot. I asked you a question. Why are you here?"

Okay. So honesty was out. Magnanimous charm it was. "I figured you were going to need some help."

"And whatever gave you that idea?" Montana gestured with a half-full water bottle. She'd avoided an open bottle of champagne when they'd settled themselves in the car, instead zeroing in on the water.

"Was I wrong?"

"No." She gazed thoughtfully at the bottle, plucking at the warped edge of the peeling label. "I . . . I felt something. In there."

"What kind of something?"

"I thought it might be you at first, once I realized you were watching me. But then I looked at you and—"

"And what?"

"I somehow knew it wasn't you. Whatever it was that was making me uncomfortable." She shifted her gaze to his, the incredible blue of her irises nearly opaque in the reflected streetlights outside the limousine. "But something was in there."

"Yes."

"So I have to ask again, why were you there?"

"I think someone's trying to kill you, Ms. Grant."

Chapter Two

Montana gripped the cool bottle of water until her knuckles turned white. The fear from earlier in the ballroom roiled through her stomach on a return trip, making her very glad she'd been too nervous to try any of the rubber chicken.

With sudden desperation, she focused on the man across from her, seated with a lazy sprawl across the bench seat of her limousine. His pose suggested supreme confidence, both in his course of action that evening and in the physicality of his body.

This was a man unused to losing.

Nothing can touch me, screamed from that insouciant pose and she couldn't say why it both infuriated her and soothed her at the same time. Because whatever else she might have felt at the moment, there was an odd sense of safety sitting in his presence.

Like nothing could touch her either as long as he was in range.

Unless, of course, he *was the one out to get you, you idiot.* Her conscience rose up to taunt her, pricking at whatever sense of calm she had regained once they were safely ensconced in the vehicle. *Damn fine time to finally get attracted to someone, Montana. Your life's in shambles* and *you're suddenly the target of a crazy person.*

An image of her mother filled her thoughts—and with it—the familiar clench of longing immediately on its heels. The last time they saw each other, her mother's frail body and fragile mind had left her with a sad despair she'd been unable to fully shake off.

Was this the underlying reason for the unease?

Even as she thought it, Montana quickly discarded it. A frail woman full of mad ramblings—and one she gave easy access to her home, at that—couldn't possibly be responsible for what was going on.

No. Montana gave herself a mental shake. The only feelings her mother engendered were the desire to scoop her up and protect her.

But Eirene would have none of that.

She arrived in her life when she chose and disappeared when she chose and no matter how hard Montana tried to find her, her mother remained elusive.

But in each successive visit—three in all over the past month—her mother had grown more and more agitated and her warnings more dire.

And through it all, she'd repeated one word, over and over.

Themis.

It was an odd word, and at first Montana hadn't understood exactly what it meant. But as she'd listened, and put her mother's words in context, she'd realized Themis was a *who*, not a *what*.

A quick Google search later and Montana had all she needed to know.

Themis was the goddess of justice, as presented in Greek mythology. The former wife of Zeus, she was said to have birthed the Moirae—the three Fates—and the Horae—the Hours. Although she'd heard of the Fates, it was their sisters, the Horae, that had oddly fascinated her. According to the ancients, these daughters were the natural personification of justice—peace, law and governance and moral justice.

What any of it could possibly have to do with her mother and her muttered instructions, Montana had no earthly idea.

And why the hell was she even thinking such nonsense in the face of Quinn's announcement?

Kill her?

"So are you going to tell me why you think someone's trying to harm me? That's an awfully large bomb to drop on a g-girl, Mr. Tanner." Her attempt at light and breezy indifference failed miserably as the last few words came out on a breathless hiccup, the plastic bottle in her shaking hand sloshing water.

He leaned forward so that those broad shoulders covered in an acre of black silk blocked everything else from view and all she could focus on was him.

The fear rippling in her belly changed instantly, morphing into something far more interesting . . . far more feminine.

Hungry.

"Call me Quinn."

The air around her grew perfectly still as she stared into those deep chocolate-colored eyes of his. In that moment, Montana found herself unexpectedly in his thrall. His eyes appeared to be deep, dark pools that held so many things.

Sensual promise. A lifetime of secrets. And—was it possible?—an overwhelming sense of pain.

He'd only asked her to call him by his name. Why did that seem like such a big thing to ask? Should she give in? Back down? She'd never felt so off balance and so oddly powerful, all in one fell swoop.

On a quick nod, she whispered, "Quinn."

"Did you get a load of anyone out of the ordinary tonight?"

"Besides you, you mean?"

"Yes."

His lack of smile broke the intimate moment and she sat back in her seat. He clearly wasn't willing to be baited and, even more clearly, he wasn't interested in any attempt at lighthearted banter.

Despite the fact he refused to humor her, the seriousness in his tone went a long way toward keeping the whispering tendrils of fear from regaining strength. Instead, she focused on his question.

"No." She glanced down at her water bottle. "And I looked."

"Well, someone was there."

"And there was that strange paralysis. It was like an electric shock all over my body, like when your hand falls asleep." Montana thought back to that moment. The panic—no, the paralyzing terror—when she lost feeling in her body. "Only, not like that."

She fought the sharp stab of nerves, focusing again on the remembered moments in the ballroom. She could only liken the sensation to what she imagined a Taser felt like, but no one had approached the dais.

Nothing had touched her until Quinn had tackled her to the floor.

"What do you think they want? And how are you suddenly involved?"

"I get involved when security matters require my attention."

"Who hired you?"

"For now, you can just assume I hired myself."

"Excuse me?" Montana heard her voice notch up, the screechy tone an embarrassing departure from the normally silky-smooth voice she'd deliberately culti-vated over the years.

"You're not the only one with interests to protect, Montana. I sensed a problem, looked into the situa-tion and seeing as how I'm right, have stepped in to handle things."

"You can't do that."

"I just did."

Quinn had just sidestepped a bullet and he knew it. Montana Grant was too smart—and too savvy and well connected—to leave this subject alone. He figured he'd bought himself twenty-four hours, at most, to get a handle on what was really going on.

Every bit of sense he possessed screamed she had something to do with the diamond smuggling out of Africa, yet even as his mind told him she was to blame, his instincts left him in doubt.

"You have no right to barge into my life."

"Actually, I do. If my suspicions are correct, some very powerful people have suddenly taken a large in-terest in you. I'd like to understand why."

There. That was vague enough to buy him a bit of time. Not much, but some. The evening's intel had given him the three things he needed to know.

He now knew how to get into her apartment. She now knew he'd be hanging around for a few days. And whoever was stalking her now knew she was protected.

And his involvement would raise the stakes.

Because whatever she was in the middle of wasn't caused by a mortal.

"When did you feel things start to change?"

Quinn watched a small furrow mar the smooth perfection of Montana's forehead as she mulled over his question. She really was a vision, all smooth porcelain skin and lush pink lips. They were decadent—plump, firm and eminently kissable.

She had a face a man *noticed*.

Of course, if she was responsible for even half the things he suspected, it was a very lovely facade that hid a truly nasty soul.

Even if the peaches-n-cream vibe she was giving off suggested otherwise.

On a small sigh, she began speaking, her voice a husky whisper in the dimly lit interior of the car. "I started to notice things about two months ago."

"What kinds of things?"

"Little things, really. Oddities. Things that in and of themselves I'd have ignored, but once I started to put them together, they seemed to mean something."

"Such as?"

"Items slightly out of order in my office. An unsettling feeling at a board meeting after all the materials I prepared vanished. An increased number of threats that seemed to have the same pattern."

"What type of threats? Against your home? Travel plans? What patterns emerged?"

"I can't explain it, but they stood out because they

were *more* sinister, somehow. Most threats against me or the company are generic in nature." She waved her free hand in illustration. "You suck, so does your company and you're going down, that sort of thing. They're unsettling, but we check them out and put them to bed. It's usually some crazy who's mad about their stock portfolio or some group who thinks we're not socially responsible enough."

"But these have been different?" Quinn's eyebrows rose. "Sinister, you say?"

"Yes. They're actually menacing."

The word hung between them and Quinn paused for a moment, searching for the next thing to say. The next *right* thing. If she was involved in even one-tenth of the things he suspected, it was no wonder she was receiving threats. But . . . something didn't quite fit.

Quinn knew the niggling doubt hovering at the edge of his mind was stupid—an angelic face and wide, guileless blue eyes didn't mean she was innocent.

Far from it.

But even as he fought to keep his normally suspicious nature intact, he admitted some small part of him *wanted* her to be innocent.

Shaking it off, Quinn pressed on with the questions.

"Has there been anything else?"

"I feel like I'm being watched."

"I'd wager the paparazzi spend a lot of time paying attention to you. Could it be that?"

She shook her head, the movement sending an errant auburn curl tumbling over her shoulder. "To your point, that's such a constant in my life, I've learned to tune it out. It's different now. And tonight it was the worst it's ever been."

Quinn let out a small laugh. "The entire room was staring at you, Ms. Grant."

A distinct shiver ran through her body and she wrapped her arms around herself. "That's what made it so awful. The entire room was staring at me and I couldn't find the threat."

Quinn removed his jacket, handing it to her. She laid the water bottle on the seat next to her and took the coat, quickly wrapping herself in it.

"Thanks."

Although he was sorry the vision of smooth, creamy skin was gone, some deep, ferocious pleasure he couldn't define reared up and grabbed him by the throat.

Montana Grant was wrapped up in his body heat.

On a rough cough, he muttered, "Better?"

"Yes, much."

"You want to tell me the rest?"

"I can hear the skepticism in each of your questions, Mr. Tan—Quinn—but the best I can explain it, something's not right. These . . . *things*. From the start, they've felt different. I felt—*feel*—threatened. Vulnerable. I know that sounds silly, but that's the best way I can explain it. Things are *off*."

"Our instincts are powerful things. That little voice is worth paying attention to."

Montana huddled down into his coat, the material large enough to cover her three times over. Even under all that cashmere and the blanket of danger that surrounded her, her eyes took on a merry little twinkle. "I couldn't agree more. I let you in the car, didn't I?"

Whatever enjoyment she had at the retort was short-lived as the small smile hovering at her lips vanished. "And then things got really weird."

"How so?"

"My mother showed up."

Although the background check he'd done on Montana indicated she and her father had been abandoned by her mother years ago, nothing he could turn up suggested it was anything ominous. Sadly—and years spent with mortals had proven it—humans had an amazing capacity to fuck up their lives and the lives of others. He'd chalked up the story of her mother as one more example of that.

"You haven't been in touch with her?"

The urge to pull her into his arms at the bleak look that filled her eyes made his hand tremble. "No. She left when I was a baby."

"How did you know it was her?"

"My father kept photos of her. And"—the word hung between them, before she turned her hands up, palms out—"I just knew."

"Clearly you're connecting the two—the feeling of discomfort and your mother's reappearance. Why?"

"I don't believe in coincidence. But it's more than that. It's the things she's said. I know it's very possible she's not well, but . . . she's oddly lucid when she speaks to me, even though none of it makes any sense."

"Go on."

Quinn saw the look of hesitation reflected in her eyes a split second before she leaned forward. "Have you ever heard of Themis?"

Quinn nearly choked on the ice cube in his mouth. How the hell did she know anything about Themis? And why was her name suddenly popping up all around him? Thoughts of how to play this raced through his mind when the car came to an abrupt, jerking halt.

In a rush of motion, Montana slid forward on her seat in the slick fabric of her evening gown. Quinn intercepted her midslide, his glass falling to the floor of the limo with a heavy thud. For the second time that night, Quinn got an armful of Montana Grant and for none of the reasons he usually held a woman solidly in his arms.

"What was that?"

"I'm going to find out."

"Tony!" Montana scrambled up and reached for the divider between the back and front of the limo.

"No." Quinn stayed her hand. "Let me check things out. Tony knows how to take care of himself. If the car's stopped, it's not for a good reason."

"But he could be hurt."

He leveled her with a direct stare. "You looking to get hurt, too?" With a quiet nod, understanding filled her bright blue eyes and she sat back on her seat.

"Don't move."

Quinn opened the door on the driver's side, crouching down along the body of the car as he inched toward the front to check on the driver. Although he wasn't sure exactly where they were, the lack of traffic made it clear they were on a side street instead of a main thoroughfare.

Which meant the driver had just turned off of Fifth onto the side street that ran the length of her building, headed toward the underground garage he would use to deliver her home.

But what happened to him?

With swift movements, Quinn had the front door open and saw the driver slumped forward over the wheel. A quick check of the man's carotid artery indicated a faint, but steady pulse and he settled the slab of driver-slash-bodyguard back against his seat. As he closed the door, Quinn finally understood what felled the large man. The car window was halfway down, leaving Tony open to the threat of an air attack.

Quinn backed away from the car, opening his senses to find the threat.

Natural or supernatural?

Holding still, Quinn listened to cold night air rush around him. Montana had already been the victim of a Destroyer attack tonight. Seeing as how the assholes traveled in pairs, was the second one lying in wait to grab her outside the ballroom if the inside job failed?

His gaze took in the quiet street. The large building on the opposite block still had several windows lit with those who hadn't yet gone to bed. About two hundred yards away, the traffic heading up Fifth was visible at the end of the street and a glance the other direction indicated the flow of traffic down Madison. From behind him, the heavy creaking of the garage entrance to Montana's building had silenced, the bright lights of the garage waiting to welcome them in.

Nothing seemed out of the ordinary.

So why had they stopped?

Quinn reached down and unsheathed the Xiphos strapped to his calf. Although modern-day warfare had become heavily dependent on guns, Quinn felt an incredible sense of comfort from the wickedly sharp knife each Warrior had been awarded upon his turning.

The solid hilt, gripped firmly in his palm, ensured any enemy who dared to get in his way wouldn't leave the encounter unscathed.

Movements slow and steady, Quinn walked the perimeter of the car. Nothing stirred except a light evening breeze tinged with the bite of late fall.

Quinn had just cleared the front of the car when Montana leaped from the backseat, rushing toward Tony's door. "Can I see him now?"

"I told you to stay in the car."

"I watched you walk all the way around. Nothing's here and I'm worried he's hurt. Maybe he had a heart attack."

Anger had him gripping the hilt of the Xiphos even harder as Quinn reached for the handle on Tony's door. Of course she wasn't someone used to taking orders, even something as simple as—

Before Quinn could even register an attack, a fireball slammed into his spinal cord, and waves of liquid fire raced down his back like demonic fingers on a keyboard. Reflexes slowed by the hit, Quinn fell on top of Montana, then shifted to look for the source of the attack as another flare of electricity barely missed his shoulder before it smashed into the body of the car.

"Stay down!"

As Quinn looked in the direction the hits had come, he immediately saw where he'd been in error. Saw the point he'd overlooked.

The Destroyer had been lying in wait, just inside the doorway of the now-open garage door to Montana's building. With measured movements, the man began to close the one-hundred-foot gap between the car and the garage. As he sauntered toward them, sparks flared off of him in the darkened evening. Although the light bathed him from behind, making his features hard to read, Quinn didn't need to see his face.

He was here to eliminate them.

The hard, reassuring strength of Quinn's body wrapped around her and Montana wondered—not for the first time—what the *hell* was going on with her life. The frantic thought was followed with swift speed by another one.

What had she possibly done to make someone mad enough to want to kill her?

Despite Quinn's earlier questions, this wasn't one of the run-of-the-mill crazies who resented her bank account or the high-profile nature of her family's company. Something had changed in the last few weeks.

This was more pointed, somehow.

Targeted.

This felt *personal*.

She twisted to get a better view, but his large chest blocked all the drama. The only thing she could take in was Quinn's heavy breathing in her ear and the increasing sound of steady footfalls as their pursuer moved toward them.

Although he was supporting his weight on his forearms, Quinn also wasn't moving off of her. "Quinn? Are you okay?"

"I'm fine. I need you to listen to me. We need to get you out of here."

"I can't leave you here."

"You will leave me here and get inside."

The helplessness she'd felt her entire life chose that

moment to reach up and grab her by the throat. She was a good person. Strived to treat others well and with respect. She wasn't better than anyone else and wealth and position didn't change that.

So why was her life more important than his?

"Did you hear me, Montana? Inside."

On a sigh, she nodded. "Yes."

"I can't let you get in his line of sight. When I lift off of you, I want you to crawl as fast as you can toward the back of the car. Use it as a shield, then head for the front of your building and get inside."

On a last plea, she whispered, "I don't want to leave you here."

His voice was tough as he spat the words at her. "I want you inside. You can't help me out here."

"I'll call for help."

"Fine. Just get out of the line of fire."

She knew that's what he did for a living. Knew he protected others. So why was it so hard to process his orders and think of leaving him there to face this monster?

"Now!"

Quinn's voice brooked no argument as his body lifted off of hers. She felt him tense, then heard a muffled curse emitted on a grunt of pain against the side of her head. Just as before, in the ballroom, her hair suddenly crackled with static and those odd tingles that reminded her of when her arm or foot fell asleep ran through her body.

What *was* that?

And then there was no time to think about it as her fierce protector urged her on. "Go!"

She scrambled out from underneath the shield of

Quinn's body, unsure of what had caused his muffled curse but innately understanding he wouldn't want her to stay and find out.

The footfalls of their pursuer grew louder, but the other man was still too far away to touch them. Did he have a gun? Was that what had made Quinn curse?

And then there were no more questions as Quinn's deep voice urged her on. "Remember what I said. Keep moving toward the front door and get inside. Don't stop."

As her heeled feet slapped against the hard sidewalk, her breath coming in deep, heavy pants, Montana couldn't stop herself from looking back. Nor could she do anything to stop what came next as the large man bent down toward Quinn.

Feet firmly planted, Montana watched as a large ball of light flared from between their two bodies.

A gunshot?

On a muffled scream, she ran into her apartment building, desperate for help.

Chapter Three

Quinn pushed at the large body of the Destroyer, the asshole's fetid breath nearly dropping him to his knees. Damn, did these guys ever bathe? This one smelled like he'd spent a month down in the subway tunnels.

With tactics honed over millennia of battle, Quinn slammed his body upward, dislodging the Destroyer's hold with practiced skill. The tattoo of a bull—his signature marking as a Warrior of Themis—twitched from its place on the back of his shoulder, desperate to get out and join the fight.

Although he wouldn't have minded the help, it hadn't completely escaped Quinn's conscience that the driver was still in the car behind him, likely to come to at any moment, so he held the tattoo in check.

Somehow, Quinn imagined, the image of him and a large animal fighting right alongside him might freak Tony out.

Go figure.

The Xiphos stayed firm in his grip as Quinn battered the Destroyer's head with the open palm of his other hand. If he could only get him into position. Get the neck exposed . . .

Another fireball exploded in front of him, slamming through Quinn's solar plexus with the speed and impact of a Mac truck. Damn, but this fucker was primed. He had to be one of the older ones if he had this much energy to draw on.

The Destroyer had thrown at least six fireballs by Quinn's estimation and each one had more power than the last. As he struggled to make sense of the fact the strikes were increasing in strength instead of diminishing, the asshole charged again and Quinn barely managed to sidestep him.

Pain rang through his body in great, echoing waves, like a vibrating gong, the fiery agony lighting up his nerve endings.

Despite the pain, his years of training and quick footwork served him well. Quinn spun around and caught the Destroyer by the arm, using the man's natural momentum to slam him into the frame of the car. A few stray sparks wafted off the metal frame of the car as the Destroyer shook off the head slam and staggered a few feet to his knees.

Quinn leaped, arm outstretched to defuse the static. The last thing he needed was the spark getting close enough to hit the gas tank. It caused him precious seconds of the battle, but Quinn knew it was a necessary precaution if he wanted to get Tony out of this alive.

Satisfied he'd eliminated any threat, Quinn refocused on his opponent. The Destroyer had regained his feet, but he staggered with drunken steps as he put some additional distance between himself and the car, presumably to get his second wind.

Fat fucking chance.

Quinn leaped, slashing the Xiphos in large, sweeping arcs, the gleaming blade reflecting moonlight as he went for his enemy's throat. The Destroyer backpedaled and Quinn saw the first hint of fear in the soulless eyes that maintained a steady focus on the slashing sword.

His bull's tail flicked in anticipation as Quinn feinted, then double-timed his steps so he was on the Destroyer before the other man could react. With the pointed tip of his weapon, Quinn kept his foe unfocused, the tight jabs enough to slow his opponent. When he managed to nick the corner of the Destroyer's rib cage—or where the ribs would be if the thing was actually human—it offered enough distraction to push the man a few more steps so the side of Montana's building was at his back.

Quinn slashed once again—harder and faster than the sharp stabs—slicing through the skin at the top of the chest. The Destroyer let out a wail of pain, the shot of electricity he was about to fire flaring off in a wild arc that petered out as it fell to the sidewalk. Quinn gave a satisfied grunt and used the momentary diversion to his advantage. With his foot, he caught the Destroyer behind the knee, dropping him to the ground.

With a pin worthy of an Olympic wrestler, Quinn subdued the Destroyer in a tight hold. The guy struggled and writhed against the concrete but couldn't break the pin.

"Who do you work for?"

"Fuck you."

"Classic answer, asshole. Why don't I make the question easier for your pea-brained intellect?" Quinn grit out between teeth clenched from the effort of holding the guy down. "Why did Enyo send you?"

"Maybe you didn't hear me? I said fuck. You. Although—" The Destroyer broke off, a subtle purr in his voice, even in the midst of his resistance. "She's a luscious piece. Hot enough to make me want to veer off my plans and enjoy some time with her."

Quinn ignored the fetid breath, ignored the physical jabs, even ignored the dark desire that beat in his veins to see this jerk carved into a thousand pieces.

All he saw was a haze of red, blood rushing in his ears like the ocean in the middle of a tsunami, as he imagined this ball of slime touching Montana. Shifting, he lifted the guy by the shoulders and slammed him down into the concrete, hard enough to make a human lose consciousness.

All it did was daze this one slightly. Damn, where was he getting his strength?

The Destroyer responded with a smirk. "She's going to get what's coming to her, you know."

"Why does Enyo want her?"

If there was any shred of emotion left in the soulless husk of the Destroyer's body, it coalesced in the dead eyes. "What does that bitch want with anyone?"

What was this? Quinn tightened his hold again, repositioning his sword so that when he did lift his arm to strike, he had the shortest distance to the guy's exposed neck.

Was it possible the Destroyer didn't work for Enyo? But how?

"One more chance, asshole. Tell me who you're working for."

The smirk gave way to an evil laugh. "You'll never guess."

Unwilling to waste another second attempting to puzzle through the conversation, Quinn made his move. With a vicious, downward slash of the Xiphos, he sliced a clean, fine line through the neck.

No matter how many times he watched it, the process never ceased to amaze him. The Destroyer's skin folded up on itself, first shrinking, then dissolving into a pool of grease until there was nothing left but a small puddle. What had started out as human—then turned to a completely evil being from greed, avarice or maybe just a lack of hope—was now nothing but a rancid, slick memory.

Sides heaving, Quinn watched the black, greasy pool spread into the sidewalk. Was he that far off from this existence? He might be flesh and bone—might even still have some semblance of a soul—but he was still a killer.

He still lived in the shadows, fighting a battle that had no end in sight.

But what did any of it have to do with Montana Grant?

Montana raced from the lobby toward Quinn as she saw him approach the ornate front doors. His shirttails hung half out of his waist and a large gash ran down the length of his tuxedo jacket, but otherwise he looked surprisingly good for having gone hand-to-hand with the scum who'd followed them.

She had to work past the lump in her throat as she reached out to touch his shoulder.

"What happened? Are you okay? Where's that guy? And where's Tony?"

Quinn rubbed a hand over the hard line of his jaw. "The guy got away."

She couldn't say why his words caught her up short, but something in them surprised her. Was it the fact that the guy who followed them got away? Or the bigger fact that Quinn Tanner didn't look like a man who ever let his prey go once he had it in his cross-hairs?

With brisk motions, she ran a hand down the arm of his tuxedo jacket, brushing at the threads that hung loosely from the hole. "Are you hurt?"

Quinn patted her hand before turning her back in the direction of the lobby. "I'm fine. And Tony's fine. He's parking the car now and then will be up. Said you'll probably want to mother him a bit."

As her mouth dropped open, Quinn held up a hand. "He said it with a great deal of affection. And not a little bit of anticipation, if I'm not mistaken."

"Oh." Her jaw snapped closed on the sweet words. "What happened to him?"

"He doesn't remember."

"But he's fine?"

"Fine. And mad. Which makes two of us." With a nod toward the elevators, Quinn's gaze was pointed. "Let me see you upstairs."

"I called the police. Don't we need to wait for them?"

"I'll come back down when they get here and I'll file a report tomorrow."

"Oh. Does this mean you've taken the job?"

He shot her a wry smile that Montana felt down to her toes. "Yeah. I guess you could say that."

The smile did a little to bolster her raw nerves as Montana walked Quinn to the private elevator that led to her two-story penthouse. Her heart beat an erratic *thump-thump-bang* and she diligently ignored it, focusing on placing one foot in front of the other in the wicked pumps she still wore.

Quinn allowed her to board the elevator first, then followed her in, the doors swishing closed sedately behind him. With a light jolt, they began ascending toward her apartment.

Her gaze zeroed in on the lights on the operations panel as she tried to focus on anything but the large, imposing man at her side. Although she'd ridden in this elevator her entire life, it had never felt so . . . small.

Or close.

And why was her pulse thudding so loudly? She kept taking deep breaths, but all she managed to do was make her heart speed up, the rushing of her blood rumbling through her head in pounding waves. The air around her seemed to waver and the lights dimmed, the elevator awash in grayish light. The doors slid open and she reached out and . . .

"Montana!"

The world went all gray and fuzzy as Quinn wrapped his large arms around her, dragging her tight against his broad, reassuring chest.

"Montana."

Her world tilted as those strong arms lifted her off the ground. The steady beat of his heart thumped against her ear as Quinn carried her across the room.

Her housekeeper had left a few lights on as was her normal custom and the room held a soft, yellow glow as Quinn settled the two of them onto the couch. Montana still saw the room through that weird gray haze that surrounded her in the elevator, but at least her breath was calming, the tight wrap of Quinn's arms around her body going a long way toward soothing her.

"Shhh. It's okay now. You need to calm down. You're just in shock. It's gone, Montana. The threat is gone."

One broad hand stroked her hair as the other ran down her back in large, soothing circles.

"What was that thing?"

"A bad man, nothing more."

"Two bad men." When he didn't answer, she added, "At my home and at the hotel. Two. And he's still on the loose."

"You don't need to worry about him. Either of them."

The pulse that had slowed under his soothing touch flared up again at the thought there were more bad people out there. If there were two, there could be more. Biding their time. Waiting. For her. "So even if it's not him, there's still a threat."

"Shhh. I'm going to find it and take care of it."

Before she could stop them—could even think to stop them—words began tumbling from her lips. "Why do they want me? I haven't done anything. Really, I haven't. I'm just me. I'm just living my life."

He continued crooning in her ear, the nonsense words a balm to her shattered nerves. "Come on, now. It's fine. I'm going to find out what's going on and I'm going to put a stop to it."

"All my life, I've tried to do right by people. Tried to be a good person."

"I know." The husky timbre of his voice against her ear continued to comfort as his hands dragged over her back in warm, soothing strokes.

Even though she didn't want to move—didn't want to give up the comforting circle of his arms—Montana shifted away and sat up. All her life she'd had to make do without the support of anyone. A stranger certainly wasn't going to change that.

Couldn't change it.

With a quick motion, she slid to the end of the couch, a cushion of distance between her and Quinn. "How do you know?"

At his wide eyes and lack of response, she continued. "You don't know me. For all you know, I'm a spoiled rich bitch who has pissed off any number of people. But I can tell you. Whatever is going on, I have no idea what it is. No idea why I'm being targeted."

"You brought up your mother before. Tell me more."

The hot, prickly heat of tears hit the back of her eyes as a tight constriction wrapped around her throat. With a deep breath, Montana fought for control. Fought to keep more useless tears from falling.

"She showed up rather unexpectedly about a month ago."

"What do you mean showed up?"

A sharp stab of anger managed to burrow through the emotion. "Don't insult me by pretending you haven't investigated my background."

Quinn held up his hands and she saw a brief moment of indecision flash through his dark eyes. On a nod, he admitted what she already knew. "Okay. I know your mother hasn't been a part of your life since you were an infant."

For some reason she couldn't name, his ready acknowledgment was a different sort of soother. As much as his hands had comforted, so did his subtle acknowledgment of the truth. "Thank you for the honesty."

"You're welcome." Satisfied he'd passed some sort of test, Quinn continued. "Your father's been gone only six months. Maybe she felt she could approach you. Thought it might be easier to deal with you, instead of you and your father."

Montana turned it over in her mind, his words making an odd sort of sense. "I hadn't thought about that, but—" She stopped short. "It doesn't *fit*."

"Why? Talk me through it."

"In my few interactions with her, my mother hasn't really spoken of my dad. She just rambles on and on with these weird comments."

"Does she seem afraid? Angry?" Quinn's voice quieted. "I'm sorry to be harsh, but do you think there's mental illness?"

"I've been through the same questions myself. Despite the odd rambling, there's some lucidity in her comments." She held up her hands. "Weird, I know. And likely it's just what I want to believe. But still. I can't explain it, but I don't think she's mentally ill."

"We have instincts for a reason."

"I do think she's ill, though. She's so frail and she coughs uncontrollably. I've tried to get her help, but—"

"She resists you? Your attempts to help her?"

Montana nodded and couldn't help the way her eyes traveled over his powerful frame as he sat there, listening to her. For someone so masculine—so imposing—he had a way about him that was actually quite comforting.

Calming.

Refocusing on the discussion, Montana sought the right words to explain the past few months. "She gets very agitated. I brought it up the first few times, that she should get help. That I'd *help* her get help, but I finally stopped the last time I saw her. I just couldn't stand it if she didn't come back."

"And you don't think this has anything to do with your father's death?"

"No, I don't think so. Did she finally contact me because of it? Who knows?"

"What do you think?"

"My father loved my mother, and from the accounts of the few people willing to discuss the subject with me, she was crazy in love with him."

"So why'd she leave?"

The question hung between them, unanswered.

Quinn knew he played with fire, interrogating Montana Grant about things she would likely prefer to leave quietly buried.

Montana shrugged, but the careless gesture didn't match the bleak emptiness in her gaze. "Why do people do anything? She must have decided marriage and kids weren't for her."

"She had an awfully nice life."

"One would think." Montana waved a hand at her surroundings, the gesture clearly indicative of the obvious wealth in the room. In addition to the Monet hanging above the fireplace, the Italian marble inlaid in the floor and the antiques filling the room alone would be worth millions. "But clearly *she* didn't think so."

"Some people are never satisfied."

"Exactly."

Quinn watched the play of emotions across her face, puzzled at the obvious retreat. Whatever vulnerabilities had gripped Montana as they'd entered the apartment were long gone, her standard armor now firmly in place.

He could no longer find any evidence of the frightened waif. Instead, a cool, collected heiress sat opposite him on the couch.

Before he could second-guess the impulse, Quinn reached out and took a thick lock of hair in his hands. The rich red strands were as soft as cashmere as he wrapped one errant curl around his fingertip.

Catching himself, Quinn dropped his hand, the moment scattering away like the last few seconds of daylight. Forcing his thoughts back to the conversation, he pressed his point.

"And you don't see any connection between your mother's recent return to your life and the attacks on you?"

"She might have abandoned me, but she's hardly a danger."

"How can you be so sure?"

Montana leaped from the couch and crossed the room to a small writing desk he hadn't seen when they'd first walked in. She reached for a folder on the desk, then recrossed the room and thrust it at him. "Take a look at those pictures and tell me what you see."

Quinn flipped the folder open, his attention immediately riveted.

The woman in the pictures was the bag lady from

outside Montana's apartment earlier that evening. "This is your mother?"

"Yes. That frail, sickly, likely crazy woman is my mother. Do you really think this woman could plot to kill me? That anyone would take her seriously if she even tried?"

Several thoughts hit him in rapid succession. Montana's mother really did know who he was.

And who Themis was.

And that her daughter needed protecting.

Chapter Four

Montana toed off her strappy shoes and slipped out of the evening gown. She gave the long wave of silver a sad glance, knowing she wouldn't wear it again. Even if it weren't covered in street dirt, tears and bad memories, she couldn't wear it again. It just wouldn't do. One of the world's wealthiest women never wore a dress twice.

No matter how much she liked it.

She dragged on a T-shirt and sleep shorts and moved in front of the mirror on her dresser to grab a clip for her hair. As she reached to twist the thick mass into a knot at the back of her head, an image of Quinn flashed across her mind and the breath caught in her throat.

That moment on the couch.

That delicious, wonderful moment when he'd reached out and taken the lock of hair that rested against her cheek. A light shiver ran down her spine as she re-lived those precious few seconds. The way her pulse had sped up as a dark curl of warmth had unfurled in her stomach.

It was only a brief moment. Not even a full minute.

But damn, it had been one of the most sensual experiences of her life.

On a soft sigh, Montana reached for a lock of hair and pulled it from the quick knot she'd twisted up, allowing it to rest against her cheek. With a small, feminine smile at herself in the mirror, she turned and padded down the hall to her office.

Time to get some work done. She didn't sleep well under the best of circumstances, but tonight's events ensured she'd see the sun rise.

As the memory of the two attacks swamped her senses, replacing that small intimacy with Quinn, a harsh, metallic taste flooded her taste buds, her insides roiling and turning like she'd just gotten off a roller coaster.

There was a nameless evil that waited out in the shadows to strike at her.

A faceless enemy who had targeted her and she had no idea why.

Desperate to stop the surge of panic, Montana inhaled a deep breath and imagined Quinn Tanner's arms wrapped around her. The image had an oddly calming effect.

Safe.

She felt safe when she thought of him.

And didn't that just beat all?

Not only was he insanely hot, but he had given her something in a few hours no one had managed to do in her life.

Ever.

He'd comforted her.

Even if his high-handed tactics made the CEO inside sit up and want to put him in his place, even she couldn't argue the man had some serious mojo when it came to the art of protection.

The fact he sported an acre of well-defined chest—a detail clearly evident without even *seeing* said chest—had nothing to do with it.

Nope.

Nothing at all.

Shifting gears as she reached her private office, Montana spoke a few quick voice instructions into a panel on the wall, then watched the door slide open.

All her paperwork was laid out on her desk, just as she preferred. Her personal assistant, Jackson, was incredibly efficient, not to mention nearly as anal as she was. Montana knew she'd find each note carefully dated and ordered by priority. A corresponding page of overview notes would reinforce all elements that needed her attention.

"Well, you may finally be in luck," she muttered to herself as she crossed the room to take the oversized leather chair behind her desk. "There's enough paperwork here to put you to sleep in ten minutes or less."

Montana swiped her finger over the edge of her laptop screen, then followed it with a typed password. If her father had taught her anything, it was to be careful with her data. He'd also spent quite a bit of time lecturing her on the importance of keeping a poker face and how to dress to impress.

Sadly, he'd taught her little else.

If Jack Grant had ever suspected he'd leave this earth, he certainly didn't expect to do it at age sixty-five. Nothing was in order, a fact she'd realized after taking the helm of the company six months ago.

On a sigh, Montana dived into the paperwork and quickly lost herself in a stack of top-level performance reviews. This latest inspiration—to review what her managers' managers had to say about the company's leaders—had sprung this morning and, bless Jackson, he'd pulled together all the required paperwork on nearly three hundred people without blinking an eye.

Montana focused on the expats stationed in the Cape Town office first. She couldn't define why, but something about the African part of the organization seemed off. Lush offices, well-respected office leaders and a balance sheet that suggested only modest success.

Something wasn't right.

With a quick shake, Montana brushed it off, willfully ignoring the idea it could mean anything.

A light knock at the door jarred her from her computer screen. She was even more surprised to realize she'd wrapped that lock of hair around her finger as she read the reports Jackson had left for her.

And then the thought was forgotten entirely as her night maid offered a small, rueful smile from the doorway. "Ms. Grant. I'm sorry to disturb you, ma'am, but . . ."

"What is it, Laura?"

Before the maid could say anything further, a lined, weathered face peeked around the doorway. "I'm sorry to bother you. I shouldn't have come. I'm so sorry."

Montana leaped out of her chair and raced across the room. "Mother! What are you doing here?"

She wrapped her arms around her mother, instructing Laura as she went to bring some tea, soup and sandwiches. Montana didn't miss the sad speculation in Laura's eyes as she headed out the door.

A glance down at the frail woman in her arms indicated exactly why.

"Mom. What's this?" Montana touched the stocking cap on her mother's head, then ran a hand down her stained, padded coat. A sigh bubbled up in her throat, but she held it back. The coat had been brand-new when she'd given it to her mother last week, as had the leather gloves she'd placed in the pockets. Weathered hands peeked out of the sleeves—sans gloves—and a soft moan escaped her chapped lips when Montana pulled off the hat.

"Come on. Let's get these things off of you and get you into fresh clothes." God only knew where the hat had come from—likely a trade with someone for the noticeably absent gloves—and the only sound thing to do for the coat was to burn it.

Montana knew enough not to suggest bathing. She'd made that mistake only once, and got an earful. Apparently, the outerwear could become as stained as she wanted, but her mother was fiercely maniacal about taking a daily bath.

"I'm sorry I came."

"Never be sorry. I've told you, I want to see you. I'd like you to stay here with me. This is your home, too, if you'd like it to be."

"Black Jack would roll in his grave if he knew I was living here."

Quinn's words echoed in her head as she worked to settle her mother. *"And you don't see any connection between your mother's recent return to your life and the attacks on you?"*

Was her mother really behind what was happening to her?

Montana tugged on one of the sleeves, pushing the doubts to the side. Her mother may be any number of things—things that pained her in a way she could never have imagined—but mastermind behind some setup to kill her only daughter?

Montana just couldn't fathom it.

The material of the jacket fell away sharply from the emaciated shoulders as Montana continued what she could only hope were soothing words. "Daddy would be happy to know you have a home."

"I have a home."

Tamping down on the urge to scream in frustration that a city shelter wasn't a home, Montana gently tugged on the other sleeve.

And fought the tears that pricked the backs of her eyes in hot jabs.

Her mother was skin and bones. Literally.

"What did you do with the money I gave you? For food."

"Gave it to Bobby and Celia. They needed it more."

Bobby and Celia likely shoved every last cent of it right into their veins, but Montana bit down on the criticism as it sprang to her tongue. Their previous visits had been all too short, and she had learned quickly that agitating her mother was a sure method for ending them even more prematurely.

"It's cold tonight, Mom. Will you stay with me?"

"Can't. I only came to warn you. And I told you to call me Eirene. I'm not worthy of the word 'Mom.'"

The words pierced her heart, but Montana ignored the sharp stabs of pain as she led her mother across the room to a large leather couch that rested against the far wall.

Not for the first time, hopeless questions spun through her thoughts, leaving only an aching emptiness in their wake. What could possibly have brought Eirene Grant to this state?

Terrified, mad and alone.

And why had she ever left her husband and daughter in the first place?

Ignoring her lifetime wish for what might have been, Montana forced brisk efficiency into her tone. "I'll be the judge of that." She reached for a blanket and draped it around her mother—Eirene—before settling her into a sitting position. "Warn me about what?"

"He's rising in power. Don't you feel it?"

"Who? Who's rising in power? You never tell me who."

"The one who puts you in danger."

"Mom. I'm not in danger." Even as she said the words, Montana couldn't keep the chill from her skin, couldn't stop the cold fingers that sent shivers down her spine.

"I tell you the truth."

Montana patted the blanket-wrapped arm. "I know you do. I know."

"But now he's here to help you. To take care of you."

"He who? The one rising in power?"

On an agitated head shake, Eirene leaned closer and Montana felt her mother's long, thin fingers close around the skin of her forearms. Her mother's grip was surprisingly strong for someone who looked so frail. "The only one who can protect you. The one I asked for."

"Mom? Who?"

"Quinn."

Montana felt her muscles stiffen, her mother's words even more effective at freezing her in place than whatever had happened to her up on the dais earlier at the hotel.

"Quinn?"

Eirene's blue eyes were bright with certainty. "Quinn Tanner, the Taurus Warrior. He'll save you. I know it."

Fuck, he was losing his touch. How the hell had he walked out of a meet like he'd been hit with a two-by-four? He'd been doing this for far too long to get tripped up by anything.

And he'd known far too many women in his very long life to let one mortal heiress make him feel like a horny teenager.

Quinn drained the last drop of his scotch as the heavy rhythm of Equinox pulsed around him. Although he wanted another one, he knew a bender wasn't the cure for this evening's ailment.

It was rarely the cure for anything. He'd learned that lesson a long time ago. Hell, he even had a few lingering scars across his lower back to prove it.

From *his* mortal days, of course.

Now everything healed. Healed as if it had never been.

Except his rotten, wasted soul, which had grown so miserable and so incomprehensibly *small* that he knew he'd never heal. Would never be whole again.

He'd suspected it for decades now, but a few months ago had proved the theory correct.

Kane Montague, his friend—his Warrior *brother*— had needed him and he'd abandoned him. In Kane's moment of need, the stubborn streak of the bull that lived inside of him stood its ground.

A fucking cop-out if he'd ever heard one. The truth was a bitch, but he was never one to shrink from it.

He'd stood his ground.

He'd put stubborn pride before a friend and it had nearly gotten Kane killed.

He'd refused to help and it had nearly killed the woman Kane loved, too.

The two of them had survived—thrived, actually, no thanks to him—after they overcame Ilsa's past and defeated the poison that had lived in Kane's blood, threatening his well-being once a year.

Now they thrived while Quinn died a little more each day.

"You want another one, Quinn?"

Josey, a valkyrie who picked up shifts at Equinox on the side to make a few bucks, flitted over to his table. The ample bosom on display normally drew his attention, but at that moment, a slight wisp of a memory swamped him.

The delicate line of Montana Grant's throat as she swallowed her water. The daring cut of her gown, slit at the thigh just enough to leave less to the imagination than was normally considered proper.

She was a vision. Pure and worldly, all at the same time. A dynamic package that suggested the elegance of pearls mixed with the excitement and daring of youth.

"Earth to Quinn." Josey flailed her green order pad at him. "Yes or no on the drink?"

"Don't worry yourself over it, Josey. I've got it right here."

Quinn glanced up and straight into the laughing pewter gaze of Grey Bennett. Owner of Equinox and the most lethal Aries of all Themis's Rams, Grey lived by a special code none of them had ever really been able to crack.

Lightning-quick reflexes.

Stubborn refusal to bend his will in any circumstance.

Lethal ability to stalk his prey.

Even after all this time, Quinn knew there was a side to Grey none of them ever saw.

A side that said KEEP OUT in blinking, neon letters.

Grey took the stool across the raised table from him. "You look like hell, Quinn. Which is the only reason I'm not going to share with you the nickname the women have adopted for you at home."

"The fact that we even have women at home is still a mystery to me."

Grey's eyebrows rose at that one. "And what's Callie been all these years?"

"You know what I mean. Women in the house who are actively having sex with the men in the house."

Grey's brows waggled at that one. "There's sex to be had inside the four walls of our brownstone?"

Quinn let out an unnaturally loud harrumph. "Do you know I actually saw a bra hanging on the doorknob in the laundry room the other day?"

Grey drew his hands up to his chest in a mock impression of Scarlett O'Hara. "Oh, the horror."

"Asshole." Quinn couldn't stop the slight grin that edged the corner of his mouth.

"Probably. That said, it looks like I need to spend more time in the laundry room." Grey's smile ratcheted up to a full-on wolfish grin. "At least tell me it had lace on it."

Now Quinn did smile, unable to stay completely somber in the face of such enthusiasm—or the image of lacy underwear. "You know what I mean. Things have changed."

"For the better, I'd say, if the shitty grins perpetually spread across Brody's and Kane's faces are any indication."

When Quinn didn't add anything, Grey reached for his glass and gestured for him to continue. "That's clearly not the only thing that has you in a foul-ass mood. Spill."

"What do you know about Grant Shipping?"

Eyes darkening, any lingering hint of humor fled from the hard planes of Grey's face, replaced by the look of the lethal killer Quinn knew him to be. "The public face suggests a multinational corporation with a successful track record for so long the Grant family makes the Rockefellers look like peasants."

"And the private face?"

"Ah, yes. The private face of the company." Grey gave his drink a swirl, the amber color of the scotch undiluted by any ice or water. His role as information gatherer for the Warriors ensured if there was a whiff of scandal he'd have already smelled it—and would know exactly whose dirty laundry it wafted from. "Sticky fingers in way too many illegal pies. A supposed 'side business' in drug trafficking and the skin trade. Complete dominance in the waters off the coast of Africa that makes the pirates who like to swim there look like choir boys."

"Africa? Is Grant into diamond running, too?"

"Yep."

"Man, you do keep your ears open."

Grey took a sip of his drink. "There are very few criminals in New York who aren't touched in some way by the grand empire that is Grant Shipping."

"No one's ever run them down? Government hasn't ever tried to go after them?"

"Nope. Between the politicians in their pockets and the layers of cover the legitimate business is able to hide, they're untouchable. Shipping's big money and their legitimate business is a behemoth. Jack Grant built a huge organization from scratch and knew exactly how to hide all his secrets."

Quinn eyed his now-empty glass, then shifted his gaze to Grey. "Montana Grant knows about Themis."

Grey's near-unflappable demeanor dropped as his eyes went wide. "Fuck me."

"Yep."

"What does she know?"

"I can't tell. All I do know is that I saved her from a Destroyer attack tonight. Two separate attacks, actually."

"Destroyers? Where?"

Quinn quickly caught Grey up, glad to have someone to confide in. Someone to work through the details and see if anything popped. "Then, in the limo ride after the dinner, between the attacks, she asks me about Themis. Oh, and she also dropped the bomb that her long-lost mother has returned."

Quinn swirled his glass, knocking the ice together before swallowing down what was left at the bottom. "You think she's as dirty as her old man?"

Grey cocked his head, considering. "She's only been

head of the company since last spring when her father died. But still, you don't live that close to the stench of filth and not get some on your designer clothes."

"I didn't get that vibe off her."

"What vibe? The whole 'I stomp the downtrodden underneath my Pradas' vibe?"

"More. There's a real fear in her. She was spooked tonight." Quinn caught himself clinking the ice in the empty glass and laid it back on the table. "Something's gotten to her. There's a level of fear there that doesn't suggest she's sitting on a company full of the world's nastiest thugs and criminals. Or that she is one, for that matter."

"She was trained by the best, Quinn. I'm sure Black Jack Grant ensured the heir to his empire knew how to toe the company line. Besides, maybe she's in over her head and has suddenly realized it. That'll scare the shit out of anyone."

"Black Jack?" As the nickname rolled off Quinn's tongue, he couldn't bite back the subtle wave of distaste it conjured. Could someone guilty of the crimes Grey outlined have a daughter as fresh and intriguing as Montana?

"Yep. Her old man's reputation is legendary."

Quinn's thoughts reverted back to those moments on the couch, her long, slender body wrapped in his arms. No matter how hard he tried to ignore the memory of their meeting—or the undoubted truth of Grey's words—Montana Grant had left a very powerful impression. She had a fresh appeal that couldn't be hidden, even under the haze of fear that had colored their meeting. "You ever hear anything about her?"

"Come to think of it, no, not really. She had a broken engagement a few years back and recently she's been making headlines."

Quinn glanced up from the mesmerizing sheen of ice in the bottom of his glass and ignored the matched shot of cold that filled his belly at the mention of a broken engagement. "That weird peace talk she facilitated?"

"Exactly. Somehow she managed to insert herself in the middle of a political nightmare and come out the victor—for her business *and* for the two countries involved."

Yet again, Grey's vast knowledge was an awesome thing to behold. "Is there anyone in New York you don't keep tabs on?"

"Not really. No one escapes my notice." Grey flashed a Cheshire cat grin before draining his glass.

"Well, then, it looks like I just landed a new client."

"Be careful, Quinn. There's no way she's as innocent as she looks. The woman's got some teeth."

Quinn flashed a grin of his own—his first true smile in way too long. "Sounds like fun."

Montana filled her coffee cup with one hand, while the other held her schedule for the day. The ever-efficient Jackson had even scheduled in small windows for coffee breaks, but—if the sleepless night she spent and the low-level headache she sported were any indication— even ten coffee breaks weren't going to make a difference today.

Her visit with her mother had sucked her emotions dry and it was going to take a few days to right herself.

How had Eirene ended up like this? And how could

her father have allowed it? He'd loved the woman. Once. Even if every drop of that was gone, he should have helped her.

Unless he didn't know.

The edges of Montana's stomach rolled over and she absently pressed the hand holding her schedule against the buttons of her suit jacket. The little girl inside of her wanted to believe her father had more noble motives when it came to the subject of her long-lost mother, but the practical woman had her doubts.

Serious doubts.

Couple that with the increasing discomfort she felt as she learned the ins and outs of Grant Shipping and her estimation of Black Jack Grant was sorely slipping.

Oh, Daddy. What have you done?

Montana was smart enough to know a company the size of Grant Shipping—especially one with interests across the globe—was often forced to work with countries that practiced a loosely moraled style of commerce. Hell, she'd even learned that lesson in business school. You greased a few palms here and there to get permits through. Understood certain payments to local government officials needed to be made to move something along. The world wasn't black and white, and international commerce had more gray areas than most industries.

But none of it was an excuse to practice out-and-out criminal behavior.

And the deeper she got into things, the more she worried her father had done just that over the last forty years.

"Darlin'?"

Jackson hovered in the doorway, his brisk efficiency

an immediate bolster to her lagging thoughts. Even if the rest of her life was going to hell, at least she had the world's most amazing personal assistant to keep her on track. Upon hearing his sweet Southern drawl she couldn't keep the ready smile from her lips. "Yep?"

"The head of Emerald Security is here to see you. Qu—"

"Quinn? Tanner?"

At her widened eyes, Jackson's tone turned teasing. "If you mean six feet four inches of solid gorgeous, then yes, that would be Quinn Tanner."

"He doesn't have an appointment."

"I don't trust him as far as I can throw him, but if you're insistent on turning him away maybe I'll meet with him. Figure out what he wants. Take one for the team, as it were."

"Real smooth, Jackson."

"I'm just saying." Jackson held up his hands, his eyes wide with mock innocence. "Besides, darling, my loyalties are only to you."

"Yes, well, I can take this one for the team all by myself." Montana headed for the outer rim of her office, intent on . . . what was she intent on?

Asking him again if he knew anything about mythological goddesses? Or firing a series of idiotic questions at him courtesy of her not-all-the-way-there mother and her mumbled warnings about danger and the saving power of the zodiac? Ooh, or maybe she'd go for broke and ask Quinn about his starring role as the Taurus?

Or maybe she could ask him a real doozy, like whether he was single or not.

Her ping-ponging thoughts were the *exact* reason

she shouldn't take a meeting with Quinn Tanner right now.

And what *about* that weird stuff her mother said? Taurus Warriors?

She stopped just short of the waiting area of her office and Jackson nearly plowed into her from behind. Smoothing her skirt, she didn't miss the whisper from behind her. "Okay, girlfriend, I get the hint. I'm not touching him."

She shot Jackson a glance over her shoulder, then moved into the outer office.

"Mr. Tanner."

"I thought we established last night you needed to call me Quinn." His broad shoulders caught her attention, just as they had the evening before, even though they were covered in a much more sedate button-down shirt as opposed to the sexy tuxedo. White cotton shouldn't be this sexy, but the crisp, pressed material drew her attention and Montana fought the rush of warmth that zinged down her spine. Damn him, this man was lethal.

Her assistant's whisper dropped even lower, so only she could hear. "Clearly, nothing I could do would make a lick of difference anyway. That man's eyes are firmly planted on you."

She tossed Jackson another pointed stare that promised the dire retribution of some hideous torture like instant coffee in the break room before crossing the outer office to Quinn. "Jackson, please hold my calls."

Despite the fact Quinn had almost a foot on him, Jackson sized him up before nodding. If she could have heard his thoughts, Montana suspected they ran along the lines of *touch her and die, maggot*. What he voiced, however, was a much more sedate, "Of course," before standing aside and allowing Quinn to pass through the outer office.

Montana mentally shook her head at men and their odd, territorial markings before leading Quinn toward her office at the far end of the hall.

"What can I help you with today, Quinn?"

"I wanted to see if you were okay."

Her breath came out in a rush as she worried the Band-Aid she'd placed on her thumb that morning after nicking herself in the shower. It was shocking just how *not* okay her life was.

Long-lost mother with possible mental illness and delusions. Check.

Crazed killer on the loose with a clear target in mind. Check.

Oversized, overbearing man capable of causing a hormone explosion from twenty paces. Check. Check.

Tearing her attention away from her thumb, she put on as bright a smile as she could manage. "None the worse for wear, apparently. And while I appreciate the concern, why are you here? Did you file that report with the police?"

"Of course. Besides, I told you I was interested in helping you."

Montana moved around her desk as Quinn took a seat opposite her, using the few extra seconds to collect her thoughts and slow her racing pulse. "While I appreciate your involvement, especially after last night's events, would you care to enlighten me on what's changed your mind?"

"Let's say I have my reasons."

"Since they involve me, I'd like to know what they are."

"Ms. Grant. I can provide you references as well as an extensive background check on my company if you're concerned about me or the quality of my work. That said, one doesn't work in the security industry without catching wind of things from time to time."

Montana had been trained at the knee of one of the last century's most revered businessmen. Shrewd and sharp, her father's poker face had been flawless but even Black Jack Grant had nothing on Quinn Tanner. His dark eyes remained impassive and his posture gave away nothing.

Absolutely nothing.

She was reluctantly impressed, even as the niggling sense of doubt that pressed on the edge of her senses rattled a few nerve endings. "And you think you've caught something about me?"

"Let's just say I take an interest in situations that I think bear closer scrutiny."

"And you think my . . . situation"—she waved a hand—"is one of those?"

"I don't think. I know."

Her mother's rock-solid beliefs picked that odd moment to come back to her. *"Quinn Tanner, the Taurus Warrior. He'll save you. I know it."*

Suspicion clawed at her with razor-sharp talons. "Does this have anything to do with my mother?"

"No."

A quick, solid, matter-of-fact response. *Hmmm. Curious.*

"She knows your name."

Quinn's dark eyes narrowed at that. "I've never met your mother, Montana. Besides, I thought your mother hasn't been a part of your life?"

"I believe I mentioned last night that she's recently come back into it."

"I can assure you, that has nothing to do with me."

Damn it, what was she missing? Although she gave the man credit for giving nothing away, he looked as if he genuinely had no idea what she was talking about.

Of course, what the hell did she know, anyway? The man worked in the security trade. His firm was responsible for the protection of the world's wealthy, from royalty to high-ranking government officials to the rich and famous who wanted to feel protected from any number of things.

Even if he did know about her mother, he'd likely know how to hide it from her.

But still . . . it just *felt* like he had no idea what she was talking about.

Did she dare mention the other things her mother said? That whole weird bit about the *zodiac* and *Themis* and—oh God, was she seriously considering any of this?—his sign.

Taurus.

On a deep breath, Montana pressed him. "Does this have anything to do with what I asked you last night? About Themis?"

Bingo.

Quinn Tanner might have a poker face, but that quick flicker at the edge of his eyes—not quite a flinch, more like a slight twitch—suggested the question hit home.

"The Greek goddess you asked me about? If you

ask me, it sounds like a code word for something. Something in the European division of Grant Shipping?"

His question was fair, even as Montana knew something hovered just under the surface. She couldn't define it, but she also couldn't quite shake the feeling she was being maneuvered.

Yes, that was the exact right word.

Maneuvered.

Like Quinn held all the cards and was just trying to get her to fold.

Chapter Five

Quinn took a deep breath as Montana's assistant entered the office with coffee service. He endured another one of Jackson's "don't fuck with me" glares, oddly satisfied to see the man's loyalty. He'd run the guy already, looking for any abnormalities, any sudden increases in his financial situation.

The guy was clean.

Other than a nice nest-egg annuity and an annual bonus he used to spend two weeks living the high life in the Bahamas every January, there wasn't any evidence to suggest he had any accounts socked away there. Or hidden anywhere else for that matter.

And he appeared to be as loyal as they came.

Although Quinn wasn't ready to rule anyone out—not even the delectable heiress sitting opposite him—he'd done this long enough to have a sense of where the dirt was hidden.

Of course, his senses had been off from the start of this project, especially if Grey's intelligence had any merit.

And knowing Grey, it had a hell of a lot of merit.

The guy knew his criminals, from the lowest pushers to the heads of every crime family in New York. If something was rotten in Denmark—or anywhere else for that matter—the ram knew about it.

"Thanks, Jackson."

The guy tossed one more glare for good measure, then left the office as silently as he came in.

"I'd like some answers, Quinn." Montana stared briefly into her coffee cup, before adding, "No matter how dumb the question may seem."

"Answer my question first. Do you think this reference to Themis has anything to do with your Greek operation? She's the goddess of justice. Anyone have a vendetta against the company? Operation Themis could be a code word for 'justice.'"

He watched her mull over the question—saw it spark briefly as something she should consider—before that crystal-blue gaze swung right back to him.

"It seems too odd. Besides, my mother hasn't been a part of Grant Shipping. She may have been hiding in the shadows, but there's no way my father would have ever let her get close to the business. Hell, get close to us, period."

"Things were bad after she left?"

Instantly intrigued by her no-nonsense professional tone as she laid it out for him, Quinn watched her face for any hint the story she told was a front. "It's hard for me to say what before was like, since she left when I was three months old. But from the snatches I've heard here and there, he loved her. When she left, something in him died."

And then he saw it. The tiniest crumble in her armor. The spark of blue fire that had flared in her eyes when she'd questioned him earlier dulled. The harsh reality of her parents' marriage dragging the very life out of her expression. "That must have been hard for you."

As if catching herself, she glanced up from her coffee, any hint of sadness evaporating from her face. "There are worse fates in life."

Quinn leaned forward, his gaze riveted on hers. "You don't believe that. I know you don't. So why don't you give me the real version of the story instead of that little sanitized story you gave me last night?"

Those delicately arched eyebrows shot up even as the corners of her mouth turned down, and when she spoke her voice was particularly frosty. "Excuse me?"

"You heard me. Enough bullshit. I want the truth."

"Thanks for the Jack Nicholson impression, Mr. Tanner, but I really don't have anything to tell you."

"I maintain my first answer." Quinn crossed his arms. "Bullshit. And the name's Quinn."

"What the hell do you want from me? *Quinn.*"

"I want your take on what's going on. Whether it's related to what's happening to you or not, the breakup of your parents' marriage has done a number on you. What do you know that you're not saying?"

On a harsh breath, Montana's face lost all color, the normal, healthy pink of her cheeks fading away. Whatever anger she'd mustered against him faded as well in the face of her words.

"It's me. She left because of me."

Montana thought her mother abandoned them because of her? An innocent infant, based on the time line of the story. Whatever Quinn expected her to say, that wasn't it.

"But you were a baby. A welcomed one, at that, if the headlines at the time of your birth are any indication."

"She didn't want me and she left rather than stay and raise me. I'd hardly call that an overwhelming motherly instinct."

Quinn shook his head, searching for the words that might help her understand. "The logic just doesn't work for me."

He saw the questions that filled her gaze, layered over the pain of abandonment that clearly lived under her skin. "What?"

"Your father was one of the wealthiest men in the world. And was at the time of your birth as well."

"Yes?"

"So what would have kept your mother from simply allowing you to be raised by the help?"

The grief that had settled around her like a shawl receded slightly. He could see it in the shape of her body as she leaned forward. The set of her shoulders as she sat staring at him expectantly. "What do you mean?"

An image of her from the previous evening swamped his senses and the urge to reach forward and recapture a loose lock of hair had him lifting his hand from where he gripped the chair. Quinn stopped the impulse just in time, instead laying a hand on the edge of her desk as he leaned forward.

"Think about it. You weren't exactly born into a family that has to suffer with things they don't like.

If—and I think it's a seriously big if, based on her recent behavior—your mother didn't want to be a mother, what reason would she have to leave? All she needed to do was hire a nanny, pat you on the head from time to time and go on with her life. But she didn't do that. She ran."

Montana nodded, those lush red curls he couldn't keep his eyes off resettling around her shoulders. "Yes."

"And now your father's dead and she's back."

"You really think they're tied together?"

"I think it's an awfully large coincidence that deserves some additional investigation. In the meantime, I need you to start thinking more objectively."

"About what?"

"Your mother. Stop thinking like her child and start thinking like a woman who's been targeted."

"It's not that easy, Quinn."

"At least acknowledge there might be something else going on. Something related to her."

At her nod, he kept on going before the emotional land mine he'd just uncovered could slow them down. "Now tell me about that large board meeting you have in a week?"

"My board of directors meeting?"

"It's a big deal. You're taking the company public. Looking at all this through a new lens, maybe someone doesn't want to see that happen?"

Whatever lingering emotion had cloaked her vanished at the potential for problems his words implied. And with that implication, the wounded child became the competent CEO. "A public offering stands to make many people very wealthy. Inside and outside the company. It's good for business."

"Not if some of your internal people have a few side businesses of their own." Quinn decided to go for broke. It was the only way to divert her. The only way to keep her off the subject she kept returning to with unerring precision.

Before she could reply, he pressed on. "Much of the business community thinks Grant Shipping is running some dirty business on the side. You go public and the people doing that are going to have a much harder time hiding it."

Quinn saw the moment his words penetrated, shifting her thoughts firmly away from Themis. "You think I'm dirty? Is that why you've taken a sudden interest in me?"

"You have to admit, the timing is awfully strange."

"Strange? For what? You sit there, blithely insulting me to the very core and you have the nerve to chalk it up to fucking timing?"

A lovely pink glow suffused her from her cheeks to the generous swell of her neckline. Quinn willfully tamped on the urge to look at the beautiful arch of her breasts, instead focusing on what he had to do: find a way to figure out if she really was as dirty as her old man.

Was it really possible? This woman was light and innocence personified and what he mentally accused her of was the worldwide equivalent of kicking puppies for a living.

Fuck. He needed to get his traitorous dick out of this and focus on the facts.

She helmed the largest shipping company in the world.

Said shipping company was up to its eyeballs in corrupt dealings.

And she was clearly messed up with some nasty—and powerful—people since she'd been targeted for several attempts on her life by supernatural beings.

"Isn't everything in life about timing?"

She shook her head, confusion now warring with anger. "Now we're having a philosophical discussion? Well, let me give you a bit of philosophy to chew on. I'm not, nor have I ever been, interested in raping the world of its gifts. I run a legitimate business with legitimate interests and I make legitimate profits. Anything else you've heard is bullshit."

Quinn saw the sincerity in the cold blue of her gaze and in the firm set of her shoulders. Felt it in the bite of conviction that laced her words.

So why did every bit of intelligence he'd managed to source suggest otherwise?

"Come now, Ms. Grant. You can't honestly tell me you believe that."

Arturo Veron stepped out of the shower and admired his wet physique in front of the floor-to-ceiling mirror in his hotel suite. Long, lean ropes of muscle corded his arms and legs, while eight thick, perfectly formed barrels rode his midsection, from just beneath his rock-hard pecs to the lower portion of his stomach.

But, as always, it was the power that rested just beneath that caught his attention. With deft fingers, he reached below the swath of hair to the long, hard length of his penis, his arousal claiming him instantly at the touch of his hand. He closed his eyes for the briefest of moments, imagining the two women he'd shared the previous evening, their moans like a remembered symphony in his head.

And then the image changed. Morphed into the one face he'd never seen writhe in pleasure, save for the rare evenings when he dreamed.

Long, lush red hair that cascaded around her shoulders in waves. Tight, high breasts, their nipples proudly pointed forward. Endlessly long legs that he imagined wrapped around his waist as he plunged himself into her.

The strength of his arousal diminished as he reached for a towel. He no longer took pleasure imagining her. Refused to accept—would *never* accept—that she'd not chosen him. Instead, he returned to his second-most-favorite fantasy—world domination.

With the towel slung low on his waist, he padded to the sink and rummaged through the items he traveled with. His BlackBerry message light winked red and he scrolled through the fifteen messages that had come in during his brief shower.

With another glance at the mirrors that surrounded him, replicating his form from all angles, repeating into infinity, he laid the device back on the counter and smiled. He took great pleasure in the idea that most of the businessmen who stayed in this suite were paunchy, their bodies going to shit as they sought to take over their little corner of the world.

Day after day they subsisted on high-fat diets rich in butter, churned out in the world's great restaurants over business lunches. Night after night, they drank their livers into oblivion with too many martinis.

He, on the other hand, was taking over the world

and looking damn fine while doing it. Butter had no effect on his body and the liquor offered a pleasant diversion, especially when drunk in proper moderation while doing business.

His BlackBerry buzzed again and he glanced at the readout, answering when he saw his personal assistant's name backlit on the screen. "Veron."

"I moved your meetings as you requested. Your schedule is fully clear to deal with Grant Shipping for the next week."

"Good. Good. And the arrangements I requested in Florida?"

"All taken care of, Mr. Veron."

"Excellent." Even better would be the mind wipe he'd do on her in the morning, so the details of said trip were nowhere to be found in the vast wasteland of her memories.

"I'll see you later today, then, Lina."

"Of course, Mr. Veron."

As he laid the BlackBerry back onto the counter, Arturo caught sight of the towel where it tented in front of him. His arousal was back, harder than before. Although he'd always loved violence, he had never known—never realized—just how sweet vengeance could be.

How gloriously fan-fucking-tastic it felt. Better than the two women who'd warmed his bed until the wee hours of the morning, truth be told.

His plans spun out before him like the mental equivalent of a chess board. He'd already made his first move, with the next scheduled for tonight.

As Arturo threw the towel on the far corner of the bathroom floor, he couldn't resist one last look at himself in the mirror as he strode toward the bedroom. His gaze caught on an image of his back, where the bull that rode high on his shoulder flicked its tail as its front paw made a stamping motion on the ground.

The beast was as excited as he was.

Thick, syrupy waves of panic lurched through Montana's stomach, an odd counterpoint to the heavy, throbbing base drum of her pulse as it thudded in her ears.

Her head spun from the rapid-fire questions and the wildly veering speculation Quinn Tanner had thrown at her. From her mother to her business to her own personal integrity, the man hadn't left a single stone unturned.

He was following her because he thought her business was dirty? Thought she was responsible for any number of horrors in the race for the almighty dollar?

An image of them last night filled her senses, the warm, safe feel of his body as he held her along with the steady thump of his heartbeat where her ear lay pressed against his chest. All that time, while she felt safe, secure and protected, he thought she was a criminal out for personal gain.

Could those moments have meant nothing to him? She reached up and brushed a lock of hair—that lock *he'd* touched with such gentle fingers—and swept it behind her ear.

And how, in what freaking universe, had his opinion come to mean so much to her?

"Do you believe it?"

His dark brown gaze gave away nothing, nor did

the harsh set of those broad shoulders. "I'm simply repeating what I've heard, Montana."

The heavy thud of her pulse intensified further at his lack of denial. "That's not what I asked you."

"Can you give me one good reason not to believe it?"

And there was her answer. The night before meant nothing to him beyond a job to be done.

Pain twisted through her as she placed a hand over her stomach. Literal, physical pain at the idea this man thought she was . . . dirty.

Unclean.

Tainted with the blood of innocents.

For reasons she couldn't quite name, Quinn's negative opinion of her hurt deeply. Of course, why did what he thought matter at all?

It shouldn't. She'd known him less than twenty-four hours. But it *did* matter.

"I have nothing to change your opinion with, other than the truth. I don't run a bad business."

The air crackled between them as storm clouds descended into that dark brown gaze. "Come on, Montana. Don't play the innocent. Your father ran one of the world's most profitable businesses for forty years. Do you really mean to tell me you think it's all been aboveboard? You're sitting on profits that make the Queen of England and the Pope look like paupers."

She didn't want to listen to this. Didn't want to listen to him voice the very same questions she'd been fighting for the past six months.

She couldn't accept the possibility she'd spent her entire life living a lie. Living with wealth and privilege while others suffered at her father's hands.

The thought she hadn't wanted to give voice to— the thought that tore her apart in ribbons from the inside out—rose up and swamped her.

Was that the *real* reason her mother left?

Had she found out the truth?

And had she abandoned her daughter to be raised in that filth?

"I would have known. Sensed—" She broke off, the words simply evaporating from her lips.

"Not to mention, your company's had wild success in the regions of the world where nothing gets done aboveboard or without a hell of a lot of arm twisting."

His words echoed her own concerns from earlier. "But that's different. That much is written into our operating policies as an organization, for heaven's sake. There are regions of the world where you just have to get things done. It doesn't mean we're a corrupt business because we know how to grease a few local palms to get our shipments in and out of port. It's standard practice and you know it."

Quinn leaped forward at that, his hands placed flat on the desk as he leaned toward her. Despite the over-sized nature of the cherry desk, Quinn's large body took up all the space between them when he leaned forward, his face inches from hers.

Montana desperately yearned for the familiar press of leather at her back, but wouldn't back down. Would not lean back in her chair, no matter how hard this man tried to dominate the conversation with his physical strength.

"Grease a few palms? Come on now, heiress. Here's what I know. It wouldn't take much to look at those situations and decide you wanted a cut for yourself."

"You can't be serious."

"Serious as a heart attack. Here's how I see it playing out. There are all these evil men you have to bargain with to get things done. Even the most basic things like setting up a legitimate business that brings more than enough commerce into the region takes almost more effort than it's worth because after you're done paying them, there's nothing left. So what do you do?"

"It's not like that. At all!"

Quinn shrugged those big shoulders, but his gaze never wavered. "Sure it is. Here you are, running a legitimate business and you have all these soulless predators who take the riches off the land—oil, diamonds and whatever else they can get their hands on. So what's any good businesswoman to do? You decide to get in on the action yourself."

A dizzying rush replaced the thudding pulse in her head as the paperwork she'd reviewed the night before registered again. South African operation.

Minimal participation in the company as they flew under the radar. Modest profits that satisfied, yet didn't raise any scrutiny. Maximum lifestyle.

"Oh God. Diamonds?" As in smuggling.

Quinn nodded his head, the heavy tenor of his voice pounding the truth home like a judge's gavel. "You've got shipping manifests running through every port in the world. How hard would it be to stash a bit of cargo in your hold? You do that, you can run whatever you want."

"But I'm not running anything."

"Somebody is."

Realization struck with the speed of an oncoming freight train and then she did lean back in her chair, allowing the soft, buttery leather to cushion her body. "That's the reason for the attacks."

"Maybe yes, maybe no. Who'd you piss off?"

As his words registered—and the evidence he didn't believe her—she leaped up, the movement dislodging her chair so it went flying behind her. "I told you, I'm not involved in this."

"I hate to be the bearer of bad news, but you *are* involved in this, Montana. To the very red bottoms of those designer shoes you're wearing."

His gaze never wavered from her as his words filled the space up between them. The urge to lean over and press her lips to his roared up, a living, breathing need pulsing with desperate heat.

What was wrong with her?

This man was the only thing who stood between her and a crazy stalker with homicidal tendencies. He thought she was a diamond smuggler and God knew what else. *And* he'd appeared in her life without reason and, despite her best efforts, she hadn't managed to get any explanations out of him.

So why was it she believed, to the very marrow of her bones, that Quinn Tanner was the only bet worth risking her life on?

The game was up. She was showing her cards and folding.

Who gave a shit if her father was rolling in his grave? Black Jack Grant had gotten her into this mess. Now it was up to her to get herself out.

"I know you don't believe me. I know it. But I need your help."

"I already gave you my help."

"Yeah, but now I need you to actually believe me, too."

Quinn was saved from answering by a knock on the door. With an impatient glance, Montana uttered a "come in." Jackson walked in with an armful of folders and laid three stapled documents out on the desk in a neat row. "I'm sorry to bother you with this now, but I need you to sign these so I can get them out tonight. The others can keep until morning."

"The shipping manifests for the new port?"

"Yep." Jackson nodded as he reached for his own BlackBerry clipped at his waist. "If I don't get these in the overnight, they won't make it to the Tokyo office on time and legal still needs to see them as well."

"It's already tomorrow," Quinn offered with a small smile, bemused despite himself at the efficient symphony playing out before him. "Where you're sending those."

Montana's furrowed brow smoothed out lightly at his interruption as she glanced up from the paperwork. "No matter how often I travel, that will never make sense to me."

"The space-time continuum?" Quinn offered.

"I guess you could call it that. All I know is that there's something distinctly odd about arriving somewhere that I lose an entire day of my life. It's unnerving."

If she thought *that* was unnerving, Quinn wondered how she'd handle a teleport through space. An image filled his mind's eye of the two of them hand-delivering those papers she signed to the Tokyo office in the flash of a moment.

The thought was followed by another . . . that he'd actually *like* to take her on a port.

Montana handed the signed documents to Jackson, then shot the man a quick, adoring look. "What would I do without you?"

"Likely spend far more time here than you already do. Now get back to your meeting. I'm sorry for the interruption. And"—he cut her off as she opened her mouth to speak—"I'll drop the last of the paperwork for your review at your place on my way home tonight."

"Truly. You're amazing."

"I know."

Quinn watched Jackson leave the office, fascinated by the man's byplay with Montana. "You and Jackson have a rhythm."

"He's wonderful. Always has been. And he's a good friend to boot."

Quinn gazed at the perfection that was Montana Grant—long, sleek red hair, porcelain skin, a lithe body that held the most fascinating, feminine curves.

To the outside world, her life looked perfect.

She looked perfect.

"You don't have many of those, do you?"

The delightful blue of Montana's eyes narrowed as she directed the full force of her gaze on him. "That's a lovely thing to say."

"Sarcasm noted. However, I didn't mean it as anything other than a statement of fact. You're wealthy and you run a multibillion-dollar conglomerate. Your company's budget is larger than most small countries. Must be hard to make friends."

The harsh set of her shoulders drooped ever so

slightly and some of the sharp icicles left her frost-blue gaze. "No, you're right. There aren't all that many inside the inner sanctum. Jackson is one of them."

"Why him?" He kept the question casual, but Quinn often knew it was the simplest answers that said the most about a person.

"Because he sees me."

Bingo.

"I see you."

"No, you see a woman who you believe runs diamonds, drugs and God knows what manner of other things. You see me as an object to be dealt with. Jackson sees me as his friend."

"But you're his boss."

"And if he left tomorrow—and I've offered him money countless times to do just that and start his own company—he'd still be my friend. In the meantime, he stays here. He says he likes it. And frankly, I like his company far too much to send him away."

Quinn thought of his own friends. Although they were brothers in arms, they were friends first. From different backgrounds, different histories, different walks of life. But they all had one thing in common.

A fierce loyalty to one another and a willingness to watch one another's back. Until, of course, your friend made a decision you didn't agree with and you fucked him over.

Damn it, no matter how many times he thought about it—his refusal to aid his friend—Quinn couldn't escape the wickedly sharp needles of guilt that wouldn't leave him.

Friendship, Quinn mused, was a pain in the ass.

Chapter Six

Montana stared at the closed door of her office a long time after Quinn left, replaying each and every moment of their conversation.

Could he possibly be right about her mother?

Was there something—some reason—that had forced Eirene Grant away all those years ago? Something so horrible that leaving her husband and baby behind was preferable to dealing with it.

And what was with those weird questions about Jackson? Even as she thought it, she dismissed it pretty quickly. Quinn, no doubt, had Jackson at the top of his alternate-suspect list if she turned out to be innocent in his mind's eye.

But damn it, she *was* innocent.

Of course, the man was clearly someone who had to come to his own conclusions, so let him think what he wanted. He'd figure it out eventually.

She was innocent of whatever wrongdoing he suspected.

And based on his suspicions—the ones he voiced—she was hell-bent on getting to the bottom of whatever else might be going on in her company.

Like a never-ending kaleidoscope of unanswerable questions, Montana shifted her thoughts back to her mother. She knew she shouldered far too much of the perceived blame for her mother's choices and she had years in therapy to show for it. Even now, as the idea of Eirene's abandonment tumbled through her mind with Quinn's added perspective, Montana wavered between opposing sides of the argument that had haunted her throughout her life.

Every rational thought in her head assured her an infant could have absolutely no fault in the choice of an adult.

But that motherless child that lived inside of her had always felt differently on the matter.

She wasn't good enough.

She wasn't worth keeping.

She wasn't worth loving.

And speaking of Quinn, why did he change the subject every time she tried to bring up Themis? Oh, he was subtle about it, but he was clearly deft at moving past that topic.

Why?

"You ready for lunch?" Jackson poked his head through her office door.

"Yes. Absolutely."

"What did the man candy want?"

Montana threw him a glance as she reached for her purse. "Excuse me?"

"Oh, don't play coy with me. You know I'm referring to the Adonis you spent half the morning with in here. Men like that don't come along every day, honey. Believe you me."

She couldn't stop the light giggle that rumbled up at Jackson's affronted tone. Affecting a more serious air as she walked around the desk, Montana added, "Based on the death glare you shot him every ten seconds, I'm surprised you're the one now singing his praises. And, besides, isn't that objectifying him if we call him man candy?"

"Just because I was worried about you didn't mean I couldn't appreciate the fine specimen that he is. And man candy isn't derogatory when used as a term of respectful awe. Which, I might add, is how I'm using it."

They rode the elevator silently and it wasn't until they neared the exit in the main lobby that Montana slowed her pace and turned toward Jackson, forcing him to slow, too. "Worried about me? Why?"

"The man's the head of one of the city's most well-respected private security firms. And it's not like we don't have a shitload of security in this place."

"Yes? So what?"

Jackson kept them moving outside, away from the prying eyes of any staff members moving through the lobby on their lunch hour. "So it was a pretty easy leap to ask myself what the man's doing with my best girl."

"Did anyone ever tell you you have way too huge a sense of entitlement for a personal assistant?"

Jackson flagged down a cab hurtling in their direction from a half a block away. "And did anyone ever tell *you* you have no idea how to manage a personal assistant? Seriously? It was your idea to take me to the Oak Room. Are you trying to give me a big head, taking me to lunch at the Plaza?"

Montana laughed, enjoying the first real easing of the tension riding her shoulders all morning. "Cheeky."

Jackson leaned in and bussed her cheek for a quick kiss as the cabdriver's launch from the curb threw them both back against the seat. "Count on it."

She was still smiling ten minutes later as they walked into the restaurant. Jackson never failed to cheer her up and his animated chatter about the curve of Quinn Tanner's ass for the duration of the cab ride was—she had to admit—right on the money.

The smile abruptly vanished as a series of stares greeted her inside the restaurant. Just as it had the night before at the gala, the feeling of being on display chaffed.

Get a grip, girlfriend. You've lived with this your entire life. What's suddenly changed?

Montana rubbed her stomach and took a deep breath, unable to understand why she suddenly felt so exposed.

And vulnerable.

"You okay, sweetie? You're pure white," Jackson whispered so no one heard his comments as they followed the maître d' to their table.

"I'm fine." Montana gritted her teeth as they were led straight to a table smack dab in the center of the room.

Seriously?

Why today of all days?

With a resigned sigh, Montana took the seat the maître d' held out for her and offered him a polite smile.

Jackson's eyebrows practically touched his hairline as he shot her a castigating look while settling his napkin on his lap. "You want to try honesty this time?"

"It's true. I am fine."

"Okay. I'll rephrase my question. What happened with Tanner this morning?"

"Jackson. Come on. It's nothing."

"I'm giving you three more seconds and then I'm calling him myself."

Montana weighed the wisdom of pulling Jackson into any of this. Although he knew about her mother, he would freak if he knew about the attack the night before. Of course, an extra pair of eyes watching her back couldn't exactly hurt, either. She weighed her options a few more beats as Jackson's dark green eyes bored into hers.

"Okay. Fine. I'll tell you. But let's order first so we're not interrupted or possibly overheard."

Jackson nodded once, flipped quickly through his menu, then laid it on the edge of the table. Their waiter took their orders and left them alone, obviously used to the business lunch crowd.

Leaning forward, Montana closed her eyes and whispered on a rush, "What do you know about astrology?"

"Not much past what I read in the *Post* every morning on the subway."

"And what about Greek mythology?"

"You mean like gods and goddesses and stuff?"

Montana nodded, surprised when the words continued to spill out of their own accord. "I mean exactly like gods and goddesses. I think they're trying to kill me."

"Kill you?" Jackson's voice was an urgent whisper as his hands clenched into fists on top of the table. "You can't possibly be serious."

"Sadly, I am."

"Even if we assume for a moment I believe any of what you're telling me—and I always believe you—what does this have to do with astrology?"

"Potentially a lot. Maybe nothing."

Jackson held up a hand. "Do I need a drink for this?"

"Probably."

With a quick wave to their waiter, Jackson flagged him back to the table. "Two vodka tonics. Double the vodka."

"Yes, sir."

Montana watched as a series of reactions flitted across her friend's face. Disbelief. Shock. Anger. One morphed into the next as Jackson struggled to find words. "Okay. What the hell is this all about?"

"You're going to think I need serious help."

"I already think that. Now spill."

Montana wanted to be offended at Jackson's frank assessment, but no matter how hard she tried, she couldn't summon much annoyance. "That's not a nice thing to say."

"We threw nice out the window my second day on the job. Would you quit stalling and tell me?"

"I've told you about my mother." At Jackson's nod, Montana updated him on Eirene's delusions, culminating with all the things she said on her last visit. "She can't stop talking about Greek gods and goddesses. I don't know if it's code for something, or if they've somehow taken on some role in her mind. All I know is the latest is that she's insisting that someone's been sent to protect me."

"Protect you from what?"

"She won't define the what exactly. Just that I need

protecting. And then there was the attack last night. And Quinn was there to save me."

"Whoa, whoa, whoa. What attack?"

Montana rounded out her story with the details of the previous evening. "So the man candy came in handy, just in the nick of time."

"You could say that."

Although he'd peppered her with a stream of questions throughout the telling of the previous evening's events, Jackson's eyes were hard emeralds, focused on her face as he took in every bit of her story. "I'm going to allow for the fact you had virtually no sleep and an early-morning visitor as the reason you didn't tell me any of this first thing."

Adding in a long-suffering sigh for good measure, Jackson continued. "What would your mother know of Quinn? And do you think she's responsible for any of this?"

"She can't be."

"Montana." His tone gentled. "You know nothing about her. And here she is, suddenly a part of your life, telling you things are going to happen and then they do. And mythology? What better cover for making you think she's nuts?"

And just like that, every insecurity she'd tried to tamp down on earlier came rumbling back to life with the strength and speed of a herd of bulls. "It's not like that."

"Isn't it? Your father's gone six months and then your mother shows up a few weeks before you take the company public?"

The truth of his words were like sharp, stinging

icicles against her skin. "It's not like that. It doesn't feel like it."

"Come on, honey. You've had more than your fair share of heartache. Now you're dealing with this. What else could it possibly feel like?"

Montana heard the edge in her voice—that not-so-subtle desperation that ground against her vocal chords. "But she's not threatening. And neither is Quinn."

"If they are a couple of operators, that's exactly what they want you to think. Besides, that man's hot enough to scramble a few brain cells."

"But it's not like that."

Wasn't it?

The steady sound of Quinn's heartbeat rushed through her ears as she remembered their previous evening on the couch. A flood of warmth filled her, skittering along her nerve endings in the exact place where his large arms had wrapped around her body.

"And you're not even supposed to be noticing those things."

Jackson leaned forward. "Hey. I'm single and un-attached. That's what happens when you have a slave driver for a boss. Surely, said boss wouldn't deny me a little bit of fun."

Montana dabbed neatly at her lips with her napkin, her spirits already rising. "And there just went that raise I was getting ready to put through to HR for you."

"A *bitchy* slave driver," Jackson added for good measure. Switching gears, her dog-with-a-bone personal assistant veered straight back to their conversation, preinterruption. "So tell me more about this astrology stuff."

"It's nothing."

"It wasn't nothing ten minutes ago."

Montana thought about Jackson's quick dismissal of anything related to the supernatural. Sadly, he was probably right. "Yeah, but it's nothing now. I was just being silly."

"I didn't mean that, Montana."

"I know you didn't. But it is silly. It's just my mother. Her being back—and me trying to come to grips with the person she is—it's got me thinking in circles."

"It takes a toll, honey. Add to that all the stress and pressure of work. A few odd thoughts here and there are to be expected."

Montana accepted his comments for what they were— a dear friend trying to calm her with logic and reason. But somewhere deep inside—in that place that not only recognized the truth, but believed it—she knew she was right.

On a groan, Jackson shifted his attention to the vibrating BlackBerry sitting on the table. With a quick head shake at the screen, he shot a longing glance at his half-eaten lunch. "The contracts department. I left one of the backup pages for the manifests on my desk by mistake and they can't finish the contracts without them."

"Can someone help you?"

"It's confidential information on that large shipment for one of the big electronics manufacturers. No one else needs to see it. I'm going to have to excuse myself and get back. Will you be okay?"

"Of course. I'll grab a cab."

"With all that's going on, are you sure you should be by yourself? I can have car service over here before you're ready to leave."

Montana waved it off, even as she was touched by his concern. "I'm fine. We're dining in the middle of one of the city's oldest hotels. Cabs line up around the block—I won't even have to wait."

"You're sure?"

"Of course I'm sure. I'm a tough broad."

Jackson gave her a big smile as he leaned down to kiss her cheek. "Yes, you are."

As she watched his retreating back, Montana wondered why she was having such a hard time believing it.

Quinn stood at the curb and waited for Montana to leave the Plaza. It galled him to stand outside and wait for her, like a pet dog left tied up outside a store while his master did as she pleased, but it wasn't to be helped. He wanted to keep an eye on her and intruding on her lunch would have gotten her back up.

Especially because she was only going to get her back up even further when he informed her he was attending her scheduled function this evening as her date.

Quinn did bless his overdeveloped eyesight—and her willingness to keep her schedule in a neat plastic cover on the corner of her desk—for the location of her lunch and the information for the evening.

Yet another black-tie charity affair would benefit from her patronage. At least this time she was attending as a guest and not as the focal point of the evening.

The only question left in Quinn's mind was whether or not she was planning on taking a date. For some reason he wasn't comfortable defining, the thought of Montana on a date left a raw, acid-filled path of fire from the bitter taste on his tongue clear to the pit of his stomach.

Quinn caught sight of Montana's personal assistant as he hotfooted it out of the hotel. The man's attention was so focused on the taxi line Jackson never even noticed him standing fifteen feet away.

Hunching his shoulders against the cool fall breeze that blew around him, Quinn figured Montana wouldn't be far behind. Twenty minutes later, he muttered under his breath as he stole yet another glance at his watch. He began to move toward the steps that led to the hotel's front door when he saw Montana's long, lean frame, clad in a designer raincoat, pass the bellman.

He watched as her eyes focused on the waiting line of taxis as she descended the steps. Pushing as much nonchalance into his voice as he could, he stepped toward her. "Fancy meeting you here."

Montana dropped the hand she had up, midwave to the front car. "Quinn. What are you doing here?"

"Waiting for you."

"Why?"

"I told you. I'm watching out for you."

He felt a small hitch in his chest when the front of her raincoat came open and she planted a hand on her hip. In that moment, he got another look at those long, glorious legs of hers, on perfect display in the designer business suit that stopped above the knee. "Then why didn't you just come with me? Why make the production of leaving earlier, only to show up a few hours later?"

"I wanted to see how you handled yourself."

"How I handled myself?"

"Yes. Are you aware of your surroundings? Are you

paying attention to who may be watching you? I'm sorry to say, you failed the test."

A disgruntled businessman stepped around Montana to grab the first cab and she stepped aside, her annoyance telegraphing itself to him in short, irritated bursts. "Seeing as how I had no idea I was being tested, I call bullshit on your results."

"You think last night wasn't a test?"

The delicate eyebrows that had arched over her eyes in annoyance snapped together in time to her question. "Why would you think that?"

"You're alive, aren't you?"

"I thought that was your doing. Not some planned mock attack by the deranged asshole who has decided to make me his next target."

Quinn had to give her credit. She might be scared out of her mind—the huddled, shivering woman from the night before hadn't strayed far from his thoughts—but she wasn't giving up without a fight.

Or a hell of a lot of moxie.

"I told you I was going to guard you until we got to the bottom of this."

Montana exhaled a heavy sigh and moved back toward the cab line, her arm already going up to signal to the next available driver. Wind whipped around her, snapping at the long, sleek edges of her coat.

Quinn reached for her, pulling her into his arms. "Did you hear nothing I said? You can't put yourself at risk."

"What has gotten into you?" Large blue eyes stared up at him, crackling with barely repressed anger and a fire that seared him somewhere low in the gut. Despite intermittent flares of frustration that suggested he back off, it didn't escape his notice that she didn't push him away.

Or pull out of his arms.

Instead, the moment spun out between the two of them, hammering a series of blows at Quinn's vigilant self-control.

The cacophony of noises in the street faded as he picked up on the sound of Montana's labored breathing; the very surroundings he was committed to keeping a watch on dulled against the brightness that colored everything about the woman in his arms.

"You can let me go now," she whispered.

"Actually—" Images slammed through his brain, all of which encompassed Montana Grant in varying stages of arousal.

The bright blue of her eyes turning a deep, dark indigo.

The flutter of pulse at the base of her throat that began to pound with the basest of desire.

The thick, heavy breaths that indicated her body's desperate need for his.

All those images and a million more flew through his mind's eye.

"Actually what?"

"Actually, I won't let you go. Not yet." Leaning in, Quinn pressed his lips against her surprised, parted ones, satisfied when she responded instantly. A small wicked moan escaped the back of her throat as her arms wrapped around his neck.

Hot, pounding desire vibrated through every fiber of his body, his muscles bunching and straining with the most primal need he'd ever experienced.

Ever.

With an urgent desperation he drew on her tongue, male satisfaction nearly a roar in his chest when she responded in kind, wrapping her own tongue around his with long, deep strokes. In perfect harmony, their lips merged and melded, retreated and rejoined.

He felt her fingers at the base of his skull, as one of her hands ran through the short hair at the nape of his neck. Her other hand held him firmly at his shoulder blades, as if she hung on for dear life.

His bull twitched under his skin from the pressure of Montana's hand on his shoulder. Although the tattoo had never been tied to his arousal, Quinn could feel the animal's impatience.

As Quinn continued to kiss the lush, vibrant woman in his arms, the tattoo grew more agitated, more active. Quinn knew Montana couldn't feel the bull, as the animal's physical presence was sustained within his aura, not his actual skin, but the sensation still bordered on unpleasant as her fingers continued to exert pressure. The increasing anxiety finally pulled Quinn from Montana's swollen lips, his concentrated focus taking over once again.

"Quinn?" Montana whispered.

He had nearly bent his head back toward her when his bull's impatience slammed through him in a wave of fury.

"Shit!" With a harsh jerk on her arms, Quinn dragged them both to the ground, cushioning her with his body as they hit the sidewalk before rolling on top to protect her. The move was so reminiscent of the evening prior, his body was almost on the move in the direction of the remembered attack.

Shaking off the last vestiges of arousal, he called

his battle-honed skills to the surface. Forcing himself to slow down and assess the moment, Quinn allowed his senses to feel for the threat. In ever-expanding circles, he reached out with his senses, seeking the telltale whispers of random electricity only a Destroyer could generate.

As the bull quieted, allowing Quinn to concentrate and feel for the threat, it registered.

Whisper light, but evident nonetheless, like short sparks that flew from your fingertips when you touched something after wearing socks on a rug.

Gotcha, asshole.

Glancing back over his shoulder, Quinn zeroed in on the direction of the current. The threat had come from the hotel, not the park across the street. That knowledge was followed quickly by one other certainty.

Her attacker had been inside the Plaza with her.

Chapter Seven

Montana held on to Quinn's hand as he dragged her in the direction of the park. She tried to ignore the sharp barbs of pain that shot up her ankles from the heels she wore to focus on the situation at hand.

"Quinn? What is wrong with you?"

The infuriating man continued pulling her along, and although his grip was gentle, it was also firm enough that she knew he wasn't letting go.

"Protecting you from a threat."

With a short, hard tug, she planted her feet and dragged on his hand. "What is going on?"

"I felt something. Back there at the restaurant. I can't explain it, but I'm sure. Someone was there."

Darts of unease flitted through her. Was someone really and truly trying to attack her?

Kill her?

The acknowledgment was enough to have her ignoring the pain in her feet and moving with a renewed burst of speed as they ran into one of the park's south entrances.

"Why are we going in here?" Even as she questioned him, Montana knew Quinn was doing his best to keep her safe. "Isn't that making ourselves more of a target?"

"I just need to buy us a bit of distance so I can call for reinforcements."

Montana kept pace with Quinn as he kept watch on both their surroundings as well as the screen of his BlackBerry. "It's Tanner. I need your help. Wollman Rink." He shoved the phone back into his slacks pocket as he dragged her several more yards toward Central Park's famed ice-skating rink.

"But there are people here. What if he tries to hurt them, too?"

"Then we take our chances."

With another hard tug on his arm, Montana came to a stumbling halt. She would have fallen to her knees if it weren't for the hard grip he had on her hands. She heard the shouts of the people on the ice-skating rink—the loud, happy hollers of small children—and knew she couldn't expose them to her problems. "I can't put all these people in danger."

Chest heaving with exertion and fear, more scared than she'd ever been in her life, Montana took some small comfort in the look that filled Quinn's dark eyes.

Acknowledgment.

Understanding.

Respect.

"Quinn. What's going on?"

A wave of fear skipped down her spine at the stealthy approach and she whirled around to find two men, nearly as tall as Quinn, walking up from the direction of the rink.

Both of them looked like they'd just stepped off the pages of *GQ*. Long legs encased in black silk slacks. One wore a black silk shirt to match, while the other had on a cashmere sweater that covered his broad shoulders with masculine grace.

Who *were* these people?

"Took you long enough," Quinn rumbled.

Long enough? Could she have heard him right? Quinn had just made his call.

Both men ignored the insult, as one pointed in the direction she and Quinn had just run from. "Brody's got the south entrance and Drake's over at the hotel. Bond Street and I are here to help."

Before any of them could say another word, a hot pulse of electricity struck her full force across the back, knocking her into Quinn. The impact was so immediate—so unexpected—her forward momentum took him down with her.

Whatever impression she might have had from the fashionably dressed men who had just shown up, nothing could have prepared Montana for what came next.

Both took off toward the path she and Quinn had just walked down, splitting out like two large cats, hunting their prey. Fascinated, Montana could almost forget the searing pain in her shoulder blades as she watched the beauty of their male bodies as they disappeared into the trees.

Suddenly, she couldn't see anything as Quinn pulled her against his chest, his hands roaming over her back in large, expansive touches.

"Does that hurt?"

"Yes." She shivered as Quinn hit a particularly sitive spot over her right shoulder blade

"Here?" He pressed the spot harder.

That was all it took. Just that one touch over the center of the attack. Great, fiery stabs of pain ran down her spinal cord, flooding her system in shock.

With a loud scream, Montana fell forward into his arms as the world went black.

Quinn didn't hesitate or second-guess his actions. Without waiting another moment, he ported them out of the park and into the Warriors' brownstone on the Upper West Side. He'd deal with the inevitable consequences later.

Right now, she needed attention.

The trouble was, attention for what?

He'd assumed from the start they were dealing with Destroyers. And while exposure to their electricity would drain a human over time, one hard hit of a fireball shouldn't have had this effect.

He glanced down at Montana's pale face as he strode through the main hallway of the mansion. Damn it, this was all his fault.

His fucking *distracted* fault.

"Callie! Get down here!"

Even the bellowing scream couldn't help allay the fear roiling through him. And retracing his actions only offered more frustrating questions.

It was obvious she'd taken the hit to her back. So he felt for damage, and even though her coat and suit jacket had taken a beating, both now bearing a large hole, he hadn't found any blood.

So what had hurt her so badly?

"What are you screaming about?" Kane's wife, Ilsa, walked out of the first-floor library, clearly intent on giving him grief, when she caught sight of Montana. "What's going on?"

"Where's Callie?"

"Get her in here. I'll go get Callie. She's in the basement looking into that research you asked her about." Ilsa stepped aside and ported away. Quinn had barely laid Montana on the couch when Ilsa returned along with Callie.

"What's happened to her?"

"I don't know." Quinn ran a hand through his hair as Callie came rushing to Montana's side. She was their resident expert on more things under heaven and earth than any one being should know. Quinn reluctantly stepped aside to let her take a look at the heiress.

And then there wasn't any time to think or wallow or worry as Callie began firing a barrage of questions. "Destroyer attack?"

"That's what I thought it was. Now I'm not so sure."

"Why not?"

"I tried to feel for damage and she passed out from the pain. A fireball wouldn't do that."

"Okay. Both of you—help me get all these clothes off of her so we can look."

Quinn held Montana up while the women worked to remove the raincoat and suit jacket. Once they resettled her on her side, Quinn could see bright, wicked slashes of red on her skin through the torn material of her blouse.

Callie didn't hesitate to take control of the situation. "Ilsa. Please go get my medicine kit and something we can cover her up with. This top needs to be cut away. She's already coming around."

Montana's long, low moan rose up in the room, fisting his heart and forcing a lump in his throat. He could actually hear the pain in the soft, mewling noises she made and it ripped at him.

"Shhh, now," Callie crooned. "We're going to get you fixed up."

Their healer and all-around Wonder Woman tossed him a glance as she worked at gently pulling the material of Montana's blouse away from her damaged skin. She mouthed the word *mortal* with raised eyebrows before returning her full attention toward the task.

"Can you help her?"

"We'll get her taken care of. Does she have a name?"

"Montana Grant."

Callie tossed him another knowing look before running a soothing hand down Montana's shoulder and upper arm. "Shhh, dear. You're safe here. I need you to take deep, even breaths."

"Where am I?"

Quinn moved around the couch to stand above her head, then crouched down on his knees so he could look her in the eyes. He kept his voice gentle as he assessed the pain that flashed in their depths. "You were attacked, sweetheart. In the park. But we're going to get you fixed up."

"Did you catch him?" She swallowed hard. "I mean. Those men. The ones you called. Did they catch him?"

Quinn's heart turned over as he remembered her words in the park. Her unwillingness to drag innocents into whatever was happening with her. Whatever he'd suspected—whatever he *thought* she was involved in— had evaporated in that instant. The woman was innocent.

He'd stake his life on it.

"I don't know. I brought you straight here. I'll find out."

She nodded and licked her dry lips. "Where's here?"

With soft movements, he ran his fingertips over her brow, then smoothed his hand over her hair. "My home."

"Smells nice. Safe."

Before she could say anything else, Ilsa came back into the room, walking this time. The goddess had clearly understood the implications of Callie's words—*she's coming around*—and didn't risk exposure by porting herself back into the room.

"I've got what you need."

"Quinn. Ilsa. I need you to hold her still. I'm afraid this is going to hurt."

Callie used the small scissors in her bag to cut away as much material as she could, leaving only a small patch still stuck to Montana's skin. "I need to remove this to begin cleaning the wound. Quinn, hold her shoulders. Ilsa, please keep her legs in place."

Quinn moved over Montana, placing his hands as Callie directed. The irony wasn't lost on him, the contrast of this moment so different from when he'd held her in his arms not even a half hour before, as they'd shared that blazing kiss.

"Ready?" Callie whispered.

Quinn and Ilsa both nodded.

"Montana. This is going to sting. I want you to hold on and scream if you need to."

She nodded and Quinn could see a lone tear where it pearled at the corner of her eye.

With one hard pull, Callie ripped the material away

from the skin. Montana screamed, the sound one of pure agony. It seared into his mind like a brand.

As he looked at the mottled flesh where Callie had removed the material of Montana's blouse, he was shocked to see a series of small metal barbs sticking from the skin.

Montana felt the scream reverberate in her throat and wondered if she could ever make it stop. Everything she was—every thought, every molecule, every emotion— was centered in that one horrible place on her back.

The world dimmed once again and she felt her stomach turning over on itself. Oh God, was she actually going to be sick?

And then she felt it.

Soft, soothing motions on her forehead and a light, crooning whisper. Both helped pull her from the maelstrom of the pain. Reaching for that comfort like a drowning victim, she focused on Quinn and the calmness his touch and his voice could provide.

Although she couldn't see their expressions, Montana could tell from the hushed whispers that something was wrong. "You can tell me."

"Shhh, darling. We're trying to figure out what to do to help you."

"Yes, but what's wrong with me?"

Quinn kept up the soft, soothing strokes. "First I need you to tell me what the attack felt like."

"Sort of like last night. Only—" Montana broke off, because she had to acknowledge it hadn't felt the same. That weird electric shock feeling was the same, but the outcome was very different. "No. It only started like last night. Then it changed."

"Changed how?"

Montana realized the questions were helping. Talking about it—focusing on the pain instead of letting it consume her—was actually helping to calm her body. "Last night felt like sharp, harsh pings of static electricity. It hurt, but it was fleeting, somehow."

"And this?"

"This started that way, and then it felt like someone was sticking a knife in me."

"Okay. That's what we needed to know. Ilsa, I need you to run and get my medical book. The one *down*stairs." Montana wondered at the emphasis on the word *down* but chalked it up to strangers she didn't know.

"Why am I here? At your house? Why aren't we in a hospital?"

"You needed immediate attention and I didn't want to wait."

His answer was ludicrous, but she couldn't quite make sense of why through the boiling anger of the pain.

Why weren't they at a hospital? Was she shot? Was that the problem?

Desperate to get her bearings and to focus on anything but the excruciating pain in her back, Montana simply kept on asking whatever popped into her head. "Oh. Who are you? The woman helping me?"

"I'm Callie. I'm Quinn's . . ."

"Housekeeper," Quinn finished.

At the sharp intake of feminine breath behind her, Montana felt her stomach drop. Housekeeper, her ass. Clearly, this woman and Quinn were involved.

Montana did wonder at how the woman's hands stayed infinitely gentle against her skin—a decidedly odd reaction for a jealous wife or lover—but still. Facts were facts and all the evidence pointed toward a relationship between these two.

Searching for something—anything—to remove her focus from the sexual politics going on behind her, Montana glanced at her hand where it splayed against the sofa cushion she faced. The Band-Aid she'd put on that morning had slipped and was coming unstuck on her thumb.

That was odd.

She'd nicked her thumb with her razor this morning, but a look at the exposed skin suggested she'd never even cut herself.

Pulling her hand closer for a better inspection, Montana looked at the skin around the edge of her knuckle.

Nope. Nothing.

Before she could analyze it any further, the second woman, the one Quinn had called Ilsa, came back into the room. "Here you go."

A few moments passed as the book was opened and Callie ruffled through pages.

"Here. Look."

Montana sensed the movements behind her and, although she was tempted to look over her shoulder, the pain had finally ebbed to a manageable state. She wasn't anxious to upset that balance but she also couldn't hide her curiosity. "What is it?"

"You know how you mentioned that it felt like knives in your skin?"

"Yes."

"There are," the woman's voice cut in over Quinn's. "I need to remove each piece one by one, so I'm going to need you to stay very still."

"Each piece? How many are there?"

"Thirteen."

Callie's eyes shifted to the book she had open, laid next to where she kneeled on the floor. The large book was one of her healing manuals, part of the collection of works they maintained in their library.

Quinn had insisted long ago that they needed to arm themselves with new technology as much as old. The wisdom of the ancients held rituals and spells that, although long forgotten by most, could still be conjured to do unspeakable harm.

His brothers had agreed and each had contributed in their own way.

Brody owned anything relating to the ancients and their religions and tools. Grey owned the histories of cultures and the underworld that ran each and every one of them. Even Max, their mysterious Capricorn, had contributed over the years. His intense fascination with space and science had ensured a series of texts on the development of air travel and cellular technology.

Hell, the man had even managed to get his hands on a series of da Vinci's works on flight.

Each and every one of them donated something to their shared collection of knowledge. Thirteen parts of one fighting unit, appointed by Themis to protect man. To leverage their individual gifts, interests and talents into one strong, united whole.

They were lucky, Quinn knew. Of the twelve contingents appointed by Themis in her Great Agreement with Zeus, only one other was still fully intact. Kane had joined their band late, so technically they weren't their original thirteen, but they still held an entire contingent of Warriors, representing each and every sign of the zodiac.

Even their twins, Pierce and Kieran, were still a pair. Opposites in every way, but productive, active members of their team.

"There are thirteen pieces in my back?" Montana's horrified whisper penetrated Quinn's thoughts. "Pieces of what?"

"That's what I'm trying to figure out," Callie said gently.

"What's that supposed to mean?" Quinn heard the harsh tone of his own voice and forced himself to calm down to avoid further upsetting Montana. "It's glass or something, right?"

Callie turned her attention toward him. "I'm sorry, but I need to concentrate."

"Of course." Leaning in, Quinn pressed his lips to Montana's head. "Shhh, now. Let Callie do her work and then we'll figure out what's going on."

What was going on? The page Callie had left open spoke of a spell from the time of Hercules and his Twelve Labors. Although much of the lore was lost, winning each of his labors hadn't been nearly as easy as the stories told and the hero had tried numerous approaches to each task before settling on the one that had worked.

Callie had opened to the page on Hercules's defeat of the Nemean lion. The difficulty in the task—aside from killing an enormous lion—was the fact that the lion's fur was impenetrable.

Hercules had tried several approaches, including a modified knife that would come apart when he threw it at his opponent, scattering into lethal pieces.

The trick hadn't worked, the varied pieces of the knife bouncing against the lion.

But clearly the technology had survived.

Quinn stared at Montana's back again, another layer of realization dawning. Only an idiot would ignore the fact that there were thirteen barbs in her skin.

Just like there were thirteen Warriors for each of Themis's contingents.

Quinn reached for Montana's hand, holding on to her as Callie began the tedious process of carefully removing each barb. Other than a sharp intake of breath each time one of the spikes was removed, Montana said nothing.

Five agonizing minutes later, a small metal bowl of thirteen wicked-looking metal shards in varying sizes sat next to the open book on the floor. Callie taped gauze over Montana's back. "You can sit up now. We've got something for you to put on. I've got a light bandage on the wound now and I'm going to go make a poultice to cover it before I put the final one on."

"Okay," Montana whispered. Quinn heard the relief in that one word and cursed himself for his inability to keep her safe.

Kissing her in front of the Plaza. What the *hell* was he thinking? But the truth was, he wasn't thinking. She'd managed to get under his skin and he was fucking up royally because of it.

Ilsa came forward with a robe. Quinn turned his back to offer her privacy, but not before he had the satisfaction of noting how the layer of pain that had covered Montana's face had dimmed. The white pall of her cheeks had faded, her skin was quickly regaining its rose-colored hue and her lips no longer trembled with the pain.

Once he heard her resettled on the couch, Quinn turned around.

Realization flashed far too late. Montana was pointing toward the open book on the floor, where she could clearly see the details spelled out an ancient healing ritual performed by the Greek gods for use of a weapon that burst into pieces.

"This has something to do with Themis, doesn't it?"

Chapter Eight

"She doesn't know?" Montana heard Ilsa whisper those words before being dragged from the room by the other woman named Callie.

Quinn's *girlfriend-slash-lover-slash-potential-wife*, Callie.

Damn it, why did that news hurt so much?

And whatever else she didn't know, she had a suspicious feeling it would make the news that Quinn had a woman in his life feel like child's play.

Even if she felt every inch the scorned woman on that score.

Shielding herself in her legendary Grant armor, she stared up at Quinn. "No, I clearly don't know. Lots of things, apparently. Care to enlighten me?"

"It's a long story."

"Well, I'm obviously not going anywhere for the moment. And based on what just happened to me, I have a right to know."

Quinn nodded and uttered a soft, "You do." Other than that, he didn't say anything more. Instead, he reached down and picked up the book, walking it over to a large cherry table that stood in the corner by an impossibly high shelf of books.

In fact, now that she looked around, she could see the entire room was covered in books. "Is this really your home?"

"Yes." Quinn stood before the shelves, scanning for something as he moved down the rows.

"Why did you bring me here instead of a hospital? And how did we get here? I know I was out, but I couldn't have been out for that long."

"I'm getting there."

Montana mentally shrugged and stopped asking questions. He was looking for something and it was obvious he wasn't going to be persuaded to talk until he found whatever it was.

Shifting gently to avoid rubbing the bandage, Montana laid her head against the couch cushion and closed her eyes.

How had she gotten here?

Was this some outgrowth of poor decisions on the part of her parents? Because no matter how she sliced it, she couldn't come up with any memory—any past dealing, any past action, heck, even any past relationship—that would explain why she had been targeted in such a personal manner.

What did she really know about them? The person her mother was now certainly wasn't the glamorous woman who had married Jack Grant and graced all the magazines and newspapers of the time.

And her father.

For all his supposed pain after her mother left, it wasn't something she'd had much experience with. He'd always kept himself very closeted and alone. When she was younger, their relationship was confined to rare occasions—holidays, birthdays, social functions—that he either trotted her out for or felt some responsibility to acknowledge her with some of his time.

That all changed when she was a senior in high school and exhibited an interest in the business. He'd taken on a more nurturing role, encouraging her to learn the business and what it meant to run a global company.

Thinking back on it, he'd been loving in his own way but very, very distant. As if he believed business instruction and time spent in boardrooms somehow equaled love.

Before Montana could continue her musings, Quinn settled himself next to her. She felt the depression of his large frame where his body pressed into the couch cushions, smelled the masculine scent of fresh air and the subtle hint of sandalwood.

God help her, she wanted him. Even though he was in a relationship. Even though she'd been attacked twice in his presence. Even though he clearly harbored an agenda he wasn't sharing.

Good Lord, what did that say about her?

"Montana." His voice was gentle. "I'd like you to look at something."

She opened her eyes to find a small volume in his hands. The bindings were old and worn, the leather pulling away at various points. She reached for it, her touch gentle as she took full possession of the book.

Turning it over, she saw the dulled imprint on the spine, the colored paint that had once filled it to denote the title and author long since faded.

A book by the Greek writer Hesiod.

"What is this?"

"You've heard of Hesiod. The Greek poet?" As she nodded, he added, "This is one of his works. Long forgotten and seldom printed."

"So how do you have it? Are you a collector of ancient texts?"

"We thought it wise to translate it into usable form several hundred years ago."

Usable form? Hundreds of years ago? What was he talking about? "Quinn. I'm sorry. You've lost me. Who is we?"

"My brothers and I."

"Your brothers? How many do you have?"

"Brothers is actually a figurative term. We're not biologically related. We fight together. Have fought together for a very long time."

"So you help one another out like brothers in arms? And the men who arrived in the park today? The ones who looked like they stepped out of a men's fashion magazine?"

He smiled but didn't say anything.

"They're your fighting buddies?"

"I'm not sure we've ever been called buddies, but yes, the men who showed up are my Warrior brothers."

She turned to look at him, a sinking feeling pulling at her stomach. The leather couch cushions that molded to her body suddenly felt like a trap she couldn't get out of.

What could he possibly be talking about? And even more disturbing, did he really believe what he was saying?

"You're not much older than me. Look at you. You're in the prime of your life. How could you have fought for a very long time?"

"I'm perpetually in the prime of my life."

Montana shook her head and tried to scoot herself forward, some insane urge to run propelling her limbs. The adrenaline that had pumped through her system only minutes before when dealing with the pain of her attack spiked once again in the urge to flee. "Whatever you're trying to tell me, it can't possibly be true."

"Montana, you said you wanted answers."

"Yes. I want the truth. Preferably something that makes any sort of rational sense." She edged farther to the end of the couch cushion, her feet finding purchase on the floor as her heart pounded a rhythm in double-time. "The real truth about why you think I'm being attacked."

"You're the one who's been asking about Themis. About all the things your mother has been saying."

"Yes. The troubled words of a woman who isn't in her right mind."

His dark eyes turned stormy and deep lines crinkled his forehead. For some reason she couldn't define, the look was oddly sexy. Scholarly.

Oh man, she seriously needed to get a grip.

Those crinkles deepened even further as he spoke. "Don't go soft on me now, Montana. You know— somewhere deep down inside—you know."

"No, I don't *know*." She stood up and moved a few steps away, casting a glance toward the door. "I don't know anything beyond the fact that you're really starting to scare me."

"Themis. Me. This—" He flung a hand around the room. "Even what is happening to you. It's not of this world."

"What are you talking about?"

Quinn reached for the book in her hands as if it were a standard paperback, his fingers deft on the pages, uncaring about the book's age. He flipped through several until settling on whatever it was he was looking for.

"Here." He thrust the book back at her. "Read this. Then we'll talk."

With that he stood and began to pace the far side of the room.

To give her some breathing room?

She glanced at his retreating back, surprised again that the panic had receded and all she felt was desire. Need.

Want.

But the fear? Even as she tried to analyze that feeling, she knew anything she felt wasn't because of the large man across the room.

With a tentative glance toward the open book in her hands, Montana read the header of the chapter, the ink still dark enough to read clearly, despite the book's age.

THE GREAT AGREEMENT BETWEEN THEMIS AND ZEUS.

With gentle movements, she resettled herself on the couch. It was time to find out what was going on.

Quinn shot Callie a text as he paced the far side of the library. He didn't dare leave Montana behind and he wasn't ready to bring anyone back in the room, either.

PULL WHATEVER FILES YOU CAN FROM MY DESK ON EIRENE GRANT.

The slight vibration thirty seconds later let him know the request had been received.

SURE.

Quinn slammed the device back in his pocket and watched Montana's form where she bent slightly over the book. Her back had to be killing her, yet she never even mentioned it.

But her eyes.

Those liquid crystal-blue eyes.

He had seen the doubt there. The wild speculation. The fear.

And he'd been responsible for putting it there.

Fuck it. What else could he do? He now had no doubt she was the victim in all that was happening. His senses had been off from the beginning and after millennia of trusting his gut more often than his head, it had troubled him from the start that the pieces didn't fit.

The attack today was the final bit of proof he needed to just trust his instincts and fuck the rest of it.

Which meant that whoever was behind the dirty, underhanded parts of Grant Shipping didn't want Montana at the helm.

But what about the Themis stuff? And Eirene? And the fact that somewhere in Eirene's mad ramblings, she had mentioned that he was a Taurus Warrior.

On a frustrated sigh, he ran his hand through his hair. None of this made any sense.

If the attack came from internal sources, it was a human problem.

If the attack was external, it was an immortal problem.

So why the hell did it feel like the two were related?

Callie caught his attention from outside the far door of the library. With a last glance at Montana, he stepped into the hallway and took in Callie's serious gaze.

"I have the files you wanted."

"Thanks." Quinn reached for them, but Callie stepped back.

"Her mother is Eirene Grant?" Before he could even nod, Callie continued, her small frame quivering."*The* Eirene Grant?"

"Callie. Yeah. Geez. *The* Eirene Grant. What's wrong with you?"

She threw the folder at his chest. "I swear, you and the rest of them." She tossed a hand over her shoulder, Quinn supposed, to suggest the rest of the household. "Do you pay any fucking attention? Ever?"

"What has gotten into you?"

"Eirene?"

When he didn't say anything else, Callie grabbed the folder back and flipped to a photo of Eirene as a young woman, smiling up with love and adoration into Jack Grant's equally loving gaze.

"Long, flame-red hair. Thin, elegant frame."

She flipped to another picture, one where the young woman stared back up at them. "Blue eyes. Remind you of anyone?"

"Montana?" The photos looked so like the woman he was protecting he couldn't see anything else. He certainly couldn't see whatever it was Callie wanted him to. "All I see when I look at that is a carbon copy of Montana."

"What about your boss, fuckwit? Do you see her

in the flame-red hair, the thin elegant frame and sky-blue eyes?"

Quinn turned his gaze toward the other room, his eyes roaming over Montana's bent head.

And the flaming red hair at her crown.

Quinn threw up his hands in a move oddly reminiscent of Callie's. "Come on, Cal. I'm not up for one of your riddles or your annoyance about years of history I've long since forgotten."

Callie shook her head and held out the picture again. "Themis and Zeus had several children. The Fates are the most well-known now in modern times, but they had others."

Quinn knew he should know what she was talking about, but he'd long since given up keeping track of the abundant fertility of the gods and goddesses who occupied Mount Olympus. Rogan had that duty and the Sagittarius didn't make it his business to give them all genealogy lessons on a regular basis. "So tell me what I'm missing."

"Themis had another set of triplets. The Horae."

"Okay. Right, the peacekeepers. What do they have to do with this?"

"One of them fell, oh, about forty years ago."

"And you think that fallen Horae is Montana's mother?" Quinn probed. "That Themis is Montana's *grandmother*?"

"Think it? Quinn. Look at the facts." Callie waved the photo once more for good measure. "The woman in this picture. The woman sitting on our couch. They belong to Themis."

* * *

Montana tried to understand the words on the page—
tried to understand what it all meant—but it just felt
like the jumbled-up words of an ancient story. An interesting story. But a story, all the same.

There was no way Quinn could really *believe* all
this.

She'd reread about the Great Agreement twice. How
Zeus indulged his ex-wife, Themis, the great goddess
of justice, and allowed her to create a race of warriors.

Zodiac Warriors.

Quinn had used the term "Warrior" and her mother
had rambled on and on about Quinn being the Taurus
Warrior.

But really?

Even if she could wrap her head around the idea
that something bigger—something supernatural—was
happening to her.

This?

It was just too fantastical.

Astrology and zodiac signs were for newspaper
columns and pickup lines. It was the early twenty-
first century, for God's sake. Astrology as a legitimate
discipline had gone out of style centuries ago.

Even as she tried desperately to come up with
some other answer, the desperation—the raw, focused
belief—she'd seen in her mother's eyes the previous
night couldn't be ignored.

"What do you think?" Quinn had stopped at the
end of the couch, his hands shoved in his pockets.

"I'm not sure."

The corner of his lips turned up slightly. "I suppose that's better than a flat-out no."

"I suppose."

He settled himself at the end of the couch, careful to keep his distance, as if she were a skittish animal who'd run off at any moment.

At least her heart had stopped racing like a frightened rabbit.

Whatever else she felt—whatever else she'd discover on this weird journey of enlightenment—she *knew* she didn't need to fear Quinn.

"This Great Agreement." She held up the book as if he somehow didn't know where she had gotten her information from. "You're a result of that?"

"Yes."

"And that's why you and your brothers felt the need to translate this book for posterity's sake, even though the volume looks hundreds of years old."

"Yes. Because it *is* hundreds of years old."

"And you're the Taurus Warrior? And an immortal?" And probably married, her conscience added for good measure.

"Yes on both counts."

From somewhere deep inside her, an ember sparked to life with each successive affirmation coming out of Quinn's mouth.

It wasn't reasonable. But it felt damn good to have a target for the confusion roiling around inside of her.

"How dare you sit there calmly and tell me all this?" She leaped from the couch, those embers flashing to quick anger without any warning.

"I'm not calm, Montana."

She knew it wasn't rational—this frustration and anger and wild rage that continued to gain strength, like a hurricane gathering force over the ocean. "You could have fooled me. You're sitting here telling me all this bullshit, you drag me in here after kissing me senseless and let your wife take care of me and then you act like all of this is just some matter-of-fact thing I should just sit here and accept. Well, fuck you!"

If she weren't so angry, the look on Quinn's face—dropped mouth, widened eyes and a flush of red creeping up his cheeks—might have made her laugh. As it were, it only fueled the fury inside of her.

"My wife?"

Mortification crept up her chest in swelling waves, but Montana kept on. There was no way she was backing down now. "Callie? That woman who took care of my back. I heard her reaction when you called her the housekeeper."

"She's not my wife."

"Fine. Your girlfriend, then. Either way, she was clearly pissed you didn't even acknowledge who she was to the strange woman you brought home. And really, who can blame her? The *housekeeper* is the best you could come up with on short notice?"

"Is that why you're so upset? But Callie's not my wife, girlfriend or any other thing that implies we have sex on a regular basis."

"Oh. Well. That doesn't change anything."

Even as the words left her mouth, her conscience leaped up and taunted her that it made a heck of a lot of difference. Which didn't diminish her anger, but merely complemented it with a massive shot of hormones because the man standing across from her—all broad shoulders and thick body and luscious hair and big hands and long legs—was doing a serious number on her libido.

Down, girl. Down.

A smile played at the corner of his lips. "So is that why you're so upset? Because you thought Callie was my girlfriend?"

"No. I'm upset because you lied to me."

"I did what I had to do. And, assuming I could get in, take care of the problem and get out, you never needed to know."

Anger, sadness, fear, longing—none of them came close to the mind-numbing disappointment she felt in that moment.

All her life, like a song that just repeated in your mind until you wanted to scream in agony, everyone did things for her own good.

She never had a voice.

Never had any say.

It was always for her *own good*. Someone else always knew best. She was the little rich girl who needed protecting.

And *this* man—this stubborn, smug, self-serving stranger—thought he could come into her life and do whatever he damn well pleased.

"You incredible asshole! You've lied to me and kept me in the dark and you have the nerve to insult me and tell me you'd have gone on that way if you hadn't been found out?"

"Yes."

Just like everything else in her life, this was one more thing she had no control over. No say. No ability to affect the outcome.

"Get out."

"Montana?"

"I'm serious. Get out and leave me alone."

Chapter Nine

Quinn paced the hallway outside the library. He wanted to walk back in—wanted to rant and rail and scream—but nothing could erase the image of her as she turned away from him.

She held the long length of her body perfectly still, her willowy frame as unbending as an oak tree.

Fuck it all, he was an idiot.

"I did what I had to do. And, assuming I could get in, take care of the problem and get out, you never needed to know."

Their conversation replayed in his mind, those smug words hitting him over and over.

The stubborn bull, always doing what he felt he had to do. Always ensuring his fucking obstinate pride had the last word.

His decisions.

His choices.

His way.

He leaned his forehead against the heavy wood of the door to the library. Her soft sobs filtered through the door, a ringing reprisal for his idiotic words.

For months now, he'd felt helpless against the choice he'd made for Kane and Ilsa and none of those self-recriminations had anything on this moment.

He'd hurt her. And he'd been cruel.

Without stopping to think, Quinn opened the door and barreled across the room, Montana's huddled form in his sights.

At the sound of his footsteps, she whirled from her position on the couch, coming to her feet in a rush. Tears stained her cheeks, but her anger quickly added color as she stared him down. "I told you to get out."

"Yeah, well, I've got a listening problem."

"No shit."

Hunger unlike anything he'd ever known flared to life from deep inside. Gods, how he wanted this woman.

He didn't deserve her. Didn't deserve to take anything from her, but damn it if he could stop himself from wanting her.

He should go.

He really should.

And then she made the decision for both of them.

With slow, purposeful movements, Montana closed the distance between them. She ran the edge of her tongue over her lips and Quinn couldn't have stopped gazing on her lips if his very life depended on it.

She was still mad, he could see that. Her back was still arrow straight and large tears still rimmed her eyelids. "I'm not ready to forgive you yet."

"I'm not either."

Oddly, none of it mattered standing there in the heat that arced between them.

He had to have her.

Now.

His gaze roved over her, reminding him she still wore the blanket Ilsa had draped over her earlier. Her bottom half was still clad in her skirt, pantyhose and heels. With a lift of her shoulders, she allowed the heavy blanket to slide down her arms and pool at her feet.

Putting on her best boss voice, she pointed across the room. "Close the doors. Both of them."

He didn't need any prompting, practically leaping across the room to complete the task. Before she could even catch a breath, Quinn again stood in front of her.

His heated gaze resumed its travels, following the line of her throat to roam over her breasts. His hands followed as he reached for her and ran one finger over her right breast, the nipple hardening under the thin material of her bra.

He might be an immortal, but he was also a man, and the light hiss that escaped her lips rocketed through his system like gasoline set to flame with a match.

"If you don't kiss me in the next two seconds, I'm going to make you very sorry you ever met me, Mr. Tanner."

Fortunately, he only needed one.

Quinn didn't need any further encouragement as he reached for Montana. Somewhere deep inside he knew this was only staving off the inevitable showdown— the one where he had to tell her that her mother was a fallen immortal—but gods help him if he could resist what she offered.

Bending his head, he ran his tongue over the edge of lace that ran along the rim of her bra, delving under the silky material. He heard her breath exhale on a long whoosh and used one finger to tug the thin barrier down, exposing all that luscious skin to his mouth.

Without looking up at her to gauge her reaction, he moved in and ran his tongue over her nipple, satisfied as the tender tip grew ripe under the heated suction of his mouth.

Montana's fingers threaded through his hair as she held him against her body, a moan rumbling through her chest cavity as he drew long and deep. With his fingers, he reached for the other silky cup of her bra and drew it down over her lush, full breast, baring her other nipple to his questing palm.

Her body was perfect. All long, supple limbs and taut flesh. He shifted his attention, wrapping his arms around her and splaying his hands across her back to move her toward the couch when he stopped suddenly. Like a blast of cold water, he felt the flat gauze bandage Callie had placed temporarily over her wound.

The image of her hurt and huddled on the couch not all that long ago filled his thoughts, pulling him up short. "Montana? Am I hurting you?"

"Hmmm?" Her gaze slowly cleared as she focused on him. "What?"

"Your back. Am I hurting you?"

The lingering effects of passion cleared completely as she focused on his words. "No, actually. Not at all."

He dropped his arms to her waist and tried to turn her. "Here. Let me look."

With gentle movements, he lifted a corner of the gauze where Callie had taped it to her back with surgical tape.

"It really doesn't hurt, Quinn."

Her words registered, but he already knew the truth. With a slight tug, Quinn pulled the bandage free of her skin. The taut lines of her back and the graceful arch of her shoulder blades were smooth and silky. As if she had never sustained an injury at all.

"Quinn? What is it? Is it that bad?"

"No, it's not bad at all. It's gone."

"Gone?" Montana twisted, her gaze roaming over her back as she sought some proof from her peripheral vision. "What do you mean it's gone? Callie pulled thirteen spikes from my back."

Damn straight, she did. And he had watched her remove each and every one of them. "Do you feel anything?"

"Well, no."

He ran his fingers across her shoulder blades, in the same spot he felt for injuries in the park. "What about now?"

"No. Nothing."

"That's because nothing's there."

Montana's gaze caught on a large mirror on the far side of the room and ran toward it. Clearly ignoring her half-naked state, she turned to look at her back in the mirror.

"Oh my God. I don't believe it. It's not possible."

Not possible? Of course it was possible, based on who her mother was. Here Montana was, an immortal all along. What a merry chase she'd led him on, those wide blue eyes smacking of innocence and ignorance.

Ignorance, his ass.

Quinn came to stand behind her, his face visible over her shoulder in the mirror as he gripped her to hold her still. "Now who's the one playing games, Montana?"

"Games?" She whipped around so fast he fumbled his hold. "What's that supposed to mean?"

"It looks like you're an immortal, too, just like your

mother. Cut the crap, Montana. Clearly you've known about Eirene all along."

Her thoughts whirled through her head in a jumbled mess. Like the speeding images you saw when you rode a roller coaster, she couldn't focus on one.

Her mother was an immortal?

And how did Quinn know that?

And he thought *she* was an immortal?

Through all the noise, one thought finally penetrated above the others. "You don't believe me?"

"It's an awfully handy excuse, don't you think? You've got this big, global conglomerate and you can come and go as you please. You're about to take the company public. You've probably set this entire thing up to your benefit. A little bit of drama to build up support for your ideas."

"What? You can't be serious."

"Look at it from my point of view."

"Quinn." She shook her head, willing him to slow down and listen. "Quinn!"

He stopped and his body stilled as she placed a hand on his chest. "What?"

"Listen to me. Please. I have absolutely no idea what you're talking about. I haven't set anything up for my own benefit. And, might I remind you, you're the one who sought me out, so you can't blame this all on me." She stopped short and stared at him. "Speaking of which, why *have* you been following me?"

A pained look crossed his face and for a moment she thought he wouldn't answer her. "There's been a lot of activity in your sector."

"My what?" Good God, she sounded like a fucking megaphone, echoing back each word he said. But seriously. What was he talking about?

"I monitor . . . things. The streets. Manhattan. Farther than that, really. I look for patterns. I've written algorithms to watch for paranormal activity and I can usually find it within all the technology that monitors our lives nowadays."

Montana knew it was silly—knew the last thing she needed to do at this moment was laugh—but she failed miserably to keep a straight face, or the laughter from her voice. "You're a geek?"

"I most certainly am not."

"You most certainly are. And this monitoring you do? What does it have to do with me?"

"About a month ago, I started to get a sense that there was a lot of activity in your sector. Your quadrant." When she only stared at him, he continued. "It's the way I monitor all the data. I narrowed it down to your block and, since your building is the entire block, I began looking into the tenants. It didn't take too long to figure it was you."

"You've lost me."

"I can see patterns, Montana. Things that most others don't. It's why I'm a good security expert. And it's what I do as my role within my Warrior brothers."

"I thought you were an ass kicker."

"I'm that, too. But we've all evolved through the years. We all do more. Than kick ass," he added.

He could call himself anything he wanted, it still didn't explain why he'd followed her. "So why did you start focusing on me?"

"Like I said, the paranormal activity around you was off the charts. Then I started—"

"Whoa, whoa. Stop there. What paranormal activity?"

"Everything has an essence. A life force. I can see those forces."

She shook her head, his explanation too fantastical for words. "You're like those weirdoes on TV. The ones who claim they're following ghosts and whatnot."

"It's not exactly like that, but it's not far off. I look for energy patterns. Humans give off energy patterns. Supernatural humans give off even more."

Oh holy shit, he actually believed this stuff?

The urge to put a few additional feet of distance between them crossed her mind, but even as she felt the urge, it was swiftly followed by another.

A desperate desire to believe him.

Because maybe if she believed him, some of the things in her life would finally make sense.

He held his hands up in a "don't shoot" gesture. "Can I finish? Please?"

She nodded, curious to hear what he had to say despite herself.

"After I got the"—he broke off as if searching for the right word—"*sense* that something was going on, I looked into your background, your father's death and your recent ascension to the head of Grant Shipping. Couple it all with the fact that you're taking the company public and my instincts went off."

"But I still don't see how they're related." She saw his skepticism in the raised eyebrows and the hard set of his shoulders, but she continued. "No, really. Explain it to me. I think I have a right to know."

"I didn't know what to think about you other than the business reputation your father built and you've inherited. Then you start talking to me about your mother and her reappearance, so soon after you take the helm. It all seems rather convenient."

He couldn't be serious. He thought her *mother* was involved? That the frail woman afraid of her own shadow was someone setting this all up to her benefit? Whatever pain Eirene's absence had caused her over the years, Montana refused to believe the woman was playing her.

To what end?

If Eirene had wanted a piece of the company, she'd have had much better luck sticking around and playing the long-suffering wife.

"So you think what? That my long-lost feeble mother is up to no good? At a time when she doesn't have to fear my father anymore, which is likely the reason she never returned in the first place."

"And you never questioned that maybe she was back for a different reason? Something tied to the company your father founded."

"But my mother hasn't mentioned one word to me about taking the company public. Not one single word. Don't you think if she were trying to set me up she'd say something about it?"

"She's been around a long time. I'm sure she knows how to be more subtle than that."

"I'm serious, Quinn. The two things aren't related. They're just not. There has to be some other connection."

"You can keep thinking that all you want. But I want to know more. Like this healing thing. You've never noticed that before?"

She'd nearly forgotten about that in the midst of their argument. With the reminder from his words, the shock of it all came rushing back. "I've never had any healing powers like this. I bleed, like anyone else. And I heal like anyone else. Here. Look."

Another thought hit her as she made her arguments. With quick movements, she tugged at the waist of her skirt, lowering it to show him a scar from her appendectomy. "Appendicitis when I was twelve. See. I've had physical problems during my life. Disease. Surgery."

She watched his eyes roam over her skin, saw him reach out and touch the thin white scar that was proof of her surgery. "I had to *heal* from that. I was out of school for two weeks."

"But this doesn't make sense."

"Let's slow down for a minute. Talk to me and tell me what you think you know." She shook her head. "No. Tell me what you know. Come on. Please."

He nodded and they walked back toward the couch. Was it possible he was softening? Montana reached for the blanket the women had covered her with earlier. Although she could still feel the brand of Quinn against her skin—could still feel each and every agonizing sweep of his tongue on her breast—she covered herself from his view.

Whatever had flared to life, whatever she'd thought she was going to prove by her little seduction attempt, was long over. It was time for a real discussion.

She could wallow in her hormones later.

Quinn took the seat opposite her on the couch and started in, no preamble. "Your mother is an immortal."

"Themis is my mother?"

"No. Her daughter is your mother. Eirene was one of the Horae."

"I'm a little fuzzy on my mythology."

"It's not a myth, Montana. It's real."

She sighed at the edge that tinged his words. "Look. I'm going to fumble a bit. This is all new—brand-new— to me. Can you cut me some slack?"

"Okay." He nodded. "Fair. The Horae are three daughters of Themis and Zeus. Sisters to the Moirae."

"The three Fates?"

"Yes. The Horae are responsible for natural justice and order."

"But Themis is the goddess of justice?"

"As an overall concept, yes. Justice as a whole. But there are subclasses of that. Natural justice, legal justice, and so on."

"Natural justice?"

"It's natural justice that the animal who lingers too long over a carcass is eaten by another predator."

"Ew."

He nodded again, but she could see a sense of satisfaction in his gaze that she'd gotten it. "Exactly. There's an order to the world. A logical way of being. Themis has overall control of it, in a broad sense, but she's allowed her offspring to control the various pieces."

"So what is my mother?"

"Eirene is the personification of peace."

"But how is that possible? I've seen her, Quinn. She's frail and sickly. She won't let me take her to a doctor, or call one in to look at her."

"She fell, Montana."

"Oh my God! When?" She scrambled to the edge of the couch, a desperate longing to find Eirene simply forcing her into action.

"Montana." Quinn's hand on her arm held her in

place on the couch. "Stop. I didn't mean an actual fall. Like today. I meant she fell. From Mount Olympus."

"She what?"

"When she married a mortal. She abdicated her role and fell. She's no longer immortal."

"Like a fallen angel?"

"Of sorts. It's not quite the same thing, but you're getting the basic picture."

"Okay. Even if I give you the benefit of the doubt on this one—and I'm not even remotely saying I am— but how the hell does someone fall from being a goddess?"

"It's not all that hard, from what I understand. You simply make a choice. That's all it takes."

Montana's thoughts raced with the implications. "They sure as hell didn't teach us that one in Greek mythology lessons."

"It kind of makes sense when you think about it. Choice is a powerful thing. Oddly simplistic, but a very fundamental power afforded all of us."

Even as every rational thing inside of her suggested she hightail it out of there as fast as she could, a part of her thought his words made sense. An even smaller—yet insistent—part believed him.

"Look. I know it's hard to digest, but it's what happened."

"And Themis just let her go?"

"I don't have all the details. It was a very private matter, but even gods talk. Her sisters were devastated when she abdicated her role. They've shared that with other immortals over the years."

"So who replaced her?"

"No one."

"But if she's the keeper of peace, that can't be possible."

Quinn let out a harsh bark of laughter. The sound was so raw—so bleak—it pulled her from her thoughts. At the matched look in his dark chocolate eyes, Montana felt the overwhelming urge to touch him.

To comfort him.

Before she could, he was off the couch and pacing the room. "Have you looked at the state of the world over the last four decades?"

"But humanity has always had problems." Montana fought for some rational explanation—for *something* to explain what couldn't possibly be true. "Come on. There were more deaths during World War II than any time in human history. If what you say is true, she was still a goddess then."

"Yes, but humanity has gotten more and more depraved with their warfare. More sinister."

"Humans haven't changed. Just the tools to see their plans through. If you are who you say you are— if you've lived the lifetimes you claim to—you have to know that."

"Oh, I do know it. But even I can see it's gotten worse."

"Humans haven't exactly shown their best sides to the world. The history books are full of that."

"But don't you think the world's gotten significantly more dire in the last forty years?"

"I'm sorry, but I just find that hard to believe."

"It's because of your mother's abdication."

He couldn't be serious. Even people who weren't overly familiar with history knew that humans had been finding new and interesting ways to kill, maim and destroy one another for millions of years. "That's an awful lot to lay at the feet of one person, Quinn."

"I'm laying it at the feet of a goddess, not a person."

"Well, now that she's a mortal, she's going to die. What's Themis's grand plan then?"

"I suspect she's decided it's you."

Chapter Ten

"Me?" Montana's eyes darted around the room, the sudden tensing of her shoulders suggesting she wanted a way out.

Well, there wasn't a way out if his suspicions were correct and he'd be damned if he was going to sugarcoat it.

"Add it up. If you haven't been immortal all along—and that little appendix story was too quick not to believe—then you're becoming an immortal."

"Don't you think I'd have known that? Felt it?"

"I know we talked about it yesterday, but I want you to really think about it. Have things changed lately?"

He saw her glance down at her thumb and he followed her gaze, wondering what was suddenly so fascinating. Before he could analyze it, Montana snapped her attention right back to him. "Oh, I don't know. Other than a deranged killer's after me and I've suddenly garnered the bodyguard services of an immortal? Is that what you mean?"

He wasn't sure if it was a good thing she was acting so sarcastic, but Quinn also decided it couldn't be all bad. It at least suggested she had decided to believe him.

Or so he hoped.

"Montana—" Before he could finish, there was a loud knock on the door.

"Quinn! Can I come in?"

Quinn groaned inwardly before hollering back, "Enter!"

"Callie told me you brought a woman with you who was injured and Brody and the guys just got back and—"

The owner of the voice—Ava—stopped in the center of the room. Their Leo Warrior's wife stared at Montana. "Callie and Ilsa told me you were hurt. Why are you sitting up?"

Ava rushed over to the couch to wrap her arm around Montana. As she fussed, Quinn could see his Warrior brothers hovering in the doorway. He shot one gaze at Montana, still wrapped in the thin blanket, and then tossed his brothers the evil eye. They all seemed to get it, as he heard a few mumbled words and a hollered, "Callie!" before all of them moved back into the hallway.

"I'm Ava. I heard what happened to you. How can you possibly look so good right now?"

Montana lifted her shoulders in confusion, but before she could say anything, Ava barreled right on through the conversation. "Come with me and I'll get you fixed up. Callie's got the poultice ready for you."

"I don't think—"

"It won't hurt that bad and it will heal you up right away."

"No, I mean, I am healed."

"What?" Ava dropped Montana's arm and turned toward Quinn. "Why didn't you tell them? Ilsa and Callie are really worried about her."

"I didn't know."

"You didn't know she was an immortal?"

"I didn't know either," Montana interjected, "if it makes you feel any better."

Ava whirled back toward Montana and for the briefest moment—the tiniest, nanosecond, really—Quinn wished for the old mousy Ava. The one who wasn't bossing all of them around like some annoying older sister.

"I saw that look, Quinn."

With eyebrows raised to the ceiling, he let out a groan. "Of course you did. Were eyes in the back of your head one of the gifts Themis threw your way on your turning?"

A very delicate middle finger shot back at him while Ava wrapped her free arm around Montana's shoulder. "Come on with me. I'll get you some clothes and I'd still like Callie to take another look at you."

Montana shot him a look of helplessness, but she followed Ava anyway.

Ava dropped the middle finger and had the graciousness to look contrite as she led Montana from the room. "I'll bring her right back. I promise. Don't worry." Seeing the lightning-quick change in Brody's sweetheart's soul, Quinn immediately felt bad about wishing she was her old, mortal self.

As soon as Ava had Montana out of the library, Grey, Brody, Kane, and Drake barreled into the room.

The curtain of awkwardness Quinn had been fighting for six months descended over his thoughts and he shoved his hands in his pockets. "Did you get him?"

Brody shook his head, disgust riding high on his cover-model-perfect cheekbones. "Fucker got past us. I swear, if I didn't know better, I'd say he had the same skills we do."

Quinn weighed the idea in his mind. "You think so?"

Brody nodded as the other guys took up spots around the room. It didn't escape Quinn's notice Kane took the seat farthest away.

Damn, but they just couldn't seem to get their groove back. Quinn knew it was his fault—his oh-so-helpful reaction when Kane and Ilsa needed him to port to the Underworld had put a permanent riff in their relationship.

But fuck it if Quinn could figure out if Kane was cold to him, or if it was an outgrowth of his own standoffishness.

And when the *fuck* had he turned into such a girl that he was even thinking about shit like this?

Brody slammed a meaty fist into his shoulder. "Yo, bro? You there?"

"Yeah. Sorry. And sorry I brought her here."

"Where else were you going to bring her?" The Leo's puzzled gaze stared back at him.

"Yeah, but here? What if she was a threat?"

Brody shrugged. "Like Kane and I haven't done the same. Besides, everyone in this house knows how to take care of himself."

"Or herself," Kane added for good measure.

"So, as I was saying," Brody continued, effectively

closing the door on the subject of Quinn's question-able choices, "I did think it might be one of us, until Callie filled us in on the spikes in her back. Not our style."

Grey added, "And while it sounds like it could be the work of an immortal, I haven't heard word one about someone horning in on our territory."

"But the spikes," Quinn pressed. "The way they exploded. It's too much like the textbooks."

"Yeah, but it doesn't have to be." Grey shook his head. "I see shit all the time, Quinn. Stuff that would blow your hair back and make the goons on Mount Olympus cry with jealousy."

Quinn had to acknowledge Grey's words. The gods and goddesses on Mount Olympus hadn't quite caught on that humans weren't exactly bumbling around in the dark any longer. They might not have immortality but they weren't clueless, either. And they sure-as-hell knew how to do some damage to each other.

"Okay. I get it, but play it out for me. What if this *is* the work of an immortal? I realize no one's seen that shit in millennia, but . . ."

"One of us would have known. Ajax has been gone for a year now. Who else is there?" Kane's eyes briefly jerked toward Brody as he mentioned the Leo's brother, executed by Enyo the year prior when he'd apparently grown greedy and outlived his usefulness to the goddess of war.

If Quinn wasn't mistaken, Brody's blue gaze dulled and his usually smiling mouth formed a straight line, but that was all the reaction he gave to the mention of his brother by birth.

"There've been other defections over the years.

Ajax wasn't the only one." Quinn thought of all the Warriors over the years who were no longer under Themis's command. Several had been lured away by the power their physical strength and immortal bodies offered. A few had simply decided their life in service to selfish humans just wasn't worth it. And still others had been killed in the course of battle.

They were immortal in a basic sense, but all of them knew decapitation would be the end of their existence.

Even Themis couldn't fix that immutable law.

"You keep up with them, don't you?" Drake probed.

"In a sense." Quinn thought about what he *did* know. "I have files on all of them, but for the ones who don't want to be found my files are woefully thin."

"Okay. Let's look at this from a different angle." Grey settled himself on the couch after pacing the room several times over. "What exactly happened to Montana in the park?"

Quinn took them through the events up until they were all together again.

"These are the spikes?" Grey pointed to the small metal bowl still sitting next to the couch.

"Yep." Quinn nodded, the image of those spikes being pulled from Montana's skin sending a renewed wave of anger rushing through him. Pulse pounding, he pointed toward the bowl Grey had picked up. "Thirteen fucking spikes. If there was any single thing that made me think it was one of us, it's the number."

"Too coincidental?" Brody asked.

"Fucking-A." Quinn nodded. "It's just too neat for my taste."

"It's also a clue," Drake added. "And where there's one, there'll be more."

"Fuck." Grey let out an exhale of breath in clear agreement with the assessment as he lifted a piece of metal from the bowl.

They all turned to look at their Aries, but not before Quinn realized what he was doing. "Are you out of your mind? Those were embedded in her skin. What the hell are you touching them for?"

There was no easy retort, no smart-ass remark, not even a cocky grin. Grey held up one of the larger pieces, holding it gingerly between the tips of his fingers. "Did you and Callie look at these when she was removing them?"

"No." Quinn shook his head. "The only goal was to get them out."

"Well, take a look at this." Grey held his hand out.

Quinn took the piece—one of the longest fragments Callie had removed. As he flipped it over, he immediately saw what Grey saw.

"Holy shit."

Mind whirling, Quinn didn't know what to make of the proof he held in his hands. Even though the slice of metal had broken clean from its counterparts, it still clearly held a good portion of the symbol it was imprinted with.

"Here. Give me the rest of them." Quinn laid them on top of the table, grateful Callie had inadvertently left behind a package of gauze. As he put the pieces together like a puzzle, awareness pricked his nerve endings with increasing intensity.

Then once he placed the last piece on top of the gauze, those fingers of awareness gripped him at the base of his neck and wouldn't let go.

In bold script, carved into the reassembled pieces

of hard steel, was the ancient symbol of the bull. A round circle with two horns that speared off of it, the symbolism unmistakable.

Quinn had seen it for thousands of years.

He wore a matched symbol on his forearm.

"Does this hurt?"

"No. Honest." Montana felt Callie probing around her back and inwardly marveled at the fact that the immense pain she'd felt not long ago had vanished as if it had never been.

"And you're not an immortal?" Ava asked her for what felt like the twenty-fifth time.

Despite the repeated badgering, Montana couldn't help but like the small woman who fluttered around like a mother hen. "To the best of my knowledge, no. How could I be something I'm having a hard time believing in?"

"But all the evidence points to you being one, if the way you just healed is any indication," Ilsa interjected. Turning toward Ava, she quickly explained the last hour and what had unfolded down in the library.

Montana listened but didn't say anything. She was torn between continued shock at the marvels of her own body, puzzled confusion as to why this had suddenly happened and a surprisingly easy sense of comfort with these women.

Truth be told, she genuinely liked Ava, Ilsa and Callie and she'd only been in their company for an hour.

Of course, she'd spent that hour practically naked and suffering from some magically disappearing wound, so Montana figured that had to do something on the bonding-o-meter.

But what the hell did she know?

Her best friend was her gay male secretary, her mother had abandoned her, her father had abandoned her emotionally and she'd spent her life surrounded by people paid to do her bidding. She wasn't exactly an expert in the friend department.

"I want to look in some of the scrolls downstairs," Callie announced, her abrupt change in direction jarring Montana from her thoughts. "Ilsa, I need your help. You're better versed in any loopholes."

Ilsa gave a wry grin. "I *am* a loophole, sister."

"My point exactly."

The two women bustled out of the room and Montana was surprised to realize their discussion of scrolls and mystical loopholes hadn't actually fazed her.

"It's sort of like falling down the rabbit hole, isn't it?" Ava took a seat next to her in the spare bedroom Callie and Ilsa had originally fashioned as a makeshift triage ward. A pile of bandages sat on one of the end tables and the nasty-smelling poultice Callie had made sat next to it in the Tupperware bowl.

It was the Tupperware that did it.

A crazy giggle bubbled up from the depths of her throat and Montana pointed at the end table. "I had no idea . . . immortals went to . . . to . . . to Tupp . . . Tupperware parties."

The laughter kept coming and she had no way of holding it back. "How do you get people to keep coming to them?"

"What?" Montana didn't miss the bemused expression in Ava's kind, brown gaze.

"The whole pay it forward thing. I have a house party and invite six of my friends." The giggles kept coming, but they were slowly subsiding into half laughs mixed with hiccups. "And then those friends have a party and invite six friends. If you're immortal, how do you get new blood?"

The word blood sent her into another fit of hysterics. "Or do the vampires keep making new women to hostess for you?"

Ava patted her arm and Montana felt her settle herself on the bed. "Despite the weirdness happening all around us, I've yet to see or meet—or even hear of, come to think of it—any vampires. And it's At-Home-Chef, not Tupperware. And finally, I'm afraid to say, it's my contribution to the household and the result of being roped into several of those parties you just referred to. Although," Ava added thoughtfully, "the witches who live next door are lovely and I suspect they'd hostess a party if we asked them to."

Montana heard the kindness underneath the nonsense and felt her throat tighten on a wave of tears. "Wi-witches?"

"Yes." Ava hesitated a beat, allowing that little tidbit to sink in.

"Wow."

"It's okay, Montana. I know it's overwhelming." Ava reached forward and pulled her close, and Montana was surprised by the strength in her small form. "It's a lot to take in. Not all that long ago, I was in the same boat. There's just no preparing for it."

"Two days ago I was just me."

"You're still you. Just enhanced."

Montana pulled back on a real laugh—not a shred of the hysterical anywhere in sight. "Enhanced. I like that."

"We're going to get to the bottom of this, too. Quinn's an amazing Warrior and he's stubborn and persistent. He'll find out what's going on and we'll all help you."

A few more tears seeped out the edges of her eyes as Ava's innate kindness penetrated the haze of panic and disbelief that she'd worn along with the blanket. With a small sigh, Montana remembered an earlier question. "They're sisters? Callie and Ilsa?"

Ava nodded and smiled. "A recent discovery."

"They haven't known each other that long?"

"That's putting it mildly. Oh goodness, where do I begin?" Her eyes alighting with a sudden twinkle, Ava added, "Since you're one of the world's most powerful businesswomen, I'll give you the executive summary."

Montana couldn't help another laugh from bubbling up. "A dubious distinction at best."

"Hardly," Ava snorted. "But I'll keep it brief anyway. Ilsa is the nymph who was selected to raise Zeus on Mount Ida."

"Excuse me?" Whatever fantastical things her mother might have told her, nothing could have prepared Montana for *this*. "She's what?"

Ava waved a hand. "I know, I know. It's too wild to believe. But it gets even better."

"Better?" Montana wanted to panic. It was the most logical thing to do and her conscience kept questioning why she wasn't running for the door as fast as her feet would carry her.

But even as the urge to flee flitted around the edges of her thoughts, she couldn't shake that immutable sense of *reality* that threaded through everything happening to her.

Her mother's mysterious arrival and disappearances, despite the time and money she'd invested over the years to find her, disappointed time and again when nothing produced leads.

Quinn's appearance and almost preternatural ability to sense danger, especially danger directed at her.

And then there was that one other fact. The one she couldn't deny, no matter how many times she thought it wasn't even remotely believable. One hour ago she had thirteen spikes sticking out of her back and now she was fully healed.

And talking about Greek gods and goddesses.

And discovering an odd sort of resonance in the information these newfound friends were trying to explain to her.

"It gets *better* than that?"

"After Zeus put a curse on her, she was rescued by Hades and became his errand girl—in a good way—and delivered souls to the Underworld. Then one of those souls punched a hole in hers and escaped."

"Her soul?"

"I think." Ava paused. "We'll have to ask Ilsa the specifics."

"Wow."

Ava nodded. "Wow doesn't even begin to describe it. Has Quinn showed you his tattoo yet?"

"No." Montana felt the blush creep up her neck and knew her pale skin gave her away. "Um. No."

"I've seen the way he looks at you. He will."

Shock replaced the embarrassment that was insistently moving toward her cheeks. "Ava!"

All she got in return was an angelic smile before Ava leaned in closer. "So tell me a bit about yourself.

I've read about you in the society columns. Is it true you dated Orlando Bloom?"

Montana rolled her eyes, the change of topic so ludicrous it was comforting.

Oddly so.

"No, I've never dated Orlando Bloom. I haven't even met him, truth be told. Apparently we were both at some resort one weekend, which in tabloid land means we snuck there under separate reservations to rendezvous for a seventy-two-hour fuck fest."

"Fuck fest?" Ilsa screamed from the doorway. "Where, and can I get in?"

"This is what happens when you expose a Scorpio to a virgin," Callie muttered, following her sister into the room.

"Hey," Ilsa complained as she crawled onto the bed. "I'm a fast learner *and* I'm making up for lost time. And have you looked at the man's abs? Can you blame me?"

"Which one is yours?" Montana asked, then realized what she'd inadvertently implied. "Was that nearly as objectifying as it sounded?"

"Oh, honey, it's a favorite pastime around here." Ava patted her knee. "And I mean that in the most nonchauvinistic way possible."

Ilsa's eyes nearly rolled into the back of her head. "The incredibly yummy, tall, rangy, broody one with short dark hair is mine." She giggled on the last word, then flopped her slender form along the edge of the bed. "Mine, mine, mine! I just never get tired of saying that. And if it's rude and objectifying, well . . . I've yet to feel all that bad about it."

Montana mentally whirled through images of the

men she'd semi-met and couldn't quite come up with which Ilsa referred to. "There are two that fit that description. Is your . . . husband?"—Ilsa nodded, her smile growing even broader, if that were possible—"Bond Street or the other one dressed like a male model?"

All three women chimed in unison, "Bond Street."

"That explains the British accent." Montana thought about what else she knew. "He's the Scorpio?"

"Yes."

Montana turned toward Ava. "What about your husband?"

"The long mane of blond hair and enough pride to take down a small village." Ava smiled. "I'll give you one guess."

Montana couldn't help but smile. "The Leo?"

"Oh yes."

Then she turned toward Callie, getting into the spirit of things. "What about your husband? Which one is yours?"

Callie's smile never wavered, but Montana saw it immediately. Her brown eyes went hard as stone and the curve of her lips took on a patently false arc. "Let's just say the player to be named later is taking his sweet time."

Quinn ported across the room to stand in the light of the late-day sun, he was so impatient to read the markings on the largest shard of silver in his hand. He turned it over again, but his first instinct was one hundred percent accurate.

The silver pieces held the mark of the Taurus.

"It's definitely one of us." His gut clenched as the words escaped his lips.

"Do you know all the other bulls, Quinn?" Grey moved up beside him, the metal bowl still in his hands. With gentle fingers, he continued to poke at the various pieces, searching for any other markings. "Do you have any sense of who it is?"

Quinn's mind whirled with the possibilities. A fallen Taurus? Another fallen Warrior trying to set him up? Enyo trying to set him up? The scenarios were endless.

"That's one possibility but not all of them. Whoever's following Montana knows I'm following her, too. Protecting her. This could as easily be a setup as a calling card."

"How'd you get involved with her again?" Kane had moved into the arc of Warriors surrounding Quinn at the window and for the briefest of moments, Quinn felt the easy camaraderie they'd once had.

Before.

Before he'd fucked it up with his lack of loyalty and stubborn insistence on being right.

He didn't deserve this. Didn't deserve the support. Didn't deserve the ready willingness of his Warrior brothers to help him.

The urge to turn away was strong, until an image of Montana lying on the couch, her skin mottled and broken with the effects of the attack, reared up to choke him. He couldn't do this without the help of his brothers. Couldn't protect her if he did it alone.

So he tamped down on the urge to move away and shared his thoughts. "She popped up on a routine screen. I narrowed in on her quadrant and slowly put together it was her."

Grey smacked him on the head. "In plain English, Your Geekiness."

Quinn sighed, thinking of how best to explain it and finally settled on the same basic explanation he gave Montana. "I've written several programs that monitor for abnormalities on all the feeds I pull all over the globe."

At the matched blank stares from his brothers, Quinn added, "Too much electricity, abnormal power surges where there shouldn't be any reason for them, concentration of immortal activity."

"You can track that?" Drake's question was a sharp reminder his brothers really had no fucking idea what he did most days.

"Yeah. Everything gives off a life force and immortals' are stronger than humans. It's easy enough to track with recording devices. Sort of like a Geiger counter for immortals."

Drake nodded. "Cool."

"Grey's club is full of them so I usually calibrate my tools in Equinox when I need to get a reading."

At the Ram's head shake, Quinn finished up. "Look. All you need to know is that I have my computers rigged to tell me when some heavy shit's going to go down. Or where it looks like some heavy shit's going to go down."

Kane added, "And what you're saying is some serious electronic noise broke over Montana."

Quinn smiled, pleased to see he might be getting through. "On several fronts. Security activity has gotten weird around her apartment building and around her office building. A ton of news stories all hit on her, taking her company public and also ending this weird pirate attack off the coast of Africa."

Kane whistled long and low, his MI6 training kicking into high gear. "She's the one who did that? She's the Grant Shipping heiress who's now running the place?"

"Yep."

"Oh, man, some serious shit is absolutely going down there," Kane continued. "Grant Shipping's been on MI6's radar for years. No definitive proof, but they're into all sorts of stuff. Her old man died about six months ago."

Quinn held up a hand. "Your turn to streamline it. I know you love the James Bond routine, but give me the high points."

"Grant Shipping runs weapons, smuggles diamonds and has even been known to deal in the slave trade. Despite all this oh-so-upstanding activity, their books are so squeaky clean they make a convent of nuns look dirty."

"Too much cover-up?" Drake questioned.

"Oh yeah"—Kane nodded—"no doubt. No one believes they're innocent, but they've been slick enough to hide all the nasty shit they're up to. Black Jack Grant's been untouchable."

"And now?" Quinn asked, a sinking feeling gripping him low in the gut. "I've already gone through the head game on this after talking to Grey. I admit I doubted her, but I know Montana's innocent. I know she is. I figured all along, but what happened today couldn't be faked."

Kane nodded in clear agreement. "She likely is. Black Jack was a wily son of a bitch and supposedly worked with a very small, very refined inner circle. If Montana's trying to take the company public, an attack by an immortal is possibly the least of her worries."

Quinn stared at the spike of metal in his hand and for the first time, felt a genuine trickle of alarm. Every time he got a handle on what was happening, the sands shifted yet again. As a lifelong disciple of Themis's mission—a *Warrior* to the core—the sense of fear was as startling as it was humbling. "What's that supposed to mean?"

"The kind of men who want her out of the way are likely as dangerous as any immortal. Hell, many of them even make Enyo look like a walk in the park."

Chapter Eleven

Montana ran her hands over the sleek lines of the indigo-blue silk sheath spread across her lap as she stared up at Quinn. "You really want me to still go to this event tonight?"

"We need to figure out who is behind the attack, and I can only do that if my brothers and I can get him out in the open."

"Him?" She raised her eyebrows as she stood up from the small couch in the sitting area of the bedroom they'd given her. The bandages and stinky poultice were long gone, replaced by a designer gown and thousand-dollar shoes.

"Likely." Quinn's voice brooked no argument and he'd shifted into what Montana already thought of as security mode.

"And he's an immortal?"

"Likely as well, but we need to confirm that." The BlackBerry at his waist must have gone off because he had the device pulled out with the speed of an Old West gunslinger.

"I'm not done grilling you." At his raised eyebrows and distracted glance from the small screen of his phone, she added, "All the immortal stuff. Just because I haven't said much about it since earlier doesn't mean I'm just going to roll over and agree with all of it."

"It is what it is." With that, he refocused on the device

Those flashes of annoyance came back in full force. She'd hated her father's constant immersion with his BlackBerry, the subtle sense she was always taking second place to an electronic device an ever-present feeling. She'd be damned if she'd tolerate it from Quinn. "You really need to learn some people skills, you know that?"

He glanced up from where he scrolled through the screen. "What are you talking about?"

"That thing, for one." She made a grab for the device, catching him off guard enough to wrest it away. "Look at me when I'm talking to you. The message will still be there in another five minutes."

He actually looked confused. Lines furrowed his brow and his eyes had taken on a distinctly unfocused gaze as he watched her hold on to the device. "It's giving me a constant stream of info on tonight's event. I've got it synched to my office."

Montana tossed said device in an arc, where it landed on the middle of the bed. "I don't give a shit. Talk to me. I run a multibillion-dollar global company and I know how to ignore mine for more than two minutes at a time."

"Montana." He was already up and heading for the bed when she reached for his arm.

"Quinn. I'm serious." On a deep breath, Montana

weighed the pros and cons of what she was about to say. After the two days they'd shared, she finally settled on the realization she likely didn't have all that much to lose.

She sat on a small settee flanking one wall. "I've spent my entire life ignored. And most of the time, I don't let it bother me beyond the fact that it's a base annoyance. But I was attacked today. And I've potentially discovered my body's changing in ways I never could have imagined. And I'm trying to talk to you about what's going to happen tonight. *Look* at me. *Talk* to me."

Whatever confusion she'd seen in the chocolate depths of Quinn's eyes morphed into a completely different sort of look. Those dark orbs turned molten as he took a seat next to her and turned to face her.

With sweet, aching movements, he ran a fingertip down her cheek, over her jaw and down the line of her throat. "What do you want to know?"

Every single shred of annoyance and anger slid in a heartbeat into long, sensuous ribbons of need. They unfurled in her belly and spread through her bloodstream. Their interrupted moments from earlier came rushing back as her body sprang to life with barely banked need.

With a shake of her head, she pulled back and shifted in her seat to add a few inches of separation for good measure. "Oh no. I can't go there right now. I need to know about myself. I need to understand."

On a resigned sigh, he sat back and settled himself on the impossibly small, decorative couch. "You're right. I don't like clients who are in the dark and I shouldn't do it to you. Where do you want me to start?"

"You've told me about my mother. While it's odd and fantastical, it makes a logical sort of sense." As if any of this were logical. "What did you find out earlier?"

"Earlier?" Quinn took a deep breath as if he were reaching for additional strength.

"With the guys? When Callie came to find me, she said you had something you wanted to tell me. That you all discovered something. What did you find?"

"The guys and I were trying to figure out what weapon was used on you. What it meant."

"You figured it out?"

"I wouldn't exactly go there. But we do have a better sense of something."

"Come on, Quinn. I'm aging here." At the idea that maybe she wasn't aging any longer, a laugh bubbled up in her throat. "Or maybe I'm not. But come on. Tell me."

"We looked at the spikes that we pulled from your back. And there were images imprinted on the metal."

"Really?" Montana had avoided looking at the metal bowl Callie had filled with the spikes beyond a cursory glance, but she had looked closely enough to see them. "I'll admit thirteen of them hurt horribly—one would have hurt horribly—but they weren't that big. How did you find writing on them?"

"The best we can tell, the spikes had been part of a larger knife that had a spell on them."

"A spell?"

Quinn nodded. "Something dark, that hasn't been used in a very long time. The moment it reached your skin, it shattered as it was designed to."

Ice-cold fingers of fear gripped Montana from the

inside out, the sensation reminding her of a long-forgotten memory of her father.

She had been fourteen and on a rare ski trip to Switzerland with her father and whatever woman he'd been dating at the time. Annoyed with the attention he lavished on the bimbo and the lack of time either of them had had for her, Montana took a lift to one of the highest mountains at their resort.

Within minutes after starting the run, she realized she was too far out of her depth as the scenery flew by. She'd finally found a place to regroup, in the midst of a few jagged outcroppings, and had stopped her descent down the mountain.

Cold wind had whipped around her and battered her body as she sat huddled between the rocks. Anger had filled her, but no matter how heated her emotions, it couldn't warm her. Couldn't keep the fear at bay.

She'd made a vow that day. A vow to ignore her father as he ignored her, taking what he was willing to offer and finding what she needed somewhere else.

So slowly, she worked her way down the mountain. It had taken her nearly two hours before she made it back to the chateau where they were staying.

She'd climbed what felt like endless stairs to her bedroom and fallen into the shower, allowing the water to run for what must have been an hour.

Long after her body had warmed, the fear that had consumed her on the mountain wouldn't leave.

"Montana? What is it?"

"Bad memories."

"About what?" Quinn moved closer and wrapped an arm around her. The motion wasn't intended to be sexual, but she felt her body come to life under the comforting gesture.

Had she ever really found what she needed somewhere else?

"I was just thinking about something that happened when I was a kid."

"Tell me about it."

In a soft voice, she recounted the story and her painstaking trek down the mountain. "I was so afraid. So fearful I was cold from the inside out."

"You probably had hypothermia." She heard the anger in his voice, felt it in the subtle tightening of his grip on her upper arm. "What the hell kind of parent lets that happen?"

"*My* parent, obviously. The only one I had since my mother chose to leave."

"If what we suspect is true, maybe she felt she didn't have a choice."

The heat of rising anger stamped hard on those cold fingers of fear clenched around her belly. She might have been unable to do anything about them as a child, but there was nothing that could keep the anger at bay now.

"Didn't have a choice?" Montana leaped up and stalked across the room, the plush carpet under her feet a soft cushion as she moved back and forth. "She had a choice, Quinn. She had a choice when she fell from her supposed immortality. She had a choice when she bound her life to my father. And she had a fucking choice when she walked out on me!"

The anger morphed yet again, into the hot swell of tears. Great, heaving gulps of anger, frustration and the pain of long years of being ignored rose to the surface, swamping her and constricting her chest as if someone sat on it. She tasted the hot, salty tears before she even realized she was crying, her voice coming out in heavy sobs.

"She chose to leave. She ch-chose to walk out."

Quinn walked toward her, his movements gentle, like he were reaching out to a hurt animal. "I didn't mean that to hurt you."

"Everyone has a choice, Quinn. She was a very wealthy woman at that point. She could have taken me out of that situation. Instead she left me in the middle of it."

"What if she thought that was the only place you'd be safe?"

The continuous loop of angry emotions that flowed through her head on a regular basis—*you're not good enough; you're not worthy enough; your own mother abandoned you*—slowed until it finally stopped, replaced by Quinn's words.

"Safe?"

"Yes, safe." Quinn's large body overshadowed hers as he moved to stand in front of her, completely consuming her field of vision with his large body and broad shoulders.

He wrapped his arms around her and Montana felt the steady thump of his heartbeat under her cheek.

"Think about it. She came back only in the last month, right?"

"Yes." The hot tears still fell down her cheeks, but they were slowing, along with the hiccups that gripped her diaphragm.

"She came back for a reason, Montana. And we're going to figure that out. But she has also brought something with her. Something that has set its sights on you."

"What something? I know she's not working with anyone." She pulled herself back and stared up into the dark depths of his eyes. "I know it, Quinn."

"Even if she's not, none of this started until she came back." Quinn tightened his grip. "She's tied to what is happening to you."

Montana gripped a bit of Quinn's T-shirt and wiped her eyes, searching for some explanation as she repositioned her head against his chest. "It could be a coincidence."

She felt the rumble under her ear before she heard the actual laugh. "I've been doing this for a very long time, Montana. I gave up on the idea of coincidence long before the Middle Ages, darling."

The low, husky sound of his voice sent a wave of shivers down her spine and she felt his use of the endearment to her very core.

What would it be like to be loved by this man?

The thought was so immediate—so intense—it surprised her.

And then she didn't wonder any longer. She tilted her face back, reached toward his neck and pulled his head down to hers.

Quinn gripped Montana's hips, his fingers curling into the terry-cloth material she wore. Sometime during the afternoon, one of the girls must have given her something to change into. Ilsa, most likely, based upon the "juicy" emblazoned across the ass cheeks of the sweatpants.

He moved his lips from her mouth, trailing a row

of kisses along her jaw, then down her throat. The heavy beat of her pulse throbbed under his lips, calling to him like a primal drumbeat of need and passion and want.

He unclenched his hands from her waist and dragged his fingertips across the top of the waistband. A small display of skin was visible between the top of the pants and the bottom of her T-shirt, the skin there calling him like a lodestone.

Montana's mouth found his again as she wrapped her hands around his biceps. Her whisper was heavy against his lips. "We're going to be late."

"Well, then"—he pulled back and smiled down at her—"let's make it worth it."

With deft fingers he delved beneath the waistband of both her sweatpants and her panties, to her velvet core. Hot liquid heat filled him to his palm and his own body hardened in response, his erection painful against the fly of his jeans.

With unerring precision, he kept up a steady pressure against her slick channel, his fingers taking control and maintaining a rhythm her body was helpless to resist.

Filled with awe, he watched Montana as the pleasure built, her head thrown back and her breathing coming in short, quick pants. Despite the desperate needs of his own body, he was in awe of her. The purity of her response—so open, so receptive—humbled him and he leaned in and captured her cries of pleasure with his mouth, sucking her tongue between his teeth.

With his free arm, he held her body against his, the length of his hand spanning the slender width of her lower back. He knew it the moment her orgasm broke.

Her entire body went still, then dissolved into a small series of explosions centered on his fingers.

Pulling her against him, he lifted her off her feet and cradled her in his arms, moving them both to the bed. Laying her gently on the bed, he followed her down and pressed his lips to where her pulse still beat a wild tattoo.

"You're amazing," he whispered against her throat.

A small giggle erupted from her as she turned her sloe-eyed gaze on him. "I was actually thinking that very thing about you."

With seeking fingers, Montana ran her hand down his stomach and over his zipper. He pressed himself against her, unable to stay away from her seeking touch, even as he knew he simply wanted to savor the moment.

Savor her.

With shaking fingers, he reached for her hand and stilled her motions. "This is about you."

"Quinn." Montana struggled up onto an elbow, her eyes dark with a mixture of desire and annoyance. "What's this all about?"

Before she could protest any further, he took her mouth in a searing kiss that was all lips and teeth and tongue. Satisfied he'd made his point—even as his heated body screamed for release—Quinn pulled back and pressed his forehead to hers. "You've had to take in a lot. Now's not the time to get into this. I don't want to rush."

"And why do you get to decide?"

He smiled at the mulish tone of her voice and pressed a quick kiss on her lips, then pulled her into his arms, settling her head against his chest. "Because I'm older and wiser than you, and I say so. Besides, I have no interest in being interrupted once we get going."

"Oh. Well, when you put it like that."

The two of them lay there for a while. Quinn soaked in the moment, the silence wrapping around them like a warm cocoon.

"Are you sure this is a good idea?"

"This?" Quinn snuggled closer and pressed his lips against her throat. "I think it's an outstanding idea."

Montana turned toward him. "I meant tonight."

"You'll be safe. I promise."

"But what about your friends? We're dragging them into this, too."

Again, he was struck by her immediate thought for others. Before in the park, and now this. Brushing back a stray, wispy curl from her cheek, he sought to reassure her. "This is what we do, Montana. We're highly trained Warriors."

"Are you sure?"

"I'm quite sure. If I could, I'd leave you behind altogether, but we're not going to learn anything if you're not with us."

Quinn pulled Montana closer and breathed in her soft, womanly scent. She smelled light and fresh, like brand-new sheets or a bright summer day, and in that moment he felt a very small piece of the heart he thought long dead come back to life.

Some of the emptiness—that vast wasteland that had filled him for far too long—wasn't quite so empty any longer.

And in two hours, he was dragging her straight into enemy territory.

Chapter Twelve

Themis stood before the Mirror of Truth and watched her daughter roam the streets of New York like a homeless person.

Because she *was* a homeless person.

A sense of despair welled in her breast. Themis wrapped her arms around her middle as the bitter taste of regret rose up on her tongue. Eirene had made her choice. She knew the consequences and she made that choice anyway.

But all that seemed to fade into nothingness as she stared at her beloved child, dying before her very eyes.

Even if Eirene didn't know the fate that awaited her, Themis did. And the cancer that ravaged her daughter's body was a vicious taskmaster, exercising its will more and more each day.

"Mother?"

Themis turned to see her daughter Atropos. "Yes, darling?"

"You called for me?" The Moirae's gaze flicked

•

toward the viewing screen. "I should have known it was to discuss Eirene."

"Her time is drawing near."

The long column of her neck arched in a graceful nod as Atropos idly fingered the shears at her waistband. "Aye."

"She hasn't done what she must. Montana is in danger and Eirene still hasn't told her what is required of her."

"Why should the girl suffer, Mother? You punish her in some ways even more than you punish Eirene. At least Reeny made her choice. Montana is innocent."

Themis's mother's heart leaped at the affection in the simple nickname. "Eirene knew the consequences of her choice. You and your sister are the ones who ensured Montana's existence."

"As if *we* had a choice." Atropos's hand flew toward the Mirror of Truth. "Clotho could no more have ignored Montana's existence than she could her own. Our niece's fate—nay, her very existence—was decreed the moment you punished Eirene."

"She has a protector now." Themis watched the mirror's screen split at her words, shifting so that Montana's image flashed on the screen.

Both she and her daughter watched as Montana wrapped herself in the arms of Quinn Tanner, her lips pressed to his in a heated embrace.

"I may be seen as the most vengeful goddess in the heavens, but I'm not a voyeur, Mother. Turn it off."

Themis did as her daughter asked, the screen winking back to show Eirene only. "The Taurus will protect her."

"You think the Warrior's presence makes it okay?"

Atropos's voice was harsh as she expressed her opinion. "Does he even know what she is? Where she came from? Your beloved Warriors aren't all-seeing, Mother."

"He's figured it out." Themis marveled at her daughter's ability to put her in her place so quickly. She truly had Zeus's temperament—steady and sure of herself, brooking no argument from anyone.

"Eirene doesn't have many days left and Montana has several trials before she ascends as the next Horae. He might have a basic knowledge of what's going on, but does he truly understand the depths of what's to come?"

When Themis didn't reply, Atropos pushed harder. "Does he understand she's becoming an immortal? And even more important, does he understand there are those who will fight to keep her from her ascension?"

"I can't interfere, Atropos. You know that. We're bound."

Delicate eyebrows arched above her daughter's piercing green eyes. "I may be bound, as are my sisters. You're not."

"I can't betray the balance. It's what I am, Daughter."

"Then we are at an impasse." Atropos turned on her heel and began to cross the room.

As she watched her go, Themis brought up another of her beloved daughters, Atropos's sister. "What does Lachesis say about it?"

Atropos turned at the doorway, her hand on the knob. "You know she doesn't share the specifics. She measures the thread, Mother. The trials each person faces are their own to experience."

"Yes, but she knows what the trials will be. What does she see when she looks at Montana?"

"The same thing the rest of us see, Mother. A victim."

The catcalls started before Quinn passed by the doorway of the upstairs game room.

Fuck.

It had never bothered him before that his office was on the same hallway as the darkly paneled game room. That was, of course, until he'd nearly gotten Kane and Ilsa killed over a stubborn bout of pride.

For reasons he couldn't quite understand, both claimed to forgive him.

But why?

The question had haunted him endlessly over the last months and he was no closer to understanding it. No closer to figuring out why they didn't hold him responsible for almost losing their lives with his obstinate, mulish, full-of-piss-and-vinegar pride.

Whatever awkwardness he'd felt earlier in the company of his Warrior brothers, it couldn't compare to how he felt now. This afternoon he could hide behind the mantle of work.

But now?

Now he had to put on his happy face and act like nothing was wrong.

Which was the exact fucking reason he now avoided the house's common areas as if they held the plague. Quinn knew he wasn't fooling anyone, either, seeing as how Callie had bitched at him just last week, letting him know in no uncertain terms that she thought he was hiding.

Which he'd scoffed at before closing his office door gently in her face.

In point of fact, he wasn't hiding. He was simply ridding the rest of the house of his presence.

Why none of them could see reason—or his point of view—was a mystery. But how did he explain it to them?

He was their leader. Self-appointed, maybe, but their leader nonetheless. And he'd failed one of his brothers.

Which meant he'd failed them all.

"Look at you, sexy. Hot date?"

Quinn flashed a middle finger at Brody as he came to a reluctant stop inside the doorway. "As if you didn't know, asshole."

"Ignore him, Quinn. We're all on heiress duty to-night," Grey added around a cigar clamped between his teeth as he threw a pile of chips into the center of a green baize-covered poker table. "Just getting in a good ass whipping of my pals here before we get ready to go."

Poker night was a relatively new addition to the house. Apparently Ava and Ilsa felt some male bonding was important, so they encouraged this little activity once a week. He supposed there was a side benefit as it also gave them an excuse to gorge on the junk food the puzzlingly slender women seemed to favor with a mad passion—cake batter, ice cream and wine.

Quinn's stomach turned over at the imagined com-bination. How in the gods names the women could stuff down spoonful after spoonful of the raw batter, let alone an entire bowl, he had no idea.

Of course, the recently uncovered news that Callie

was a nymph *and* Ilsa's sister meant they had a lot of catching up to do.

But still.

Their capacity for gossip and junk food was moderately frightening.

"Does everyone know their positions?"

"Drake and I scoped it out a little while ago," Kane offered. His brothers might be in the middle of a game, but their professional skills were honed to a sharp point and each man knew his duty this evening. "The peace organization running the dinner seems top-notch and we got lucky. Not only are there a bunch of high-profile donors, which has ratcheted up security, but the governor plans to be there, which means they doubled the security staff for the event."

Quinn reached for his BlackBerry and reviewed the message he got earlier. "The organizers have placed Montana at the front table. If the governor is there, that will likely help us even more."

"Why aren't you porting her in and out?" Grey's question was nonchalant, but Quinn admired the tone of respect underneath. His brothers had his back, but they weren't above questioning his choices.

"She needs to make an appearance in the publicity line, for starters. And there's one other little matter."

"Oh?" Grey's eyebrows rose over his piercing gray eyes.

"She doesn't know about teleportation yet."

"Damn, that's a big one," Brody added. "Ava was a bit shaken about it, but she learned to like it quickly enough. You need to tell her."

"I know." Quinn needed to tell her a lot of things. Tossing a book at her to read a few elements of their lore and history wasn't the same as actually talking to her and giving her the ins and outs of who and what they were.

"She had a lot thrown at her today."

"It is a lot, Quinn. But parsing out the knowledge is only going to make each conversation harder to have." Drake's voice was gentle, his more mild-mannered approach to everything—as usual—spot-on.

Quinn knew it would. But how in the hell did you tell a mortal woman that you could fling her body through the time-space continuum without freaking her out? And further, how did you explain to her that she likely had the ability to do it. Or would, within a matter of days or weeks.

Fuck.

"You gonna take the perimeter or sit with her?" Drake knew it was time to switch topics, even as he threw his cards on the table, disgust riding high on his face.

"Sit with her. After what went down this afternoon, I don't want her uncovered."

"I'll just bet you don't," Brody added, "in more ways than one. The gal's not going to stand a chance against the big, bad bull."

Brody's grin maintained its usual cocky demeanor and Quinn couldn't quite say why the urge to punch it off his face hit him square in the gut. But all Quinn could see in his mind's eye was Montana, taking her pleasure at his hands, and the idea of spoiling that—hell, of even *comparing* it to any woman he'd known before.

She was different.

And he was different when he was with her.

Quinn nearly pushed himself off the wall before he got himself under control and held his place.

The smile fell from Brody's face and the easy, comfortable friendship that filled the room quieted immediately. With raised eyebrows and a voice that had gone hard as hammered steel, Brody added, "You okay, Quinn?"

"She's not like the others, Talbot."

Brody held up his hands. "Got it."

On a last nod, Quinn turned and left the room. He might have moved firmly into the camp of House Asshole, but he knew his friends had his back.

If the easy friendship and camaraderie between them was gone, well, he had no one to blame but himself.

Montana kept her cashmere wrap firmly around her shoulders like a protective shield as she stepped out of the limousine in front of the Waldorf. Quinn had gotten out before her and was now standing guard near the car door, his body between her and the open crowd.

It was silly, really, she argued with herself as she walked next to Quinn toward the red carpet entrance. The cashmere would do nothing to protect her from a crazy killer with an agenda, but there was something about the fabric cocoon that reassured, even as it kept her warm.

"You okay?" Quinn whispered as they stepped up to a small marked spot on the edge of the carpet and posed for pictures.

"Ms. Grant! It's a big week next week!"

"You're taking your father's legacy public. Do you think he'd be pleased or angered?"

"Who is your date?"

She forced a smile as they posed and ignored the questions, Quinn's hand tightening around hers on that last question.

Date?

Even in the midst of all that was happening—the danger, the threats and the overwhelming sense of menace—the thought of being on a date with the large man standing next to her thrilled her to the depths of her toes.

Her thoughts slammed her back into the bedroom before she finished getting ready for the gala. Warmth filled her and her mind grew slightly fuzzy as her body tingled with remembered pleasure, the result of his expert touch.

Was he still thinking about it, too?

Was he as sorry as she was they didn't finish what they'd started?

Although she appreciated his gentlemanly restraint, a part of her wished they'd not only been late, but had never even left the house. Whatever imagined protection a cashmere wrap and the man by her side semi-promised, being wrapped in his arms for an evening of pleasure was a hell of a lot safer.

For your body, maybe, her conscience whispered. *But not your heart.*

Before Montana even realized it, her grip on his fingers tightened as the memories of the pleasure they had drawn from her body left her desperately wanting more.

Quinn looked down at her from his impressive height as he led her to the entrance, a knowing smile curving his strong lips and boldly chiseled chin.

Oh shit, am I in deep.

The ballroom was set up in a similar fashion to the evening before, but there was an additional round of security each person was required to pass through. "The governor's attending"—Quinn leaned over and whispered—"which works in our favor."

Montana expected this would make her feel better, but she was surprised as she discarded her wrap and purse and laid them in a plastic bin that the nerves buzzing in her stomach weren't diminishing.

Moving through the metal detector, her gaze scanned the room and the crowd of blue bloods who were shedding their garments in a similar fashion. She watched a doddering old couple she'd known for years link hands after the man retrieved his wife's purse, the actions so natural and easy, she could tell they'd spent their lives together.

The comfort of that thought quickly gave way to a far more startling one.

"If he's supernatural, he could get in here anyway."

Quinn's hand settled itself on her lower back. "It's okay, Montana. I'm here with you, and the guys are scattered around the ballroom."

"How'd they get tickets? This has been sold out for months."

"There's not an event in this city Grey can't get a ticket to."

"But how'd they get here so quickly? They weren't even ready to leave the house when we did."

"It's a long story I owe you an explanation on later."

Forcing her most stern executive face, Montana narrowed her eyes. "Quinn Tanner. You can't leave me in the dark on this stuff."

Quinn navigated them through the ballroom. "Fine. They ported here."

"Is that what I think it is?"

"What do you think it is?"

"Teleportation? As in flashing yourself from point a to point b? *Star Trek* shit?"

"Exactly."

Every time she thought she had a handle on what was happening to her, the sands shifted yet again. Whatever comfort she'd managed to glean back at the house evaporated in the news that Quinn and his Warrior brothers could imagine themselves in different places and travel there instantly.

Travel that wasn't some fantasy created for a generation of TV viewers.

"Oh my God."

Quinn pulled out a chair for Montana as they reached their table. "Gods actually, sweetheart. You can blame it all on them."

Quinn had timed their arrival to minimize cocktail hour chitchat, but even he couldn't keep Montana protected from the well-wishers who came up to their table.

He watched as she greeted each individual by name, again impressed to see yet another facet of her personality. Although he'd observed her from a distance the previous evening, to actually watch her body language and hear her conversation up close and personal offered another layer of clarity to the question that had captivated him like no other.

Who was Montana Grant?

Fascination warred with the baser needs of his body as he thought of the stolen moments they'd shared back at the house.

She was strong and vulnerable, sensitive and tough. She could manage a global business and yet still yell at him for his BlackBerry social skills.

In short, she was amazing.

"She's a special lady." A shaky voice interrupted Quinn's thoughts. Turning, he saw the older couple he and Montana had walked in behind when they entered the ballroom.

"Yes, she is."

"You her new beau?"

Quinn let out a slightly uneasy chuckle, especially when he spied Brody wiggling his eyebrows from where he'd positioned himself at the next table. Clearly, whatever tension had risen between them back at the house was gone under the Leo's good-natured need to tease him whenever the opportunity arose. "I have an interest in Ms. Grant, yes."

"You stupid?"

Brody let out a loud cough and covered his mouth with his palm. Quinn simply stared. "Excuse me?"

"Montana Grant's not a woman you have an interest in, boy-o. She's a woman you hang on to and don't let go. Like my Marcy there."

Quinn nodded politely at Marcy and, despite the lines of age, saw the beauty in the curve of her cheek and the elegant lines of her neck. "Your wife is a beautiful woman."

"Damn straight." The older man shifted and took the empty seat next to Quinn. "I knew her father for a long time."

"Oh? Marcy's?"

The old man shot him a look that clearly screamed *keep up*, before he said, "Montana's."

"Got it." Quinn wasn't sure where this was going, but didn't want to be entirely rude. The old gentleman seemed harmless enough and Montana appeared to be deep in conversation with his wife.

"Miserable bastard, Black Jack Grant." The guy leaned toward Quinn as if attempting to whisper, but his voice still echoed loud enough to be heard by everyone in a radius of three tables.

"You seem to like his daughter well enough."

"Montana's an angel. Her father, on the other hand. He took whatever he could without a care for anyone else. It's a miracle she turned out as perfect as she did."

The older man leaned in one more time, and this time, he did lower his voice to a modulated whisper. "Her father was into any number of things, but I can tell you that little girl isn't. I may have retired going on ten years now, but I keep my ear to the ground. Watch my investments. She's taking that company public and a whole lot of people are going to lose all the special interests they've cultivated over the years. Watch out for her."

"I will, sir."

The man stood and nodded. "Protect her. She needs it."

Quinn watched the man collect his wife and move them on toward their seats. He didn't miss the small smile that ghosted the edges of Montana's mouth.

"You like them, don't you?"

"I do." Montana took her seat and he did the same. Their table was still empty, although he presumed it would be filled at the last minute by the governor and his security detail. "They've clearly got a special love. A lifetime of stories, just between the two of them."

He might be more comfortable with his computer programs and his constantly buzzing BlackBerry, but even Quinn saw the wistful longing in her face. "It's a rare thing."

"That it is."

"But that doesn't mean it's impossible."

"Oh yeah? That sounds surprisingly romantic, Quinn." The thoughtful smile morphed into something much bigger. "The women shared quite a few details about the men of the house with me earlier. But they were suspiciously silent about you. What's your story? Have you ever been in love?"

"No."

The word seemed to hover between them. He saw Montana's thoughtful gaze and the extra few beats of silence before she continued. "Ava said you're the strong, decisive, silent type."

"She also calls me an ass hat on a regular basis. Or so I hear."

Montana giggled as she reached for her water glass. "You heard correct."

"I knew it!"

"She actually says it with a high degree of affection."

"I'll just bet she does."

"No. Really." Quinn couldn't help but be captivated by the subtle blush that covered her features as her blue eyes shined with suppressed merriment. "Come on. Out with it. What do the other ones call me? I'm sure Ilsa has a few choice names."

"Callie called you a *stubborn* ass hat. And I think she might have used raging fuckwit once, too."

"Ah." Quinn wanted to be angry, but for some reason, it just wouldn't come. He loved each of those women—would lay down his life for any of them—and he knew he was an object of ridicule for his endless list of rules and overt management of every situation that came up.

"But Ilsa didn't call you anything."

"She probably didn't want to use such shocking profanity in your presence."

Montana cocked her head and stared at him and Quinn felt a sudden sense of unease skitter under his skin. He rarely felt vulnerable or exposed, the combination of his willful attitude and sheer physical strength ensuring vulnerability didn't ride high on his list of emotions.

"No, she just calls you Quinn. With a great deal of respect, I might add."

In that moment, under the watchful gaze of Montana Grant, Quinn felt as naked and vulnerable as the day he was born.

Arturo ported himself into Montana Grant's penthouse, his gaze scanning the long hallway that ran through the inner portion of the apartment. He sensed the low-level hum of humanity as he oriented himself inside her home. The penthouse took up the entire floor of the building and had to be at least eight thousand square feet.

Arturo felt the pride rumble through his chest as he thought of his own homes, scattered throughout the world. Penthouses in Rio, Rome and Hong Kong.

A villa in the South of France. A beachfront mansion in Malibu.

Moving down the hallway, he focused on the various rooms, glancing into each as he passed. A small study. A formal living room. An entry into the large kitchen that ran along one side of the apartment, windows all along the length of the far wall. One of the people he'd sensed upon his arrival—a housekeeper— stood with her back to him as she stirred something over the stove, humming to herself.

As he continued to walk, Arturo focused on the only door in the hallway with a closed door.

That had to be it.

Montana's home office.

He tried the handle and wasn't surprised to find it locked. The thumb pad next to the door added a further clue that some serious security barred whatever was inside. Although he didn't have a visual of the office to complete the port, he didn't worry about getting in. The little trick he'd figured out centuries before had served him well over the years.

Standing before the door, he started into the port. The heavy drag of gravity that took hold just prior to weightlessness was the moment he waited for.

The moment of transition where the *real* power was to be found.

With a focus that had become as second nature as breathing, Arturo held himself at that exact moment, rendering his physical form invisible, but holding himself in this time, in this place. Once he had his body in a sort of stasis midway through the teleportation, he moved forward, stepping through the closed door.

Instantaneously, his body reassembled, the door at his back. As Arturo looked around, he confirmed his instincts were correct.

Montana's office was behind the locked door.

"I can't believe nothing happened." Even as the words left her lips, Montana knew how stupid they sounded. It wasn't as if she *wanted* to be attacked in public.

"He's toying with us," Quinn muttered, his lips a harsh slash across his face.

"Do you think so? I was sort of hoping he just went away."

Quinn stopped in the lobby of the Waldorf and pulled her aside, her back to the wall and his back to the crowd. In her heels, she could see over his shoulder. Brody, Kane and Drake were fanned out in the lobby and she knew Grey had gone on ahead of them all and waited outside the hotel.

"Montana. I don't want to scare you, but you need to understand this problem isn't just going to go away. We have to take care of it for that to happen."

She knew it. Deep inside, in the places where she allowed only raw truth, she *knew*.

It was the place she kept the thoughts of her parents. It was the place she worried about never being loved for who she was. It was also the place she now kept the acknowledgment that things were happening outside her control . . . like the idea that she had the healing powers of an immortal.

"So you think tonight was only a game?"

"Yes, I do. Which means we need to figure out his next move."

"You're sure it's a man?"

The ice-cold set of Quinn's gaze grew even frostier, if that were possible. "No."

"You think a woman's doing this?"

"Enyo, the goddess of war, is my sworn enemy. It's highly possible—and very probable—she's involved."

"But this isn't about you. It's about me. Someone's targeted me. Why would this woman target me?"

"She's a goddess. Remember that."

"Fine. Goddess." The hard-won sense of calm that had descended as the interminable dinner stretched on and on evaporated as if it had never been. "What the hell does she want with me?"

"It's a theory I'm working on. It may be her—it may not. Either way, she's a wild card I can't afford to ignore."

Again, the sense of unreality dragged at her. "This just gets worse by the hour."

"Come on. Let's get you home so you can get settled in for the night."

Quinn's words painted an immediate picture in her mind of snuggling down in her bed in her warmest, softest pair of pajamas. "The comforts of home and my own bed."

His eyes flashed from cold and hard to a warm, molten chocolate at the mention of her bed and suddenly, the thought of warm cotton pajamas held no interest.

None at all.

Chapter Thirteen

Arturo settled himself on the soft, overstuffed couch on the side of the room. He'd toyed with settling into the large leather chair behind Montana's desk, but this would be more intimate.

More suitable for what he had in mind.

He flicked a glance at his watch and noted the time. It would only be a few more minutes. Montana's little toady was nothing, if not punctual.

To pass the time, his gaze continued cataloging the contents of the office.

Neat rows of papers sat atop the desk.

Floor-to-ceiling bookshelves ran along the wall opposite him, full of everything from college textbooks to paperbacks to any number of photos and knickknacks.

The evidence of a life.

All so fucking pointless.

A noise from outside the hallway registered, like a reward for his ability to control his behavior. A light beep sounded and the door unlocked with a soft snick.

Light expanded in the room as the door opened.

Arturo stretched his arms out so they spread across the back of the couch cushions.

Master of all he surveyed.

King of the castle.

A fucking god among men.

"Oh. Hello."

"Jackson." Arturo allowed a slow, seductive grin to spread across his face as he unfolded his long, lithe body from the couch. He didn't miss the flick of confusion that rode high on Jackson's face, nor did he miss the appreciative glance that assessed the width of his chest.

Moving forward, Arturo allowed his own gaze to travel the length of Jackson's body in a seductive greeting. "It's so lovely to see you again."

Quinn pulled himself back from Montana's body by sheer force of will. Gods, what was wrong with him? He was standing in the lobby of the hotel, for fuck's sake.

In plain sight.

With her protected by the width of his body and nothing more.

He'd been attracted to women in the past—hell, a lot of women, if you added up the millennia of his life—and none of them did this to him.

Made him forget who he was, where he was or what he was.

This one slender woman managed to do all three while also wiping out any lick of sense he possessed at the same time.

He was a Warrior of Themis and he had a job to do. And it involved protecting this woman who made him bat-shit crazy with need, lust and want.

Pure, simple *want*.

He wanted her. And it was supremely humbling for a man who had always known how to control his baser natures in favor of doing his job.

"Come on. Let's go. Drake just signaled me the limo is here."

In minutes, they were all piled in the car, Montana's elegantly clad frame surrounded by five Warriors.

So why weren't the snapping jaws of awareness and unease quieting?

Or stopping altogether.

He glanced around at his Warrior brothers. Although none of them ever fully relaxed, he could see they'd gone off of high alert once everyone was settled in the moving automobile.

They were highly trained in combat and had survived thousands of battles, both large and small, as a team.

If his brothers weren't concerned, why was he?

"You do these often?" Brody was the first to speak, shooting his question toward Montana.

"Events like this?" At Brody's nod, she continued. "Sadly, yes, I do."

"Kane and Grey here"—Brody pointed to the men on either side of him—"live to wear tuxedos. I, on the other hand, prefer—"

Kane cut him off before he could continue. "—to look like shit on day-old toast. He thinks he's sexy, with his Indiana Jones wardrobe and two-day growth of beard. I say he just smells."

A series of "amen's" went up around the car.

Montana giggled and Quinn relaxed ever so slightly at the calming sound. If his brothers were good at anything, it was their ability to play off one another and lighten the mood.

Spirits clearly lightened, Montana dived in with questions. "So tell me. I thought there were more than five of you. You're tied to the zodiac, right? Twelve signs? Where is everyone else?"

"Missions, mostly," Grey filled her in. "And there are thirteen of us, not twelve. Gemini's always a pair."

"Twins," Montana added, in comprehension.

"Exactly. Part of the strength of our signs is that they make us a diverse group. But as you'd imagine, that diversity doesn't always make us the easiest bunch to get along with. Some of the guys prefer life outside the brownstone. Heck, life outside of New York, if you can imagine that."

"But you all help one another. Look out for one another."

Quinn felt the impact of Montana's statement like an atomic bomb and he couldn't stop his gaze from narrowing in on Kane. What he didn't expect was the Scorp's ready confirmation. "Yes, we do."

"Speaking of those missing in action lately," Drake added, "I know Max has been obsessed with playing Mr. Corporate Executive, but he checked in earlier to see what's on everyone's radar. I told him about Montana's situation and he said there's huge interest in her taking the company public."

"With all the growth happening at Capricorn, I'm surprised he still has time for us." Grey's words held the sharp edge of disapproval and Quinn shot him a questioning stare.

Were Grey and Max on the outs?

Or was it something more? Something Grey heard in

all the knowledge, gossip and overall information that traveled through his nightclub on a regular basis.

Montana's words interrupted his train of thought. "Max St. Claire? The head of Capricorn Communications?"

"Yep."

"He's an immortal Warrior?"

"On his good days." Brody's eyes flashed again. "Personally, I think he really likes playing Mr. Corporate Executive."

"What he really likes is the Harvard degreed pus—" Quinn almost laughed out loud at Grey's pained expression as he caught himself just in time. On a rough cough, the ram added, "He, um, really likes his job."

Quinn felt Montana's shaking body next to him as she laughed in reaction to Grey's testosterone-laden honesty. He smiled along with her, but it only expanded the puzzle, to Quinn's mind.

He'd just have to grill Grey on it later.

Montana's voice held a note of teasing as she aimed that glorious smile at Grey. "I'll just bet he does. As a fellow corporate executive, I can confirm there is a lot of Harvard-degreed ass to be found if educated sex is what you're after."

"Damn it, I *am* in the wrong business," Grey muttered with a wicked smile of his own.

Before Quinn could say anything, the rest of his brothers did it for him with an echoing series of "yeah, right's."

Montana leaned over and placed her hand on his forearm, the light touch matching the amusement in her gaze. "You're in tune with one another. It's lovely."

"Lovely?"

"In a very manly sort of way."

The crystal blue of her eyes, the long sweep of eyelashes and the subtle curve to her jaw captivated him and in that moment, without anything other than the basest of instincts to go on, Quinn knew he'd never be the same.

Montana felt the answering tug of Quinn's gaze and wondered how a human body could live through such roiling highs and lows. From the advancing disaster that seemed to be tied to her professional life to the dizzying changes in her personal life, none of it held a candle to Quinn Tanner.

Large and overbearing. Forceful, yet gentle. And so freaking sexy the thought of simply ripping off her clothes and allowing him to have his way with her continued to build under her skin with the increasingly powerful beat of jungle drums.

"Manly, you say?"

"Yes. Lovely and man—"

Whatever else she was about to say faded to nothingness as she flew forward through the air to sprawl across Brody, Kane and part of Grey.

Drake and Quinn nearly followed her, but both managed to brace themselves far quicker than she could, her heels not allowing her feet to find purchase on the floor of the car to hold herself still.

Before she could understand what was happening, Brody held her outright and muttered, "Neither of you are touching her. Go."

And then Kane and Grey simply disappeared.

Evaporated.

"Oh my—" Quinn pulled her back to the seat next to him, his body quivering with tense anticipation.

What in the hell was going on here?

And then Kane reappeared in the exact spot he'd been before and Montana couldn't stop the startled scream from erupting in her throat.

Abstractly, she heard Brody's muttered, "I told you you should have said something."

"Driver's gone," Kane said, his face an unreadable mask as he gave his fellow Warriors the details. "Grey's already headed into the park, but it's Destroyers. The frame of the car had a shitload of electricity stamped all over it. I defused it, but it was one helluva clear calling card."

"Tony? They got Tony?" She calmed the urge to scream again and forced herself to focus on the problem at hand. "And the park? Again?"

"We're on Fifth heading toward your apartment, so the park was the ready place for them to take him. We'll find him, Montana," Kane promised. Although his words were meant to be reassuring, she knew what he didn't say. Whether they'd find Tony dead or alive, *that* was the real question.

And then she felt Quinn's arm wrap around her shoulders. "We'll get to the bottom of this."

"Are you going to evaporate, too?"

"Yes. I'm going to port." His voice was solemn and she could see him searching for the right words. "It's part of us, Montana. Like I told you before."

Montana fought to catch her breath. "But it's real. Really real." Absurdly real.

"Yeah." Quinn's eyes remained steady on hers, almost as if he were willing her to believe in him with the sheer force of his gaze. "It's real. And it's part of you, too."

And then he leaned down and pressed his lips to hers. Although quick, the kiss held passion and . . . reverence?

Need.

And promise.

"I can't leave you here, so I'm going to port you home and then come right back."

"Take me with you. Please."

"I can't do that."

"I can't be in that house by myself. I can't know that you're here, fighting for me. Fighting for someone in my employment, and left me behind. Besides, you said it yourself. This is a part of me. I'll heal. If anything happens, I'll heal."

"I can't take you along."

"You will take me along."

"Montana. You're not trained. You can't get in the middle of this. It's your house or the brownstone, but you'd better decide quick, or I'll decide for you."

"Fine. The brownstone. I'll go knit by the fucking fireside with the other women."

Although it galled her, she hoped the company of the other women would at least diminish the feeling of helplessness that overwhelmed her.

Quinn didn't say anything, but reached for her hand. Before she could say anything, the weight of the universe bore down on her shoulders.

And then she was flying.

* * *

"Here. Take her." Montana heard the words before she fully caught her bearings, the image of a kitchen shimmering to life around her.

Quinn thrust her at Callie before barking orders toward Ilsa and Ava. "Central Park. East side bordering Fifth Avenue. Destroyers got our car and they appear to have kidnapped the driver."

Ilsa stood immediately, with Ava close on her heels. "On our way."

Montana watched in awe as both women simply disappeared. Quinn gave her one last glance before he followed suit.

"Son of a bitch." She muttered to herself, whatever feeling of uselessness she'd felt in the car multiplying into infinity.

"Not one of his finer moments. But that's our Quinn for you." Callie patted her arm and led her to the raised stool in front of a ginormous butcher-block counter. "Come on and sit down. This may take a while. Or," she added philosophically, "they could be back in ten minutes. You never know."

"But Ava and Ilsa went with them?"

"Yes. They're immortals and Warriors in their own right. They can help them."

"But you're an immortal and you didn't go."

A small light dulled behind Callie's eyes and again, like earlier in the bedroom when she'd asked about the woman's husband, Montana got the feeling she overstepped her boundaries.

"I'm sorry. I know you all have roles. Jobs to do. That was horribly insensitive of me."

"It's the truth. And you've been thrown into the

middle of something you no doubt are struggling to understand."

Montana marveled at the remarkable woman as she moved toward the stove to reach for a tea kettle. "I'll fix us up something while we wait."

Anxious for something—*anything*—to do to feel useful, Montana reached for her BlackBerry in her small purse, looking for Jackson's good night message. He always shot her one after he left the house, a funny little ritual that always made her think of the Waltons.

He even put "Good night John Boy" in the subject line of the e-mail.

She suppressed a giggle at the idea she'd even managed to hang on to her purse. Funny, the things a person could manage by sheer subconscious thought, she mused.

When the screen showed no message, Montana laid the device back on the counter. "Will they be okay?"

"They've lived this long." Although the words were callous, Callie's voice was gentle when she turned from the stove and moved to the sink to fill the kettle. "They know what they're doing and they'll be fine. But Quinn would have been in more danger if you'd gone."

Even as the words galled her, Montana knew they were true. "Of course."

"What you need to do is focus on learning all you can. You're an immortal, of that I have no doubt. But you're a rising one and that means you've got a lot to learn. Some of it comes naturally, but a lot of it's honed over time."

"A rising immortal?"

Callie brought two steaming mugs of tea over to

the counter and placed them down. Montana took in the rich, earthy aroma and felt the small measure of comfort begin to unlock the fist in her stomach. "I know you recently discovered her, but your immortality is directly tied to your mother."

"How do you know this?"

"I know a lot of things."

Montana laid a hand on Callie's forearm. "Look. Tell me what you want or don't tell me, the choice is yours. But it's very clear you know things, likely far more than you let on. Please don't talk in riddles and hints. It's not fair."

She saw a measure of respect fill Callie's gaze and Montana felt a shot of satisfaction after two days of nothing but confusion. It was small, but it was victory all the same.

The small woman nodded, decision stamped across her face. "That's fair. What do you want to know?"

Quinn triangulated himself back into the park, the sound of grunts and groans ensuring he wasn't far off the mark. Ilsa and Ava were several yards in front of him and he gave a low whistle to catch their attention.

His stomach still full from dinner—even if it was rubber chicken and chewy mashed potatoes—ensured Quinn felt the ease of the port on his body. Even after millennia of holding the ability, it never failed to amaze him on some base level. But, like all gifts, it came with a price.

Extreme fatigue or hunger weakened the body and it weakened the ability to port. Food, sleep or the mother of all cures, an orgasm, was the only way back to full strength.

While he thoroughly enjoyed the last method, he'd found regular sex more and more of an impracticality as their world advanced and evolved around them.

He avoided bringing women home to the brownstone, as the compound was far too dangerous for a mortal to see. Its existence on both the human plane and the immortal one—damn near all of the breadth and depth of the mansion existed on Mount Olympus—ensured a human simply couldn't be exposed.

And as their work grew more sophisticated, his free time had diminished to practically nothing.

So he found a woman when it was convenient and they both knew what they were getting out of the brief fling, and then he moved on.

"You ready or not?" Ava whispered in his ear. She practically quivered with anxiety and he saw her shift on the balls of her feet.

Although Ava had no idea of his thoughts, Quinn couldn't help compare her question to his feelings for Montana. The forgotten images of his previous flings were nothing compared to the moments he shared with Montana.

Was he ready?

Ready for commitment? Ready to share his life with someone?

Should he be worried that those questions didn't seem nearly as scary as they would have even a week before?

"Yes. I'm ready."

Ilsa pointed in the direction of the battle taking place with his Warrior brothers. "There are ten left." Ilsa flashed both her hands up to show the count as well. "I already saw Drake and Grey dispatch two of them."

Quinn reached for the Xiphos strapped to his calf, suddenly aware his weapon was in the trunk of the limousine. Although his brothers had ported in with their weapons strapped to them, he'd known he'd have to go through security. Unwilling to deal with the hassle of explaining a ten-thousand-year-old knife, he'd stowed it in the trunk before entering the Waldorf. "Shit."

Ilsa saw the movement and pulled a wicked blade from a scabbard strapped on her back. "We stopped in the basement before we left. Thought you might need this."

Quinn leaned forward and bussed her cheek with a kiss. "You're an angel."

"Nah, but it's sweet of you to think so."

As he felt the weight of the hilt in his palm, the soothing flash of steel as he turned it under the park's streetlights, a humbling thought came over him.

These women that had come into their lives—lovers to two of the Warriors, family members to the rest—and they looked out for them. Took care of them. They thought about preparation for battle differently and because of it, they brought a unique dimension to the Warriors' ongoing battle with Enyo.

He and his brothers were better because of them.

Better fighters.

Better men.

On a quick cough, Quinn brought his attention to the matter at hand. "Focus on whoever's having the toughest time as your priority. And stay out of the way of their tattoos. Grey's ram in particular. Those horns hurt like the devil if they stake you."

As the war cry rumbled up into Quinn's throat,

the signal for the three of them to charge into battle, a fireball hit him square in the back. Ilsa and Ava both grunted in pain and they fell to their knees beside him.

Struggling to his feet and turning to face the attacker before another hit could strike him from behind, Quinn watched six more Destroyers come out of the trees and brush of the park to form a wall. As the six soulless minions linked arms, a shot of electricity arced from the hand of the last Destroyer, headed straight for them.

Chapter Fourteen

Quinn lifted the sword just in time, deflecting most of the fireball with the broadside of his weapon. Of course, his arm rang like a son of a bitch as his skin absorbed wave after wave of electricity.

Fuck, it hurt. But it was better than a direct hit.

Before he could hold either of them back or instruct otherwise, Ava and Ilsa moved forward in unison, their focus on opposite ends of the linked Destroyers.

Although the assholes clearly thought working in unison would elevate their power, it also weakened them. In order to form the link, it was obvious they couldn't break physical contact. The women used that to their advantage as their swords slashed in wide arcs in front of them.

Quinn followed quickly, watching their backs and offering a second line of defense. The tattoo that rode high on his shoulder twitched to be released and Quinn didn't hold the beast back.

Unfolding from his aura, the large bull stamped the ground as it faced their attackers.

Although an exceptional fighting aid, the size of the beast and the close proximity of the fight meant the animal could inadvertently harm Ilsa or Ava, so Quinn waited. And watched. And allowed Ilsa the room she needed to finish her task.

As the battle played out before him, Quinn realized these women he'd come to care for had far more talent than he'd suspected.

Or bothered to give them credit for.

Ilsa sliced at the shoulder blade of the Destroyer on her end of the line, toying with him and luring him into breaking ranks. As if on cue, the slash—deliberately not fatal—did enough damage that the guy dropped arms with his brethren. Ilsa wasted no time. In whip-quick slashes, she went for the neck, nearly severing the head in the process.

Immediately, the body began to disintegrate, the form of the Destroyer no longer supported by the evil ooze that filled him.

Satisfied Ilsa could handle herself, Quinn switched his focus to Ava. Although she'd only trained as a Warrior for a little over a year, her skills were superior. She slashed at the Destroyer who'd thrown the fireball, nailing his neck in one, clean sweep of her sword.

Two down.

"Ava! Ilsa! Move back!" The women had taken care of the ends of the line.

He was taking the rest.

As soon as the women pulled back, Quinn moved forward and let go of his restraint. The bull leaped to his side, slamming into the Destroyer who now held the end position before the asshole could work up a fireball. Leaving the beast to focus on the end, Quinn shifted to the opposite side of the line. All the while, he shouted to Ava.

"Keep watch on them. I think only the ends can fire on us when they're linked."

He heard Ava's agreement, pleased when she stayed behind to act as backup.

Quinn leveraged his footwork—one of his biggest assets for a man of his size—and kept himself in constant motion. His blade whistled through the air as he parried another fireball, the shot of electricity winging through the length of his sword and sending another shock through his arm.

Fuck, but these guys were loaded.

Anger mixed with adrenaline as he leaped forward, ignoring the pain as he thrust his blade. In one sinuous motion, man and beast leapt at their opponents. Quinn's blade arced through the air, neatly severing the head of the Destroyer on the end as the bull ripped out the throat of its opponent on the opposite end of the line with a clamp of his powerful jaws.

Two more down.

Ilsa moved in when Quinn and his tattoo retreated, her aim steady and true, her war cry unmistakable. With lithe, graceful movements, Ilsa thrust her weapon at the Destroyer's midsection, barely missing him when he sidled away from the slash of her weapon. As the man reached to grab her—the long reach of his arms more than capable of grabbing her smaller frame—Ilsa ducked low and came up at him from underneath.

Her blade pierced his neck in the vicinity of where an Adam's apple would be if the asshole had one. The puncture wound took him down immediately and the husk of his body fell forward over her blade.

"Yes!" Ava screamed as Ilsa pumped a fist in the air.

One more down.

As Quinn advanced on the last Destroyer, he had a moment of surprise when the guy held his ground. Something registered in the back of his mind, but it was only when he took his last step forward, the tip of his sword pushing easily into the weak flesh of the Destroyer's arm in his sights, that Quinn realized his miscalculation. His dress shoes slipped in the ooze from the Destroyer Ilsa had killed, knocking him off balance, the ground rising up to meet him in a rush.

Quinn's Destroyer reacted immediately, the sword poke having done nothing to diminish his strength. Quinn felt the slam of the asshole's body as it knocked the wind out of him. Distracted, he couldn't keep a focus on the Destroyer and on his aura, and the bull folded back up on his body, unable to help deal with the threat.

As Quinn struggled to keep his grip on his weapon, his opponent used both hands to slam his sword arm against the pavement. Distantly, Quinn heard the sword clatter away as fire crawled up his arm and into his chest. While he knew he'd heal, the pain lingered and Quinn struggled to shift his body to gain the upper hand.

If he could just get the guy over . . .

Like a wrestler working to pin his opponent, Quinn struggled and heaved, seeking the upper hand. Seeking to expose his back once again so he could let the bull back out.

Muscles straining, Quinn nearly had the guy over when he heard a loud sucking noise, followed by a face full of ooze as the evil minion's head went skating away off the top of his body. The shit stung and Quinn glanced up to see Ilsa smiling at him, her hand outstretched to him.

"Thought you could use some help."

"You thought right." Quinn gave her a hand as he used the other one—still stinging from being slammed on concrete—to wipe at his face. "I owe you one."

"Damn straight. Come on. The guys need us. Grab your sword."

As Quinn reached for the discarded metal, he was awed to watch Ava and Ilsa race on toward the continuing battle.

Damn, but they were some mighty warrioresses.

There was a time the idea he'd been saved by a woman might have bothered him.

As he looked at the six grease spots fanning out on the ground, Quinn realized just how much times had changed.

And how very happy he was about that fact.

"Is this about the meeting? About Montana taking the company public?" Jackson felt the waves of pain as they lapped over, around, *in* his body and marveled he could still speak.

Could still ask questions.

"I don't need to tell you anything."

Jackson watched Arturo Veron pace the room from where he slumped on Montana's desk chair and wanted to scream in frustration.

He knew he was a dead man.

Had known it the moment he'd seen Arturo on the couch.

But instead of running, he'd let his fucking hormones drop his guard and here he was paying for it.

The harsh, tangy scent of blood filled his senses. Although his nose was broken, making it hard to breathe, he couldn't keep the taste from his tongue. With the bitter flavor of truth, Jackson knew the only thing he could possibly do was try to leave some sort of message.

Some sort of sign Montana would understand.

"You're killing me anyway. What have you got to lose?"

"More than you could imagine, little one." Arturo pranced around the room again, his gaze lingering over various elements in the room. Photos. Mementos. The files Jackson had walked in with.

As Arturo flipped through those once again, he spared him a glance. "You really know a lot about the inner workings of Grant Shipping."

"I'm a secretary, nothing more."

Jackson knew the words were a bad idea. They would only taunt the asshole, but he was unable to stop them. For his cheek, he got another round of electricity.

Where was this guy getting it from?

Jackson's gaze roved the room in a wild arc, desperately searching for the source of the pain.

But it all seemed concentrated in the man's fingertips.

How was it possible?

Rivers of pain ran through his body, violent hammers playing a rapt pattern on his nerve endings. God, how did anyone survive this?

With renewed clarity, Jackson acknowledged the truth.

No one did.

And with that clarity came the whisper of a memory. Could he reach it? Grab it through the pain?

Montana.

It was something she'd said. Something at lunch earlier. The comment had seemed out of place at the time and she'd quickly dropped it.

"What do you know about astrology?"

"Not much past what I read in the Post *every morning on the subway."*

"And what about Greek mythology?"

"You mean like gods and goddesses and stuff?"

"I mean exactly like gods and goddesses. I think they're trying to kill me."

The small moment of triumph that he managed to remember the conversation was quickly drowned out by the stark reality of the man standing opposite him.

Was it even possible?

Was this man a god?

Or was the pain so horrible—so mind-fuckingly intense—that he'd believe anything?

"You're a god. Aren't you?"

Arturo moved forward, but he held his body in check. No outstretched hands. No random bursts of electricity. "You're brighter than she gives you credit for."

Drool oozed down his chin, but Jackson ignored the indignity. He had to find out what he could. And then he had to find some way to tell Montana. "What are you?"

"Who, darling. Who. I'm an immortal Warrior and I've got a bone to pick with your best gal pal."

Jackson gritted his teeth, willing the pain to subside. Willing himself to stay conscious. "Why her? She's an angel. Surely you know that."

"She's a threat. One I aim to erase."

Oh man, this guy was off. And Montana was in danger because the asshole thought he knew something. "How can she be a threat? She's the head of a global company, not an immortal. You've been in meetings with her. You're going to be on her board of directors."

"Ah, but you know so little. So very little."

Oh shit, this was bad. Jackson's eyes darted around the room, searching for something—anything—that could help him warn her. To make Montana understand what was happening around her.

As his body sank lower in the leather chair, his frame no longer able to fully support him, Jackson's gaze alighted on a small button, visible on the underside of the desk.

An alarm?

He tried—desperately tried—to remember Montana's instructions the first time she showed him the room. The first time she trusted him into her inner sanctuary.

No. Not an alarm.

Something even better.

As the reality of what he had to do filled him, Jackson knew he had to keep Arturo talking. "I've known Montana Grant for a long time. She's not a fucking immortal."

Arturo raised his hands and Jackson leaned forward, swiveling the chair as he went. He had one shot at this. One try to let his bound hands at the back of the chair hit the button.

As the chair swiveled, Jackson braced himself for

the pain. Instead, the shot of electricity he expected to light up his body erupted in a shower of sparks against the wall near his head.

And as he marveled at the avoided electric charge, his fingers hit the button, depressing it as they flew past, powered by the momentum of the chair.

Arturo reached forward and spun the chair to complete Jackson's rotation, his face mere inches away. "She *is* a fucking immortal. Or will be when her mother breathes her last breath. And you. Will. Look. At. Me. When. I. Talk. To. You."

Jackson knew he was losing precious seconds. He could only hope the tape would give Montana what she needed to know. "She's innocent."

"She's innocent of nothing. And I will not rest until she is dead."

Another round of electricity slammed into his body, and Jackson blindly heard the bleak sounds that fell from his lips.

The sound of death, he thought abstractly. Those moans were the sound of death.

Before Jackson could say anything in response—could even *think* of any words—a large bull rose up behind Arturo.

What the fuck?

The scream lodged in his throat as light exploded before his eyes, a shower of sparks that could rival the Fourth of July on the Hudson.

As if on cue, the bull leaped over the desk even as the sparks still rained down over all of them, his enormous body crumbling the old varnished wood of the desk.

And then there was darkness.

* * *

Montana was on her second cup of tea when people began reappearing in the kitchen. The tense knots in her body loosened as she counted arrivals.

Ilsa and Kane, wrapped around each other like two long-lost lovers. Brody and Ava in almost the same position. Drake. Grey. And finally, Quinn.

"Oh my God! Are you okay?" Montana leaped toward Quinn, reaching for him so she could run her fingers down his chest even as her gaze roved over the ravages of battle. The pristine white dress shirt he'd worn under his tuxedo sported several rips, two patches of blood, a very odd spatter of green stains and so much dirt he looked like he'd rolled in a mud pit.

Quinn laid his large hands over top of hers. "I'm fine. We're all fine."

"What happened to you?"

"We kicked ass!" came a resounding cry from over her shoulder.

The lot of them looked beyond tired, but aside from that, none the worse for wear. Everyone had spots of blood on them and a few had those odd green blotches that matched Quinn's shirt, but no one was broken or bleeding.

"And you're all okay?" Montana whispered, unable to fully find her voice in the face of whatever battle they'd all just fought.

Callie had given her some clues—how the Warriors fought their archenemy, Enyo, and her soulless minions, Destroyers—but it was an entirely different sensation to see the evidence standing before her.

"You fought Destroyers, right?"

"We sure did." Quinn's victorious smile was broad

and infectious. In fact, as she gave him an answering smile in return, she had to acknowledge she'd never seen him so carefree.

So joyful.

"We fought and destroyed eighteen of them, to be precise," Drake offered up.

"Our girls can kick some ass," Kane added, giving Ilsa another squeeze.

Montana took her stool and stared into her half-drunk mug of tea. "Where did they all come from? And why were they after me?"

The easy camaraderie and boisterous comments faded in the face of her question.

"You know . . . ," Brody started, then faded off.

Montana didn't miss the pointed stare he shot Quinn, or the fact that the Taurus took the seat next to her, placing his hand over hers again. Although she felt comforted, it couldn't fully erase the creeping knot of worry that quickly reasserted itself in her stomach. "We're trying to figure that out."

"No. Really. What would this Enyo person want with me?" At the questions that filled Quinn's dark gaze, she added, "Callie told me all about her."

Montana saw the speculative look rise in Quinn's eyes and she cut it off. The steady fire that had simmered under her nerves for the past hour leaped to life. She wouldn't sit back and be talked about.

Damn it all, she would *not*. They might have left her behind, but she was an active participant in what was happening, whether she liked it or not. They'd damn well start giving her that baseline of respect.

Waving a hand in Callie's direction, Montana didn't give Quinn a chance to say anything. "And before you go shooting Callie dirty looks, you can just stop it right now. I have a right to know what's happening to me. You all went out and fought on my behalf and left me here to sit and wonder if you would all be okay. If you'd even survive. I have a right to know."

"She's got a point, Quinn." Drake offered, taking a seat on the opposite side of the butcher block. Callie had already laid out a huge platter from the fridge and Drake had a piece of friend chicken in his hand. "We need to tell her what we know."

"We know fucking little. Still," Quinn growled. Even as she wanted to snap back at him in anger, Montana had spent enough time with the stubborn man to know that the lack of information frustrated him.

And in that frustration came the anger.

Calming her tone, Montana reached for her mug and took a fortifying sip, willing the warm brew to soothe the increasing tension that refused to settle. "So tell me what you *do* know and we'll take it from there."

The rest of the Warriors took seats at the large, square counter as Callie bustled around grabbing various drinks—clearly favorites—for each of them. Brody had already snagged another large platter of fried chicken from the fridge so that each end of the table had a platter. Grey was the only one who made his apologies and then disappeared to his nightclub.

Once everyone was settled, Montana began her line of questions. Funny, the lot of them sitting around the table reminded her far too much of her weekly staff meetings.

Which immediately made her think of Jackson. A

distracted glance at her BlackBerry still showed no message.

Where was he?

Laying the device down once again, Montana took a deep breath and applied her best work tone and manner to the discussion.

"You killed off a horde of Destroyers this evening. I can only assume, by the vague descriptions you've provided of them, these are also the same creatures who've gone after me four times now."

"Yes. Although, we still don't know if that was a Destroyer in the park earlier today. It could have been something else," Quinn added. "But yes. If we count the park and twice last night—at the benefit and then afterward—and then this evening outside the car, it's four times."

"And you think Enyo's behind it." Montana shot a glance toward Callie. "She's the goddess of war, right?"

Callie nodded as the assembled table offered up a varied set of "yeses."

"Although . . ." Ilsa's unfinished statement hung over the middle of the table, like a thunderstorm ready to produce rain.

"What, babe?" Kane reached over and rubbed her back, the motion so simple—so easy—Montana felt a nasty swipe of envy strike at the very center of her stomach.

What must it be like to be that in tune with someone?

That *comfortable*.

Before she could dwell on it any further, Ilsa continued her point. "Six months ago. The night I found you." Kane nodded. "I was attacked by Destroyers. We never did figure out why."

"I've fought off more than a few in random attacks over the last several months," Drake added. "One went after Emerson a few weeks back, too."

Montana saw the quick gazes of the women at the mention of Emerson's name, whoever that was, but the moment faded as quickly as it arrived.

Hmmmm . . . clearly there was a story there. Or some really good gossip.

"How'd she know it was a Destroyer?" Quinn questioned. "And why are they randomly going after mortals?"

Drake shook his head as he stared into a now-empty glass of scotch. "The electricity. She knew enough from what we've told her to put two and two together and got herself over here before the asshole could do any damage."

"Yeah. I bet that's the only reason she showed up." Brody added before Ava slammed an elbow into his gut.

Oh yeah, Montana thought, *definitely* something going on there.

Quinn drained the last of his scotch and, in a move that mirrored Drake's, he stared into the bottom of the glass before glancing at each person surrounding the table. "Look. We can sit and wonder about this all day. It doesn't change the fact that a horde of Destroyers methodically attacked Montana's limo and then another group added to their numbers and attempted a surprise attack on Ilsa, Ava and me. The shit-storm of the century's going on and we need to figure out what the hell it is and why Queen Bitch has her nasty paws all over it."

"Is it possible she's helping someone?"

Seven pairs of eyes turned to look at her in unison.

"I'm serious. That's an awfully large distraction. Is it possible she's taking your attention away from the main event?"

"Like what?"

Montana wasn't sure what brought it on, but in that moment, a series of thoughts clicked into place with frightening clarity.

The random nature of the attacks showed no rhyme or reason.

The Warriors protecting her were just distracted for several hours, on top of a completely nonexistent threat at the evening's event.

And she had no BlackBerry message telling her good night.

"My house. Oh my God. They're at my house."

Chapter Fifteen

"Hold on to my arm and don't let go." Montana reached for Quinn's outstretched arm. Five minutes of arguing that she needed to stay behind didn't change her mind, so here they were.

Wasting precious time.

What he did make her stay back for was the quick ports in and out of her apartment, ensuring the other Warriors ended up in the right place. A muttered explanation of a needed visual barely held her back from grabbing on to his arm, but ultimately she acquiesced.

Montana knew every second counted and these men could do a hell of a lot of damage if necessary.

"Come on, darling. Hang on."

That heavy sense of gravity, like all of her weight was centered in her feet and then she was flying. The sensation would have been dizzying if it had lasted longer, but in no more than a heartbeat, she and Quinn stood in the front hallway of her apartment.

Without even seeing the carnage, she knew her home had been violated.

"Where is it?"

Montana appreciated Quinn didn't play dumb or try to hide what she was about to see. "Most of it is in your office. Come on."

"But my office was locked."

"Locked to a mortal, maybe. But immortals have a way."

"But you said you needed a visual to port."

Why she could even say that—why that simple point stuck out in her mind—was a mystery. But Quinn stopped and turned toward her. "Yes. You're right. Who's been in your office?"

"Just the staff. Jackson." A harsh sob choked her throat. "It's Jackson, isn't it?"

Quinn nodded, his jaw hard as granite, his eyes dark, fathomless pools of black. "You don't have to see this, darling. The guys have secured the place."

"I have to."

Quinn stopped her, his hand on her forearm to hold her still. "What if I don't want you to?"

The dark pools of his eyes changed in that moment. Softened as he looked down on her with so much compassion it made her ache.

But she needed to see what was in the other room.

Needed to know.

Reaching up, Montana twined her arms around his neck and laid her cheek against his chest. The heavy, steady thud of his heart reassured and comforted her.

The solid tempo of his pulse—quiet strength in the face of what she was to endure—offered the serenity she desperately needed to go on.

Fortified emotionally, she pulled back to look up

at him. "I have to do this. He's one of mine. Can you understand that?"

"Yes."

Quinn reached down and pressed his lips to hers. It was a silent offering, simple and somehow pure, in the midst of a whirling storm of evil and madness.

When he lifted his lips from hers, his gaze stayed steadfast on her. "Are you ready?"

She nodded and linked her fingers with his.

As they walked down the hallway toward her office, the only home she'd ever known suddenly looked horrifyingly foreign.

Separate. Cold. And she knew she'd never live here again.

As Quinn held her hand, they approached the door to her office. The heavy door was open, the light from the hallway spilling into the room. She saw Quinn's brothers first, where they moved about the room, looking for God knew what in the sheer disaster that covered the floor.

As Montana stepped across the threshold, she saw where they'd laid Jackson on the couch, his body battered and nearly bruised beyond recognition. The men had wrapped a blanket around his body like a shroud and Montana could only imagine the damage underneath.

Montana ran to him, dropping to her knees next to the couch. Everything from smashed wood chips from the destroyed bookcases to randomly strewn papers crunched under her knees, but Montana paid them no mind.

Gently laying her hands over Jackson's where they folded under the blanket, she leaned forward and wept.

* * *

"Quinn. You need to see this," Brody whispered in his ear.

Quinn glanced briefly at Brody before shifting all his focus back on Montana. He didn't know how to help her cope as she lay with her head pillowed on her friend.

Brody kept his voice low, but the insistence wasn't lost on Quinn. "I need you to see this and we can't do it with her here."

Reluctant to leave her, but even more reluctant to cause her any further pain if he could avoid it, Quinn followed Brody to a small room next to the office.

"What is it?"

"The guy was smart enough to turn on video."

"The attacker?"

"No. Jackson. He didn't get much, but what he got tells one helluva a story."

Quinn followed Brody to a security system that could rival NASA and sat down in front of the various sets of equipment. The security system was so like his own that he lost no time in navigating through the film of Jackson's last moments.

Quinn had to admit that the entire apartment, and Montana's office especially, really did have some slick security. In the office alone, four cameras caught all the detail from different angles, so there wasn't an inch of the room that was missed.

On his first viewing he watched the camera focused on Jackson. The man was strung to the desk chair, his hands bound behind his back, his face dripping with blood. Quinn was reminded of the proud way the man had looked out for Montana in her office earlier that day. His respect grew immeasurably as he watched

Jackson question his attacker before thousands of volts of electricity slammed through him.

"Fuck," Quinn muttered. "Would you look at that? It's got to be a Destroyer."

"That's my guess," Brody agreed.

"What the fuck?" The tape continued, but Quinn felt the absolute bottom fall out of his stomach.

"Is that what I think it is?" Brody leaned closer to the screen, reaching for the toggle to rewind the film.

Quinn didn't need to see it again. He knew what it was that leaped on Jackson.

It was an exact match for the bull that rode on his shoulder and lived within his skin.

Montana huddled in a blanket on the couch in the sitting room off her bedroom. Ava, Ilsa and Callie continued to check on her, but for the most part kept their distance by staying in her bedroom.

Abstractly, Montana played with a tassel on the end of the blanket. The entire evening—hell, the last forty-eight hours—felt like a nightmare within a nightmare. The attacks directed at her had been bad enough, but this?

Jackson?

And the horrible person who got him also killed Laura in the kitchen and Tony earlier in the park.

These people had depended on her, were loyal to her, and what had it gotten them?

Death.

Grisly murders, all three.

Oh God, what was this horrible curse? What could anyone possibly want with her that they'd do this evil thing to innocent people?

The nausea that had filled her stomach when Quinn informed her about Laura and Tony rose again, and leaning forward, she took long, deep breaths to try and calm her body.

"It's okay, sweetie." Callie was by her side in a flash, a small wastebasket at the ready.

"No. No, I'm fine." Montana sat back and allowed Callie to take a seat next to her. The small woman wrapped an arm around her, pulled her close.

"Get it out, sweetheart. It's okay."

"It's my fault."

"You know that's not true."

"It is, Callie. I never got the BlackBerry message. I never checked on him. On any of them. I never thought."

"Your place has top-of-the-line security, Montana. You couldn't know."

"But we did know." The words fell from her lips, half sob, half accusation. "We did know. We knew we were dealing with an immortal and I never thought to secure my home. My *family*."

The sobs racked her body, the grief a living thing inside her chest. Without her knowing it, Quinn came in and relieved Callie, wrapping her up in his big embrace.

"Shhhh. It's okay."

Through the pain and the self-recrimination, Montana knew one thing. "It's not okay, Quinn. Whatever else you say to me, don't say that."

"All right. I won't."

They sat there for what seemed like forever, but couldn't have been more than a few minutes.

"I'm going to show you something. I need you to make an identification and I need you to understand something."

She nodded and stood. With exquisitely gentle movements, Quinn leaned down and picked up the blanket where it lay near her feet. "Here. Hold this so you don't trip."

She followed him down the hall, huddling deeper into the blanket when she caught sight of the open office door. "I can't go back in there."

"We're not. I want you to look at something on the security monitor."

"The monitor? But I didn't leave it on."

"Jackson did."

"He what?" Montana let the blanket fall to her waist as she followed Quinn into the small security room that operated everything in the house as well as the cameras that surrounded the apartment building. "How could he have?"

"He's a smart guy and knew we needed information. Even tied up, he managed to get to the security button, turning the recording on. He didn't get much and I'm sorry to expose you to what he did record, but the faster we can move on this, the better shot we have of catching this asshole."

Montana took in the racks of cold metal built into the security room. A wall of screens stood sentinel, capturing the daily life inside and outside the apartment. Although she almost always kept the security off inside the house, Quinn must have turned everything on because the screens lit up like a billboard.

"It's on tape? Jackson's last minutes?"

"Yes. And while I'm sorry to say that, he was so brave to help us—to give us this to work from."

Montana nodded. "Of course he was."

Quinn settled his hand on her lower back, the motion meant to reassure, and pulled her toward the rolling chair that sat before a computer keyboard. "You've got four cameras in that room, each recording on a separate deck. We're going to watch the camera on his attacker. I need to see if you can ID him."

"Ohh . . . okay."

Montana took a seat in the chair and waited as Quinn fiddled with a few dials. Grief tore through her again, great suffocating waves of it, along with cold terror for what she was about to watch. It clawed at her stomach and she was grateful she'd avoided nearly all of her meal at the benefit.

Quinn stopped fiddling with the machines and turned to her, his gaze understanding yet firm. "I'm sorry to ask you to do this, Montana. Are you sure you're ready?"

She looked up into his face and saw his concern. Saw it in the deep creases around his eyes, in the harsh line of his jaw, in the tense set of his shoulders. And in that moment, she needed only one thing.

"Tell me something."

"Anything."

"Tell me you're not immune to this," she whispered, the answer to the question more important than any other she'd ever asked. "Tell me this isn't just a job anymore."

With exquisite gentleness, Quinn kneeled down in front of her and pulled the swivel on the chair until he was directly beside her. She felt the press of her knees in the hard wall of his stomach muscles and shifted, opening her legs to straddle him.

His touch gentle—so gentle she barely felt the brush of his fingertips—he ran the pads of his fingers down the side of her face before cupping her cheek.

"This isn't a job, Montana." He kissed her forehead.

"It's not a game or simply a vendetta." He pressed his lips gently against each eyelid as he murmured each word.

"I will find whoever did this. I will hunt him to the ends of the earth and beyond if I have to. I will keep you safe and I will avenge your loved ones." Quinn pressed his lips to hers and she felt them tremble.

"I believe you," she murmured against his lips. "I believe you."

Chapter Sixteen

Quinn's eyes never left Montana's face as she watched the tape. He refused to miss one moment of what she was dealing with. Her pain would be a beacon he could wrap his arms around and hang on to.

He had told her the truth.

He wouldn't rest until he found the one responsible for this. The threats to her, the deaths of her loved ones—he would see this through, no matter who was involved.

"Oh my God."

Her sky-blue eyes, red-rimmed from crying, opened wide as she leaned forward toward the bank of security monitors.

"You recognize him?"

"Oh my God." She whispered the words over and over, her features morphing from grief to shock. She reached forward and hit the pause button. "I know him."

"You do? How?"

"It's Arturo Veron. He's one of the members of my new board of directors."

Shoulders heaving on a loud sob, Montana dragged the blanket back around her body. "I spoke with him this morning. He's Jackson's . . ."

She broke off, a mix of shock and anger coloring her cheeks a bright red.

"He's Jackson's what, Montana?"

"He always flirts with Jackson. I thought maybe . . ." A loud sob pierced her calm. "I just thought about the two of them and thought maybe he might make a nice boyfriend for Jackson. I don't care for Arturo personally, but I thought he might make a nice partner. Why'd I think that?"

"You didn't know. You were only thinking of your friend. Why didn't you like him?"

Montana shrugged against the heavy blanket. "It's nothing I can explain, exactly. There's just something false about him. Artful."

"Has he done anything to you?"

"You mean up until now?"

"Anything to give you pause? Before now?"

"No, that's the problem." Tears welled in her eyes as her breath caught on another heartbreaking sob. "Even this morning, the reason I called him was to thank him for an excellent lead he gave me on a small shipping company in Cartagena. He's always been a gentleman. But he's not. He's a murderer. A murderer I invited into my life. Into my home. He's even been here before."

The knowledge Arturo had been in this apartment dropped the last clue into place. "You didn't do this, Montana."

"How can you say that?" She flung a hand at the screen before her. "Look what he did to Jackson. Arturo played him." The words dripped from her lips. Quinn could handle the anger—he could even handle the tears—but the underlying sense of self-recrimination killed him.

"We suspect that's the case, yes." Quinn offered quietly. "There's more to the tape. There's something else I need you to see."

Montana reached for the security equipment and toggled back through the scene to watch it again. "That son of a bitch. He knows our routine. Our schedule. I talked to him just this morning and all the while he was planning to fuck with us."

Quinn's voice was quiet in the darkened viewing room. "I'm sorry, Montana."

"I want to play the rest."

"Of course."

Quinn wasn't even aware he was holding his breath as the scene he waited for came on screen. Voices echoed from the speakers embedded in the ceiling and walls.

"She's innocent."

"She's innocent of nothing. And I will not rest until she is dead."

Montana flinched once at the puzzling words that referenced her, then again as Arturo launched a fireball at Jackson, the man crying out in agony.

And then she saw it.

The large bull that rose up from behind Arturo, filling the screen with menace and a dark evil that was visible, even in two dimensions.

"What? How?" Quinn's gaze returned to Montana, even as her focus never left the screen. "What is it?"

She flattened herself in the chair as she watched

the animal leap and scrabble over the desk, destroy-ing it with its weight.

Quinn flipped the switch before she was subjected to Jackson's final screams, then turned the unit off en-tirely so she couldn't even look at a still image of the carnage.

"What was that?"

"It's the mark of the Taurus."

"But how? How do you know that?" Montana pressed herself farther into the seat and with her feet flat on the floor began to propel herself away from him.

"I am a Taurus Warrior and I have a matched ani-mal that sits on my shoulder."

She kept the chair moving a few more feet before hitting the far wall of the room. "But that's not possi-ble." She pointed to the screen. "That's an animal. A full-grown animal. Where was it? Before the attack, where was it?"

"It lives in Arturo's aura. He's a Taurus Warrior, too."

Her words tripped out on a rush, stumbling and fumbling over one another. "But you should know that. Shouldn't you have known that? He's like you. Themis made you both. You should have known."

"It's been a long time, Montana. We don't all get together like some annual meeting of salespeople."

"But—" She tugged the blanket harder around her-self, the pink blush riding high on her cheeks sud-denly falling from her face as if she'd fallen ill. "Wait a minute. You just said something. You mean you've got one of those, too?"

Raw acid churned in his gut at the fear that covered her as clearly as the cashmere she wrapped so closely around her body. "It's in my aura. It's a fighting aid."

"But he killed with it. That means you can kill with yours, too."

"It helps me defeat Destroyers and any other threat I take on."

"But you could. You could turn it against someone. You could turn it against me."

"Montana." Quinn moved forward, but she curled in on herself. "You need to listen to me. I'm here to help you. I will help you, as I promised you before. I won't rest until I find him."

With a fierceness he didn't expect given her half-catatonic state, she leaped from the chair, the blanket discarded at her feet. "I was fine before you showed up! You brought this on me. You and these . . . creatures," she spat. "You're not even human. You're some kind of fucking animal!"

Callie and Ava came running in at the commotion and Quinn eyed them, desperate for someone who could get through to Montana.

"Shhhh, sweetie. It's all right." Callie moved toward her, but Montana inched away until her back was against the far wall. "Stay away."

"Montana—" Callie and Ava both said in unison.

"Stay back! Both of you. None of you are human."

The women lifted their hands in a gesture to imply they weren't getting any closer, but both of them shot him a puzzled look.

Quinn ran a hand through his hair. Well, didn't that just fuck all; they had no idea what to do, either.

Quinn moved closer, his steps soft. "Montana. I need

you to listen to me. We're going to get to the bottom of this and we're going to get Arturo."

And then Quinn's heart broke as he saw the tears that ran freely down her cheeks, her arm up and trembling where she slumped against the wall.

"Please. Please stay away from me."

Indecision ate at him. He couldn't—wouldn't—leave her there, but the overwhelming number of things they'd thrown at her today had clearly pushed her to the breaking point.

And then Jackson's death broke her.

"Montana. Please." Quinn kept his gaze level on hers, willing her to understand. "Please let me help you."

"Montana." A soft, ethereal voice floated over all of them from the open doorway. "Listen to the man. He is the only one who can help you."

They all turned in that direction, but Quinn didn't need Montana's next word to explain who stood in the doorway.

"Mother," Montana exhaled on a cry.

The events of the last hour replayed themselves in her mind on a continuous loop as Montana drew circles with her finger in the design on her duvet.

Jackson, Laura and Tony—all senseless deaths.

The eventual realization that Arturo Veron was behind the attacks.

The unbelievable knowledge that a bull—an honest-to-God *bull*—lived in? on?—as part of Quinn.

And then her mother's arrival, at the very moment the entire room likely thought she needed to be committed.

"Fuck," Montana whispered out loud, the expletive

the only suitable word to describe the wildly racing emotions whipping though her system.

"Your father used to use that word and I used to yell at him. I don't like that language."

"It seemed like the only suitable response."

Eirene harrumphed as she settled herself at the foot of Montana's bed. If it were possible, Eirene looked even more frail than a few days before. The skin over her hands was paper-thin and deep, dark circles set off her eyes. Her tone, however, still bore the implacable mark of parenthood.

Those bright liquid-blue eyes, so like the ones that stared back at Montana each and every morning from the bathroom mirror, were clear and lucid.

"Funny." A small smile ghosted Eirene's lips. "That's exactly what Jack used to say."

Montana wasn't sure if it even mattered at this point—or why the thought even occurred to her—but she blurted it out anyway. "Did you love him?"

At her mother's joyful expression, Montana wondered if her mind wasn't playing tricks on her.

"Oh, aye, I loved him. Loved him like a fool. Even long after I shouldn't have, I loved him."

"Did Daddy do the things Quinn thinks he did?"

Eirene's gaze narrowed from joyful memories to focus more closely on her daughter. "What do you think?"

"I'm afraid that I think yes."

Her mother nodded. "I'm afraid you think correctly."

"Is that why you left?" Montana whispered. "Because you couldn't stand to be with him any longer? Because he didn't deserve your love?"

"No." Eirene shifted and Montana noted the pain in her gaze at the movement.

Scootching up, Montana settled herself against the headboard, beckoning her mother to do the same. "Here. Come sit here." She fluffed the pillows and made a comfortable pallet, pleased to see her mother move slowly to settle herself.

Once comfortably seated against the pillows, Eirene let out a soft sigh. "I left because I didn't deserve him. Or you."

"But you just said Daddy did bad things."

"And I still didn't deserve him."

Montana shook her head, desperate to follow the trail of the conversation. "Could you give me something? Anything that helps me understand."

On another small sigh, Eirene turned so they faced each other. "Your father was always a bad boy. In life and in business. He'd throw in a couple shipments that weren't on the manifests to make a few extra bucks under the table. Or he'd run a few things on the side to make a few more bucks. My mother thought I was oblivious to it, but I kn-knew."

A harsh cough racked Eirene's frail body as she struggled to clear her throat and catch her breath.

Montana reached for her, but her mother's hand was surprisingly strong on her forearm, stopping her from coming any closer.

As another round of coughs filled Eirene's chest, a dispiriting sense of helplessness descended over Montana again, reminding her of the bleak moments when she and Quinn first arrived home. Was anyone in her life whole? Untouched by pain and suffering?

And was it all because of her?

Montana ran to the bathroom for a glass of water, then pressed it on her mother, urging her to drink. When the horrible coughs finally subsided, Eirene finished her story.

"As I was saying, my mother thought I was oblivious to Jack's baser natures, but I knew. Of course I knew. Not only wasn't I born yesterday, but I was so in love with the man, I followed him every chance I got when we first met."

"You followed him?"

"Like a modern-day stalker. Only I had the benefit of invisibility."

"You what?" That crazy sense of unreality settled over her again and Montana wondered—yet again—if her life could get any weirder.

And then she looked at her mother—really looked at her—and Montana was forced to acknowledge the truth. No matter how hard to believe these tales seemed—how insane, really—it was real.

All of it.

Themis.

The Warriors.

Supernatural abilities.

All of it was real.

Eirene's voice broke the silence. "What is it, Montana?"

"It's all true, isn't it?

Without preamble or explanation, Eirene simply nodded. "Yes."

"She's been in there forever," Quinn grumbled as he filled another trash bag of detritus from the floor of Montana's office.

"Shut up and help us with this." Callie shot him a warning glare. After Brody and Kane had ported the bodies back to the brownstone so they could map out a way to contact the police, Callie had mobilized the rest of them into action.

Which, in Callie-land, meant manual labor.

"Has Brody called you back yet?" he asked Ava for the tenth time in as many minutes.

Ava let out a soft sigh, but her voice was gentle when she spoke. "Quinn. You know they can't just call the police. They have to have the right story and then, even once they do come up with something, they have to wipe the officers' minds. It takes time."

Of course it did. Surprisingly, they didn't have to deal with mortal fatalities all that often, but it did happen. Themis had given them many gifts—individually and as a unit—and the Vulcan mind-meld, as most of them fondly thought of it, could be counted on in a pinch.

It also worked quite well for dealing with bureaucrats when trying to change property ownership and any other nosy entities that simply wouldn't understand why the same individuals came and went from the same place, never appearing to age.

For all its conveniences, the modern world was a big, fat pain in the ass a good portion of the time.

"Callie. Maybe you should go check on them. I don't want to leave Montana."

"Would you stop it already?" Ilsa pointed her broom at him. "It's her mother. Would you give them some privacy and let them talk? It's not like the girl hasn't had a big day."

"But she looked at me—" Quinn broke off, the words drying up in his throat.

"Like a leper. Actually, like a murderous leper," Ilsa added for good measure.

"Not quite what I was going for."

"But accurate," Ava added, holding Ilsa's trash bag open so she could drop in an armful of debris.

"Yeah. She did," Quinn muttered as he reached for a huge handful of waste and slammed it into the half-full trash bag beside him.

"It's a lot to take in. It took me a while to accept it, Quinn. You have to give her a chance."

Quinn whirled on Ava. Despite the good intentions behind her words, he couldn't hold back the anger. "But you came around. You didn't look at Brody like a"—he shot a pointed stare at Ilsa—"fucking murderous leper."

"Quinn—" Ilsa tried to break in, but he cut her off with a wave of his hand.

"I thought we were making progress and then she stood there and stared at me like I was an animal. Worse. A predator, out to harm her."

Never one to back down from a fight, Ilsa moved up in his face. Although he had her by more than a hundred pounds, the goddess formerly known as Nemesis wasn't one to be cowed by that. "And what reason did you give her to think otherwise? I heard you talking to the guys and Kane filled in the gaps. You stalked her because your precious equipment gave you a few clues that put her on your radar. You then follow her and drag her into any number of dangers. And to boot, you tell her you think she's running diamonds and human slaves on her boats. Would you trust you? Because other than a nice ass, I'm not sure what else you've had to sell yourself to the poor woman."

The anger that seethed through his veins like thick, molten lava evaporated, like water turning to steam. How in the hell did these women manage to make sense and put him in his place, all at the same time? "You think so?"

"I know so." Ilsa patted his arm, her rapid-fire change of mood oddly comforting. "Give her some time to come around. She knows you're one of the good guys. She does, Quinn. Give her some space."

"Well said, Ilsa." Montana's voice rid him of whatever lingering anger still vibrated in his chest as Quinn turned to see her standing in the door. "I especially liked the nice ass remark."

Before he could answer—could even take a step toward her—Brody's shouts rang out through the apartment.

"Quinn! The monitors!"

The Leo raced into the office, the Scorp on his heels. "Arturo's outside. Fucking outside! It was on your monitors at home. He's got to still be here."

Montana momentarily forgotten, Quinn felt a rising fury fill his veins. "Where?"

"Roof."

Quinn didn't wait—didn't even think to discuss it with his brothers—he simply acted.

As he came out of his port on the roof of Montana's apartment building, Arturo Veron stood across the flat stretch of concrete.

The bull that lived in the man's aura already stood by his side, breath coming from the animal in heavy pants that steamed up the air. "Well, this should be fun."

Quinn's own bull filled the space next to him as it unfolded from his aura. "Bring it on, motherfucker."

Raw anticipation filled his veins as Quinn stalked toward Arturo. Unstrapping the Xiphos he'd replaced earlier on his calf, he flicked his wrist in the moonlight and watched the light reflect off the wicked edge of the blade.

A comparable light flashed back at him from his opponent.

Let the asshole think they were well matched.

Unwilling to toy with Arturo, Quinn leaped immediately, man and beast engaging simultaneously. Although not enough to take Arturo off his feet, it did have the effect of knocking him off balance and he stumbled precariously close to the edge of the roof.

Quinn continued pushing, his bull feral with the need to engage its opponent when a stray line of voltage hit him square in the back.

What the hell?

On an unspoken command, Quinn kept his bull at his back as he turned to face the latest threat. Four Destroyers stood opposite him across the roof, their frames lit up with electricity.

What the *fucking* hell?

An arc of light came barreling at him as the Destroyer on the end launched a fireball. Before Quinn could block it, Kane let out an ear-piercing war cry as he materialized on the roof, his Xiphos outstretched to deflect the shot.

"Thanks, brother."

"Don't mention it." Brody materialized behind Kane and the two of them went to work on the line of Destroyers. With his own personal cavalry in place, Quinn turned back toward Arturo. "Nice friends you've got there. And now it all makes sense. You made a deal with Enyo."

"I don't deal. And I certainly wouldn't deal with that bitch."

Arturo's bull leaped, but Quinn's beast easily deflected it, their forelegs locked in battle as they butted heads. Quinn fought to hold to his feet as the power of his bull rocked through him. "Oh no? Then how'd you get her little boys?"

"She's not all-seeing," Arturo shouted through gritted teeth as he opened his stance wider to accommodate the battle.

"Yeah, but she's awfully protective of what's hers." Quinn tightened his grip on his Xiphos and ran forward. "Just like I am."

Bracing himself for the harsh sting of resistance, Quinn swung in a large arc, slicing his Xiphos through the neck of Arturo's bull before bringing the blade in a downward arc through his opponent's chest.

Arturo screamed, his own blade clattering to the concrete near his feet.

Quinn wasted no time. With an upward slice, he caught the edge of Arturo's shoulder just as the man backpedaled. "You took what belonged to her."

Quinn slashed again, this time nicking a kidney as Arturo fumbled over his feet and accidentally presented his back.

"You took the people she loved."

He slashed again, barely missing Arturo's body as

the asshole got lucky on a sidestep. Quinn stumbled as his blade met air, but the movement gave him the additional momentum he needed. With unconscious orders honed over millennia of battle, Quinn and his bull acted as one, using the benefit of their forward movement to catch Arturo off guard.

Before the asshole could regain his balance, Quinn pushed him off the edge of the roof.

He watched as the duo landed on the sidewalk below. Quinn knew the fall wasn't fatal—had it confirmed as Arturo struggled below—but before he could gather the strength to port below and finish the job, he heard shouts from behind him.

Whirling, Quinn watched as Brody finished off the last standing Destroyer.

As silence descended over the rooftop, Quinn's gaze lit on the far corner where the door to the rooftop stairs stood open.

Montana stared at him in the moonlight, her gaze firmly riveted on the bull at his side.

Chapter Seventeen

"Are you okay?" Quinn fought the urge to reach out and touch Montana to reassure himself as they sat in her living room. Callie hadn't had a chance to clean the kitchen and Quinn hesitated to bring Montana to the site of Laura's death.

The living room seemed like a natural alternative.

Wrapped in large, oversized terry-cloth robes, Montana and her mother occupied opposite ends of the cream-colored sofa. He sat just to the side in a stiff wing-backed chair that recalled the time of long-dead French despots.

"I promised Montana I'd tell her the entire story. But I want you to hear it, too." Eirene started in, turning her liquid-blue gaze in his direction.

Quinn vacillated between shock at how much Montana and her mother looked alike and the sad acknowledgment that Eirene wasn't long for this world. Even if he hadn't put it together from her physical frailty, the racking coughs that convulsed her body every fifteen minutes confirmed it.

"I'm sorry I haven't told you sooner, Montana," her mother began. "But I didn't know how to tell you. I always thought I'd have more time."

"More time for what?" Montana rubbed Eirene's arm where they sat next to each other. Quinn marveled at the inherent warmth in her actions and wondered yet again how he had ever suspected Montana of such a horrible series of crimes.

Her innocence shone through in everything about her—her care for others, her unwillingness to put those around her in jeopardy, even the questions she asked.

She was a thoughtful person, with an innate kindness that came through in her every action.

And why did he find that so compelling? Like the warmth of a fire on a cold day, he wanted to get closer.

For the first time in his very long life, Quinn had to admit he wanted someone to let him in.

He wanted Montana to accept him. Welcome him.

"What is it, Mother?"

"I have cancer." Eirene's statement was so simple— so direct.

"Oh God." Montana's breath rushed on an exhale of air.

Without thinking, Quinn reached for her hand, lacing his fingers with hers across the small chasm that separated her position at the end of the couch and his seat on the chair.

"Why did it take you so long to tell me?"

Quinn heard the words, but he also sensed the deeper despair underneath. Even he—who had seen more than his fair share of death, destruction and the horrors man could inflict upon each other—had to admit Montana had suffered through more in one day than anyone deserved in a lifetime.

"Come now, my child. You knew. I agree you deserved to hear the words, but surely you knew."

Quinn saw it—the almost imperceptible nod of her head—and the lone tear that ran down her cheek. "Yes. I knew."

"Please don't be upset, my darling. It's necessary. For you to fully ascend, it's necessary."

Quinn leaned forward, Montana's hand still tucked firmly within his. Even though he'd come to the same conclusion earlier in the day, the truth of it was hard to fathom. "Will she really ascend to your position?"

"It is my mother's great curse on me. Not only will my mortal body die, but my daughter will take my place in the pantheon."

"But how?" Montana's eyes were wide as she processed the news. "I'm a mortal woman. I bleed, I ache. I told Quinn that earlier. I had my appendix out as a kid, for heaven's sake. That's not the constitution of an immortal."

"For as long as I live, you *are* a mortal." Eirene's smile was gentle as she continued. "But *my* mortal body is dying and you are called to fulfill the promise Themis made to me forty years ago."

Quinn felt his earlier anger renew, even as the object of it was his boss and leader. "But Montana didn't agree to this. Why would Themis do that to her?"

"I gave up a great gift and I was told the price."

"But Montana is innocent! It isn't her price to pay." Quinn knew yelling at the woman wouldn't change anything. Wouldn't make it any less so. If he had learned anything over the last ten millennia it was that his boss had her own set of rules.

Her own way of seeing the world.

Her eternal quest for balance often led to some very odd choices.

Of course, his conscience taunted, that same insistence on balance made Ava an immortal and gave Kane and Ilsa freedom from their personal demons.

You can't only take the good, boy-o. His father's words rang in his ears. The village seer, his father had always had an odd mix of worldly wisdom. Of course, it was coupled with bouts of depression so severe his descent into alcohol and drugs ensured he walked the fine line of madness at least fifty percent of the time.

But Quinn hadn't ever been able to argue against the core truth of his father's words.

And he couldn't now.

Unwilling to raise his voice to Eirene, Quinn tried a different tact. He gave Montana's fingers a quick squeeze before pushing ahead with his question. "With all due respect, if you knew this, why did you ever get pregnant?"

"I tried everything in my power not to. But my sisters had other ideas."

The realization slammed through him as he quickly tallied up Themis's many children, all accounted for in the Pantheon. "The Fates."

Eirene's eyes dulled as another spasm shook her, but not before she nodded in the affirmative.

Montana laid a hand on her mother's back, holding her through the worst of it until the coughs subsided. She pressed some tea on her mother. "Here. This should help. And then we're not asking any more questions and you're going to rest."

The teacup shook in Eirene's hands as Montana's words registered. "I can't stay here."

"You will stay where you're safe. I've been understanding enough up to now, but you will not stay on the streets."

Quinn leaned forward. "You need to listen to your daughter, goddess. There's a place for you. Where we can protect you. At the Warriors' house. We'll take care of you."

Indecision crept into her pained gaze before Eirene slowly nodded. "All right. Thank you."

Montana opened her mouth to speak, but her mother took her hands. "Thank you, my darling. Thank you." Resettling herself, Eirene picked up the thread of her story. "As I was saying, my sisters, the Fates, stepped in."

"But why? Not that I'm not happy I'm here," Montana quickly added, "but pregnancy prevention is an easy enough thing."

"Not when you've tempted fate, darling. And besides, I knew the moment I found out—you were meant to be." Eirene's lips tightened into a straight line. "Even as I wouldn't wish this on you."

"What am I, exactly?"

"You mean you haven't figured it out?"

"Figured what out, Mother? I'm just me."

"The peace talks you facilitated off the African coast. The continued efforts you expend for goodwill between nations around the world."

That light blush Quinn was growing so fond of spread up the fine column of Montana's neck to settle on her cheeks. "But that's just Grant Shipping. Goodwill is part of being a global company."

"But you've taken it a step further."

"But how? We simply defused a difficult situation."

"*You*, Montana. You returned peace to a hopeless situation," Eirene said gently. "Upon your ascension, you will replace me as the goddess of peace. It's a role that's long been missing from the world and you've already begun to show your aptitude."

"You are the third Horae," Quinn added, Eirene's words confirmation of his suspicions. "Just as Callie thought you were."

"I knew your nymph many millennia ago. She is a woman of amazing talent and understanding. And she's correct. Upon my death, Montana's ascension will be complete. That's why she's under attack. That's why you need to protect her, Quinn. Until she's fully ascended, she can still be killed as a mortal."

Montana's gaze drifted toward the hallway and Quinn knew she pictured the ravages from her office just down the hall. "And based on this evening's events, it's an immortal who wants me dead."

Montana found Quinn a half hour later, in the same place she'd left him on that chair in her living room.

"You can't possibly be comfortable, folded into that thing."

Even more uncomfortable were the lingering memories of how she treated him earlier.

Had those words really come out of her mouth? And had she actually suggested he was some sort of dirty animal. Especially after she saw what his animal—no, his tattoo—was capable of.

A blush crept up her neck at the remembered violence of her words, the irrationality of her fear. On a small shiver, she wrapped her arms around herself, burrowing her hands in the long sleeves of her terrycloth robe.

"I hadn't noticed." Quinn looked up from his Black-Berry.

She watched the long, elegant sweep of his fingers as he placed the device back in its case, then back into his pocket.

Clearly her lecture earlier had sunk in.

So why couldn't she tear her gaze away from the long lines of his fingers?

Because you can't forget what those fingers are capable of.

Ignoring the errant thought, she tried to focus on what she'd come to do.

Apologize.

Even if she couldn't think of any words that would be remotely adequate to make up for what she'd said before.

"You're still getting messages? It's after midnight."

She saw him hesitate, the indecision stamped in his dark gaze before he took a deep breath. "Brody and Kane are back at the house. They contacted the police, who are now in possession of the bodies. Jackson, Laura and Tony will be well cared for now. Brody ensured they were placed in a good precinct with a detective who will do right by them and their families."

"Thank you." Montana wondered if that was the right thing to say. What did you say to news like that? "You don't have to hide it from me, you know."

When he didn't reply, she added, "I'm sorry I flipped

out on you before, but you don't have to keep anything from me. I won't break again."

"I know it's a lot, Montana. And I'm sorry. Sorry you have to deal with this. Learn about it this way. Sorry you had to see it."

"Actually." A half laugh bubbled in her throat. "I'm the one who owes you an apology. Those things I said to you before. To Callie, Ava and Ilsa. I was horrible to all of you, when all you were trying to do—all you've been trying to do—is help me. And before . . ."

She left anything else unsaid.

What did you say? How did you begin to apologize?

Quinn pressed on, ignoring whatever discomfort she felt. "We've asked you to absorb so much in the last twenty-four hours. I should have removed you from this situation as soon as I knew what was going on."

"It's my home."

"A home that was breeched by violence."

Montana saw the riptide of emotion that hurtled across his features. The anger that hardened his lips and jaw. The haunting certainty in the set of his shoulders that he had somehow wronged her. And worst of all—the look of pure anguish as he turned that dark chocolate gaze on her.

"The moment I understood what had happened, I should have removed you from this place."

"I needed to be here. Laura, Tony and Jackson. They belong to me, Quinn." It was clear he understood as the harsh set of his jaw softened and the small line that cut a deep groove between his eyebrows relaxed.

On a singular nod, Quinn agreed. "Yes. They were family."

"And you fought for them. You fought for what is mine. With your bull." She stopped, reaching for his cheek, the stubble at his jaw line a very real reminder that he was a man. A man with a gift, yes, but a man all the same. "With your talents. You did that for me."

As if remembering himself, he looked around. "Where's your mother?"

"Callie and Ava brought her to your home. Callie had a few ideas for her cough and wanted to get her tucked in as soon as she could."

"We should go as well."

"We should."

Montana knew it was the right thing to do. She was beyond exhausted. The painful reality of the day's events—if she were willing to give in to them—could easily keep her in bed for a month.

So why did she feel the exact opposite of tired? How could she feel attraction? *Now?*

Her entire life was upside down and all she could think was how badly she wanted to touch the smooth skin of his flesh underneath the tuxedo shirt he still wore, open at the throat and uncuffed and rolled at the sleeves.

The roller coaster of emotions that had grabbed hold of her since Quinn landed on top of her at the previous night's benefit coalesced into one desperate, aching need.

"I want you."

His gaze snapped to her with the speed of a run-away train.

"What?"

"You heard me."

"I heard the words, but I must have misunderstood. There's no way you want me, unless it's the idea that you want me gone." Before she could say anything, he held up his hand. "I don't blame you for that."

Before Montana could second guess herself—or stop the one thing she wanted so desperately her skin practically hummed with it—she reached for Quinn's hand and pulled him to a standing position. "I want you, Quinn Tanner. All of you, and not a few stolen moments, either."

Montana knew this was the worst time to suddenly develop an amorous streak, but she couldn't stop. The revelation of her mother's illness gave her the final piece she needed to let herself go.

Life was meant to be lived, and for far too long, she'd allowed herself to simply go through the motions.

Oh, to the outside world she looked busy, happy and fulfilled, her life one high-profile event after another. But as the woman who slept alone each and every night, she knew her life was anything but.

Twining her arms around the heavy, corded muscles of his neck and shoulders, Montana lifted her face to his. "Take me away from all this, Quinn. Take me away and make love to me."

When his lips took hers in rough possession, Montana knew she wouldn't have to ask twice.

Montana's mouth met his and her eager response offered the proof behind her words.

Despite all that had happened—all she'd seen over the past thirty-six hours—the beat of attraction that hummed between them was mutual.

Thank the gods.

Desperate for her, Quinn took her lips over and over, in a driving need to get as close to her as he could. His fingers played with the waistband at her robe, tugging at the tie until the knot loosened, the material falling open in front.

With questing fingers, he reached for her, running his hands over the smooth skin of her stomach, up the ridges of her rib cage until he reached the heavy globes of her breasts. As her body filled his palms, he used his thumbs to tease her already-erect nipples, satisfied as they grew harder under his touch.

His own body grew harder by the minute, and he shifted one hand to her lower back to pull her closer. With their lower bodies flush, his erection pressed against her stomach, a hot brand between them.

Quinn felt the world around them grow smaller, so that the only things in it were the two of them and the pleasure that grew and expanded, arcing between them like lightning.

It was only as her head fell back and his lips moved in a deliberate path down her throat that a small piece of the world broke through.

Quinn's half-lidded gaze took in the flush of pleasure that rode high on her cheeks—along with the increasingly frantic movements of her hands as she pressed them to the small of his back—and the reality of where they were sunk in.

He couldn't make love to her here.

Not in this place of death.

"Montana," he whispered against her.

"Mmmm." Her hands shifted so that she was now cupping his ass, pulling him even tighter against her.

"Baby." He pressed his forehead to hers, willing some semblance of calm into his body. "We can't stay here."

Quinn held himself still as he waited for his words to register. He felt it the moment they did, her questing fingers hovering over his stomach muscles just above the waistband of his slacks.

"What?"

On a harsh drag of air, Quinn moved his hands to take hers. "Let me take you away from here."

"Where? Your house is full."

The smile spread before he could help it. "We actually have more rooms than you think, but I had somewhere else in mind."

"Where?"

"Do you want to go to Texas?"

"Now?"

"Now."

The sensual haze that had turned her sky-blue eyes almost violet subsided as logic fought for purchase. "Let me go get some clothes."

"You don't need to do anything but stand still and hang on."

"Oh. Right."

"Ready?"

She nodded, and Quinn couldn't help but smile at the small crease of apprehension on her forehead. "I promise. We'll be there before you know it."

Before she could even reply, he launched them into the port, an image of the Warriors' ranch in the Texas Hill Country filling his mind's eye.

The heavy rush of the universe pulled on them both, before whirling them through time and space to the very spot Quinn pictured in his mind.

"Oh!"

Montana's moue of surprise was the first thing he heard as the rush of air subsided and his feet found firm purchase in the front hallway of the house. "Here we are."

"Holy shit." Montana's arms were still wrapped around his waist and her body still pressed sensually against his, but her eyes roamed around her surroundings, taking in the oversized two-story foyer. "This place is beautiful."

"I'll take that as the highest compliment coming from one of the world's wealthiest women."

A small frown touched the edges of her lips. "I can still appreciate a beautiful home."

Quinn smiled and leaned down, pressing a quick kiss to her lips. "Of course you can. It doesn't mean the compliment is any less appreciated."

An answering smile greeted him, followed by the quick assessment of a situation that he was coming to realize was her hallmark. "You're right. And seeing as how I really have no interest in discussing architecture with you, is there any reason you didn't port us straight into your bedroom?"

"I wanted to make sure no one was here. We come and go as we please, but no one keeps their things here permanently."

"And you didn't want to land us on top of anyone?"

Quinn laughed at the image, but acknowledged she was correct. "Especially since my plan is to make love to you in the largest, most luxurious bed here."

"First choice for any good seduction scene."

"Bingo."

Hands entwined, Quinn led her down the long hallway into the wide-open kitchen. A quick scan showed no glasses on the counter or dishes in the sink, confirming this was a very good idea.

As he turned to see Montana pulling the folds of her robe closed with one hand, her modesty suddenly on display, he couldn't help pulling her close for another wild kiss.

The ranch house was a *very* good idea.

Montana pulled the ties of her robe closed as she followed Quinn through an oversized living room that looked like it could easily host touch-football games, then on toward a curving staircase that ran along the far wall.

It was a stunning home. She'd always loved exploring new places and seeing how every individual put their own stamp on a place.

The Warriors' home was no different. Where the brownstone had been elegant and refined, this home had a rustic quality with a decidedly masculine underpinning. The two large-screen TVs that bookended the living room only added punctuation marks to the thought.

Quinn ran a finger down her face, capturing a lock of hair between his thumb and forefinger. The gesture was so sweet—so reminiscent of the night before when he brought her home to safety—that her pulse tripped and she felt the low, insistent tug of attraction reassert itself.

"Was this a bad idea, Montana? Coming here? Would you rather just go back to the brownstone?"

She knew it wasn't. Just because they'd taken a few

moments out of the pleasure building between them didn't mean it was a bad idea. The question was, how to put her brain on hold to just sit back and enjoy it.

"No. You were right to leave my apartment." After what had happened there—to Jackson and to Laura and then her behavior afterward—it wasn't the place to make love to Quinn.

They needed somewhere new to take the next step on their journey together.

"I'm glad we left."

"Good. Since I'm quite sure we have the place to ourselves." Quinn leaned in and scooped her up in his arms. She felt gravity shift as those large arms came around her, followed immediately by the loud rush of air she was coming to associate with him.

With a thud, Quinn landed on his back on an enormous bed and she bounced on top of him.

The moment felt so wonderful—so carefree—she couldn't stop the joy filling her chest. "I wouldn't call it graceful, but it is highly effective. And what do we have here?" Montana scrambled to the side of his large body where he sprawled across the duvet. "A bed."

Quinn rolled to his side and propped himself up on an elbow. "I figured we'd done enough talking. But I promise you, before we leave here, I'll tell you everything."

"No more questions?"

His sideways nod was solemn in the dark light of the bedroom. "No more questions. I promise."

"Well then." Montana leaned forward, one hand flicking at the studs of his tuxedo shirt. "I love a man of action. What did you have in mind before we leave?"

Quinn's hand captured hers, the thud of his heart heavy under her palm. "Let me show you."

Moonlight spilled through the floor-to-ceiling windows, allowing in enough light to see every inch of Montana's perfect body. Her fingertips pressed against his chest and he removed the hand that covered hers to allow her continued exploration.

His own exploration was considerably less complicated than removing tuxedo studs, as he reached forward and once again tugged the tie at her waist. Because she was on her side, half the robe fell away to reveal one breast. He reached out to remove all of her robe, his hands caressing the smooth skin of her shoulders as he pressed the material away.

He urged her back until she lay on the bed, then pulled away and ripped at his shirt. What was left of the tuxedo studs in his shirt flew around the room and landed with a musical tinkle.

"Effective." She smiled up at him.

"Efficient," he added, before leaning down to cover her mouth with his.

Quinn wasn't sure how it happened—wasn't sure how he was able to make himself slow down—but in that moment, all he wanted was to show her how much he cared.

How safe and protected she was.

His movements slow, he dragged out the kiss, branding her lips and mouth with his tongue. As he continued the deep, drugging exploration of her mouth, he used his hands to paint the warm, fascinating canvas of her body.

With one long sweeping motion, he ran his hands

over her body, from the base of her throat down over the peak of one breast, through the valley of her stomach to settle between the warm, welcome opening between her thighs.

Hot, liquid heat met his questing fingers and he couldn't help but pull back and smile at her. "That's one damn fine welcome, darling."

The dark, sensual haze that had turned her eyes a rich shade of indigo in the moonlight went even darker as he pressed one finger against the slick opening of her body.

"You're certainly taking your sweet time about it."

With deft pressure, Quinn leaned down to whisper in her ear, "Count on it."

And then there were no more words as he used his fingers to make love to her, his gaze never leaving hers.

His body ached to be buried inside of her, but he wouldn't—nay, couldn't—change this moment if he wanted to. Time stretched out, breaths mingled as she rocked against his hand, taking her pleasure.

Quinn felt the moment spread out before him in wonder. The warm responsive woman in his arms, the absolute trust in her gaze as she gave herself up to the pleasure he created, the unique sense that no matter how many lifetimes he'd lived, he'd never shared a moment like this with anyone.

He felt the pressure build, the tightening response of her body around his fingers before she let go on a soft moan.

Satisfaction curled in his belly as he watched her shatter. This beautiful woman—*his* woman—had found release and he refused to let it end there.

Shifting his position on the bed, he rained kisses over her sensitive skin. He savored the light, salty taste of her sweat-slicked skin and the dark, ripe flavor of her breasts as he ran his tongue over the darkened tip of one nipple. She writhed under his mouth, the soft moans a symphony as he focused on her.

Only her.

Shifting yet again, he continued the exploration with his mouth, moving lower toward the epicenter of her pleasure. Before she could catch a breath, he pressed his lips against her, his tongue probing deep within to drive her to madness once again.

He heard her sharp intake of breath—her sweet cry of pleasure—before he took her again, his tongue exploding with her rich, sensual taste. He focused on the tight bundle of nerves of her clitoris, heightened to the brink with sensitivity, and knew the moment she lost control again.

Beyond reason, beyond need, beyond want, he worshipped at the altar of her pleasure.

Montana wasn't sure she could breathe. Hell, she wasn't even sure she wanted to. The sheer magic of being held in his arms—of being pleasured by Quinn—had left her completely sated.

Quinn's head pillowed against her stomach and she toyed with the short, soft locks of his hair.

"Is that an acquired skill? Or one of Themis's gifts? Something special to subdue your subjects?"

He lifted his head, his dark eyes like midnight as he gazed up at her. "None of the above. That was something special created just for you, baby."

Her heart rolled over at his words—at the tender,

sexy affection she heard on the word "baby"—and her insides turned all soft and gooey.

"I find I have a decided urge to return the favor. And look at you." She pushed on his shoulders to get him on his back. "You're still wearing pants. That's not very conducive to what I have in mind."

"Far be it from me to stop you." His sexy grin lit up his face.

"Exactly."

The tight ridge of Quinn's erection pressed against the silk of his dress slacks and a thrill ran through her at the obvious promise of what was to come.

Impatient, she dragged at the fastening to his slacks, then pulled on the zipper, satisfied when she found no further barrier. Her gaze shot to his, his eyelids at half-mast as her fingers hovered around the most sensitive part of him. "Commando, eh?"

If she wasn't mistaken, a light blush suffused his cheeks as he opened his eyes. "I just never got used to it. Something underneath my clothes."

"Oh, I'm not complaining." Montana reached for the hard length of him. "Not at all."

His eyelids drooped again as a bolt of sheer, feminine pleasure suffused her veins.

Was there anything sexier than a man at his most vulnerable?

She shifted position, tugging the pants off the rest of the way and dropping them to the floor, then straddled his legs with hers. Leaning forward, she took his hard length between her hands and, with the pressure of her palms took him on a ride.

As the clouds shifted outside the window, moonlight streamed into the room, highlighting his features as she dragged him through his sensual paces. Quinn's eyes closed and his back arched to put him more firmly in her hands as pleasure built in her own body.

Quinn moaned low and deep in his throat as he gave himself up to her ministrations. Although she'd thought to use her lips and tongue to give him the same pleasure he'd given her, it would have to wait.

She had to have him. Had to hold his body deep within her own.

Shifting forward, she maintained contact on his skin with her fingers, using them to guide his cock deep inside of her.

As Quinn's hands reached for her waist, holding her above him, his gaze once again sought hers.

"I want you." The words floated over her and Montana already felt the long, answering pull low in her belly.

Leaning forward, seating him even more deeply inside of her, she pressed her lips to his. "I want you, too. Desperately."

Moving back into position, she rose on her knees and fell back to him, his strong fingers on her hips like a guide.

As Montana rode him—this incredible man who bore the heart of a warrior—she allowed the moment to take her completely.

What was this between them? This raging need that grew, even as they gave to each other.

How was it possible?

And how had she ever lived without it?

Chapter Eighteen

Montana stumbled toward the kitchen, where the smell of coffee was a powerful lure. Dawn was just breaking through the floor-to-ceiling windows of the ranch house, suffusing the kitchen in a warm glow.

Which was sort of how she felt.

Gloriously suffused.

The door of the kitchen's Sub-Zero refrigerator stood open as she moved into the room, her mind already imagining the first sip of liquid gold. Goodness, had she *ever* felt this good before?

How had he managed it? In one night, Quinn had found a way to make her feel both secure in the knowledge of what was happening around her while also making her feel like the sexiest woman on the planet.

The smile spread across her face as she moved toward the open refrigerator. "Quinn Tanner, I didn't think you had it in you, especially since I came three times last night, but I think I may actually be having an orgasm, that coffee smells so good."

The door to the Sub-Zero closed, followed by the

image of a large man with dimples, an acre of exposed chest and the greenest eyes she'd ever seen. "I wasn't aware coffee could do that. I'm going to have to have a cup myself."

Montana screamed before she could stop herself, the realization of what she'd just announced, coupled with the very large stranger standing before her too big a shock to the system.

"Whoa!" The man's hands went up in a "don't shoot" gesture as he backed slowly away from her, a carton of cream held high in his grip. "I'm sorry I scared you."

"Where's Quinn?" Although her heart still hammered and she wasn't quite ready to drop her guard, the sight of such a large man holding up dairy creamer was going a long way toward calming any sense of fear.

"He wanted to check some things on his computer. He's in the security center."

"Oh." The slow burn of embarrassment crept up her face and Montana wanted nothing more than to turn tail and run. Damned curse of the redhead.

"I'm sorry I scared you." He extended his free hand, his movements gentle. "I'm Rogan Black. One of Quinn's Warrior brothers."

She took his hand, the width of his palm nearly double hers. "Which one are you?"

That grin was back and an irresistible twinkle lit up his emerald gaze. Turning, he presented her with his back. "I'll give you one guess."

There, high on his shoulder, in the same place Quinn's bull perched, was a large bow and arrow. Montana stared at it, fascinated by the sheer elegance of the mark.

"It's not an animal."

"'Fraid not," Rogan said as he moved toward the

counter and reached for a couple of mugs. "Now. I'm dying for some of this orgasmic coffee."

"Look. I. Um."

He turned, the edges of his smile going serious. "Don't worry about it. You've had quite the forty-eight hours, from what Quinn's told me. It was nice to hear a smile in your voice."

Who was this man? Where the other Warriors had seemed . . . *fierce,* this man had a gentle nonchalance about him and a manner that couldn't help but put a person at ease.

Which was funny, really, since he was about six foot four, with shoulders the width of the refrigerator and a set of muscles that could give the Terminator a run for his money. Gentle would not normally be the first word to pop to mind when confronted with a man Rogan's size.

Rogan poured them both a cup of coffee, then handed her a steaming mug. With a glance toward the counter, he added, "Cream?"

"That's okay." She gazed down into the dark brew, then looked back up at the large man where he perched on a stool at the bar that ran the length of the kitchen.

"Ah, a real coffee drinker, eh? I just don't have that skill."

She took a few steps forward. "Is that why you just dumped about a pint of creamer in there?"

"Yep." He reached for a sugar bowl she hadn't noticed at first and simply picked it up, dumping a liberal amount on top of the cream. "Sugar, too."

"Obviously."

Montana took a seat opposite him. "So you're the Sagittarius?"

"Guilty."

A large plate of breakfast pastries—scones, croissants and danishes—sat at the edge of the counter and he dragged them over. "Would you like one?"

Why the hell not. If she truly was *ascending* as an immortal, Montana suspected calorie counting was about to become the least of her problems. "Sure." As she bit into the flaky croissant, she nearly moaned in pleasure, but caught herself just in time.

The suggested coffee orgasm was bad enough.

"Where did this come from? We're in the middle of Texas. Right?"

"Right. The Hill Country to be exact, about an hour outside of Austin. But the pastries I picked up in France."

"No way."

"Yes, way." There it was again, that nonchalance, coupled with a merry little twinkle in his gaze.

"I really have descended into the Twilight Zone."

"It can be a lot to take in. It's also a gift, even if it doesn't feel like it right now." Rogan polished off a chocolate chip scone in three bites and was already reaching for a cheese Danish. "The thing to keep in mind every time you get surprised is that the rules have changed."

"What rules?"

"All your life, you've believed in the basics of human existence. Gravity. Mortality. Cycles. I'd imagine someone in your position of wealth has also had a sense of security that's pretty rare, even for humans."

Was he right? Had she always felt secure? Safe?

Montana mulled it over in her mind, twisting the thought through the prism of thirty years of living. And

had to admit that he was one hundred percent correct.
"I guess I have."

"Taking all this in would be difficult for anyone.
But your frame of reference is even more skewed for
this to seem impossible. Pay the problem to go away."

"I haven't done that."

His smile was gentle, but his words were firm.
"Oh no? Tell me, before you realized what was going
on, that you didn't just think Quinn and his security
firm could take care of this problem and let you go
back to normal."

Damn, but he was good.

"Who are you, Rogan Black? Oh wait, let me guess.
You're the group shrink."

His laugh echoed around the kitchen. "I am a Sagittarius Warrior, in service to the great goddess of justice, Themis. And I'm no shrink. I just call them like I
see them."

"That's all?"

"I've got a few other tricks up my sleeve, just like
the rest of my Warrior brothers, but playing Freud
isn't one of them."

"Don't let the asshole fool you, Montana." The insult came barreling across the length of the kitchen,
where Quinn stood in the doorway. "He's as fucked
up as the rest of us."

Quinn tried desperately to tamp down on the harsh
stab of jealousy that had pierced his gut the moment
he walked into the room and saw Montana and Rogan having a lovely little breakfast chat.

Fuck, this was embarrassing.

"You got a problem, Tanner?"

"Quinn?" Montana's eyes were wide as she stared at him from across the room. "What's wrong?"

"Nothing." Quinn sauntered over and grabbed a croissant from the counter. He took a large bite as the pleasant surprise of butter-based satisfaction whistled a happy tune through his taste buds. "Where did this come from?"

"Paris," Montana and Rogan said in unison. Quinn didn't miss the small smile that passed between them as he took another large bite of the flaky pastry.

"It's good," he muttered.

"Your verbal skills are amazing this morning, Quinn." Montana leaned over from the stool where she sat next to him and pressed a kiss to his lips. "Mmmm. But you're nice and buttery. Good morning, grumpy."

"Good morning." Quinn kissed her back, then turned a glare on Rogan. "Fuck you."

"I didn't say anything."

"Oh no, not you with the innocent eyes. Did he tell you, Montana"—Quinn motioned toward Rogan with a free hand as he reached for another croissant—"what he does all day?"

"We hadn't gotten that far," Montana admitted.

"I'll save you the trouble of asking, Montana," Rogan added. "I roam the globe, searching for rogue members of the Pantheon."

Quinn noticed Rogan didn't mention the goddess he'd yet to find in all his years of travel. "Yeah, well, you missed one, oh great one."

"What?" Whatever merriment lingered behind Rogan's green gaze vanished in a heartbeat.

"Arturo Veron. Former Taurus Warrior."

Rogan shook his head as he dumped about a half pound of sugar in a fresh cup of coffee. "He's clean."

Quinn thought of the security video that confirmed Arturo Veron was anything but clean. "No, he's not."

Whatever humor had fueled Rogan's earlier, playful remarks, it had all evaporated in the suggestion he hadn't done his job. "Quinn. I've kept up with him. This life wasn't cut out for him, so he left. It's not a crime and clearly it was the right choice. He's made a fucking fortune in emerging technologies."

"He makes Steve Jobs look like a pauper," Montana added. "That's why he was invited to sit on the board of directors for Grant Shipping. He knows global business like the back of his hand. He was a natural fit and I was thrilled when he accepted the position." Montana stared into the depths of her mug. "*Was* being the operative word."

"Well, whatever intel you've got is wrong. Arturo broke into Montana's home last night and killed several people very close to her."

Rogan shook his head. "I'm telling you, it's not possible."

"And I'm telling you," Quinn countered, "you missed something. Arturo Veron is as dirty as Enyo."

Enyo paced in front of the large obelisk in Central Park—Cleopatra's Needle—as the cool air whipped around her body. She felt nothing of the cold, the long cashmere coat she wore doing much to keep her warm.

Whatever the coat didn't take care of, her anger managed and then some.

With a brief flick of her gaze, she stared up at the

obelisk. Although she had never considered herself a woman who lived in the past, this site haunted her and she visited it more often than she cared to admit.

Had the end of it all started here?

And what could she have done differently?

Enyo didn't want to acknowledge it, but the last year had been an ass kicking. And while she might be a raging demon without a shred of decency to everyone who knew her, the one person she never lied to was herself.

Everything changed last year. The Summoning Stones were going to be the key to regaining her dominance over the Warriors, and in the blink of an eye—and because of Ava Harrison, that fucking princess with a conscience—it all evaporated.

In preparation for the battle, Enyo had increased her army of Destroyers to ensure she'd get the stones. And what did it get her? Diminished power and a group of out-of-control assholes who were increasingly going rogue.

Fuck her father and his damn bargain with Themis. Why should she be punished for it? She was the daughter of Zeus and Hera, for fuck's sake. She was the goddess of *war* and nothing—no force on heaven or earth—should diminish her power.

But lost battles diminished it. And using her power to create Destroyers diminished it.

And it wasn't fair.

Her father's weird guilt complex over Themis put her in this position of weakness. And it was time it stopped.

Enyo stared up at the obelisk again and thought about her little Destroyer problem. They might have

been created as soulless minions, but her evil foot sol-
diers smelled blood in the water, that much was clear.
And lack of a soul didn't mean complete lack of intelligence or inability to exploit an opportunity.

Which was exactly what they were doing.

"Interesting place for a meeting." Arturo Veron
materialized in front of her, his broad shoulders swathed
in Armani. Despite the temperature, his only acquies-
cence to the weather was to shove his hands in his
pockets.

Enyo refused to tell him about the latent power
she still believed the obelisk held and instead shot him
one of her coldest stares. "I thought you had a business proposition for me."

"Ah, a woman with purpose. I like it."

She flashed him one of her rare smiles before si-
dling up to him. "You'll like me a lot less if you insist
on continuing with the small talk." At that, she extended one long finger and pressed it against the hard
wall of his stomach. Heavy voltage assailed his taut
form and Enyo took a small moment of pleasure as he
fell to his knees.

Pulling her finger away, she stepped back and
planted her fuck-me pumps. "Now. Tell me what the
hell you want."

Arturo waved a hand before regaining his feet. His
voice held the edges of strain, but beyond that, she
had to give him points for a quick recovery.

Which immediately made her wonder how he'd
be in bed.

Hmmm . . . maybe she *was* being a bit hasty. She
had, after all, been lonely since killing Ajax. There was

nothing to be done for it, but if she could snag a few side benefits out of this one, she was all for it.

She'd lived a long life and some of her most favorite sexual escapades involved the bleeding edge of depraved. And this one's dark eyes suggested a level of immorality that would be absolutely delicious.

Enyo burrowed inside the cashmere, but she made an effort to soften her tone. "So tell me, what do you want?"

"I need your help."

"Interesting approach."

"Themis's boys are guarding something I want."

"And why should I help you?"

Arturo rose to his full height and lobbed a verbal volley Enyo wasn't expecting. "I know all about your recent losses. Maybe if you worked with me, you might have a chance to win one."

"And what would you know about any of that?"

"You'd be surprised what I know. But, truth be told, that's not why I'm here."

"So what do you want from me?"

His gaze burned a path down her body, in spite of the layers she wore against the whipping wind.

"The Warriors are guarding a little prize. Two of them actually."

Despite herself, Enyo was intrigued. "Prizes?"

"Oh yes. Themis's daughter, the fallen Horae, Eirene, and her daughter, Montana Grant."

Enyo had heard for years about Themis's missing daughter, but she had no idea the woman had been found. Or that she had a daughter.

She kept a wary eye on Arturo as he stalked closer.

"If you're so sure about this, what do you need me for?"

"I'm building a team."

"Maybe I'm not into team sports."

Arturo moved in even closer, his gaze narrowed on her mouth. "Maybe you should be." Before Enyo could reply, Arturo leaned over and purred in her ear. "Themis, her daughter, her granddaughter and a whole heap of Warriors. Come on. You know you want to."

She did want to—that was the damnedest part.

Of course, she wasn't one to be completely led around by her urges. If there was one thing she'd learned over the last year, it never hurt to have reinforcements.

"Let me just make a quick phone call."

Satisfaction hummed in Enyo's veins as she moved away from Arturo and walked on the opposite side of the obelisk. She felt his eyes on her back as she moved and took some small measure of satisfaction she had at least that.

Did she trust him? Absolutely not.

Was she going to take advantage of what he offered?

Abso-fucking-lutely.

She scrolled through her address book until she found her sister's number.

Oh yeah. This was going to be fun.

"You seemed awfully pissy at Rogan." Montana eyed Quinn across the kitchen as she finished drying the last of the mugs to put them away.

Quinn still sat at the bar, tapping away on his BlackBerry. "He was flirting with you."

"He was talking to me, Quinn."

"It pissed me off."

"Is that the real reason why you're upset?"

"Partly." Quinn laid the device on the counter. "I'm more pissed off he missed Arturo."

Montana placed the last of the mugs back in the cupboard. "Mistakes happen."

"Not when they involve you."

"Arturo's kept up a good disguise. Well-respected businessman and all that. We appointed him to our board of directors to launch the company public, for pete's sake."

Quinn reached for the buzzing device. "Sorry, Montana, but that excuse isn't fucking good enough for me."

"You're not infallible and neither are your brothers."

"I should be. We all should be. Otherwise what the hell good are we?"

She eyed the BlackBerry as a slow boil began in her veins. "Would you get the hell off that thing?"

"Why? So you can lecture me on how wrong I am? I know what I know, Montana. I have a job to do. We all do. And we let one of our own fucking betray us. And if that weren't enough, he hurt you. Wants to hurt you more. How the hell is that supposed to make me feel?"

His words echoed between them, reverberating off the surfaces of the kitchen.

Tossing the hand towel she still held onto the counter, she stormed toward the living room, hollering over her shoulder as she went, "I don't care what Arturo's done. Frankly, I don't even think most of this is about Arturo. You have this belief you can control everything. Well, I've got news for you, Quinn: You can't. No one can."

Frustration and fury kept time with her stomping feet as she stalked into the living room and up the stairs. Her bathrobe flared around her ankles as she moved, whipping against her calves.

Stubborn, asshole jerk. That's what he was.

Thought he could do everything himself.

Thought he was infallible. Or needed to be.

Thought the weight of the world rested on his fucking shoulders.

She stalked through the bedroom door and ran head first into Quinn. "Fuck! What the hell did you do that for?"

"You're mad."

"No, Quinn. Not mad. Furious. There's a huge difference."

Quinn reached around her and closed the door. "If this little fight ends like I hope it does, we don't need anyone walking by the door."

The sly twirl of desire fluttered through her veins at his words, but she resolutely tamped down on it. She'd never been a prisoner to her body and damn well wasn't going to start now.

She was pissed off and she was entitled to it. "Don't you dare fuck me with your eyes and don't think that just because I'm still horny from before I'm going to willingly forget this."

"I don't think that."

"Good."

A wicked smile spread across his face. "I'm still going to fuck you blind once we're done fighting."

Oh my.

Well.

Just . . . oh my.

"In the meantime, why are you mad?"

She scrambled to keep up, the thought of how she went blind in his arms not that many hours ago still too immediate for comfort. "You were acting like a jerk down there."

"Rogan didn't do his job. I was addressing that. Don't you do that at work?"

"Yeah. But what does that have to do with this?"

"It has everything to do with this. This isn't just a part of me, Montana. It's my job, too. It's how I live my days, years, centuries. I'm a Warrior, and along with my brothers we ensure the safety of humanity."

"Fine, so it's your job. It doesn't change the fact that you lambasted Rogan because you were pissed he was talking to me."

"You were laughing back."

"Because he's funny."

Lines creased his forehead and his jaw was iron hard. "Rogan failed on this one, Montana. You, of all people, should understand that feeling. And the anger that comes when a job isn't done right."

"Yes, but aren't you taking this a bit too far? He's not beholden to you."

"We're all beholden to one another. That's the only way we work. I failed and I've paid the price. He should, too."

And that's where she heard it. The telltale thread of frustration underlying his words that had absolutely nothing to do with Rogan, or Arturo, or even her.

It had to do with Quinn.

"Want to tell me about it?"

His dark eyes shuttered, going all hard and flinty. "Not particularly."

"Too bad. Spill it."

Montana took his hand and walked them both over to a small sitting area on the far side of the room. Tugging on his hand, she sat on one end of an over-stuffed love seat. "Come on, Quinn. Tell me about it."

Chapter Nineteen

Quinn felt the pull of her hand in his. He felt the insistent tug of his heart even more.

Did he dare tell her? Did he dare admit his failure? Could he show weakness in front of the woman he loved?

Loved?

Quinn's gaze roamed over Montana as he took the seat next to her. Her long, lush red hair curled about her shoulders and her blue gaze was quietly trusting.

She believed in him.

And in that moment, it all came clear. The last six months tiptoeing around his Warrior brothers. Castigating himself for his decision to leave Kane and Ilsa at the entrance to the Underworld. The pain and embarrassment of watching the Scorp and his woman as they both desperately tried to show him they didn't hold what happened against him.

Was that love too?

Maybe it was. And sometimes you did things to each other that you not only had to ask forgiveness for.

But you had to accept the forgiveness when it was given.

"Last spring Kane found Ilsa again."

"Again? She didn't mention that."

Quinn caught her up to speed on Ilsa's history, the goddess's role as Hades' deliverer of souls and her own poor choices prior to meeting Kane.

"Well, it's clear they're in love with each other," Montana said as he finished the story of how Kane and Ilsa met, remet and fell in love. "All's well that ends well there."

"It did end well."

"But you can't help being mad at yourself."

The gentle, dulcet tones of her voice scraped at him. At the image he held of himself since the incident. "I didn't help them when they needed it most. And I did it out of stubborn, arrogant pride. Arrogance they had to pay the price for."

"It sounds to me like Kane and Ilsa have come out the other side just fine. It's you who keeps paying the price."

"Well, what am I supposed to do? I left them in a place they might never have come out of."

"But they did come out of it. Rose above it, too, if the way they look at each other is any indication."

Why didn't she understand? Why couldn't she see it from his point of view? And who was she to even suggest he couldn't see reason? "You haven't done anything to your mother, yet you persist in believing you did something to drive her away."

Montana's spine went rail-straight and whatever gentleness underlying her previous words evaporated. "That's different."

"Is it? Because from my point of view, you're pretty damn innocent, yourself."

Her sky-blue eyes went as blank as glass. "She's my mother, Quinn. And she left me. I hardly think it's the same thing."

"Are you sure, Montana? Because you sit there with this big huge blind spot of your own you're unwilling to look past, yet you have no problem poking at mine."

Fuck. Did he even say that out loud? What the hell was this, share your feelings with Oprah?

Quinn leaped off the couch and paced across the room. His heart raced from anger, from panic, hell—from pure unadulterated embarrassment at admitting his feelings.

"You have no idea what I feel like. You can't possibly know what it is to be abandoned. By your own mother, no less!" Montana's voice punched at him in loud waves, rising to match the same volume she'd used in the kitchen.

But this time, there was pain lancing through each and every word.

Pain he had caused by going down this road and poking a wound that would not heal for her.

"The one person in the entire world who is supposed to love you unconditionally."

"She loves you. It's clear to anyone who has seen the two of you."

"Well, fuck love. She might love me in her own way, but where the hell has she been for thirty years? Answer me that!"

And he couldn't.

He could tell her over and over what he thought.

He could even tell her what he saw when Eirene looked at her.

But he couldn't give her any reason—anything with substance—the explained why Eirene had chosen to go away.

"Ah. See. Now you're quiet. Damn fucking straight. I can't believe you even think it's remotely the same. Especially when your anger over Kane and Ilsa is so stupid and pointless!"

"Pointless?" Quinn felt as stupid as she accused as the words sputtered from his lips. "You have no idea what I've been through. No idea how it went down."

"Based on your stubborn behavior, I have a pretty good idea. You're a great, huge, overgrown ass hat, just like the women said you were!"

Quinn wanted to hold on to his anger. Wanted to keep it held tight in his palms, like a hot coal, just as he'd done for the last six months.

But the anger wouldn't stay put and he found the urge to make a fist and hold it all tightly against himself was gone. In that moment, standing before this amazing, incredible, infuriated woman, whatever was left of his anger simply floated away.

"Stupid?"

With slow, measured movements, he crossed the room, his eyes never leaving Montana's.

How could this one tiny woman have shown him the way? Pointed him toward the path to forgiveness, to absolution, to . . . love.

Because that's what she'd found a way to do.

In only a few short days, she'd gotten under his skin and changed everything.

Everything.

"That's really the argument you're going to use?"

"If the shoe fits."

Quinn leaned over and placed his hands on the slender width of her shoulders, pulling her forward to stand before him.

He ran one finger down the curve of her cheek, then pulled that lock of hair that mesmerized him so between thumb and forefinger. "Let it go, Montana. It's the only way."

"What if I can't?"

"Of course you can. And I'll be right here to help you."

Montana wanted to believe him, but the hurt she'd held for so very long wasn't quite ready to release her.

Adopting her most petulant voice, she added, "You can't even wear my shoes. And for the record, I don't think Prada heels would look all that good on you anyway."

The edges of his eyes creased with the sweetest crinkles as Quinn added, "Maybe not heels, but Grey insisted I own a pair of their dress shoes. For men. Claims he's going to instill some bit of fashion in me somewhere, even if it's just my feet."

"If you're trying to be funny . . ." She broke off, not sure where she was going.

Could he be right? And could she really live a life where she felt as adequate as the next person?

A life where she believed she could be loved.

"I'm trying to make you smile. And make sure that you're not only listening to me, but hearing me as well.

You're an amazing woman and I believe the person who knows that most of all is your mother. It was her mistake, Montana."

Montana knew he was right. She'd spent the last few days trying desperately to work that out in her mind.

"The people we love have the power to hurt us. But it's not a reflection of us."

The urge to rant and rail had passed and Montana found curiosity took its place. "Are you still talking about yourself?"

"I'm actually talking about my father."

"Oh." The idea of Quinn having a father was an odd thought.

"Oh shit is probably more like it. He had his fair share of problems, amazingly accurate visions at the top of the heap."

"Visions? Like a seer of some kind?"

"Exactly like that."

"When did he live?" Had she really just asked that question? Maybe it was starting to get easier, believing in this world that was rapidly coming to claim her.

"He was born around 550 BC. I was born almost twenty-five years later."

"Oh my God." The man was over twenty-five hundred years old? Montana reached out and ran a finger down his cheek, unable to keep from touching him. "But you . . . you look like you."

"Perpetually thirty-six." Quinn smiled. "And I was an old man for my day."

"It's not possible." Montana shook her head. "I mean, I understand what immortal means. But to think you were born then. That you've existed for that long."

"And I'm quite young compared to many of my brothers."

"How old are they?"

"Several are upwards of ten thousand years old."

Montana fought to grasp it, the insane idea that these people had lived so many lifetimes. "How did you become a Warrior?"

"Themis's agreement with Zeus allowed for the development of twelve sets of thirteen Warriors each. And she hit a wall after a while. She just couldn't find enough men. She'd had several defectors by the time the Greek empire was developing and had become selective about who she pulled into service."

"But she saw something in you."

Quinn nodded. "Apparently so. I was one of the generals in the Greek army who fought in the Battle of Marathon. Late after the battle, she found my body. I was close to my last breath, but she found me and offered me a choice."

"And you took it."

"I did."

"But why?"

"I'd survived my father's words and fists so many years, until making my own way. I was proud of that. Proud of my strength. I guess I just didn't want to give it up yet."

"You're a leader."

"I'm a Warrior."

Montana smiled, the modesty of his words in direct opposition to his behavior. "You're a leader among leaders, Quinn Tanner. Clearly Themis saw that."

She leaned in and pressed her lips to his. "I see it."

Quinn's arms banded around her as his mouth

pressed to hers. She opened for him; the long, slow sweep of his tongue was an exquisite brand. Immediately, she felt her body respond, arousal burning a fire low in her belly.

What was this? She'd been in love before—had even thought to marry someone—but even with Stephen, it had never been like this. She hadn't wanted this badly. Hadn't needed.

She hadn't *craved*.

Opening herself up to what only Quinn could offer her, Montana allowed him to walk her backward toward the bed. As they fell on top of it, a heap of giggling limbs, Quinn whispered against her throat, "Now I have a promise to keep."

Quinn pressed Montana back against the mattress, need and longing already pumping through his veins. She made him want to the exclusion of anything—of everything—else.

The desire—bone deep and seemingly endless—that welled up inside of him made him desperate for her.

His woman.

His Montana.

Where their lovemaking earlier had been slow and measured, all he could think about now was taking her. Driving her to the peak and back again. Burying himself so deeply inside of her he could brand her as his mate.

Montana's need was as frenzied as his own. She already had the T-shirt he wore up and over his head and was clawing at the jeans he'd put on before breakfast.

"I want to feel you. Now."

He smiled against her neck. "That's an awfully tempting invitation."

Her answering smile had a world of promise in the curve of her lips and the light in her eyes. "Actually, I have a far more tempting idea."

With surprising speed, Montana levered herself under him and had him on his back in moments. As he gazed up at her he saw the blue of her eyes had darkened in sensual invitation. "Tempting?"

"Very much so."

Before he could maintain the witty repartee—or hell—even a coherent thought, Quinn's world tilted on its axis as her hand snaked between them to make a tight fist around his cock.

The epitome of every fantasy he'd ever had—and a few he'd never even thought of until right now—was the responsive woman in his arms. She drove him wild and by the seductive smile on her face, she damn well knew it.

"I believe you said something about going blind, Mr. Tanner?"

The long lines of her body rose up from where she straddled his thighs. The perfect curve of her breasts, the slender arch of her waist where it met gorgeous, lush hips. His voice strangled, he struggled to focus on her words and not on the distracting sight of her body. "I might have mentioned something like that."

"Well, then, I guess I'd best get to it."

All Quinn could do was offer up a silent prayer of thanks to whatever gods had brought her to him—and sit back and enjoy the ride.

And what a ride it was.

Her hands were everywhere at once, over his shoulders, across his chest where her fingers set off a shock wave of sensations as she brushed against his nipple, down the length of his rib cage. Sensation after sensation filled him as she took him along on the most passionate ride of his life.

Quinn felt his body falling deeper under her spell, his body separating from his mind as she lavished herself on him.

Over him.

Around him.

With a light push, she forced him onto his side and, before he understood her intention, he felt the light, questing touch of her fingertips as they traced the outline of his bull tattoo. He stiffened, immediately concerned the bull would come to life under her touch. Although he could hold it within his aura, it wasn't always so easy to keep it from moving.

"It's beautiful."

Quinn didn't know what to say; didn't know how to react. So he said nothing as she continued her ministrations.

Her breath feathered across his back as she spoke. "I had no idea. And I'm so sorry for what I said."

"It's a lot to take in."

"You're too kind." On those words, Montana leaned in and pressed her lips over the smooth skin of his back, right above the head of the bull.

He didn't think it was kindness when he was just being honest, but the words never made it. Instead, she turned the tables on him again as her hand snaked down the front of his body.

Stars exploded behind his eyes as he rolled to allow her better access, then erupted with another wave of sparks as she took him with her mouth. Mind-numbing sensations coursed through his body, but it all centered in his cock. Pleasure exploded along his nerve endings as her mouth did the most wicked things. Quinn tried to keep up—tried desperately to stay focused—but every attempt at a coherent thought died before it could fully form.

She wrung every sensation out of him and just as Quinn thought he couldn't take any more—just as he reached for her to drag her up the length of his body so he could bury himself inside of her—she began again.

A long, heated drag of suction as she swirled her tongue along the underside of his cock. With clever fingers, she added pressure and he felt the telltale tightening at the base of his spine as she used both her hands and her mouth on him.

"Montana." Her name dragged from his chest on a rush of air.

"Hmmm." She never broke contact, the word humming around his cock and sending another round of hard shocks through his system.

She never let up.

She simply stared up at him with that liquid-blue gaze and that was all it took.

Quinn gave himself up. Vulnerable, naked—physically and emotionally—it was in that moment he knew.

He was hers.

He'd be hers until the stars fell from the sky and the heavens exploded.

Forever.

Unable to bear it another moment, he reached for her shoulders and pulled her forward. "Montana."

His body on the brink of madness, she only made it worse as she slowly crawled up to settle herself on top of him. Her husky voice showed him she wasn't unaffected by what lived between them. "Quinn."

Fingers trembling, he reached for her waist and settled her over himself. Hips arching, his body fought a desperate battle for more pleasure as he pushed upward to drive himself even deeper within her.

When she began to move, Quinn gave her the lead as she rode him. He felt the sweet curves of her ass as she fell back onto him over and over again and gazed on the glory of her breasts as they moved in rhythm with her movements.

As her inner muscles clamped around him, Quinn let go. Arching upward, he used his hands to drag her down, their lips and tongues merging in tempo with their bodies.

A low moan began deep in his chest, carried forth in the power of his orgasm. And as he gave his body up to the heat that raged between them, Quinn's promise was turned on its ear.

As Montana cried out above him, her orgasm overtaking her, Quinn went blind.

Montana stretched like a cat. The satisfaction of being made love to before nine a.m. was such a welcome change of pace she wasn't sure she could ever go back to board meetings.

Board meetings . . .

The thought lodged in her mind and like an insistent insect, buzzed in her ear, refusing to be ignored.

Board meetings.

Florida.

"Oh shit." Montana sat straight up and glanced at the clock. "Quinn." She pushed at his shoulder to get his attention. "Quinn."

"What? I kept my promise, didn't I?"

"I know. But I didn't."

Quinn shifted and rolled to his side, his gaze alert. "What's that supposed to mean?"

"The board of directors meeting in the Florida Keys. It's in a few days at our resort. I have to get it all canceled. I can't risk these people. I have to get this taken care of."

Montana reached for her robe and dragged it on. "I can't believe I forgot this. I can't believe I was so irresponsible. It's like Jackson died for nothing. And Laura. And Tony."

"Montana." Quinn dragged at the back of the robe, but she flitted out of his reach.

"Would you get *up*?"

"Montana." All traces of sleep left his voice as he said her name in three crisp syllables. "Calm down."

"I have to take care of this."

"*We* will take care of it. Let me get dressed and I'll have you back at the brownstone in five minutes."

As she watched him drag on his clothes from the night before, Montana couldn't help but wonder if she had five seconds.

How could she have forgotten Jackson so quickly? Or the threat that hovered, just waiting to strike?

True to his word, Quinn had them both back at the brownstone in less than five minutes. Montana had immediately asked after her mother and Callie directed her to a second-floor guest room.

"Find out anything else?" Quinn scrubbed a hand over his jaw as he looked up at Brody and Rogan. Both men had followed him into the security center and they'd been suspiciously quiet as Quinn scanned the continuous stream of reports from the various monitors.

Brody started first. "Her mother's worse. I didn't think it was possible, but she is. Exponentially worse than last night when they brought her here."

"Why didn't you call us back here?"

"We didn't know. Ava and Callie just found her about fifteen minutes ago. She fainted in her room."

Another reason Montana would be beating herself up.

Fuck.

"Something else arrived a little while ago."

"Here?"

"At Montana's. Ilsa and Kane stayed there last night, keeping watch."

"They didn't have to do that. Arturo left his message all over Montana's office. What reason did he have to go back?" Even as he said the words, the look on Brody's face left Quinn with the sinking suspicion he'd misjudged.

"Yeah, well, apparently there was a part two. Pull up the feed you've got going on Montana and look at the security in her building." Brody pointed to the screen as Quinn typed in a few keystrokes.

It wasn't lost on Quinn that Rogan moved up first to look at the data.

"A messenger delivery?"

"He checks out clean and the service has no record of who gave them the package that was delivered to Montana's doorman." Brody pointed toward an envelope Quinn hadn't noticed on the edge of his desk. "Take a look."

Quinn flipped through the various sheets of papers, not sure of what it all meant. "These are dossiers on each of the new board of directors."

"Yeah. With personal details about each individual as well as details on each of their families," Rogan pointed over his shoulder at the photo on top. "Joy Justice, head of Justice Cosmetics."

Quinn scanned the page again. It was only on a closer look that he saw what he was supposed to see. "Joy Justice has three children, ages five, seven and ten. And their names are circled."

"It's like that on all of them," Brody added. "Everyone has a weak spot and Arturo's going to use that to his benefit."

"So we get there and get all of them into protective custody. I run a fucking security business. It's what I do, Talbot."

Brody shook his head. "Look at the last page."

As Quinn flipped to the very last page, after the dossiers, he saw it. The thin disk clipped to the page, the kind used to capture photos on a digital camera.

"We haven't had a chance to watch it yet, but we think he's got them already. Hostages."

Montana tucked her mother in, rewrapping the blanket around her frail form. Eirene had gotten worse overnight, and Montana couldn't help but wonder how long she really had left with her.

And she'd spent the time with Quinn.

"He's a wonderful man, Montana."

The guilt racking her system threatened to choke

her as Montana gazed down into Eirene's knowing blue gaze. "He's a distraction, Mother."

The blankets fell away as Eirene reached out. "He's your future, Montana. You were right to spend the time with him. To heal from the horror of yesterday."

"How can you say that?"

"Because I can see your happiness. For the first time, my sweet precious baby, I can see it. On you. Around you. When you're with him, you're right where you're supposed to be."

"Moth—"

Eirene held up a hand to stop her. "It's your time with him and you need to take it."

"But you needed me last night."

"Callie took care of me just fine." Eirene released her grip on Montana's forearm and smoothed the covers. "Besides, orgasms are good for immortals. Aids in building up strength."

A choked laugh caught her by surprise. "Mother!"

Eirene actually looked a bit offended. "I was young once, too, Montana. I know about these things."

"I'm sure you do."

"Damn straight," her mother grumbled and Montana couldn't stop the small giggle. "And there's something else I know. Men like Quinn Tanner don't come along every day."

"No," Montana mused, an image of his dark eyes filling her mind's eye. "They don't."

"You have to reach out and take joy where you find it. I did that and despite all my other regrets, I've never once regretted that."

"You mean you and Daddy?"

"Yes. Oh, he was magnificent. Jack Grant, the bold businessman out to conquer the world."

Montana smiled at the sweet ache in her mother's tone and the wistful yearning that filled her gaze. "Sounds pretty special."

"It was. And it made me realize I didn't know what special was before that."

Montana settled herself on the bed and leaned forward. The oversized sweatshirt she'd pulled on before leaving the ranch house was warm and cozy and she reveled in the feeling of connection.

A conversation with her *mother*.

"You had other beaus before Daddy?"

"Oh yes. Mount Olympus is quite the scene, actually. Gods, demigods, immortals and so on. There's always someone to keep an eye on and my sisters and I had our eyes on many."

A bittersweet sort of awe filled her chest as Montana thought of her mother as a young woman.

Not as a mother. Or a wife. Or even a frail human. A young, healthy woman with the world at her feet.

"Sounds like you had fun."

"I did. And it was fun. And then I was the first to get serious with someone and things changed. I was engaged once before, you know. Before I met your father."

"You were? Was that guy a mortal, too?"

"Oh no. He was perfectly acceptable in every way. Everyone loved him, my mother most of all. The problem was, I didn't love him." The haze of memory in Eirene's gaze shifted back to the present. "Just like you didn't love Stephen."

"You knew about that?"

"Darling. Just because I've not been physically present doesn't mean I haven't watched out for you. I knew from the first he wasn't right."

"Because you didn't like him?"

"Because he wasn't right. The two of you didn't fit. Just as Arturo and I didn't fit."

The sharp, pointed flare of understanding stabbed at Montana, her chest going tight at her mother's words. A coincidence. That had to be it.

It had to be.

Desperate to keep her voice calm and not overreact, she pressed Eirene. "Arturo?"

"He was a gorgeous man. I'll give him that. Dark Latin features and the most incredible bedroom eyes you've ever seen. But it just wasn't enough. He was a pretty package and that was all."

Montana thought of the man she knew as Arturo Veron. A beautiful exterior wrapped around a depraved, dishonest soul. "How'd you meet him?"

"He was in service to my mother. One of her Warriors."

Her stomach flipped over at the truth. "Like Quinn?"

"Exactly like Quinn. Arturo is a Taurus Warrior, too."

Chapter Twenty

"Your mother dated Arturo Veron?"

"She was engaged to him, too." Montana walked through what she'd learned from Eirene, including the history of her courtship with Arturo. Her increasing discontent with him. And finally, the Warrior's anger when Eirene broke the engagement.

"Did she give you a sense of when this happened?"

Montana couldn't help but be impressed at Quinn's security room. He sat at an oversized leather rolling chair before a bank of monitors that would have made NASA weep with envy. Pulling her gaze away from an image of the front entrance of Grant Shipping on one of the monitors, she nodded. "Several millennia ago."

"Which makes more sense."

"How?"

"I couldn't understand how I missed him. I've got intel on all the individuals joining your board of directors and he never popped for me. He never registered and I haven't been able to figure out why."

"You think he defected from being a Warrior before you ever became one?"

"We'll have to confirm with your mother when she ended the relationship, but that's exactly what I think."

"Do we have to tell her?"

"You didn't?"

Montana knew it wasn't fair, but she just couldn't bring Eirene any more grief. "At first, I was so surprised I couldn't say anything. And then the more I thought about it the more I realized I didn't want to upset her."

"She needs to know. And if she does know, she may be able to offer us some additional information."

She couldn't hold back the small sigh. "I know you're right. I just wanted to spare her the pain."

Understanding and acceptance filled the depths of Quinn's gaze. "I know."

"Do you want to know something else?" Montana moved forward and laid a hand on his shoulder. With her other hand she ran a finger down the stubble on his chin.

"What?"

"I think your interest in finding out more means there's finally something you're not taking responsibility for."

His hands fisted in the bunched material of the sweatshirt at her waist. "Maybe I'm mellowing a bit."

Montana bent forward and pressed her lips to his. "The guys will be shocked."

"We'll keep it as our little secret."

Montana moved into his lap, their lips never breaking contact. As one moment spun into the next, she marveled at how desirable Quinn made her feel.

The soft, sure press of his lips let her know how much he wanted her. She reveled in the deft stroke of his hands, gentle, yet knowing, as he touched her. And the sense of security—of protection—she felt each and every time he wrapped his large body around hers.

Settling into his lap, her head against his shoulder, Montana allowed her gaze to travel the width of the security screens again before alighting on a stack of papers next to his keyboard. "What is this?" Montana grabbed the papers, Quinn's answering "Wait" seeming to come from a distance.

"But . . . but these are my board of directors." The pain and guilt over Jackson, Laura and Tony roiled in her stomach like a bad meal. "What is this, Quinn?"

"Arturo's next targets."

Ice-cold fingers seized her nerves as she flipped through the dossiers. "Does he have them, too? These people he's clearly targeted."

"I'm afraid so."

Montana stood and moved back several steps. She didn't deserve the warmth of Quinn's arms or the feeling of safety to be found there. She didn't deserve to feel anything while these people suffered. "Where? Why didn't you tell me?"

"We believe they're being held in Florida. I was about to find you when you found me."

"But they're in danger."

Quinn's dark eyes offered a solemn promise, as did his words. "We're going to get them back, Montana. We'll get them all back."

"But they're in danger because of me. Just like Jackson and the others."

"They're not going to end up like Jackson and the others. I promise you that."

"Damn straight, they're not." With the clarity that can only come in the midst of adversity, Montana knew what had to be done.

What role she had to play.

Quinn stood and moved toward her. "What do you mean?"

"We're going after him. If I'm the one Arturo wants, he can have me. And we're going to take him down."

Arturo finished checking on the last of his hostages, before slamming the heavy iron door to the room in disgust. The Florida warehouse had proven a perfect place to hide people, but *fuck all*, if he wasn't rethinking this part of the plan.

These people were so damn annoying he was tempted to kill them all and punt with a new idea.

Stalking toward a makeshift office, Arturo scanned through what he'd missed the past fifteen minutes on the various security cameras he had on Montana.

It had been so easy. Was the woman that trusting or just that stupid?

Three successive board meetings at Grant Shipping and he was able to get communications equipment inside the building each and every time. He had cameras and listening devices in all key areas of her office and she was oblivious.

He didn't even need to use any of his immortal skills to do it.

Gods, how did these humans live like this? They

had the most voracious appetites to fuck one another over in every way imaginable, yet they still believed in one another.

Trusted one another.

"I thought we might find you here."

Arturo whirled around from the screens, Enyo's long, lean form filling the doorway of the makeshift office.

An unexpected wave of panic shot through his stomach in short, hard jabs. *Fuck.* How did this woman manage to throw him off? One look from her and he felt his balls shrivel up.

Painting on the cocky grin he'd worn since his birth so many millennia ago, he lifted his eyebrows and projected as much disdain as he could. "We? You weren't kidding when you said you wanted to bring reinforcements. And how thoughtful of you. I've always had a special fondness for twins."

Enyo moved through the door and on her heels was an equally tall, equally lithe woman with matching features. Even though they were obviously sisters, Arturo couldn't help but notice some very clear differences.

Where Enyo had a sheen of refinement and, dare he say it—elegance?—her sister looked like she'd walked straight off a battlefield.

From the tips of her shit kickers to the tight leather that covered her ass, the woman screamed "Don't fuck with me" like a blinking neon sign.

Enyo moved in even closer and Arturo fought the inclination to back up a few steps. He'd be damned if he'd give her the satisfaction. "Eris and I aren't here to indulge your perverted little fantasies." She let out a small, tinkling laugh that ran like razor blades down his spine, "not that I don't enjoy a good perverted fantasy or two. But, be that as it may, I think our relationship needs to stay strictly professional."

"You do?"

"Yes. Sadly, Arturo, I've thought about it and decided I needed to test our partnership before we attempted any 'partners with benefits' relationship."

Enyo reached out and stroked one long finger down the front of his jeans. He watched, mesmerized, as the rich bloodred of her nail stood out in stark contrast to the dark color of denim. And fuck, if she couldn't make him respond. His cock shot to attention like an overeager schoolboy raising his hand.

"Of course, if you act like a good boy and do what I ask, I may change my mind."

Willing his body under control, Arturo nodded toward the other woman. "So Eris is your sister?"

"Yes. I had this sudden realization that she and I hadn't spent nearly enough time together lately, so I decided to remedy the situation."

"And what does your little family reunion have to do with me?"

Enyo shot a glance over her shoulder where Eris waited in the doorway. "A lot, actually."

Eris stepped forward and came to stand next to her sister. Under any other circumstance, Arturo would revel in the close proximity of two women, especially when one had a hand still planted firmly on his groin.

But something about the two of them set off warning bells.

"We decided that you've got something we want." Eris's voice was low and dark, evoking all the warmth of a torture chamber.

"What's that?"

"The goddess of peace."

Arturo flicked a wrist. "She's a means to an end."

Enyo pressed harder against his jeans. Even though it was just the pad of her index finger, the threat was as clear as if she'd taken a knife to his balls. "Then you won't mind if we call dibs on her. When you offered me access to the Warriors, Eirene and her daughter, you didn't say I couldn't pick and choose."

Arturo weighed the situation. He could always agree and then fix things to his advantage on the boat. He'd planned this for quite some time. All he needed to do was bluff his way through and then leave the Warriors to deal with the *ladies*.

"Fine. Eirene is yours."

At the satisfied smile that spread across Enyo's face, Arturo knew he's made the right choice. Hell, he liked to live on the edge and it was his own damn fault he invited a nest of vipers into his midst. Might as well play out the hand and use them to his advantage.

They walked in here like the Olsen twins, but it was no secret on Mount Olympus the two women were rarely in agreement on anything.

If he played his cards right, he could use them to distract the Warriors while he took care of Eirene and Montana and then he'd still get his prize at the end.

He really did enjoy a pair of sisters every now and again.

Extending a hand toward the monitors, Arturo pasted a smile back on his face. "Ladies, let me show you what I had in mind."

* * *

"You're not going to be the lure, Montana." Quinn shook his head as a wave of—frustration? Anger? Bone-numbing fear?—rocked his gut. "Arturo is dangerous and he's been working on this for far longer than any of us know. He's methodical and stubborn and you're not walking into the middle of that."

Montana shook her head as she pointed a finger at her chest. "Quinn. I am the bait and there's nothing we can do to change that. This isn't going to stop unless we make a bold move. You all can protect me. Hell, if someone would teach me, I could protect myself with this supposed immortal power I'm gaining."

They were all assembled back in the kitchen, more heaping plates of food bookending the countertop, as Quinn, Montana and the other Warriors sat and planned their strategy.

Rogan and Drake took the end of the table, plowing through matched plates of lasagna while Kane and Ilsa sat next to them with a map of the Florida Keys spread out just beyond their own plates of food. Brody and Ava stood at the counter with laptops open and Callie kept herself busy baking a batch of brownies while interjecting into every single conversation.

"Montana's right. You have to let her go on this, Quinn."

Quinn bristled at Callie's interference. "I don't have to let her do anything."

"Actually, you do," the nymph shot back. "This is her destiny. And you have to let her live it."

Raw fury pumped in his veins—at the situation, at Callie's flippant remarks about fate and destiny and, damn it, at the fear he couldn't protect Montana. "Her destiny is fucked up because of a shitty decision Themis made about Eirene. That has nothing to do with Montana."

"It has everything to do with her." Callie shoved the large mixing bowl across the counter and stalked over toward him. The entire kitchen went silent at her outburst, everyone still as statues. "You can't keep her from this."

"I have to keep her safe."

Callie got in his face and refused to back down. "You have to support her and believe in her and do everything you can for her. But you can't take this away for her."

And there it was.

Just like with Kane and Ilsa, the truth reached up and slapped him in the face.

Just as he couldn't take away their pain. Or their trials. Or the roadmap of their destinies.

He couldn't do it for Montana.

Throwing his napkin on the table, he stalked from the room. The truth hurt, but the knowledge he had to let Montana enter the battle tore him to ribbons.

"I know you don't care for me very much, but I'd like to say something to you."

Quinn stared at the screen before him—whatever he'd sat down at his computer to do bogged somewhere in his brain. He couldn't think. Fuck, he couldn't even function on autopilot.

Montana wanted to walk straight into Arturo's plans.

Plans the ex-Taurus had no doubt been honing on for quite some time. He might not know Arturo Veron personally, but Quinn knew himself.

Knew what he was capable of.

Knew the stubborn, methodical ways of the bull that rode on his shoulder and influenced his life.

Whirling in his chair, Quinn's gaze landed on Eirene, where she waited at the door to the security center. He stood immediately, reaching for her frail forearm and leading her to his chair. "Please sit down."

"I hate this," she grumbled as she lowered herself into the seat. "I knew it was my destiny eventually, but I hate it."

It was the first he'd heard anything from her but a serene view of the world and it was a surprise. "Illness. Sickness. The life of an immortal ensures these aren't worries. Hell, they're not even fleeting thoughts."

Eirene nodded as she folded her hands in her lap. The blue of her veins was visible in stark relief against her paper-thin skin. "I thought myself so unbeatable. Even those first years in my mortal body, I thought myself invincible. And now look at me." Eirene looked down at her body, disgust riding her features when she glanced back up at him. "I'm dying."

"Yes." A callous acknowledgment for a callous situation.

"And I'm leaving my baby at the most difficult trial of her life."

"Seems like you've done that from the first." The words were out before he could stop them and strangely, after he'd spoken, Quinn acknowledged he was glad he had. This woman had given Montana a lifetime of hurt and he wasn't all that willing to cut her any slack, despite the evidence death was waiting to claim her.

Eirene sat up straighter in the chair. "I have. And I've also realized what I lost due to my own stubborn will."

"Your immortality?"

"No. I've never regretted that decision. A decision made out of love. It's what came after I regret. I lost my family because I thought I knew better. I thought I could outrun the Fates."

"The Fates didn't dictate your choices with Montana."

"No, they didn't. And it is I who must live with that."

Choice.

It always came back to that. The choices people made and the choices they didn't.

Wasn't that the very concept running ice-cold water through his veins? The choice Montana was insistent on making, to go after Arturo.

To put herself in the line of fire. Just as he himself had time and again through the years, fighting for what he believed in.

Just as Kane and Ilsa had.

With immediate clarity, Quinn saw what he'd chosen to ignore the day he took the Scorp to the entrance of the Underworld.

It wasn't about holding our loved ones back from making the hard choices, it was about supporting them when they did.

Eirene's words pulled Quinn from his musings. "She can do this."

"Are you sure she's ready?"

"If there's one thing my husband gave that child, it's a spine. She can handle whatever's thrown at her."

"But Arturo's dangerous. And he's been planning this—whatever this is—for a very long time."

Eirene's gaze flew to his face, then to the stack of photos he had left next to the computer. "Arturo?"

"You haven't spoken to Montana?" At the panic riding high in her gaze, Quinn backpedaled. "What did you think I meant?"

"I came to talk to you about Montana becoming an immortal. That she's up to the task."

"You didn't come to talk to me about Arturo Veron?"

"What about Arturo?"

"Your former lover who is behind the attacks on your daughter."

There was a moment of stunned disbelief, then a dark, keening moan began low in her chest as Eirene leaned forward and hugged herself. Quinn leaped toward her, but she pushed him off, her strength several times that of what he expected from someone in her condition.

"He's doing it. He promised he would. Years ago he promised he'd have his revenge and now he's making good on his vow."

"Eirene." Quinn tried again, laying a hand on her back. Her body was so thin, he could feel the vibration from the heavy wails echoing through her chest. "Eirene!"

Kneeling down, Quinn tried to find some way to get through to her. "Please listen to me. You have to tell me what you know. You have to tell me what happened. You have to give me the information so I can protect her."

Nothing he said got through, the woman's wails only getting louder as paralyzing fear gripped her in its claws. Quinn was afraid to leave her, yet unsure of how to help.

Trying once again, he whispered what he hoped

were soothing, hushing sounds. Then, voice firm, he tried once more. "Eirene. You must listen to me. You must help me take care of Montana."

At the sound of her daughter's name, the mournful cries subsided, even as she continued rocking in place. Satisfied he'd done something right, Quinn pressed her once more. "You have to help me help Montana. You have to tell me what you know. What did you mean, he promised?"

Eirene lifted her head to look at him, rivers of tears running down her cheeks. For several long moments, all he heard was the whirl of the computer equipment behind him and the heavy, thready sounds of her labored breathing.

Quinn had almost decided to go get Callie anyway when Eirene spoke. Her voice—normally husky with the pain she endured—was quiet and scratchy in the hush of the room.

"Arturo was never my lover. No man was until Jack. But when I walked away from Arturo, he promised me he'd come find me. When I least expected it, he told me, he'd hurt me in ways I could never imagine." Another sob burst forth on a keening wail.

"Why Montana? Why now?"

The sobs continued, but through it, Eirene gave him the information he needed. "He couldn't hurt me before. I was as immortal as he. Even more so, as a goddess."

"And now?"

"Look at me!" Her voice cracked on her scream as Eirene slapped a hand against her chest. "He can do nothing to me my body hasn't already done. But my daughter. My Montana."

Quinn fought the clawing frustration, desperation to get as much from Eirene as he possibly could. "But why *now*?"

"I always knew Jack protected her and kept watch over her. He wasn't immortal, but his money bought a hell of a lot of protection. But not anymore."

Eirene gripped his arm, her voice so devoid of hope Quinn felt it all the way to the soles of his feet. "Arturo wants Montana. He found the one thing that could hurt me above all else."

"You have to think about it, Montana. And *see* your destination."

"Think about it *how*?"

Ava and Ilsa stood at the far end of a long room in the basement of the brownstone, the walls filled with bookshelves at certain stretches or weaponry mounted on the wall at other stretches.

Montana looked at the women, about as far away as the length of her corporate boardroom, and wondered again what they meant.

How did you *think* about teleportation? Or a port, as everyone called it. And what in the world made her think she could ever do this?

"It's like shoe shopping," Ava shouted, inspiration lighting up her face.

"Excuse me?" Montana stared down the length of the room.

"Seriously, Ave." Ilsa gave her a sideways stare. "Shoe shopping?"

"Yes." Ava nodded vigorously. "You know how you see a pair of shoes and you just *know*?"

"No—"

"Yes—"

Ilsa's "no" matched Montana's "yes" at the same time.

"Great!" Ava gave Ilsa her own sideways stare before instructing again. "Okay. So you see this pair of shoes and you know they're perfect. They'll fit right and they'll be the exact match for this outfit you have and you just *know*. Focus on that knowledge."

Shoes and teleportation.

Holy shit.

"Okay." Montana took a deep breath. "So let's presume I know what I'm doing. How do I get over there?"

"Think it," Ilsa hollered across the room.

Think it.

Think it?

"Okay."

Eyes closed, Montana took a deep breath and tried to assimilate everything the women had told her. *Think* about where I'm going. *See* my destination. *Know* I'll get there.

"Now!" Ava screamed.

With startling clarity, an image of the women standing at the other end of the room rose up in her mind's eye.

Think.

See.

Know.

Think.See.Know.

Thinkseeknow.

A rush of gravity pulled at her, weighing on her limbs like nothing she'd ever felt before. A scream seized her throat, but before she could release it, the gravity vanished and she was flying.

And then crashing on top of Ava and Ilsa in a huge heap.

Loud giggles suffused the air as Ava and Ilsa screamed in unison. "You did it!"

Montana scrambled up, the three of them shoving at each other like puppies to get into a sitting position.

A quick glance around confirmed she was actually at the other end of the room. Wonder filled her as she tried to stand, but an overwhelming sense of dizziness dropped her flat on her ass. "I'm here."

"You're here," Ilsa confirmed.

"And you two didn't somehow do this? Or play a trick on me? Or come get me and bring me down here with your own port?"

Both women shook their heads as they regained their feet and held hands out to help her up. "*You* did this."

"But how?" A wild sense of euphoria was quickly replacing the dizziness as Montana grabbed their hands and got to a standing position. She'd gone skydiving several years earlier and had been on an adrenaline high for several days afterward.

Thinking about this—heart racing, blood pumping and an odd little dose of pride to boot—and she had to acknowledge skydiving had nothing on teleportation.

"I want to try it again."

"You sure?" Ava gave her hand a squeeze. "It's a lot to take in and you didn't eat a whole lot at lunch."

"Does that really have anything to do with it?"

"It has a ton to do with it. Didn't Quinn tell you?" Ilsa demanded.

"He gave me that book to read. The one you guys used when trying to figure out what was in my back."

"The man gave you a freaking book to figure all this out?" Now it was Ava's turn to make demands. "I swear, he is so fucking bullheaded sometimes."

Montana wasn't sure why that was so funny, but she couldn't stop the giggle. "He is a bull, Ava."

"Not technically."

"But the tattoo. The one I freaked out about. It's a bull that comes to life."

"A bull lives in his aura. That's all." Ilsa must have seen her skepticism, because she added, "It's not a real animal, per se. It's just . . . Ava? Help."

Ava sighed. "Brody tried to explain it to me and I still don't fully understand it. But it's one of their gifts from Themis to fight with. It's a physical manifestation of their sign that comes to life and helps them fight in battle."

"But Rogan's wasn't an animal."

Both women whipped their heads around toward her, Ilsa sputtering out, "You saw Rogan naked?"

"Just his chest." Montana shrugged. "And he only has a bow and arrow on his shoulder."

"Oh good Lord, you saw that man naked. Be still my heart." Ava clenched a fist to her chest.

"Your husband's pretty good-looking, Ava," Montana felt compelled to mention.

"So's mine," Ilsa added. "Doesn't mean we're dead. That man is a serious piece of eye candy. Hot. Hot. Hot."

"I thought he was nice." Montana recalled their discussion in the kitchen. How Rogan had offered her the pastries and joked about coffee.

"Nice? The man is a royal ass kicker, of the highest order." Ilsa pointed to Ava. "You've been here longer. You explain it."

"I haven't met him all that many times. He stays away from the brownstone most of the time." Ava glanced down at her wedding band with a small smile and Montana wondered if she even realized the subconscious gesture. "And Brody and I've been traveling quite a bit as well."

"It sounds like everyone's in and out around here. But he told me what he does. Traveling on missions to hunt down rogue immortals."

"He told you that?"

"Well, he didn't. Quinn sort of mentioned it while going all jealous on his ass for talking to me."

"Oooh, the bull's jealous," Ilsa taunted, shooting Ava a large grin.

"Quinn also got mad at him for missing the details on Arturo."

"It's a big mistake," Ava added. "Which must be why Rogan's sticking around here to help."

Ava's words doused whatever brief reprieve the women's camaraderie offered and Montana refocused on the task at hand.

She *could* do this.

Before the women could say anything further, Callie hollered into the basement, "Can you guys come back up to the kitchen?"

"Want to port there?" Ilsa asked the question, a bright twinkle in her eye.

"I'd love to."

"Remember. You have to think about it," Ava said. "I'll go on up ahead of you. Ilsa—you stay here. We'll both keep an eye on you. And then once we're up there, you're eating something."

Montana watched Ava simply disappear and turned toward Ilsa. "Does it get easier?"

"I wouldn't use easier. But it does get less unexpected."

On a nod, Montana acknowledged the thought. "Well, I guess that's something."

"So go on. You can do it. Picture the kitchen and you're off."

Montana closed her eyes and pictured the acre of counter, the table that even now likely held several oversized men ready to do battle in her honor.

Picture the kitchen.

Think. See. Know.

Picture the kitchen.

She felt the increasing pull of gravity, starting with her feet and working its way up her body.

Picture the kitchen.

A small memory of her and Jackson laughing in the kitchenette at work assailed her and she smiled with the memory.

The gravity took over fully, then the light rush of air and she was flying.

As she landed, Montana stumbled forward, but managed to keep her feet. "Well. That's better than last time," she muttered to herself.

With a satisfied smile, she focused on her surroundings.

And realized she was no longer in the brownstone.

Chapter Twenty-one

"Where's Montana?" Ilsa's voice rang across the kitchen.

Quinn glanced up from where he was busy settling Eirene into a mound of blankets on a deep armchair Drake had pulled in from the living room. "What do you mean, where's Montana?"

"She just ported from downstairs. She did a good job of it, too. Where is she?"

The mere idea of Montana porting was startling enough. But why did the women think she'd been successful at it? "She's not here."

Ilsa's jaunty smile fell immediately as Ava rushed over to her. "You saw her into the port?"

"Of course. I told her to picture the kitchen. And then she nodded and disappeared. She knew where she was going, Ava."

"So why the hell isn't she here?" Quinn barreled toward the women, a series of berating words halting on his lips when he caught sight of Ilsa's stark gaze.

"I don't know."

He wanted to yell and rail at them. Needed to blame someone for the situation, but at the bleak look in Ilsa's gaze, he couldn't say another word.

Damn the gods, was he going soft?

"Okay." He caught himself, rubbing a hand over the coarse stubble along his jaw. "Where could she have gone?"

"She knew the kitchen. I told her to picture it. I told her she had to see it in her mind," Ilsa added. "Where else could she have ended up?"

"Her own kitchen?" Eirene offered in a quiet voice.

Quinn turned toward her. "Do you really think so?"

"It would be the only logical explanation. If she was going to accidentally picture somewhere else, wouldn't it be her own home?"

Before anyone could offer another suggestion, Quinn was already into his own port to Montana's.

Montana looked around, surprise warring with a satisfaction she'd managed her way through a second port, albeit accidentally, to her kitchen at work.

"Holy shit on toast," she muttered to herself. She'd always thought the phrase—one of her father's favorites— was an odd one, but somehow it fit. "I actually did it."

Ava's last words reminded her that she hadn't eaten in a while and although she didn't want to alarm Quinn by not showing up in the kitchen, eating something before trying another teleport was probably a good idea.

If only she knew the number to the brownstone. Or Quinn's number.

At the thought of calling him to let him know where she was, Montana realized she did have his number, on a card he'd left her on his first visit. She headed toward her office, thinking she'd grab one of the granola bars she kept stashed in her desk drawer. She'd call him to let him know she was all right and then be on her way.

Damn, but this was the way to travel. Even if it was a bit disorienting.

Just as the entire week had been.

A surge of grief snatched away her sense of happiness and accomplishment. Tears pricked the backs of her eyes as she moved down the plush carpeting toward her office. How could it have been only yesterday she and Jackson had walked down this very hallway?

The sharp, bitter taste of guilt swamped her. He was dead because of her. No matter how many ways she looked at it—no matter how Quinn's reasoned, rational argument that the responsibility lay solely with Arturo—she could not escape the simple fact Jackson was dead because he was a part of her life.

As Montana moved down the hall, the anger coalesced into something else. Something tangible.

Something she could *use*.

If the port was any indication, she really was becoming immortal. With all the abilities and power that came with it. The confusion and fear she'd carried since learning of her fate morphed into newfound understanding and strength. The disquieting uncertainty about the unknown gave way to the gentle calm of purpose.

Something vital and alive beat within her now.

She would have vengeance against Arturo.

The edge of awareness hit her first as Montana rounded the entryway to her office. But the realization she wasn't alone wasn't quite fast enough to stop her forward movement.

"Well, what have we here?"

Arturo Veron stood across the room, his arms crossed in a casual pose as he leaned back against the bank of windows that ran almost the entire width of her office.

Like a camper encountering a dangerous snake, her entire body went stock still as she assessed the threat.

He knew she was there.

But would he strike?

And even more important, could she get out of the line of fire before he did?

"How did you get in here?"

"I can get in lots of places. But"—he pushed himself off the wall and moved a few steps closer to her— "I'm sure you understand that."

"But I've got security. You can't just come and go as you please."

"Actually, sweetheart, I can. The joys of having immortal powers. But you've begun to learn all about that, haven't you?"

"I don't know what you're talking about."

The slap that knocked her across the jaw—quick and brutal—happened so fast Montana didn't even blink. One moment Arturo was halfway across the room, a shitty grin planted across his face and the next he was on top of her, the crack of his hand and the pain shooting through her cheek leaving a loud ringing in her ears.

"I think you know exactly what I'm talking about."

"What do you want with me? You're an immortal. Why bother with me?"

Arturo stared down at her, satisfaction riding high in his gaze. She wanted nothing more than to slap the superior sneer off his face, but didn't dare provoke him until she got some answers.

If she could get what she needed to know—what Quinn needed to know to do battle with Arturo—she might have a prayer of porting herself out of there.

Assuming she didn't screw that up just as she did this one.

"You really don't know?"

"Know what?"

"Gods, you're a dumb piece of goods. I thought so after that first meeting and you've done nothing to change my mind. You, my dear, are the heiress to a fortune made in illegal arms, the slave trade and diamond smuggling."

When she said nothing, Arturo's smile spread like an evil Cheshire cat's. "And you sit there like a princess with no fucking clue."

Montana listened to his words, like icy slaps to her consciousness.

She *did* know.

Or had at least suspected.

And for the last six months, she'd left things as they were, too unwilling to find out the truth. To see her only remaining parent as what he really was— damaged and flawed.

"You've done all this because of my father?"

"Your father's hardly worth my time."

"Then what do you want?"

Whatever Montana expected—whatever she imagined he could possibly say—none of it matched the reality.

"You mean your whore of a mother never told you?"

Icy fingers of fear clawed at her belly at his words. "My mother?"

"Do you know? Can you possibly understand? Do you know that I've slept with any number of women in my life and none—not one—can hold even a molecule of space in my mind. But your mother. She loved me—told me so—and then discarded me as if I were nothing."

The sheer unreality of the last few days coalesced in that moment. "This is about my mother?"

"It's all about your mother. It always has been. When your father was around, you were fucking untouchable. But no longer. Through you, I can have my revenge." Harsh laughter spilled from him as he stared down at her, and with stark clarity, Montana knew she had to get out of there.

No waiting to find out information.

She couldn't even wait to find out what he'd done with the hostages.

She needed to get help, as far away from this madman as possible.

Ilsa's encouraging words rose up in her thoughts. *Think. See. Know.* Refusing to lose another moment, Montana concentrated on the words.

Thinkseeknow.

That oddly comforting tug of gravity pulled at her feet. Pulling at her . . . heavier . . . heavier.

And then nothing as Arturo's arm snaked out and grabbed her by the wrist, pulling her toward him and into his arms.

* * *

"Nothing," Quinn slammed a hand down on the countertop in frustration as he looked at the somber expressions across everyone's faces. "She wasn't there."

"Quinn." Kane's voice broke the quiet. "Something was delivered at Equinox. Grey just called."

"I wasn't gone that long."

"Yeah, but it was long enough." Kane shoved a tablet at him and hit Play on a video already loaded up.

Quinn saw it immediately. Montana's wide-eyed fear as she sat in a chair with Arturo's hand on her shoulder. "What the fuck?"

Kane reached over and pressed the screen, the video coming to life. "Hello, gentlemen. And ladies. I hear there are a few of those now, too."

Arturo laughed at his own joke, before adding, "Lucky for me, Montana doesn't know a fucking thing about porting and landed here in her office by mistake."

Quinn backed away from the smug byplay on the screen, his mind already halfway across town.

"Quinn! Where are you going?" Brody grabbed hold of his forearm.

"To Grant Shipping." He shook off Brody's hand, but the Leo was quicker and grabbed him again, tightening his grip.

"She's not there. I checked the security cameras. As soon as we started the video."

"But I have to go there. The cameras don't mean shit."

Brody wouldn't let up and all Quinn could see— all he could *feel*—were the precious, priceless seconds passing by.

As the bottom fell out of his existence, Quinn was forced to acknowledge the truth.

Arturo had Montana.

"We watched the tape, Quinn. We wound it back and watched it. They're not there. He's taken her. You need to watch the rest of the video and see for yourself."

On a deep, ragged breath, Quinn turned back to the oversized screen and hit Play. Arturo's mocking words began again, and then came the moment he was waiting for.

The demand.

"I think there's no more fitting place to have our little rendezvous than at the place where it all began. The Grant yacht, *Dreamtime*."

"The yacht?"

Quinn couldn't wrap his head around it. Was it the panic, weighing him down like an anchor? Or was it Arturo's depraved ramblings that seemed to say something, yet said nothing at all.

Where it all began? Where *what* began?

"Kane, play it again. Just the end. That jumble in the middle we'll shoot to the security team at Emerald—he doesn't mention anything about Themis or immortality so my staff won't be any wiser. I've already given instructions and they'll know how to handle the hostages. I want to hear the last part again."

Arturo's words floated into the air, filling the kitchen once again.

"I think there's no more fitting place to have our little rendezvous than on the place where it all began. The Grant yacht, Dreamtime."

"Yeah, motherfucker, we get it," Quinn grumbled. "But I still don't get what started there."

"My romance with Jack."

"What?" Quinn whirled around to see Eirene, who stood next to him. Her slender frame wobbled slightly, but she gripped the edge of the counter for balance.

"My first date with Jack. He took me out on the *Dreamtime*. I don't know how Arturo knows that, but it's the only thing that makes sense. My romance with him is what *began* there."

Quinn turned toward the team and saw the faces of his fellow Warriors—his brothers, and now his sisters as well—staring back at him. All ready to do battle.

All prepared to help him save Montana.

"Let's get the weapons we need and we'll leave in fifteen minutes. There's no way he's just letting us board the boat. And no way it'll be easy, so pack well and arm yourselves to the teeth."

"I'm going with you." Eirene's voice was quiet and oh so tired, but firm with purpose.

Quinn reached for her arm to lead her back to the chair, but she pulled it away. The movement clearly cost her a lot, by the sharp intake of breath, but she stood her ground.

"Eirene, come on. You need to stay here and rest."

"She is my daughter. You can't expect me to stay here and wait here while you try to save her."

"But I can't take you into this. Arturo has something planned. He's not going to make this easy."

"Then it will be hard." The blue of her gaze, so like Montana's, bore into his own.

So like the woman he *loved*.

Oh gods, was it really that easy? He loved Montana. Such a simple concept when it was with the right person.

So all consuming.

So life affirming.

So *real*.

And as he looked into the eyes so reminiscent of the woman he loved, he knew he couldn't deny her anything.

"I've nothing left, Quinn. Nothing left to give her but myself. I am the reason this started. I'm the reason she's trapped with a madman. I will see this through."

Quinn nodded and stretched out his hand to her. "All right. We'll see this through together."

Montana opened her eyes to darkness. She lay on her side, and despite a stiff ache that gripped her entire body, she offered a silent prayer of thanks she wasn't bound. From what she could tell, she was on some sort of makeshift bed—a cot, most likely, from the feel of it. She couldn't see a thing, but she could hear water in the background.

Water?

Were they still in New York? Or had Arturo taken her somewhere else?

How long had she been out?

And did she even have enough energy to port?

She hoped.

"I heard you stirring." Lights slammed on and Montana immediately closed her eyes against the stark, almost painful shot to her eyes.

"Where are we?"

"You certainly are impatient for death, aren't you? Must be all those motherless years. Makes you feel worthless and meaningless. Sort of how you felt when I took care of your friends, eh?"

Montana fought down a wave of nausea as his eyes filled with an odd, manic glee at the taunt.

Don't show a reaction. Don't show a reaction. Don't show . . .

The cot tilted wildly as Arturo grabbed her by the forearm and dragged her to her feet. Montana stumbled forward, off balance from the stiffness that still suffused her body.

"They were cowards, you know. Jackson sniveled for his life, the little loser."

Montana stood to her full height and looked him in the eye. She couldn't change what had happened, but she could defend Jackson's memory. "No, he didn't. I saw it. Every bit of it. He was smart enough to get you on the house video cameras. You and your bull."

Arturo's dark gaze went wide at her words and Montana felt a momentary shot of victory until he shoved her away. The ground rushed up to meet her and she landed in an awkward heap on her left side.

Staring up at him, she felt her newfound strength pumping through her veins. Strength and an absolute certainty that she would find a way out of this.

She was a rising immortal and she was a woman in love. And she'd be damned if she was going to give it all up without a fight.

Quinn would find her. And in the meantime, it was time to do a little damage to Arturo Veron.

"You think you're so clever. Well, you're not. You're a fucking waste of skin and my mother was right to leave you. To get away from you."

"You dare speak of the whore?"

Montana shifted, struggling to a sitting position. There was no way she'd lie at his feet like some defeated opponent. Arturo was nearly on her—his fist lifted in threat—when a loud clapping noise rose up from across the room.

"Nice try, asshole. You beat up women, too? Well, doesn't that just add to your list of desirable qualities?"

Montana's gaze never left Arturo's, but she saw a look of fear skitter across his features before he turned toward the open door.

"This doesn't involve you. I told you to meet me at the boat."

The taller of the two stepped forward. She was long and lean, and clothed in a Chanel suit Montana recognized from this year's collection. "Actually, it does involve me."

Who were these women?

Montana couldn't help but stare at them as they moved across the room. Both looked like models . . . with murder on their minds.

There was no doubt they were sisters, but where the one in Chanel had a sexy, worldly vibe, the other one, clad head to toe in leather, looked like a serious ass kicker.

The woman in Chanel moved forward, her gaze speculative as it roamed over Arturo's body. She laid one long finger against the black T-shirt he now wore, her bloodred fingernail pressed against his heart. "You've been especially naughty, Arturo. Normally, that's a trait I admire in my men, but you've lied to me, and, oh yeah"—the woman moved up into his personal space—"you've stolen my Destroyers for your own use. Don't think I didn't notice."

"Enyo. We had a deal. We made it just this morning."

"Oh, I have no problem keeping my end of the bargain. You know as well as the next person I have no love for Themis's boys. But if you think you're running the show, guess again. We head to the *Dreamtime* when I say we do."

At that, a needle-sharp prick of awareness speared through her. The *Dreamtime*? The Grant yacht? That's where they were taking her?

Arturo's voice wavered between anger and clear touches of madness. "You bitch! This is mine. I've waited too long to have my revenge and you don't get a say in it."

"Actually, I do." Before Arturo could reply, a long stream of blue fire lit up the air around them. Montana stood still as visible sparks shot from the woman's fingertip into Arturo's chest.

The man's body jerked from what had to be a jolt of electricity that would kill a human. Montana watched in increasing horror as Enyo kept up the current, slowly driving the asshole to his knees.

Although her curiosity ran high to understand what was happening, Montana knew she needed to get out of there.

Whatever was going on, she didn't want any part of.

And she needed to get to Quinn.

Think. See. Know.

The air around her seemed to wiggle, like the heat rising off of asphalt on a hot day.

Damn it, Montana. Focus!

Thinkseeknow. Thinkseeknow. Thinkseeknow.

The light tugs of gravity at her feet grew stronger. Drowning out her surroundings—the warehouse, the immortal fight taking place before her, the threat to her general well-being—Montana put everything she had into focusing on her port out of there.

Thinkseeknow.

The heavy pull of gravity suffused her body in thick, lapping waves and then it morphed into a fast weightlessness that set her free.

The room disappeared, but just as the image of Enyo standing over Arturo faded from view, Montana felt long, slender fingers wrap around her ankle.

Chapter Twenty-two

Quinn mowed through the plate of lasagna Callie had pressed on him as he listened to Drake's reconnaissance report. He knew he needed the strength the food provided, but the thick noodles and rich cheese tasted about as delectable as day-old socks.

He needed to get to Montana.

Every second away from her was agony.

And no matter how many times his brothers assured him he needed to act with as much knowledge as they could gather, it galled him to remain inactive.

Their Pisces had spent the last twenty minutes in the harbor around the *Dreamtime*, getting the lay of the land. Between his superior swim skills and the protective bubble that surrounded him whenever he was submerged in water, Drake was best suited for the job.

Add in the fact the Pisces had spent a great deal of time in the Florida Keys and knew the location of the boat dock for an immediate port in and they had the perfect person for reconnaissance.

"What do you have?" Quinn barked the question as soon as Drake materialized in the kitchen, still dripping onto the floor. "Does he have Montana there?"

"I didn't see Montana and I didn't hear anything to suggest Arturo was onboard. I did defuse the explosives he's got rigged under the boat, but I couldn't get on the ship. There are a horde of Destroyers walking the decks and no doubt a shitload of security cameras to boot."

"And the hostages?" Quinn barked the order.

"All accounted for. I already gave your lead man in the Keys a heads-up and the team's going after them now."

"Does Arturo actually think we're just going to appear onboard?" Rogan snorted as he took the last bite on his own plate.

"We don't have a choice and he knows it." Quinn slammed his empty plate on the table. "How are we going in?"

"There's a string of warehouses along the docks. It's the same place he's had the hostages and they're being cleared out now so we don't have to risk any collateral damage. I'll port a few of you there so you have visuals, then everybody comes back with a buddy. We'll head in from there."

The time for planning was over. They had secured their weapons and everyone had eaten as much food as Callie could put in front of them. "Let's go."

"Quinn. I'm ready to leave when you are." Eirene's quiet voice penetrated the tense atmosphere from across the room. Indecision still warred within him. Quinn respected the woman's desire to be a part of the rescue effort, but he didn't want to take her into the battle and he didn't want her slowing them down. They'd already lost precious hours as it was.

She'd fallen asleep a short while ago and he'd hoped they'd be able to depart unnoticed.

"Eirene—"

"Young man, I am not having this discussion with you again." The thin sound of her voice strengthened with each word, her determination unmistakable. "I know I'm weak and I know I'm a liability. Leave me behind there if you need to get Montana out, but you are taking me with you."

Brody and Kane hid twin guffaws behind heavy coughs and the rest of the room suddenly found other things to do as Eirene continued her castigations. "This is it for me, Quinn. Arturo has set this all up because of me and I'm going to see it through."

He nodded. He wasn't going to win this argument and, in a rare moment of remorse, he had to acknowledge it wasn't fair of him to try to leave her behind. "Of course, goddess."

Eirene walked across the room, her gaze clearer than he'd seen it all day. Whether it was a burst of strength or simply determination and renewed purpose, Quinn didn't know.

As she reached his side, she laid a hand on his forearm. "Let's go kick Arturo Veron's slimy ass."

A round of shouts went up around the kitchen. Quinn lifted Eirene in his arms and moved to stand next to Drake. The shouts echoed in his ears as the three of them ported from the brownstone.

"What the hell?" Montana kicked her legs, but the tight grip on her ankle wouldn't lessen. "Get off me!"

"Where do you think you're going?"

"Who are you?"

"You don't need to know who I am or anything else."

"Yeah. That's a comforting answer." Montana gathered herself and then shook her leg, finally dislodging her ankle from the woman's hands.

The sister—the shit kicker, as Montana had come to think of her—had grabbed her ankle just as she ported out of the warehouse.

With a quick look around to ensure she was where she had intended, Montana saw the comforting lines of a hard teak countertop in the yacht's library-slash-bar.

Backing away, Montana knew she couldn't outrun the woman, nor could she go head-to-head in any sort of immortal battle, so her best bet was to forage for food and increase her strength. With slow movements, Montana inched her way toward the bar, casually flicking her eyes at the dish of bar nuts that sat perpetually full on top.

Thank God for regular cleaning service and the yacht's active role in entertaining clients. She'd been here only a few weeks prior and things were still in good order.

And food was out on the counter.

Arm extended, Montana reached for a handful of nuts, idly tossing a few in her mouth in a casual gesture. "Who are you? And was that woman Enyo?"

"You don't need to know anything."

"Actually, I think I do. Especially seeing as how you all look at me with the barely repressed urge to kill me. I at least have a right to know who I'm dealing with."

Shit Kicker shrugged her shoulders and took a seat

on the couch. Although her pose looked casual, Montana had no doubt the woman could move faster than a cobra.

And she looked about as mean to boot.

"I'm Eris. And yes, that woman giving Arturo a good ass kicking is my sister, Enyo."

Montana made a big production of waving a hand, even as she reached for another handful of nuts. "You'll have to forgive me, but I'm a bit rusty on my Greek mythology. I know she's the goddess of war, but that makes you who?"

"The goddess of strife and discord is my official title."

"And your unofficial title?" *Miserable bitch* crossed Montana's mind, but she kept the jibe to herself.

"Eris works just fine."

Montana saw her hesitation for the briefest of moments—really, if she hadn't been concentrating so hard, she wouldn't have even noticed it. But there was something in the gray depths of the woman's gaze that Montana recognized.

Feelings of inadequacy and discontent with life had a way of doing that to a person. Although Montana couldn't ignore the fact the woman who stood before her personified those traits, she acknowledged those two feelings seemed to have fully disappeared from her own life.

Because of Quinn, a small voice whispered in her ear. Even the thought of his name filled her with joy and she knew it was true. Quinn Tanner had showed her what she was missing and forced her to look at her life—and herself—in a completely different way.

So what was up with Eris?

"Let me guess. You hate your job and you're sick of being stuck in middle management. The boss doesn't appreciate you and you haven't had a date in a year."

Okay, maybe she needed to dial it back a bit. Riling this woman up was not the way to make things easier on herself.

So why was it working?

A small smile ghosted Eris's lips and the look was oddly transformative. She was almost . . . pretty?

"You've got style, heiress. I'll give you that."

"Thank you. I think." Montana grabbed another handful of nuts, even choking down the walnuts she hated in hopes of getting as much fuel in as possible. "So really. How'd you get involved in all this? I've heard your sister's name but not yours. How'd this become your problem?"

"I've been bored and I needed something to do. Enyo mentioned the Warriors and I got interested."

"Lucky me. And why do the Warriors interest you?"

"No reason in particular."

Montana heard the lie from a million miles away, but decided to hold on to that line of questioning. "So what does Enyo want with me?"

Eris leaned toward her, several long locks of hair falling forward. The woman really was pretty. If she'd ease up on the dominatrix look, she might actually be *really* pretty. "Look. Enyo couldn't give a shit about you other than the fact that screwing with you pisses off Themis. She wants the Warriors. But she also wants to fuck that little shit Arturo over. You're just caught in the middle."

"And you and Enyo want to help us?"

"I wouldn't go quite that far."

As answers went, it wasn't a comforting response, but it was something.

If she could only get out of there and warn Quinn and the others. If they could regroup and find a way to have this battle on their terms instead of whatever Arturo had already orchestrated, the situation might not seem so bleak.

Might not *feel* so stacked against them.

Did she have enough energy to port again? Montana tossed a quick glance at the bar nuts and realized she'd polished off about half of them.

Was that enough protein to boost her strength? Enough to complete another port?

She'd managed the trip here, but that whole shimmering thing at the beginning wasn't very helpful. And it was probably the reason Eris had known she was about to escape.

Before Montana could finish weighing the pros and cons, another thought tripped past the others. What if Quinn was already on the boat? She couldn't leave him here to fend for himself.

And she had no doubt Arturo had already given her Warrior the address for the final showdown. If there was anything she knew from Arturo's scheming, it was that this had been building for far longer than any of them knew and the ex-Warrior was ready to close the deal.

Montana avoided looking at the nuts again, even as she prayed the fuel had done its job. With sharp focus, she remembered Ilsa and Ava's instructions and . . .

Didn't even attempt to move as Eris slammed her hand forward, gripping Montana's wrist.

"Look, heiress. You might have a poker face in

business, but I've seen you eyeing the door and scarfing those nuts for the last five minutes. You're not getting out of here, so you may as well sit down for a while. Besides, Arturo planted a horde of Destroyers up on the decks. I know my sister has a fondness for them, but they creep the shit out of me, so I, for one, would rather stay here until your cavalry arrives."

Montana could only stare and wonder why the lack of poker face comment was so insulting. She had a damn good poker face.

Black Jack Grant had made sure of it.

So put it to your advantage, Grant.

If she couldn't get herself above deck, maybe it was time to do a little digging of her own. This woman had secrets. She'd bet her life on it.

Eris continued, obviously unaware of the poker face insult as she dragged Montana over to the couch. "This little showdown's been a long time in the making, so sit back and relax. Your boyfriend will be here before you know it."

"Why are you bored? Nothing at home keeping you busy?"

Eris shrugged, but her stare went a hard, gunmetal gray.

Direct hit.

"I wouldn't say that."

"I mean, it must be hard. Humans seem to have no problem doing strife and discord all by themselves these days. Not much for a girl to do in that situation."

And then Montana went in for the kill.

"You have a husband? Kids?" It was the question she hated above all others, so she projected every single ounce of pity into it as she could.

Eris's back was stiff against the couch cushions. "I'm not married."

"Oh, well, that's okay. Boyfriend?"

"No."

Ooh, this just got better and better. "Shame. But it must be hard in your line of work. Hard to find time to date. Or a man who's willing to put up with your professional life."

"I do okay."

"Oh sure. Sure." Montana pushed even more sympathy into her tone. "Is the dating scene on Mount Olympus decent?"

"What do you care?" Eris squirmed on the couch, but her grip never wavered. "You're seeing one of the Warriors, aren't you? Quinn? That's what Arturo said."

"What does he know? The Taurus has been my shadow, but that doesn't mean I'm interested." The lies tripped off her tongue and even as she knew why she said them, Montana couldn't help but feel the words burn.

She loved Quinn. Loved him with everything she was and everything she would ever be.

And she might never see him again.

Even if the lies saved her, the words hurt.

"Besides, they're all some serious eye candy. I can't believe they've been around so long and so few of them have been snatched up. It's a travesty, actually."

"They are fine-looking men," Eris admitted.

Finally! Montana nearly pumped her fist in excitement. Something other than ass kicking lay under the surface with this one. "Which one is your favorite?"

"No one in particular."

"If you say so." Before Montana could say anything else, the entire boat rocked as if they'd hit a huge swell. Eris dropped her wrist as both of them were thrown to opposite edges of the couch.

Since she knew they were docked in port, that could only mean the cavalry had well and truly arrived.

Quinn.

Screams erupted above deck and Montana stared at the ceiling of the room, hope slamming through her in lockstep with abject fear for Quinn.

Unable to bear another moment wondering about him, Montana launched herself into a port. She knew this boat better than anyone on it. It was time to put the knowledge to good use.

As the rush of air took her, she heard a long string of curses from across the room.

Quinn slammed his elbow into the windpipe of the closest Destroyer and tried to assess the space in the center of the deck. Although the yacht was large, there was a literal horde of Destroyers on deck.

Where the fuck was Montana?

Quinn swung his arm, sword fully extended, toward the shoulder of his current opponent. Although it wasn't a death blow, it should damn well slow his fire. The guy had lasered a series of fireballs at Quinn's chest and he was now gritting his teeth through the pain and the heat. It was about fucking time the asshole got a little something-something in return.

Pulling back his arm Quinn thrust his blade, allowing his opponent had no time to regroup. No time to sidestep the blow. The sword removed the Destroyer's head in one clean swipe and a loud sucking noise followed the movements of Quinn's sword.

Score.

He glanced quickly down the line, where each of his brothers—as well as Ilsa, Callie and Ava—all fought their own opponents.

But no Montana.

And no sign of Arturo.

Refocusing, Quinn parried a rogue fireball with his sword, then shifted on the balls of his feet to lend Drake a hand. The Destroyer he battled had given up all pretense of throwing electricity and instead had gone for the body, grabbing Drake in a headlock.

Quinn lifted his blade arm and slashed downward, again going for the beefiest part of the guy's shoulder.

If he'd learned anything over the years it was that in their human form they felt enough pain that battle wounds slowed them down and messed with their focus.

Amidst the screams and shouting, the battle cries and the loud, crackling electricity flying around the ship's deck, Quinn's fear grew. He channeled it into combat, but he couldn't stop the frustration and anger from roaring through his mind in equal measure.

Where was she?

And when would the real battle with Arturo begin?

Montana held her ground in the small alcove off the deck. She shifted from foot to foot in impatience and an odd eagerness to see this through.

She *wanted* to be out there—desperately wanted to help them—but she knew she had to hold back. She wasn't an immortal yet and she didn't have an effective weapon.

There was no way she could do anything but slow the others down as they battled the Destroyer threat out there.

What she did have on her side was the element of surprise. Arturo and Enyo weren't going to know what hit them—literally. Tearing her gaze from where Quinn fought next to Drake, she glanced down at the lethal Sig Sauer that her father had kept locked on the yacht.

Yet again, Montana had to give Black Jack credit. He might have been a lousy father for all the day-to-day stuff, but he'd ensured she knew how to handle a weapon.

And the cool piece in her hand was going a long way toward reassuring her she could survive this.

Of course, it wasn't likely to do much permanent damage against an immortal.

So where were Enyo and Arturo?

And where was Eris? Even if she had to run up from below deck, she should be here by now.

One by one, Quinn and his mates leveled the deck until all that remained were a series of greasy spots. As the last Destroyer fell, a shout went up through the group.

Joy filled her at their victorious faces and Montana couldn't help but revel in their victory. As her hand reached for the door to push it open, it slammed outward on its hinges.

Before she could lift the weapon or get off a shot, Arturo had her in his grip and sent them both whirling into a port.

Chapter Twenty-three

The air whirled around her, shimmering like an eerie, ethereal mist as the gun in her hand clattered to the floor and slid away.

Where were they?

She could see the deck—with everyone on it—but it was like she stood in a pool of water behind glass and couldn't reach any of them.

What was this?

She became aware of Arturo's clench on her shoulder, his fingers digging into her collarbone, and she registered pain.

Arturo's voice boomed next to her ear. "Drop the weapons."

The sound of her weapon hitting the ground caused Quinn to whirl in their direction, confusion riding his features like a mask before he spun back in the direction he'd been facing.

Couldn't he see them?

"Quinn!" Montana couldn't stop the shout, even as Arturo's fingers dug deeper into her shoulder.

Arturo's voice was as menacing as his grip. "I've got your woman and there's a knife pointed right at her. So I suggest you do as I say."

Quinn faced them again and acid burned through her chest at the confusion and panic she saw in his eyes.

Was it really possible he couldn't see them?

His name was on her lips again, breath filling her lungs to cry out when a sharp pressure registered in her desperation to get to Quinn. Glancing down through the filmy mist, Montana saw the long, sharp knife that pressed to her side.

She'd seen matching weapons on Quinn and his brothers. And she'd read about them in the texts Quinn had given her about Themis and Zeus.

Arturo had a Xiphos pressed against her rib cage. The weapon might have been millennia old, but it was so razor sharp it could have been forged yesterday.

Terror filled her as Montana admitted the raw, aching truth to herself.

She was still a mortal.

And Arturo had her right where he wanted her.

What was going on?

Icy sweat ran down his back as Quinn fought to get his bearings.

He knew Arturo was there with them. Heard the man's voice and Montana's cries.

So where *were* they?

Drake made a motion from across the deck, catching Quinn's eye. The Pisces mouthed the word "invisible," even as Quinn shook it off like a pitcher throwing off his catcher.

Before Drake could do anything else, Ilsa grabbed

a pillow from the couches that ran the perimeter of the boat and slid it across the deck.

The pillow's forward motion stopped, as if by some invisible force.

But how was it even *possible*?

Quinn ran through the various gifts from the goddess. Invisibility wasn't on the list—never had been—and he knew no Warrior who could do that.

Had Arturo traded up when he defected from the Warriors? Or did he know something the rest of them didn't?

"You've been a sniveling coward all along. Show yourself if you want to prove you've still got the goods." Although he fought to hang on to a sense of calm so he could assess the threat, all he could imagine was Montana in the grip of that monster.

"This is between you and me, Arturo. Show yourself and let us end this as the true Warriors we are."

Arturo's voice quavered around the edges, but his words rang out across the ship's deck. "She will pay. She will pay for the sins of her mother."

"She's done nothing."

"She exists! That is enough." Arturo's voice shook harder and Quinn caught the slightest shimmer of a mirage about twenty feet away.

Gotcha!

Deep down, Quinn sensed all he needed to do was keep the man talking. They were all tired—each of them had ported several times—and the shit wore you down. Whatever skill Arturo possessed to make himself invisible, Quinn also knew the immutable laws of their bodies couldn't be breached.

Depletion of energy weakened powers and the asshole was running on empty.

If he could wear him down, he could get a real read on Arturo's position.

Quinn caught movement from the corner of his eye. The rest of the Warriors moved up behind him, a phalanx of support fanning out across the deck.

"I've done some checking up on you, you know. You might have been chosen by Themis, but you're a bit of a fuckup, aren't you?"

Quinn had to hand it to Rogan. Although the archer hadn't caught Arturo the first go-round, he'd made up for it in record time. Rogan had spent the morning hitting up his contacts and going through the Warriors' archives. They had some gaps in their knowledge, but Quinn had enough of what he needed to keep the traitor off guard and talking.

"I'm not a sniveling servant like the rest of you. Themis thought she could control me. Own me!" The air shimmered again and Quinn could just make out the silhouette of two bodies.

His heart clenched as he took in the subtle curve of Montana's cheek before her image winked out again as Arturo got himself under control.

"So you thought you'd make a little gigolo of yourself on Mount Olympus. And a mercenary for the gods, to boot. Which clearly worked out so well, seeing as how you kept fucking every skirt—including client's wives—instead of doing your job."

A sloppy laugh floated into the ether. "Can I help it if I'm irresistible?"

Quinn ignored the rank irritation of the laugh and

went in for the kill. "Until you found the one woman who didn't think you were irresistible. Right?"

"What would you know of that?"

Fucking direct hit.

The air shimmered for the briefest of moments and then Montana and Arturo filled out before him.

Everyone leaped to attention immediately. Quinn ported for Montana, dragging her out of Arturo's grasp just as his brothers leaped on top of the fallen Taurus.

Quinn dragged her away, desperate for the feel of her in his arms.

"Oh gods, are you okay?" He pressed his face into her hair and breathed deeply. His heart pounded so hard he shook and all Quinn could do was hang on to her.

"I'm fine, Quinn. I promise you, I'm fine."

Pulling his head back, he ran his hands over her frame. "Did he hurt you? I will fucking kill him if he hurt you."

"I'm not hurt. I'm not."

Quinn bent his head to press his lips against hers. Soon the grunts and groans mere feet away from them faded into nothingness as he reassured himself of the woman in his arms. Montana kissed him back in kind, the press of her lips firm against his. Reassuring. Life affirming.

"Oh gods, I thought—"

Quinn broke off as a stab of pain shot across his back and down his spine. Montana screamed as he twisted in agony and without warning, Quinn felt his knees give way as he fell to floor.

"Sorry to interrupt your little reunion, but we're far from done here."

Quinn struggled to his knees, unwilling to fall before anyone. Unwilling to leave the woman he loved without protection. "Look what the cat drag—" He broke off as he saw what Enyo had in her grip.

"Mom!" Montana screamed as Enyo pulled Eirene forward like a rag doll.

"The bull dragged me, actually." Enyo flicked a glance to where Arturo struggled in the twin grips of Drake and Kane. "And look at what I found as I searched around the boat."

Quinn struggled to his feet, ignoring the flames that licked every part of his body. He had to get Eirene out of Enyo's grasp, but he had to keep Montana safe. "You're behind this?"

"Sadly, not all of it. Lucky for me, I know how to improvise."

"You bitch!" Arturo screamed from where the guys held him. "This is mine! My revenge. Mine!"

"Oh for fuck's sake, Arturo. I told you you could have Eirene."

"Mom?" Montana's voice trembled behind him, where he shielded her with his body.

"Get her out of here, Quinn," Eirene pleaded.

"We won't leave you."

Enyo pulled Eirene closer and laid a finger against her neck. One bloodred fingernail stood out in sharp relief against the thin skin of Eirene's frail body. "No, you won't."

Sorrow filled Montana and she winced as Enyo dragged her mother forward.

Had it really come to this?

Enyo's gaze never wavered off of Quinn. "Let go of Arturo. Now."

She trusted Quinn implicitly, but would he comply with this? Could he?

Quinn took one of her hands in his and squeezed, before turning his full focus on the avenging goddess. "You made a bad deal on this one, Enyo. Since when do you get yourself involved in Warrior politics?"

"Since it benefits me."

"The traitor would betray you as fast as he did us. The moment you turn you back."

"He actually did that already. However, it's lucky for him I like all of you a lot less than I do him. So let him go. *Now*. Oh, and be good boys and give him his weapon back, too."

"Kane. Drake. You heard the bitch. Let him go."

Montana took in Quinn's words. No matter what happened—no matter the outcome—she would be forever grateful Quinn put her mother first.

And in doing so, he put her first.

"Thank you," she whispered.

Quinn squeezed her hand again, but before she could squeeze it back, a loud, piercing scream rent the air as Arturo leaped forward.

A war cry echoed off his lips and before Montana could move, Arturo landed on top of her.

The bull that rode high on his shoulder sprang to life and Quinn shifted on his heel to give the animal its head. Man and beast leaped toward the threat, pulling back at the very last moment.

Throwing himself to the side, Quinn tumbled into

a heap on top of Brody, to keep from landing on top of Arturo and Montana.

A Xiphos rose in the air, lethal despite the trembling hand that held it, as Arturo stared mindlessly at Montana, his murderous intent clear.

Before Quinn could move—before any of them could get closer—Eirene screamed. With a strength born of desperation, Eirene threw herself against Arturo, the Xiphos piercing her heart.

Great white light suffused their surroundings and a shrill ethereal scream pierced the air. Without care for whatever else was to come, Quinn leaped forward, his own Xiphos extended to slash at Arturo's throat.

The traitor fell immediately; Eirene's weight, coupled with the slash to his neck, dropped him to the deck floor.

Quinn was on the move immediately, intent on dragging Eirene off of Arturo when a warm hand pressed against his shoulder.

Themis.

She stood before them, taking immediate control of the situation.

"Well, just in time. Look who shows up right on cue." Enyo mocked the goddess, but Quinn saw the edge of fear that tinged her gaze.

Themis took it all in stride. "And look who's made yet another bad choice in whom to ally herself with."

"Your days are numbered, Themis. Arturo told me all about his defection. How little control you really have and how easy it was for him to leave you." Enyo took a few steps back, even while her words dripped with vitriolic acid. "Your power is waning, old woman. And your Warriors will turn against you, one by one."

"Just as your Destroyers have? Your supposed minions to whom you gave no choice?"

"They belong to me."

Quinn watched on in amazement as Themis maintained her composure. "And that is the great difference between you and I. I do give my Warriors choice. It is their greatest gift."

"Enyo!" A woman appeared on the far side of the deck along with Rogan. She raced forward and only as she got nearer did Quinn notice the resemblance. "What have you done?"

"I did as I promised."

"You weren't supposed to kill her. Not Eirene."

"You weren't here and I needed to improvise. She simply got in the way." Enyo shifted her gaze, effectively ignoring her sister and anything else she might have to say. "Your days are numbered, Themis. Just wait."

Enyo shifted into a port, reaching for her sister as she disappeared.

"Mother!" Montana skirted around him to run to her mother. Tears streamed down her face as she reached for the woman. Before she could fully pull her into her arms, Themis laid a hand on her back.

"Please, Montana. Allow me."

With gentle movements, Themis lifted her daughter and walked her body over to a line of couches that surrounded the deck. Gently laying Eirene down, Themis knelt before the body as tears flowed freely down her cheeks.

"Oh, my daughter, what have I done?" The goddess leaned forward and pressed her forehead to Eirene's. "What have I done?"

Eirene's lips moved, air trickling through them in a whisper. "Mother."

"Yes, my darling child. I am here."

With stiff movements, Eirene extended her hand toward Montana. She raced forward and reached for her mother's hand. "Why did you do that?"

"I've failed you all my life, Daughter. But no longer. You shall live. And you shall love."

Montana leaned forward and pressed her lips to her mother's forehead, her shoulders shaking with grief as Eirene's grip slackened in her hand.

Quinn moved up beside Montana and reached for her as the rest of his family gathered around behind them.

"Goddess. Can we help you?"

Themis lifted her head and turned her tear-streaked face to his. "Nay, Warrior, you cannot. Only I must bear the knowledge I turned my daughter away out of my own stubborn, unrelenting pride."

Quinn swallowed around a lump in his throat, Themis's words cutting so close to his own image of himself, he could barely stand upright. Kneeling beside her, Quinn leaned forward to lay his hand over Themis's. "I know of stubborn pride, goddess. Let me help you."

When Themis turned toward Quinn, her blue eyes looked like enormous jewels. "Choices, Quinn. It is always about choice. You made a choice once, but when it mattered, you came through, last year on the cave in Mount Ida. Now you must make the choice to forgive yourself."

"But how?"

"Embrace what you have been given. Protect this woman with your life and love her fiercely. Care for her and allow her to care for you. Do the same for your Warrior brothers and sisters."

"And what of Montana? Must she rise to replace Eirene as the Horae?"

At that, Themis stood and moved to her granddaughter. Both women wept openly for Eirene, but Montana stood taller as her grandmother approached.

"Montana. My dear, sweet child. I cursed you before I knew you. Bestowed it upon you before you ever had a chance to live. You, too, have a choice. There is a position for you with the immortals, but only if you choose. I won't take that gift from you."

Montana's gaze drifted to where Eirene's body lay on the couch, then moved back to Themis. A smile broke through the tears, bright and oh so luminous.

"I accept my inheritance and my destiny, Grand-mother. I accept it proudly. For you. For me. And most of all, for my mother."

Quinn's heart filled with love and pride, joy and excitement as Themis extended her arms and pulled Montana into them. "You continue to make her proud, just as you always have."

At those words, Montana pulled back, shock and a lifetime of questions stamped across her face in equal measure. Before she could say anything, Themis nod-ded as her own smile graced her features. "Aye. She was always there. She always watched over you. Loved you." Themis pressed a kiss to Montana's forehead. "Always."

Stepping back, she led Montana to Quinn and joined

their hands together. "Choice is a gift. I will never take it away from another. You have my vow."

She then crossed the deck of the yacht to lift her daughter's body into her arms. "She will have a proper burial on Mount Olympus."

And with that, Themis and Eirene disappeared.

Turning, Quinn pulled Montana into his arms. "I love you. With everything I am, I love you. When you were mortal, now that you're immortal, none of it matters. All that matters is you."

"I love you, too, Quinn. And you know what this means?"

"What, my love?"

Montana smiled as she pressed her lips to his. "You're stuck with me for the rest of days."

Quinn wrapped her up in his arms. As he looked her—the woman he chose—he then shifted his gaze to his assembled Warriors. "I choose you, Montana. Just as I choose my brothers and sisters. Always."

Montana whispered against his lips. "Always."

Epilogue

Montana stood before the press of news cameras in the Grant publicity room and leaned into the microphone. "Thank you for coming." The room quieted immediately as another round of flashes erupted through the assembly.

"Corporate responsibility is our greatest requirement as a global organization. It is with great regret and deep sorrow that I stand before you and share with you that the Grant Shipping organization has not acted with responsibility or accountability for many, many years."

A loud murmur ran through the room like a flash of wildfire, but Montana held up a hand for quiet. Her gaze shifted to Quinn as she did so and she took immeasurable comfort just in his presence. The quick wink he gave her bolstered her up and she took a deep breath before continuing.

"I have begun a full investigation across all areas of the company and I am committed to corrective action for every wrong that's been committed in the forty-year history of Grant Shipping. I begin with one of the most egregious errors—our treatment of the peoples along the coast of Africa."

Hands raised, but Montana ignored them, unwilling to answer any questions until she completed her task. "We have regrettably been a part of contributing to the pain and suffering of these people and effective immediately, each port berth owned by Grant Shipping will become a resource for food, water, medicine and whatever else is needed to aid these ravaged peoples. And this is only the beginning."

Montana finished outlining her plan to repair and rebuild all areas where Grant Shipping had committed atrocities and then took questions.

As she stared out at the sea of faces, clearly anxious to ask the most damning questions she'd ever encountered, Montana felt the weight of her existence lift from her shoulders.

She was in control of her company, her life and her destiny. And now that she had made the most important choice of her life, the rest seemed so easy. Simple.

As her gaze once again drifted to Quinn, she couldn't keep the words from rising to her lips. Couldn't stop herself from mouthing the words *I love you*.

And in the end, that was the only choice that really mattered.

CAPRICORN/TAURUS STAR CHART

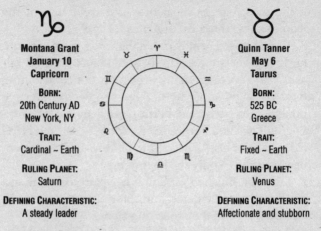

♑

Montana Grant
January 10
Capricorn

BORN:
20th Century AD
New York, NY

TRAIT:
Cardinal ~ Earth

RULING PLANET:
Saturn

DEFINING CHARACTERISTIC:
A steady leader

♉

Quinn Tanner
May 6
Taurus

BORN:
525 BC
Greece

TRAIT:
Fixed ~ Earth

RULING PLANET:
Venus

DEFINING CHARACTERISTIC:
Affectionate and stubborn

The magnetic pull of Taurus to Capricorn offers a sensual feast for the two lovers lucky enough to find each other.

While the Capricorn woman often has to break through the stubborn pride of her Taurus mate, his sensible, focused need to protect will guarantee he keeps her safe and secure.

Taurus is a mate for life, seeking a woman who will love him for the long haul. The same stubborn nature that makes him hard to live with at times, also makes him a life-long partner who will love his mate through thick and thin.

Once they can overcome their own natures—his stubborn one and her focused one—to trust in love, Quinn and Montana will have a lifetime of warm, devoted passion to sustain them. Natural leaders, their magnetic personalities and devotion to each other will ensure a prosperous—and happy—marriage of equals.

GLOSSARY

Ages of Man—the stages of human existence, as identified by the Greek writer Hesiod. Most often associated with metals, the Ages—Gold, Silver, Bronze, Heroic and Iron, reflect the increasing toil and drudgery humans live in. The world only thinks the ages are myth. . . .

Cardinal—a sign *quality*, Cardinal signs (Aries, Cancer, Libra, Capricorn) mark the start of each season. Those born under Cardinal signs are considered dynamic and, like each season, forceful in its beginnings. Cardinal Warriors are equally dynamic, forcing change with their impatient natures and independent spirits.

Chimera—with the body and head of a lion, the tail of a snake and the head of a goat extending from the center of its back, the chimera is one of the eleven monsters of Mount Olympus. Created by the goddess Echidna—the Mother of all Monsters—her menagerie is a favorite resource of terror for Deimos and Phobos.

Corybants—legendary male dancers, clothed in armor and playing drums. Their loud, rhythmic playing was said to drown out the cries of the baby Zeus so he wouldn't be discovered in his hiding place on Mount Ida.

Deimos—the son of Ares and Aphrodite, he is the god of dread. He is the brother of Phobos.

Destroyer—a soulless creature created by Enyo from an emotionally damaged human. They take on the appearance of men, but their bodies are nothing but husks, filled with a superconductive life force. They can be slowed and hurt, but quickly recover. The only way to kill a Destroyer is by removing his head. Each Destroyer Enyo creates takes some of her power, an innate balance agreed to during the creation of the Great Agreement.

Element—just as all signs are Cardinal, Fixed or Mutable, each sign also possesses an elemental quality of Fire, Earth, Air or Water. Each Warrior has an elemental nature to his sign, allowing for additional powers for those who have learned to develop them. These elemental qualities exist beyond those granted to all Warriors—immortality, the ability to port, rapid healing and above-average strength—and have begun to express themselves as the Warriors have grown more comfortable in their abilities and better understand the full range of their skills.

Enyo—the goddess of war, Enyo is the daughter of Zeus and Hera. Equipped with the ability to create anarchy and death wherever she goes, she was offered up to Themis by Zeus for their Great Agreement. Before

Zeus allowed Themis to create the Sons of the Zodiac, she had to agree to a counterbalance to the Warriors' power. Enyo provides the balance, at constant war with Themis's Warriors. For each battle Enyo wins, her power grows. As such, for each she loses, her power is diminished.

Equinox—a nightclub owned by Grey Bennett, Aries Warrior. Each Warrior has a role within the whole and Grey's is to keep an eye on the underbelly of New York for Enyo's likely crop of new Destroyers. What none of the Warriors knows is that Grey carries a secret—one that will lead him to his destiny or to his doom. . . .

Fixed—a sign *quality*, Fixed signs (Taurus, Leo, Scorpio, Aquarius) mark the middle of each season. Those born under Fixed signs are considered quite stubborn and persistent. Fixed Warriors are equally stubborn and persistent, unwilling to yield to their enemies.

Great Agreement—an agreement entered into during the Iron Age (the Fifth Age of Man) by Zeus and Themis. Fearful that her beloved humans had no protection from the trials of life, Themis entered into an agreement with Zeus that created the Sons of the Zodiac. The Sons of the Zodiac are Warriors modeled after the circular perfection of the heavens and each Warrior carries the immutable qualities of his sign. Under the Great Agreement, the immortal Warriors will battle Zeus's daughter Enyo, the goddess of war, for the ultimate protection, quality and survival of humanity.

Hera—wife of Zeus and mother of Enyo.

Iron Age—the Fifth Age of Man, generally thought to be about ten thousand years ago, where humans toil in abject misery. Brothers fight brothers, children turn against their fathers and anarchy is the rule of the land. During this age the gods have forsaken humanity. It is during this time that Themis—desperate to alter the course of human existence—goes to Zeus and enters into the Great Agreement. During this age, the Sons of the Zodiac are created.

Hades—god of the underworld and brother to Zeus and Poseidon.

MI6—the British Government's foreign intelligence service, also known as the Secret Intelligence Service (SIS).

Mount Ida—the legendary site in Crete where Rhea hid her son, Zeus, as a baby from his father, Cronus.

Mutable—a sign *quality*, Mutable signs (Gemini, Virgo, Sagittarius, Pisces) mark the end of each season. Those born under Mutable signs are the most comfortable with change, making them easily adaptable and resourceful. Mutable Warriors are the first to see the big picture, able to adapt and shift their battle plans at a moment's notice. Their ability to see issues from multiple angles make them strong Warriors and a comfort to have watching your back.

Nemesis—the Greek goddess of divine retribution. The name Nemesis means "to give what is due."

Phobos—the son of Ares and Aphrodite, he is the god of fear. He is the brother of Deimos.

Port—shortened form of teleport. The Warriors and Destroyers both have the ability to move through space and time at will. Porting will diminish power.

Prophecy of Thutmose III—a prophecy, carved on the walls of Thutmose III's tomb and not discovered until the early twenty-first century. The Prophecy outlines the power of the Summoning Stones of Egypt, for those who are Chosen by them.

Sons of the Zodiac—created by Themis, the goddess of justice, upon her Great Agreement with Zeus. The Great Agreement stipulates for a race of Warriors— 156 in total—that will have the traits of their zodiac sign. Tasked to protect humanity, they are at war with Enyo. A Warrior is immortal, although he may be killed with a death blow to the neck. Removal of a Warrior's head is the only way to kill him. The Warriors' strength may be reduced from extended time in battle, multiple ports and little food. A Warrior's strength will be replaced with food, sleep or sexual orgasm. Each Warrior has a tattoo of added protection that lives within his aura.

Stregheria—an ancient Italian practice of witchcraft, which formed the basis for Emmett the Sorcerer's poisonous spell placed upon Kane Montague, Scorpio Warrior.

Summoning Stones of Egypt—the five Summoning Stones of Egypt were crafted during the reign of Thutmose III. For those who are Chosen—and there will be a Chosen One in each age—the Stones give the user the power to control the universe. Each of the five stones represent a different element—death, life, love, sexuality, and infinity.

Tartarus—a prisonlike pit that exists under the Underworld. Zeus's father, Cronus, is housed in Tartarus at Zeus's hand.

Themis—one of the twelve Titans, Themis is the goddess of justice. Disheartened that her beloved humans toiled in misery and abject drudgery, she petitioned Zeus to allow her to intercede. With Zeus she entered into the Great Agreement, which provided for the creation of the Sons of the Zodiac, 156 Warriors embodied with the traits of their signs. Originally she envisioned twelve of twelve—but upon reaching her agreement with Zeus gained an additional twelve Warriors so Gemini might have his twin. Themis's Warriors live across the globe, battling Enyo and keeping humanity safe.

Titans—the original twelve children born of Uranus (Father Sky) and Gaia (Earth). Themis is one of the Titans, as is Cronus, Zeus's father.

Warrior's Tattoo—the Warrior's Tattoo is inked on his body, generally on his upper shoulder blade (right or left). The tattoo lives within the Warrior's aura and, when the Warrior is in danger the tattoo will expand as an additional form of protection. The tattoo is never separate; rather, it provides additional protection through the Warrior's life force.

Xiphos—an ancient Greek weapon, the Xiphos is a double-edged blade less than a foot in length. The Warriors each carry one, strapped on their calves. Although a Warrior may deliver a death blow to a Destroyer's neck when in close range, the Xiphos provides them with an additional tool in battle. Although a Warrior may use any Xiphos—or any weapon—when necessary, each Warrior was granted a Xiphos at his turning. Although it is nothing more than metal, many Warriors find a personal connection with their Xiphos through millennia of battle.

Zeus—the king of the gods and ruler over Mount Olympus. Zeus is married to Hera. Zeus's first wife was Themis, the goddess of justice and one of the Titans. Zeus entered the Great Agreement with Themis, which resulted in the protectors for humanity—the Sons of the Zodiac.

Read on for a sneak peek
at the first book in a sexy
new series by Addison Fox,

BABY IT'S COLD OUTSIDE:
AN ALASKAN NIGHTS NOVEL

Coming in November 2011 from
Signet Eclipse.

New York City
The Sunday after Thanksgiving

Jane Austen had it wrong, Sloan McKinley thought
miserably as the black Lincoln Town Car drove her
ever closer to the bright lights of the George Washing-
ton Bridge and the Manhattan streets she called home.
A man in possession of a good fortune only wanted to
get laid.

Of course, she thought reflectively, that made rich
men really no different from poor ones.

Despite the fact that dear old Jane was being cheeky
in her pronouncements on the proclivities of wealthy
young bachelors, Sloan knew her point was valid all
the same.

What she didn't know was why her mother thought
an endless parade of Scarsdale's finest—men who she'd
known since birth, played Little League soccer with (until, of course, it became unseemly to play a sport after
growing breasts), seen puke outside their limos at prom

and heard from every girl at school who did or did not have a package worth paying attention to—was going to be the answer to her daughter's walk down the aisle.

Case in point: one Trevor Stuart Kincaid IV—Trent, to all who knew and loved him. If the asshole stuck his hand on her knee and allowed his pinkie finger to creep up her inner thigh one more time, she was likely to go all Terminator on his Armani-covered ass.

"I'm glad your mother suggested this. It's a far more enjoyable drive back to the city with someone."

Sloan shifted yet again, firmly pushing his fingers away as his other hand inched closer on the backseat. "She's full of ideas."

"Good ones, I'd say. Speaking of good ideas"—his bloodshot eyes twinkled in the reflected lights of the streetlamps on the West Side Highway as Manhattan, and her escape, drew ever closer—"why haven't we ever gone out, you and me?"

Perhaps because Mitzi Goodby shared with our entire class at our fifteen-year reunion just how shitty you are in bed, how you enjoy the occasional cocaine bender and how you are a bad tipper. But Sloan said none of that and instead opted for, "I think we've likely just been in different places in our lives."

"It looks like we're in the same place now."

"We're probably not as close as you think."

"We can easily fix that."

Sloan caught the driver's raised eyebrows in the rearview mirror and shot him a glare. While she knew she wasn't in any danger—Trent was a world-class jerk with opportunistic hands, but that was about it—she also knew most people only saw what they wanted to see when they looked at her. Blond hair, all-American blue eyes and a five-foot-eight-inch frame had a way of doing that to a person.

The gangly ugly duckling Trent remembered from

high school—which was one of the many reasons they never *had* been in the same place, at least emotionally— had been replaced by a swan.

But it was the duckling that Sloan couldn't seem to shake loose.

People thought they were so discreet, but Sloan knew what was said about her. The only daughter of Forrest and Winifred McKinley had been *saved*, as far as the wealthy matrons of one of New York City's most elite suburbs thought, by the overpowering influence of genetics. The gawky teenager had long ago been re- placed with a grown woman with poise, intelligence and flawless skin—a fact for which her mother would be forever grateful.

What Winnie wasn't grateful for, however, was the fact her only daughter was still unmarried at the oh so advanced age of thirty-three.

Oh, the *horror*.

So whatever fears her mother had harbored when Sloan was a teenager—that she'd never get married, have babies and take Winnie's place as one of the movers and shakers of Scarsdale—were still firmly in place. And, Sloan was happy to note, she'd become the town charity case to boot, based upon an over- heard conversation between her mother's best friends— Betsy and Mary Jo—just before everyone sat down to Thanksgiving dessert.

The memory of that whispered conversation still rang in her ears, no matter how hard Sloan tried to fight it.

"You know Winnie's just been sick over this. I mean, can you imagine? She went to her reunion alone."

"Oh, Mary Jo, it's just so sad. Sara told me when she brought the twins over the other day that Sloan was the only one in their entire class who didn't have a date."

"It's not natural. What's wrong with that girl?"

"You know she's always been independent."

"Independent is having a cocktail by yourself at the Plaza before your lunch date arrives. Not going to your high school reunion alone."

Sloan released the tight fists that had formed at the memory, the bite of her nails digging into her skin finally registering.

"So what are you doing this week? I've got Coldplay tickets for the Garden on Wednesday night." Trent's invitation pulled her back from her maudlin holiday memories.

What would be the harm in going on a date? Sloan wondered. *Except for the bad tipping and the drugs,* she amended in a quick reminder to herself.

Still. Some good music, a nice evening out. A quick glance at Trent's clueless face and overheated gaze, and she knew what the harm would be.

She wasn't interested—in him or in his personal choices—and she'd long ago stopped trying to fake it.

Sloan was prevented from replying by a buzzing from her coat pocket. She pulled out her cell phone and quickly forgot Trevor Stuart Kincaid IV as she read the message from her best friend, Grier.

SOS. DESPERATE FOR HELP. ANY CHANCE YOU CAN COME TO ALASKA AND SAVE ME? THIS WHOLE INHERITANCE MESS HAS GONE OFF THE RAILS.

Trent gazed at the phone, a mixture of irritation and jealousy filling his features. Sloan hit REPLY and tossed a brief apology at the problem. "A friend of mine. Her father passed away, and she's dealing with his estate."

"Oh. That's too bad." His tone was flat with irritation, but she'd managed to stamp out the jealousy.

"It is a shame. It was very unexpected. Sorry. Just give me a minute." Sloan tapped out a quick text of her own.

WHAT'S GOING ON? I THOUGHT THE LAWYER SAID THINGS WERE
MOVING ALONG FINE. P.S. MOM'S STRUCK AGAIN. YOU'LL NEVER
GUESS WHO I'M SHARING A CAR BACK TO THE CITY WITH.

Sloan hit SEND and turned her attention back to
Trent. Her exit was coming up soon, and now was the
time to firmly extricate herself from whatever ideas her
mother had put into Trent's head. "Thanks for sharing
the car back with me."

"So you never answered me on the Coldplay tickets. You up for it?"

"I'm sorry, Trent. It's a full week workwise, so I
should pass."

"You can get out on the town for one night. The
concert doesn't even start until eight."

"Yeah, but I really shouldn't."

The features that had been distantly annoyed veered
straight toward firmly pissed, evidenced by the narrowed eyes and tightly drawn lips. "Seriously?"

"I'm sorry."

"I really don't get it. Your mom makes this huge
fuss about coming over to dinner. We take a car ride
back together. What the hell am I supposed to think?"

"Um, that two people who've known each other
since they were five shared a car back to the city?"

Trent ran a hand through his perfect hair. "What a
fucking joke. You come on to me all night and don't
follow through?"

A slow burn started low in her stomach, her rising
anger the culmination of a long weekend full of those
subtle clues that said she was a failure in the only area
her family chose to place value. "I'm forced to repeat
that we shared a car ride. If you thought that was a
come-on, it's not my fault."

"High-society bitches. It figures."

Sloan abstractly heard the ringing bell of her phone,
letting her know another text message had come in,

but she ignored it, the rising heat of battle creeping up her neck.

How dare he?

When it was roaming hands hoping to get lucky and a few suggestive comments, she could handle it. But *this*? To borrow his phrase: *Seriously?*

"Look. Whatever impression my mother gave you isn't my fault. I know *I* wasn't the one giving off vibes I was interested."

The car had come to a stop outside her building, and she could hear the driver opening the trunk for her luggage. Trent's face was a cold mask of irritation and indifference. "Whatever. Your mother wonders why you're not married. You can't even go on a date, you're so fucking repressed. We've arrived at your castle. Have a nice life, Princess."

The door opened before Sloan could say anything, and then she realized she didn't want to.

All she wanted to do was escape.

"Sloan, he's a slimy rat bastard. He's just pissed you didn't want to have sex with his sorry ass."

The tears had stopped over an hour ago, leaving behind the worn-out effects of a good crying jag, coupled with raw, angry frustration. Even now Sloan wondered why she'd let him say those things.

And why she was even bothering to give Trevor Stuart Kincaid IV another second of her time.

"Yeah, well, we can thank my mother for whatever expectations she put in his head. Hell, she's so desperate at this point, she probably insinuated I haven't had sex in about five years."

"It's not any of her business anyway, even if it's five days." Thank God for Grier. Her champion, no matter what the subject.

It had only been two years, Sloan thought defensively, not five.

Well, shit.

Had it really been two years?

A quick mental tally indicated her math was correct. And the knowledge only added to the well of gloom Trent had managed to open. Firmly tamping down on the rampaging self-pity, she turned her focus to her friend.

"So what, exactly, is going on up there?" Sloan asked.

"Where do I start?" Grier quickly got her friend up to speed on the rapidly deteriorating inheritance battle she was waging in her father's chosen hometown of Indigo, Alaska.

"What does your lawyer say about all of it? Shouldn't this be a bit more straightforward? It's an inheritance, for Pete's sake." Sloan hesitated for a moment, but decided that since it was Grier, she'd keep on going. "I mean, do you think he's qualified to handle this? He is practicing in the middle of nowhere."

"No, he really has been wonderful. And he seems as puzzled as I am by the town's reaction. They've all taken Kate's side, which is just a load of bullshit, but I haven't figured out a way around it."

"Wait, wait, wait." Sloan's attention caught on the mention of a new name. "Who's Kate?"

"Are you sitting down?"

"Out with it."

"She's my half sister."

Sloan almost dropped the phone on that news. "You have a sister? And it took you this long to tell me?"

"She's the holdup. She claims I don't have a right to my father's estate."

"Um, isn't it called a will for a reason? He willed it to you."

"Well, the will was changed relatively recently and she's making a fuss."

"And your lawyer can't do anything about it? You can't even get in to see your father's things?"

"Nope. While it's moving through the legal sys-'em, neither of us can touch anything. That's why I'm ...ill at the hotel."

Sloan refrained from pushing harder on the lawyer angle. "So tell me about this sister of yours."

"From what I can tell, she's about as warm as a python, and instead of the word 'sister,' I think 'bitch' would be a far more appropriate moniker."

"It's not just her grief talking? I mean, she presumably knew the man."

"I wish." Grier snorted, her disgust more than evident even though more than three thousand miles separated them. "That I could understand. I could even understand if it made her prickly, but the attitude I'm getting is just way off the charts. She's actively waging a campaign to alienate me."

"Have you tried talking to her?"

Grier never had any problems winning anyone over; her effervescent personality drew people to her like a lodestone. Sloan knew grief drove some strange actions, but the idea that Grier's half sister was actively shutting her out was a surprise.

"Oh, Sloan, I've tried everything on the rare occasions I can get her to even look at me. Friendship. Sisterhood. Hell, I've even tried to boss her around as her older sister. *Nothing* works. And it's very clear the entire damn town's on her side. Whoever said small towns were interested in newcomers was smoking crack. These people won't give an inch."

"They won't talk to you?"

"Talk to me?" Grier snorted. "As little as possible. Everyone except for my lawyer cuts me a wide swath."

"They've taken her side?"

"So it seems, even though no one seems to like her all that much, either. I swear, the girl's more frozen over than the ground up here, and that's saying something."

At the suggestion of the mysterious half sister's frozen personality, Trent's similar words brought Sloan's own problems back to the center of her thoughts. Sloan wasn't able to stop the suspicious tightening in her throat or the renewed wave of anger that roiled in her stomach.

"So what do you say?" Grier asked. "Will you come up here and help me? You could call it research and use it to put together an article or two."

The offer was more tempting than Sloan cared to admit. But really? What was she going to do in Alaska? Yeah, she could write, and she had four more articles on deadline that she really wanted to hit out of the park. Although she was fortunate with steady work, the life of a freelancer meant she was always looking for more.

And a trip to Alaska could be some good fodder for a few articles. A few weeks ago, she'd talked to a travel editor looking for some fun pieces with a unique twist.

Alaska.

Miles and miles away from *here*.

Before she could debate it any further, Grier's voice dropped a few octaves and Sloan heard in her tone the undeniable cadence of desperation mixed with abject misery. "Sloan. *Please*. I really need you up here."

Sloan stopped teetering on the edge of indecision as Grier's words registered. "I'll book my flight in the morning."

As she hung up the phone a few minutes later, Sloan couldn't stop the flutter of hope that filled her stomach.

Maybe a trip to the middle of nowhere was just what the doctor ordered.